PASS~~ION~~

Travis grasped the hands that were caressing his cheeks and pressed them to his lips. As his gaze remained fused to hers and he absorbed her presence, his lips and tongue played sensuously in her palms. When Rana moved closer to him, his arms slipped around her body and his lips seared her right ear. As they drifted down her throat, she trembled and swayed against him, enslaving his senses. His mouth brushed over her bare shoulder and traveled back to the hollow of her neck. When Rana's arms encircled his waist and she arched her body against his, Travis's hands slipped into her cascading tresses; he cupped her head and lifted her lips to his. Their shared kiss ignited smoldering passions that roared into a blaze of urgency and formed an all-consuming force too powerful to contain . . .

ZEBRA'S REGENCY ROMANCES
DAZZLE AND DELIGHT

A BEGUILING INTRIGUE   (4441, $3.99)
by Olivia Sumner

Pretty as a picture Justine Riggs cared nothing for propriety. She dressed as a boy, sat on her horse like a jockey, and pondered the stars like a scientist. But when she tried to best the handsome Quenton Fletcher, Marquess of Devon, by proving that she was the better equestrian, he would try to prove Justine's antics were pure folly. The game he had in mind was seduction — never imagining that he might lose his heart in the process!

AN INCONVENIENT ENGAGEMENT   (4442, $3.99)
by Joy Reed

Rebecca Wentworth was furious when she saw her betrothed waltzing with another. So she decides to make him jealous by flirting with the handsomest man at the ball, John Collinwood, Earl of Stanford. The "wicked" nobleman knew exactly what the enticing miss was up to — and he was only too happy to play along. But as Rebecca gazed into his magnificent eyes, her errant fiancé was soon utterly forgotten!

SCANDAL'S LADY   (4472, $3.99)
by Mary Kingsley

Cassandra was shocked to learn that the new Earl of Lynton was her childhood friend, Nicholas St. John. After years at sea and mixed feelings Nicholas had come home to take the family title. And although Cassandra knew her place as a governess, she could not help the thrill that went through her each time he was near. Nicholas was pleased to find that his old friend Cassandra was his new next door neighbor, but after being near her, he wondered if mere friendship would be enough . . .

HIS LORDSHIP'S REWARD   (4473, $3.99)
by Carola Dunn

As the daughter of a seasoned soldier, Fanny Ingram was accustomed to the vagaries of military life and cared not a whit about matters of rank and social standing. So she certainly never foresaw her *tendre* for handsome Viscount Roworth of Kent with whom she was forced to share lodgings, while he carried out his clandestine activities on behalf of the British Army. And though good sense told Roworth to keep his distance, he couldn't stop from taking Fanny in his arms for a kiss that made all hearts equal!

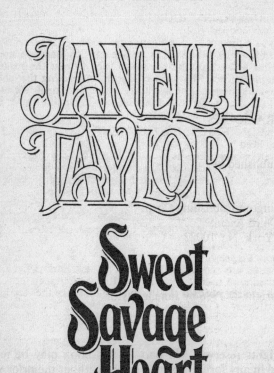

JANELLE TAYLOR

Sweet Savage Heart

ZEBRA BOOKS
KENSINGTON PUBLISHING CORP.

For:

Kay Garteiser, a dear friend who has such a special and supportive "romantic spirit;"

Virginia Brown, my very good friend and a superb writer;

Virginia Driving Hawk Sneeve, from whom I've learned so much about the Sioux chiefs and the inspiring Dakota Nation.

Raised on the Plains with a spirit just as wild,
Lives an Indian princess half woman, half child.
On her wits and courage she was taught to depend,
Now, to the whiteman's way, she is forced to bend.
Will it be justice or only a selfish game?
Who will step forth her wild heart to tame?
Indian is her heart, but white is her skin;
Is there a way for her two facets to blend?
Once free as the air, is this deed right or wrong?
Blithe child of nature, now where does she belong?
When fate opens a new path, where will it end?
For who has the power to tame a wild wind?

Chapter One

Dakota Territory
May 3, 1867

It was a busy time of year with the spring buffalo hunt and the constant flood of whites onto the ancestral lands of the Sioux. It was a time of great peril and many changes—for the Oglala tribes in the Lakota branch of the Dakota Nation and for a white girl who had lived for ten years as the daughter of Chief Soaring Hawk of the Red Arrow Band. Sadly, tragically, Soaring Hawk had been slain; the band was now ruled by his son, Lone Wolf. Indeed, times were rapidly and painfully altering for the flaming-haired, blue-eyed girl who was trapped between two warring cultures and who seemingly belonged to neither world. But she desperately wanted to find inner peace and the answers to the mysteries and influences that controlled her life and continuously plagued her mind and daily existence during these troubled times. The North/South war had ended and the whites had turned eyes of conquest toward the west; now an ominous conflict was brewing in these lands and another one was brewing within the heart and life of

7

Wild Wind.

The warrior Buffalo Slayer urged his horse toward the mottled stallion that carried their new chief, Lone Wolf. The younger brave informed the stalwart warrior of the inquisitive "wild wind" who was rapidly blowing down their backs. The seasoned warrior glanced over his bare shoulder, frowned in vexation, and told his braves to continue toward their meeting point with other Oglala and Hunkpapa hunting parties while he halted to order his adopted sister back to camp. The warriors and braves were amused by the willful but beautiful Indian princess who would have gladly performed the Sun Dance to become a warrior. Many in this group had been rejected by her, but in such a way as to inspire more hunger rather than resentment or discouragement.

Lone Wolf dismounted and tied his reins to a bush. He fretted over *Watogla Tate's* ceaseless streak of defiance, her impulsive ways, her annoying independence, her refusal to obey his commands. She wanted to race the wind on her white stallion, which only she could mount and master. She wanted to perform the duties and practices of warriors—to hunt, track, raid with his band, and sit in the ceremonial lodge and be a part of the talks and votes. She still wanted to shadow him as she had since becoming his sister ten winters ago. It was time she realized they were no longer children, he mused in annoyance. It was too late to change past years, when he and his recently deceased father, Soaring Hawk, had allowed her to do as she pleased and had actually enjoyed and boasted of her immense skills. How foolish that had been.

He asked himself if it mattered that she could ride and fight better than many braves. Did it matter that her lance or arrow never missed its mark? Did it matter that she could swim as skillfully as the otter? Did it matter that she could track a disguised or aged trail? She was a

8

female! He had been chief one full moon. His band and others were observing his leadership and prowess. If he could not properly control his own tepee, they would look upon him unfavorably.

He knew he must convince her that a woman cannot change her sex, or her role in life; such things are controlled and decided by the Great Spirit.

Lone Wolf reluctantly admitted that he and his father had been too lenient with *Watogla Tate*. During the past year, his father had been too weak from a soldier's bullet—it was this viciously consuming wound that had finally claimed Soaring Hawk's life—to battle this headstrong creature who had been thrust into their lives long ago and had been accepted by them at the direct command of the Great Spirit, *Wakantanka*; and he, Lone Wolf, had been too ensnared by his responsibilities, his love for her, and his many adventures to realize what was happening to his cherished white sister. But now, with Soaring Hawk gone, it was up to him to discipline and train her.

Yet the constant verbal fights they waged were wearing thin on the warrior, for he had more vital matters to consider and handle. Feeding and protecting his people and guarding his sacred lands against white conquest weighed heavily in his mind and heart. These days she provoked his anger faster and caused it to run deeper. Others were teasing both him and her. During these perilous times, he needed the full respect and support of his band and their Lakota brothers. He could allow no mark of weakness or ridicule to stain his face or threaten his leadership and the Lakotas' survival. His sister had left him no choice; she would have to be forced to obey his orders!

Lone Wolf wondered how he could reach her, how he could stop these foolish dreams of hers. He hated to force her into a marriage to settle their war of words and wills,

9

but he must, or all that he knew and was could be in peril. The hostilities with the white man were increasing; he needed the total confidence and loyalty of his people. Her misbehavior was casting bad shadows over both of them. She was closing off all paths to escape, except one. Countless braves and warriors from their tribe and other tribes desired her. She had spurned each one. Soon she would have to marry and begin her own family. Perhaps a mate and children would tame her wild spirit.

Lone Wolf stood tall and alert as he awaited his audacious sister. She had become aware that her presence had been discovered and she had ceased her stealthy approach. He was glad he had told Buffalo Slayer to guard their backs, for now he could force her home before their Lakota brothers discovered her embarrassing defiance.

Her hair was unbraided, and the wavy mane swirled and tangled in the breeze she created with her fast pace. As the locks whipped wildly in the wind, they seized the sun's rays and reflected its fiery glow. If she had not been his sister, he might have been stimulated by the shapely legs, revealed by her raised skirt, as they deftly gripped the horse's sleek body. His sister was slender, but firm and nimble. She could move as rapidly and agilely as a bee but appear as lovely and delicate as the flower upon which it landed. Although her flesh was nearly as tanned as most Indians, it was a different shade, a color that favored newborn colts in early spring. He envisioned her compelling winter-sky eyes, no doubt filled with determination and eagerness. Truly she was a beautiful and body-stirring creature, though one who had refused to use such magic to lure a mate.

The girl's shapely body grew larger against the horizon as she closed the remaining distance between them. Lone Wolf worried over her conduct and his necessary response to it. He wondered if it was her white blood that

10

was causing the unrest and rebellion within her. After all, *Watogla Tate* was his adopted sister; she was all white. She had once been a captive of the fierce Kiowas, until his brave father had attacked their camp after they had encroached on Oglala lands. He had won many *coups* by stealing weapons and horses and by taking many captives. This white girl had been nearly eight winters old then, and a sacred vision had commanded Soaring Hawk to adopt her.

Lone Wolf could close his dark eyes and recall the pathetic creature whom his father had brought into their tepee after that raid. She had been so dirty and afraid, too scared to talk or move or cry. There had been bruises and scratches on her skinny body and tangled knots in her filthy hair. Her grimy dress had been torn in several places, but thankfully she had not shown any feminine traits at that early age. Those gray-blue eyes had appeared so large and so full of terror and sadness. She had been a slave to the Kiowa chief's second wife, and she had been intimidated and abused by the hateful woman in this demeaning position. To reflect upon such cruel treatment of an innocent and helpless child evoked new anger in him against his enemies, the Kiowas. Silently he raged. A small child should never be treated as an enemy!

The day Soaring Hawk had returned from that raid, the Great Spirit had spoken to him through a vision, telling him to take that captive child into his tepee as his daughter and to name her *Watogla Tate*, Wild Wind, for Soaring Hawk had won his victory and her capture during a violent wind storm: it was a name well suited to the girl, who could behave just as unpredictably as a wild wind. From that moon to this one, the white girl with flaming hair had lived with them. How she had changed during the past years! he reflected now.

Wild Wind had learned to protect herself, physically and emotionally. She had worked on defensive skills and

11

had sharpened her senses as if her very life had depended on them. She had once confessed to him that she would never allow anyone or anything to hurt her again. Perhaps that persistence and determination and the motives behind them were the reasons why he had assisted her in her training, training that had done as much damage as good for her as well as him. Many times he had dreamed that her destiny did not lie with his people. Many times he had dreamed of her leaving their camp to travel a long and dangerous path, a path that led to the destiny she had been born to live. For years he had been preparing her to face and conquer that perilous challenge. But with her practiced skills and honed instincts had come the belief that she was as effective and as proficient as any male warrior. And, he vexingly confessed to himself, perhaps she was. Yet she had become an Indian maiden and would have to exist as one.

For many years they had not spoken of the deaths of her white family or her abuse at the Kiowas' hands. Perhaps with a wounded mind, the injuries to body and spirit were suppressed, as her white childhood had been. Perhaps secret resentment against her Kiowa captors was inspiring her to refuse marriage to any Indian. Maybe deep inside she did not feel as if she belonged here. Perhaps she was training and waiting for the Great Spirit to return her feet to her destined path. If outsiders had not continued to mention her white skin and blood, it would have been forgotten by her, his people, and their Lakota brothers. But the more they endured this vicious war with the whites, the more her white skin, blue-gray eyes, fiery hair, defiant ways, and high rank were noticed and scorned by his and other bands. Too many saw a white enemy in a place of honor in the Oglala camp, not Soaring Hawk's daughter or Lone Wolf's sister. It was a tormenting situation, which needed a swift and acceptable resolution.

No matter what his sister did or said, he knew she had a tender and caring spirit. She was as lively as a muskrat. She was as gentle as a doe. Her smile could be as warming as the sun and her laughter as musical as a watery cascade. Sadly, Wild Wind rarely let such special traits show, as if exposing them would endanger her hard covering and bring about more anguish.

The Indian princess now pulled on the reins to halt her stallion. She tossed her leg over his back and gracefully dismounted. It did not require keen eyes or a sharp mind to detect the change in her brother's attitude today. Quivers of uneasiness teased over her body and a knife of cold reality stabbed into her racing heart. The fact that Lone Wolf had reached his limits in patience and tolerance was exposed boldly in his ominous gaze and rigid stance. He did not smile or relax as she joined him. She was alarmed by the resolve and barely leashed anger that she read in his expression, though fear was something she detested in herself and in others. It was as if she were trapped upon a landslide, and she sensed there was no way she could halt her movements or prevent her injuries.

She wondered why she felt an outsider with the people who had rescued her, adopted her, and raised her as one of their own. She could not comprehend why she seemed so restless. Even if she did not think and behave like the other women, this was the only life she knew; yet she could not accept her designated role in it. There was an unknown hunger that ate at her heart and mind daily and denied her peace and forced her to disobey. It was as if an uncontrollable force was pushing her toward a vital challenge that continued to elude her. *Help me, Great Spirit,* she prayed. *Help me understand who I am and what I am seeking. Help me find my rightful place. Help my brother and our people understand and accept why I cannot be as they desire me to be.*

13

Exasperated, Lone Wolf decided to take a rash but stern path with his sister. *"Tokiya la hwo? Takca yacin hwo?"* he queried, tersely asking her where she was going and what she wanted. Before Wild Wind could respond, Lone Wolf scolded to embarrass her, "Why does my sister race after warriors as a fool without honor and wits? Anger fills my heart and head, *Watogla Tate.* Have you no pride, no shame, no sense of duty and loyalty? Do you not see how you are destroying my love and respect for you? Do you not see you are stealing the peace in our tepee? Does it mean nothing that you are staining my honor and rank? Do you think only of Wild Wind and her desires? You—"

"I want to observe your first talk with the Hunkpapas as our chief. Pride fills my heart and excitement clouds my head. I will stay hidden, my brother. It is a great day for us. Please, let me—"

"Inila!" Lone Wolf harshly ordered her to silence, rebuking, "Do not cut into the words of a warrior, your chief! Have you learned nothing of our customs and laws since living with us for so many winters? You defy our ways and bring dishonor to your family. I can allow no more disobedience," he warned coldly. "You bring shame to the tepee of Chief Lone Wolf and to our band of Oglalas. You shame Wild Wind. We made you the daughter of our chief and the sister of Lone Wolf. We loved you and protected you. Why have you dishonored and pained us? You cause my warriors and others to laugh at me. How can warriors ride behind a fool? How can they follow the commands of one who cannot control his own tepee? Your disobedience and dark pride prove that there is no Indian heart within a body without Indian blood. Each moon you become more white than Oglala. It brings sadness and anger to my heart to view such evil within my chosen sister."

Wild Wind was stunned momentarily by his vehemence and incisive words. He had become annoyed with her of late, but never had he spoken in such a manner or behaved so coldly toward her. Something was terribly wrong today. Though she was one who normally could control her expressions and reactions, she helplessly paled beneath the golden glow of her silky flesh. Eyeing him intently, she asked, "Why do you speak such cruel words to your sister, Lone Wolf? I have lived by your side for many winters, and I wish to be like you. Can you deny that I am as trained and skilled as your best warrior? Why must I waste such skills and prowess when my people are in danger of being no more? When I see wrongs, where is there honor and bravery in remaining silent? What excitement and courage is involved in gathering herbs and wild vegetables, or putting up a tepee and taking it down, or rubbing foul brains into a hide to cure it, or cooking meals and serving men like a slave? Such acts require no skill or wits. They can be done by old women or young girls, or by our captives. They can be done asleep!" she shouted at him in an unusual display of anger. "I do not want to be enslaved by a tepee, by a woman's boring life. I want to feel the sun and wind upon my body. I want to feast on danger and freedom as you do. I want to put my skills against fate's powers. I wish to be a warrior, not a helpless woman! Let me help our people."

Lone Wolf shook his head in mounting frustration. "You are a female, Wild Wind. You are the most beautiful creature alive. Why do you make yourself ugly with shame and defiance? If you love me and honor me, find a worthy warrior and join him. Be as you are, my sister, a woman of great value and pride and courage," he urged.

"You wish me to marry and leave our tepee? You wish me to be miserable? You wish me to let our people suffer and die because the pride of warriors will not allow

15

women to join them in battle? I must not! I cannot!" she blatantly refused, her eyes sparkling with fury.

"You are eighteen winters old, a woman. It is time to accept your place as Grandfather willed it. Do not force me to—" At her wounded expression, he halted briefly. He was softening, and he could not permit that to happen if he wanted to win this battle.

"Force you to do what, my brother?" she quickly demanded, her heart pounding in trepidation.

Lone Wolf breathed deeply, wearily. "I am your brother and chief, and I must be obeyed. If you do not cease your childish and rash behavior, I will be forced to punish you before the entire tribe. Then you will feel the shame that you bring to me and my camp. If you do not find a mate before the Sun Dance, I will choose one for you and have you joined after the ceremony. I have spoken."

Wild Wind could not believe what she was hearing. "You would not do such brutal things to your sister!" she debated fearfully, for she perceived the danger and seriousness in this threat from him.

"You are my sister only as long as you behave as my sister. For many moons you have behaved as white. If you are my sister and you are Indian at heart, you will obey the laws and ways of our people," he shockingly informed her, his voice clear and crisp and intimidating.

"Father would not wish you to hurt me and punish me this way. It is wrong, my brother," she argued frantically, though she knew Lone Wolf saw the situation from a completely different viewpoint. She had been raised by the Oglalas and she knew their customs and ways; yet something strange and powerful was pushing her away from them and was preventing her from sealing her life with them. If only she could understand and explain what was influencing her thoughts and actions, she reflected miserably.

16

"Father is with the Great Spirit, Wild Wind. He was too weak to battle you. If love and respect lived in your heart and head, you would not shame and hurt your brother and people. Do you wish to make us regret your rescue from the Kiowas? Do you wish to make us regret you are Soaring Hawk's daughter? Is there hatred and bitterness hiding within you toward all Indians? Do you seek to punish all with red skin for the cruelty of our enemies? In the past three winters, you have become more white than Indian. I fear such changes will bring much trouble to our camp and to those of our Lakota brothers. There is a powerful force that is driving you from us."

"You words are not true, Lone Wolf!" she shrieked in dismay. She licked her suddenly dry lips and tried to slow her racing heart. "I love you and loved our father. I would do nothing to hurt you or our people."

"Your words do not match your actions, my sister," he replied, refuting her frantic claims. "There is no deeper wound than dishonor. You know the way of my people: it is better to die in honor than to live in shame. If you are truly Oglala, become one with us in all ways."

"Do you say that the only way to prove my love and loyalty is to marry a man I do not love or want? Must I deny all I am and feel just to prove I am your sister and the daughter of Soaring Hawk? If you loved me as I love you, brother, you would not wish such an empty and cruel life upon me. Perhaps I have acted too boldly and recklessly, but it was to seize your attention and to earn the right to defend our lands and people. If I cannot live in peace and love in our tepee, then I will leave our camp and your life," she warned him.

She expected him to relent slightly. Instead, he responded, "Perhaps that would be best for all, Wild Wind. Your will was too strong for Father to master, and it pained him to watch your arrogance and rebellion grow

17

as swiftly as the spring grasses. I cannot reach you. Soon, I will be forced to put my people first. I cannot allow you to darken my honor and rank. I cannot waste time and strength correcting or punishing you each sun. Think on Rides-Like-Thunder of the Cheyenne as a mate. He is a great warrior with many *coups*. By all females he is called handsome, and he has many skills upon the sleeping mat."

Her cheeks grew as fiery as her hair at his last remark and her gray-blue eyes widened with astonishment. He continued slowly and confidently, "It is time for my Cheyenne brother to have his own tepee. He has many horses and skins to trade for a wife. He is strong and brave; he can protect his family from all evil. In his camp, you will forget your foolish ways and words. He has spoken with me about you. He wishes to join soon. I say we accept his offer. Do you agree?"

Anguish and panic ruled her senses. "You despise my white blood so much that you would send me to another camp, to a stranger, to become his slave by the joining law?" she inquired anxiously. Tremors assailed her body as she observed his resolve. Normally she would have battled him with obstinate words and actions, but she knew he was gravely serious. She dared not push him today.

"Many warriors have asked for you as their mate; each day the offers for you grow larger. Black Hawk and Prairie Dog have asked to approach you. No maiden has received such great offers of trading. The other women grow jealous and angry. You must not reject so many noble warriors. The warriors challenge each other and joke over who will tame the wild wind. For peace, you must choose one, or I will do so. Is there a warrior who stands taller and braver than than Rides-Like-Thunder?"

"You would sell your own sister for the biggest price? I do not wish to marry your Cheyenne brother or any other warrior. I am young, Lone Wolf. I am not ready to become a wife and mother. There is much to learn and see. I do not love or desire any of them," she protested. She had allowed several handsome braves to steal kisses, but they had had no effect on her. What was so special about the joining of bodies on sleeping mats? she wondered. Once she was wed, her freedom and joy would be lost forever, and her restless spirit would be corralled. If only Soaring Hawk were still alive . . . Her Indian father had understood her hunger for life, her many differences from the others of the tribe. Sometimes they had talked for hours of the mysteries of life and the variations in people. He had never pressed her to be anything more than she was. Why had he been taken from her during this confusing period in her life? Why could she not consent to her brother's commands? She knew why: somewhere there was a special existence and a man awaiting her. She would have to resist Lone Wolf's orders until her destiny was revealed to them. If only the Great Spirit would open her brother's eyes to the truth, he would understand why she was refusing to comply with his wishes, and perhaps he would find a way to help her locate her path to happiness.

"I will invite Rides-Like-Thunder to visit our tepee. You will see that he is the best choice for the daughter of Soaring Hawk and sister of Lone Wolf. Do not rashly close your heart and mind to him. He is a good man and my friend. You are my sister and I love you. That is why I choose the best man for you. Accept him and my words," he coaxed. He did love her, and this matter was difficult for him. He was distressed by her rebellion and selfishness. How could he reach her?

"Would Rides-Like-Thunder be the best choice if he were of our tribe? Or is he the best because he will take me away from your camp and tepee? Am I so repulsive that my own brother wishes to be rid of me?" she

19

challenged him, her emotions in turmoil. "Why are you blind to the truth, Lone Wolf? Grandfather must guide my steps."

Lone Wolf reasoned, "Good changes will be made in Wild Wind in another camp. If you remain here, you will not try to become a good wife. Your defiance will vanish in the Cheyenne camp, for you will learn that such ways and words are wrong. You will learn to be Indian again. You will find love and desire. If you wish to choose another warrior, do so before the buffalo hunt ends. If you do not, I will accept my friend's offer after our tribes hunt together. I will allow him to take you as his mate after the joint Sun Dance. If Rides-Like-Thunder were of this camp, my choice would be the same," he added honestly. "If you desire Black Hawk or Prairie Dog and promise to become a good Oglala wife, I will accept your choice of either warrior. I do not wish to hurt you, my sister. Do not make it so."

Unaccustomed tears glimmered in her eyes, for she could not alter or resist the Indian ways. She had lived with the Oglala Sioux long enough to know she must obey Lone Wolf's words or be banned from her tribe. Where could she go? How would she survive? Did she want freedom that badly? Even if Rides-Like-Thunder was the best choice for a mate from any tribe, she did not love him or want to marry him. She wanted happiness and freedom; she wanted to comprehend this fierce and intangible hunger that chewed at her mind and body. She wanted and needed . . . what the Great Spirit had not yet revealed.

How could she yield to defeat when such a powerful urge to seek her real destiny pulled at her? As surely as the sun rose, it was wrong to marry Rides-Like-Thunder, or any man, just now. But how could she prevent it until she understood who and what she was? Why must she sacrifice her joy, her freedom, and her body to another

20

person? What about her desires and her honor? Was she of such little importance?

"Niksapa hantans ecanu kte," Lone Wolf encouraged her tenderly.

Wild Wind bravely fused her blue gaze to Lone Wolf's ebony one and mentally questioned his last words: "If you are wise, you will do it." Suddenly she lost the will to resist him. This battle between them was too vicious and demanding and destructive. If the Great Spirit had other plans for her, He would see them exposed and fulfilled before it was too late. For now, peace with her brother and people was the important thing. She replied, "As you command, I will choose a mate by the Sun Dance, or I will leave our camp forever. If you open your senses to the words and desires of the Great Spirit, you will know your order is wrong. I beg you, Lone Wolf, seek His will for our lives before you stubbornly go against it. Your words and anger have pierced my heart as fiery arrows. I was a child when I came to the tepee of Soaring Hawk and Lone Wolf; you have made me as I am. Now you punish me for the skills I have learned and the hungers I feel. I know I am a female, for I experience the sting of that sex each day. Why must being a woman destroy my chances for happiness? A captive could perform the same duties you ask of me. Why can there not be more to my life, Lone Wolf? Why is it wrong to ride with the sun and wind? Why is it wrong to learn and practice warrior skills? Is it not best for a woman to be able to protect her tepee and family when her warrior is gone? Have you forgotten how many camps have been raided and destroyed while warriors were hunting or fighting?"

Her voice became strained with heavy emotion as she continued, "Why are women not taught to defend their camps and lives? Why must they flee into the forests or be abused by their captors? Without homes and families, the warriors will have nothing and will cease to exist, as

21

the white man cunningly plans. You know their clever strategy: leave nothing and no one behind and the Dakota Nation will perish. Why is it wrong to know how to track and hunt when the warriors are away and food is needed? Must women, old ones, and children suffer and die because of male pride? Why can we not listen to the words of the council, which also affect our lives? Did not Grandfather also create females? Did He not also give us cunning and courage? Why must we hide these traits? Women have feelings and wishes; why can we not speak them? We are allowed to do no more for our families and people than animals do for their own kind or slaves are commanded to do for their owners; yet we are above animals and slaves in all ways. Women are Oglalas too, Lone Wolf, the children of the Great Spirit. Where and when has Grandfather said we are beneath males? The taste of cowardice is bitter, my brother. Explain these things that trouble me, and I will obey all orders," she vowed.

Lone Wolf declared impatiently, "We have spoken of such matters many times, my sister. It is our way. Grandfather chose the paths for males and females long ago, and He has not changed them. Oglalas must be Oglala. I will waste no more words and strength on such useless talk," he told her, for he could not think of words to refute her arguments, and this dismayed him. "You refuse to see right and to do it. I wish it were not so. Think on your honor and deeds, my sister, and we will speak when I return." He secretly hoped his wits would not fail him at such a trying time. If only her words did not sound so logical, or go against all he had been taught . . .

"It is useless to speak further, my brother and chief. You see only your feelings and thoughts; you care nothing for mine. All people are not the same, Lone Wolf. One day you must face this truth and you must learn the value of women. If you could become a female for only one sun and moon, you would learn much. I agree that many of my deeds are rash and my words are often too quick and sharp, but my honor exists only as long as I remain true to myself and all that I believe. We will not speak on this matter again. I will obey your wishes or I will leave before the buffalo hunt," she announced, a new confidence filling her at that irrevocable decision. If her brother felt she would leave before complying with his commands, he might back down . . .

Lone Wolf watched his adopted sister mount and ride for camp. Wild Wind was smart and brave. She would think on his words and her behavior, then yield to his orders. After the passing of one full moon, she would become the mate of his Cheyenne friend or another of her own choosing, and all would be as it should be . . .

Wild Wind returned to camp and closed the flap to her tepee to signal privacy. She had much thinking to do but did not know where to begin. For as long as she could remember, or would permit herself to remember, she had lived as an Oglala. Yet she was not Indian, and the trader's looking glass impressed this reality upon her more and more each day. She had tried to be like all of the other Indian maidens but had failed. She was making Lone Wolf and others angry and sad, yet she could not help herself. She wanted and needed something more than this confining life offered her. She was not Soaring Hawk's daughter, but she could not recall her dark past. Who was she? Where did she belong? How could she become all she wanted to be? "Help me, Great Spirit, for I am lost in mist and cannot find my rightful path. I do not wish to dishonor or sadden my brother, Lone Wolf, but I cannot yield to his commands. Please show him I am not like the females of his kind. Please reveal my purpose in life to him. My time is short, Grandfather, and I need

23

your help and answer. Do not fail me because my skin is white, for my heart is Indian."

Suddenly she began to weep, for the truth pounded inside her head: No, Wild Wind, you are not Indian and your place is not here . . .

A similar confusion was taking place far away in Texas, near Fort Worth. Rancher Nathan Crandall was wondering if he was experiencing a cruel joke or a miracle as he digested the news he had just received. He swallowed to remove the lump in his throat that temporarily prevented him from questioning the astounding mystery that had been presented to him. The hands that gripped two breathtaking canvases by renowned artist Thomas Mallory were wrinkled by advancing age and scarred by countless hours of hard manual labor often done in harsh weather. His grayish blue eyes glanced from the two small portraits of an Indian princess to a large portrait of his deceased daughter, Marissa Crandall Michaels, which was hanging over his fireplace. The deteriorating portrait, which Thomas Mallory was now studying intently, had been painted in 1847, when Marissa had been eighteen. Nathan found himself wondering in confusion how the two portraits he held could look like Marissa when they had been painted so recently and his daughter had been dead since '56?

This talented and adventurous artist had arrived in Fort Worth three days ago. Nathan's foreman, Travis Kincade, had met Thomas in the Silver Shadow Saloon and had become intrigued by his work and tales. Travis had learned that Thomas had been traveling the West for the past three years, painting portraits of trappers, soldiers, Indians, and settlers. When he was not doing portraits, he was painting landscapes, portrayals of customs and adventures, and wildlife. Nearing the end of his often perilous trek and before returning east, Thomas had traveled to Texas to capture rugged lawmen and infamous outlaws in evocative oils.

Returning home, Travis had informed Nathan of the master craftsman's arrival. As Marissa's portrait was in dire need of expert attention, Nathan had sent Travis back to town to bring Thomas to the ranch to examine his daughter's portrait and to discuss its restoration.

At first glance, the eagle-eyed artist had gaped at the portrait that he was being asked to revitalize. To explain his curious reaction, Thomas had pulled two canvases from an oversized leather satchel, unwrapped them, and handed them to Nathan. "I brought along some of my favorite paintings to let you judge my work for yourself. Now you can understand my astonishment, Mister Crandall. They could almost be the same person. Such resemblance . . . It's incredible."

The owner of the Rocking *C* Ranch tried to master his shock in order to think clearly and calmly. "Who is this girl? When did you paint these? Where?" Nathan demanded hoarsely, the questions suddenly tumbling over each other from his dry mouth.

Thomas Mallory pulled his probing gaze from Marissa's portrait and focused it on the anguished expression of his eminent host. "Her name is *Watogla Tate*. She's the daughter of Chief Soaring Hawk of the Sioux. I spent most of the winter and spring traveling through the Dakota Territory, painting chiefs and warriors. When I saw that girl, I had to paint her. So much beauty and vitality for a maiden of eighteen years. No artist or healthy male could ignore a face like hers. Nor that one," he added hoarsely, motioning to Marissa's fading portrait.

"*Wato* . . . what?" Nathan asked anxiously.

"*Wa-to-gla Ta-te*," Thomas repeated. "It means Wild Wind. Clearly she isn't Indian, not with that red hair and

25

those gray-blue eyes. I wonder how those Sioux got hold of her and why they made her a chief's daughter." He turned to continue his study of the painting, which was desperately in need of repairing and retouching.

Nathan placed the smaller paintings on either side of Marissa's portrait and stared at the images side by side. The sixty-three-year-old man ran shaky fingers through mussed hair, the color of which shifted more from blond to silver with each passing year. As time seemingly halted, Nathan visually compared the Sioux Indian princess, *Watogla Tate*, to his deceased daughter, Marissa. His heart began to pound forcefully.

With an eye for detail, Thomas Mallory pointed out each matching or similar feature. Both women had large eyes, but Marissa's were a cornflower blue, whereas Wild Wind's were the color of a Texas winter sky just before dusk, an entrancing gray-blue. Each set of eyes exposed an air of mystery and sensuality. Thick red hair in masses of waves and curls tumbled over slender shoulders to small waists, hair that came alive with fiery color, that seemingly flowed wild and free like the rain-swollen river whose banks could not confine its abundance and energy. Marissa's portrait had been painted inside while *Watogla Tate's* had been painted outside, and therefore Wild Wind's tresses revealed golden highlights that Marissa's lacked. Both women seemed to exhibit a love for the outdoors, displaying sun-kissed golden flesh with a barely noticeable smattering of pale freckles. The shapes of their noses, faces, and chins matched perfectly. It was eerie. "This resemblance is fascinating. I would like to meet your daughter. Perhaps she could pose for a new portrait after I complete my repair work on this one. I would guess it's around . . . twenty years old?" he hinted as he critically eyed the aging portrait.

Nathan nodded. Despite his reluctance, he had to think, to remember those painful times. "I'm afraid that isn't possible, Mister Mallory. Eleven years ago, Marissa was murdered by Kiowa Indians. The red bastards attacked her stagecoach and slaughtered everyone on it but my seven-year-old granddaughter. They kidnapped her. For years I searched for Rana and offered large rewards for her return. Nothing. I couldn't bear the thought of her being enslaved and abused by those murdering savages, so it seemed easier to accept her as dead, like her mother. She was eighteen this March, if she's still alive." Nathan's eyes were glued to the canvases. "After years of torment and doubt, have I found my little Rana? Look at her. She's the spittin' image of my Marissa. It has to be my granddaughter. But how did the Sioux get her away from those Kiowas? Their territories are far apart and they're fierce enemies. How could a white captive become a Sioux chief's daughter? How can she look so dadburn happy?"

Mallory turned and glanced at the distressed man. "It seems I've brought the image of a ghost to your home, sir. I'm truly sorry." After looking at the portraits and at Nathan again, he shook his head and refuted his words. "Not a ghost, but wonderful news of your missing granddaughter. She has your eyes, sir. How marvelous to create such a happy event. You must be ecstatic to discover she is safe and happy."

"Hell, no!" Nathan shouted. "The only thing that will please me is to get her back home where she belongs. And, by God, I will."

"But what can you do to recover her, Mister Crandall? Even if you can prove she's your granddaughter, Chief Soaring Hawk wouldn't turn his daughter over to a white man. Most of those Sioux despise white men. You can't blame them, with whites and soldiers taking their lands, killing off hundreds of them, and herding the survivors onto reservations like cattle. Those treaties are worthless to both sides. I had a terrible time getting into their

27

camps and getting permission to paint some of them. Conflicts are brewing all over that territory; that's why I had to get out so fast. Settlers are pouring in, and the Indians don't like it. If this girl is your granddaughter, perhaps she doesn't even recall her childhood. Eleven years is a long time away from family and civilization. Chief Soaring Hawk and his son, Lone Wolf, seemed crazy about her. Besides, those Indians are nomads. How would you locate her and steal her? I was told the Sioux are the largest and mightiest Indian nation in the West. It could cause a war."

"I'll get her back the same way those Indians snatched Rana from her home and family—by force! She's my granddaughter; she belongs here with me. Travis will help me get Rana back," Nathan declared confidently, nodding toward the young man who had been his ranch foreman and like a son to him for seven years.

Travis Kincade had gone unnoticed during the conversation between Nathan Crandall and Thomas Mallory. He had been sitting in a large chair in the rear of the room and had listened intently as his friend and boss had questioned the artist about the intoxicating girl in his paintings, a woman whose expression and pose blended perfectly with the wildness and striking beauty of the landscape behind her.

"What do you think, Travis? Is this my Rana?" Nathan asked, even though he knew without a doubt that she was Marissa's child. He was charged with a variety of uncontrollable emotions as he looked into the face that mirrored his lost child's features.

Travis joined the men before the fireplace. Seeing the girl's clothing had brought to life a flood of haunting memories and suppressed feelings. Long ago he had lived as a Lakota warrior, and an Indian maiden had gotten him into peril; she had not only ruined his existence but had also nearly cost him his life. Repressing his past, he compared the two women. Both were of medium height and possessed shapely figures of the variety that could entice moisture above a man's upper lip and a tightening in his pants, though such reactions only supported his belief that most women were nothing but trouble. He unknowingly focused his full attention on the fascinating creature in a heavily beaded white buckskin dress. Her unmarred complexion glowed as if the sun had turned to lather and had bathed her in its golden foam, permanently staining her silky flesh.

In one portrait, the girl's hair was in braids and she was wearing a beaded headband and matching braid ties. In the other, his favorite, her thick hair fell wild and free to her waist. If the sun's rays had not caused it to seemingly burst into fire, her wavy tresses would have appeared a medium auburn shade. A small medicine wheel, made of quills in the sacred colors with a breast feather dangling from its center, was secured just above her right ear. Travis knew a Sioux medicine wheel had to be earned before one could wear it, as a warrior must earn a *coup* feather. He wondered what brave deed had prompted her tribe to gift her with it. As more turbulent memories stormed his vulnerable mind, he tried to deter them, as he had for years. He could not quite succeed.

Travis's green eyes settled on the girl's winter blue ones. Unlike Marissa's knowing look, which revealed she had tasted some of life's wanton offerings, Wild Wind's alluring gaze had a glow of innocence, a glow that hinted at eagerness to explore life. Oddly, he warmed at the undeniable spark of magic and vitality that flowed out to him from *Watogla Tate's* expression. She was a rare beauty who could strike a man speechless or halt him in his tracks. She was trouble of the highest degree and had probably crushed many men. For years he had noticed Marissa Michaels's portrait and beauty, but it was the Indian girl's image that affected his respiration and pulse; it was Chief Soaring Hawk's adopted daughter who caused his curiously susceptible mind and body to do more than stare. And this was most unusual considering his sardonic attitude toward women, an attitude that had been forced on him.

Travis became aware of the silence and the fact that the two men were staring at him. He scolded himself for his foolish reaction to a mere painting of a beautiful woman, one who doubtlessly used her looks as a potent weapon. "It could be her, Nate, or just a wild coincidence. But you'll surely pay hell if you try to steal her from Soaring Hawk and his Oglala band. Didn't you hear Mallory? She's considered the chief's daughter."

Nathan and Travis stared at each other as if speaking without words. Nathan realized his mixed-blooded, twenty-seven-year-old foreman knew what he was talking about, for Travis Kincade had been born and reared as Hunkpapa, one of the most powerful tribes in the Lakota branch of the Sioux Nation, as was the Oglala tribe, which had his granddaughter. Before settling on the Rocking C Ranch seven years ago, Travis had been a defensive and wary loner, a drifter, and a devilish rogue who had been a master of many skills and charms and had used them without mercy or hesitation whenever necessary. Born and trapped between two warring cultures, Travis had grown up too fast and too hard. Although he and Travis were now very close, Nathan knew there were things Travis had never told him or anyone, things that haunted the young man and had made him cynical and rebellious.

After leaving the Indians at the age of eighteen, the troubled youth had wandered from place to place, observing and learning about life and people, and constantly honing his skills and body. The fearless and cunning man had worked many jobs inside and outside of the law. Even when he had ridden as an Army scout and

U.S. Marshal, he had owed loyalty to no man or force but himself. Travis had become a man of immense physical prowess. Confident and self-contained, he had always sought the danger, excitement, challenge, and intrigue of any new and stimulating adventure. Then Nathan had crossed Travis's path.

Travis was also recalling his first meeting with Nathan Crandall. It had been the second time the young man had almost lost his life. The first had been at the hands of Indians and, when Nathan found him, Travis had just experienced the treachery of a spiteful white vixen. Nathan had come across the critically injured youth near St. Louis, during a Rocking *C* cattle drive. The older man had personally doctored him back to health. Some of the most difficult challenges Travis had had to face had been controlling his restive spirit, learning to trust and love, and yielding to his new fate during his physical and emotional healing process. Nathan had brought him to this ranch to recuperate, but he had been persuaded to stay on as foreman. Over the years the two had formed a deep, strong bond of friendship, dependence and loyalty. Nathan had become like a father to him and had made vast changes in his character and his way of life. This ranch had become his home and part of his responsibility. He had found acceptance and respect here; he had found happiness and a sense of belonging; he had found himself, his place in life—things that had been stolen from him nine years ago . . .

He had been born the mixed-blooded son of a Hunkpapa woman and a white man, and had been raised in the Lakota way. When he was eighteen and a seasoned warrior, a lethal and unjust travesty had destroyed all he had been and had known and loved. His mother's people had accused him of being a traitor and had tried to slay him. Their treachery and betrayal had cut him deeply and painfully; it had sapped his belief in good and

31

evil, and had shaken his faith in the Great Spirit. It was as if all he had done and had become had been in vain. If they could believe he was guilty of such wicked deeds and could order his torture and death, their past love and acceptance had been lies; his entire life had been a cruel lie. Because of one man's and one woman's greed and treachery, he had been forced to become a renegade.

Even after all these years, reflecting on that betrayal sliced through his heart and soul like an enemy's white-hot knife. By turning against him so bitterly, the Hunkpapas had robbed him of many precious things: his very existence, his honor, his trust, his hopes and dreams, his confidence. And, for awhile, they had stolen his heart and soul. They had made him become leery, resentful, hostile, hard. They had taken part of his self-esteem and, for the first time in his life, had made him feel worthless, scared, weak, helpless. For a man's desperate lie and a woman's selfishness, he had been sentenced to death by his own people and, fleeing that injustice, he had become an outcast, forever estranged from his Indian lands and ways.

Two years after that tragic episode and just as he was beginning to feel and to care once more, an evil white woman had attempted to ensnare him, and, failing that, destroy him. His bitterness, mistrust, and cynicism had increased. To avoid being hurt or betrayed again, he had tried to resist any feelings or contacts that could lead to more anguish and rejection. Then Nathan Crandall had entered his life . . .

Nathan had accepted him for himself and had proved there were people who were not selfish or traitorous. Despite what the Kiowa Indians had done to his daughter and granddaughter, Nathan had not resented him or held him accountable, though most whites hated all Indians and they persecuted all of them for the evils of a few. As for "half-breeds," they were despised and scorned by both sides. It was only because his mother had been a war chief's daughter that the Indians had accepted him, until a grasping foe had maligned him and turned his mother's people against him.

Not so with this white friend. Nathan was a rare man, a good and kind man. Nathan would never turn against him unless he was convinced Travis was guilty of some crime; then Nathan would doubt it until he was given absolutely unquestionable evidence. And, despite such evidence, Nathan would probably try to rationalize the deed and pardon him. After all this man had done for him and was to him, Travis hated to think of Nathan being hurt by this fantasy of regaining his missing granddaughter. By now, that girl was no longer white, no longer his family . . .

Nathan saw Travis's look of deep concern and affection. "That's my daughter's child, my own flesh and blood. Surely you don't expect me to sit here and do nothing?" he asked softly.

"Of course not. We'll just have to do some clever planning before we take off to Soaring Hawk's camp. If that's Rana, there's no telling what she's been through since her capture. We'll need to walk this path slowly and carefully, Nate. First, we have to make certain she is Rana Michaels; then we'll have to figure out a safe way for you to stake your claim on her to get her free of the Oglalas and back home. She's probably been there a long time and might not want to leave. This won't be quick or easy, Nate."

"Nothing good or right ever comes fast and easy. I'm used to hard work and patience, Travis; but this time, it's damned difficult to practice them." What if Travis was right? Nathan reflected silently. What if Rana had forgotten her family? What if the Indians refused to release her or she refused to come home with him? After all, during her childhood Rana had seen him only a few times. He looked at Thomas Mallory and asked, "Can I

33

buy those two portraits of Rana? Name your price."

Thomas replied, "Normally I would say no; but this time I'll agree. We can discuss a reasonable price later." He glanced at the clock. "I must be hurrying along. I have a dinner engagement tonight. The restoration of your daughter's portrait should require five to seven days. If we have a deal, Mister Crandall, I'll complete my work in Fort Worth tomorrow and return here Sunday afternoon."

Nathan shook hands with the artist. "I'll have one of my hands pick you up at the hotel around three Sunday afternoon. Thank you for bringing me the news of my granddaughter's survival and her location."

"I wish you luck in accomplishing her return. As your man said, it won't be an easy task to recover her. We can discuss her and your impending journey Sunday evening when we have more time."

Travis remained before the immense fireplace while Nathan escorted the artist to the waiting buggy. When Nathan returned, he poured himself and Travis a whiskey. The younger man turned and watched his older friend as the man collapsed wearily into a chair. "I know this must be hard on you after all this time of considering her lost forever. Are you sure it isn't best to leave her where she is, Nate? Stealing her back could be as traumatic for her now as her abduction was years ago. Look at her, Nate. That isn't the expression of a miserable, lowly captive. Clearly she's done well for herself. Those Oglalas are her family now. I would think long and hard before I interfered. I know what it's like to be caught between two warring peoples, and I know how hard change is. She can't replace Marissa." Travis almost hated the idea of a "Marissa" coming to live with them. She could turn their lives inside out and wreak havoc on their emotions. He instantly realized that his was a selfish attitude and scolded himself. If she was Rana, she

34

deserved to be rescued and given another chance.

Nathan drained the last sip of whiskey from his glass, then placed it on a side table. "Even after all these years, Travis, it's impossible to understand Marissa's behavior. If she hadn't taken off with that conniving gambler, she would still be alive. I can close my eyes and picture her sashaying into this very room to announce she was eloping with Raymond Michaels. I tried everything to change her mind. We argued for hours. I threatened to whip her and lock her in her room. Hell, I even threatened to have Michaels beaten and jailed. I refused to give them my blessing or permission. I told Marissa she would be disinherited if she ran off with that piece of cow dung; I thought that would change Michaels's mind about latching onto a wealthy girl. I knew Marissa was spoiled and headstrong, but I didn't think she would give up all she had for a man whose reputation was as black as his hair or that fancy suit he wore. It was like Michaels had cast some evil spell over her. I was a fool to call a gambler's hand. I always thought he would drop her before the wedding, but that greedy bastard held out with dreams of getting his filthy hands on my money. Perdition, I would spend it all to get Marissa and Rana back!"

"You can't blame yourself for Marissa's mistakes."

Nathan sighed heavily. "I'm to blame for some of them, Travis. I let her have her way too long. If my Ruthie hadn't died with that fever when Marissa was ten, she would have known how to handle our feisty child. When I realized Marissa was dead serious about running off, it was too late to stop her. Hell, I would have married her off to one of the neighboring ranchers or one of my cowpunchers! How could a girl raised so easy choose a hard and dangerous life like Michaels offered? Traveling from one dirty town and loud saloon to another; always being around drunks and whores and gunslingers; going up and down that treacherous river on one of them big boats so Michaels could lie and cheat while he plied his dirty trade. You know what kinds of things go on in those saloons and riverboats. It wasn't any place for a lady like Marissa or a small child. Surprised me Michaels kept them around for seven years. I kept hoping Marissa would come to her senses and return home. She never could see the evil in that man, or wouldn't admit she could to me or herself."

"You sure you want to dig this up tonight?" Travis asked. He knew how painful this subject was for Nathan. Besides, he had heard most of this tale before and it always made him angry. Travis loved and respected the older man; he would risk any peril to defend him. During the seven years since Nathan Crandall had saved his life, Travis had learned much about Nathan, and his defiant, selfish daughter.

Travis had met plenty of vixens like Marissa and had forgotten all except two vicious bitches. Conniving, greedy females rubbed him the wrong way. He despised vain, spoiled creatures who only cared about themselves. Marissa's eyes told wicked tales and seemed to shout them louder than a cannon roared, though Nathan was too much the loving father to hear them. It had taken years after that horrible incident for Nathan to find happiness and peace of mind, and he had still been suffering when they had been thrown together. Maybe that mutual need for love and peace had sparked the rapport and bond between them. Together they had healed each other's wounds. Now some evil force was thrusting this imposing girl into Nathan's life and emotions. She possessed the power to hurt Nathan as deeply as Marissa had, and he could not allow it. If she was like her mother, she could destroy Nathan Crandall.

"Maybe I am partly to blame, Travis. Maybe I should have let Marissa have her way. Maybe I should have tried to buy off Michaels. Hell, I made sure Marissa learned about his other women and deceits. She wanted to stay deaf and blind to his weaknesses; she refused to believe my reports. Michaels turned her into a spineless, empty-headed fool who would follow him anywhere! Maybe I was too busy with the ranch to see what was happening to my little girl. Maybe if I had remarried and had given Marissa a mother who could supply love and guidance, then she wouldn't have gone bad. Women can be such fools when it comes to a handsome face and charming front. Michaels thought all he had to do was outwait me, then move in here and take over. I've wished a hundred times I had shot the bastard. Hell, he tried to have me killed twice! If those Kiowas hadn't murdered him, me and him would have tangled eventually. If Michaels had truly loved her, I would have done anything to help them. Why didn't my little girl listen to me?"

Nathan picked up his glass and poured himself another drink. Travis remained silent and observant, a lingering trait from his Indian upbringing. "If it had been anyone but my child, I would have said she was getting what she deserved. I loved that girl, Travis. If only she could have admitted she was wrong and let me help her get away from that snake. If we'd only been given a little more time . . ."

Travis empathized with Nathan as the older man was forced to retrace a torturous path. "Just before she was murdered, she and Michaels seemed to be at their last stand. I told her over and over that she could return home with Rana any day or night. Maybe I shouldn't have sent money for food and clothes. Maybe poverty and shame would have opened Marissa's eyes and driven her home. But I couldn't let them go hungry and naked and sleep in barns or over saloons. I wonder if he even let her keep the money. Knowing that beast, he probably took it and gambled it away. Those two girls saw plenty of

37

hard times. No, I should have given in to her pleas; maybe they would still be alive."

"No, Nate," Travis argued. "Marissa would have had to have been the one to break it off with Michaels. He would have destroyed you and this ranch. Let this matter rest," he urged. Travis had never seen Nathan so insecure, so determined to place the blame on the wrong head. He knew that Nathan was being plagued by doubts and self-recrimination, but the man did not deserve them, for Nathan had done what he had thought was right for his child and for himself. That was not true of his own father. Jeremy Kincade had duped and betrayed his child for selfish reasons.

"I can't, Travis. I have to think about Rana. You and her are all I have left. If you had been here years ago, Marissa wouldn't have looked at another man. I could have left the ranch to you two. You know I think of you as the son I never had. If I can't get Rana back, it's yours. If I do, you two will share it."

Travis smiled. "You've done plenty for me, Nate. I wouldn't be alive now if you hadn't found me and taken me in. I know I gave you lots of hard times and smart mouth, but you turned me around. If Michaels hadn't been pulling at Marissa with pretty words and smiles, you could have turned her around too," he encouraged his friend, even if he did not believe these last words. He wondered how Marissa had turned out so badly with a good father like Nathan Crandall.

"The last time I saw Rana, she was a beautiful, vivacious child. Marissa had brought her to visit me for a month, probably trying to change my mind about taking them in before winter started. I could tell she was getting tired of always moving around and ignoring Michaels's lies. She was tense and moody. She was weakening, Travis. I should have pressed her harder. She looked so weary and sad. I think Michaels was starting to give her a hard time, maybe threatening to get rid of her and the child if she couldn't get any money out of me. You should have seen those two girls together, Travis. Little Rana had arrived a quiet, shy, frightened child. She loved it here on the ranch. I watched her open up and come to life. After a few days, she was full of laughter and chatter, always following me and the boys around and asking countless questions. I think that was the first time since her birth she was getting enough food and rest and play. She thrived on the sunshine and attention, and she wasn't timid or afraid anymore."

Nathan's voice and expression went cold and harsh. "They only stayed two weeks. That no-good Michaels showed up and took them away. The minute he walked in the door, I saw a change come over Marissa and Rana. He sapped the life and joy right out of their bodies. He was a cold and clever bastard, but I saw through his little game. He had been giving me a taste of what I was missing. He figured I would relent. I was hoping my daughter had regained some of her pride and spunk and she would stand up to the vermin. God forgive me for saying that only Marissa and Rana would be welcome here. Michaels called my bluff and I lost Marissa. If she hadn't died, I think she would have returned home within a month. She's gone forever, Travis, but I can get Rana back with your help. Will you take me to Soaring Hawk?"

Even if he disagreed with Nathan's explanation and plans, Travis realized he had to yield to his friend's plea. The truth was that he did not know how he felt about this matter. "I'll do what I can to get her back for you. Just make sure you understand the consequences if she and the Oglalas don't agree with our actions. You know the government sent every Union soldier they could find into that area to subdue the Dakota Nation. Maybe they have rounded up and fenced in some of the tribes, but those Oglalas and Hunkpapas will never make peace with

39

whites who are stealing their lands. Those ex-Yankees don't realize who they're challenging in Red Cloud, Gall, Sitting Bull, Crazy Horse, and Soaring Hawk. Blind lambs to the slaughter, Nate. Even if we can get in and out alive, bringing Rana back with us will be nearly impossible. We could stir up more trouble and danger for the whites and Indians by stealing part of Soaring Hawk's family. Do you want to risk causing a new bloodbath?" Travis observed the effect of his words on Nathan. Travis was not afraid to risk his life, but he did not want to risk Nathan's.

"I want her, Travis. I need her. Help me do this the right way. Once Soaring Hawk hears the truth, surely he'll let Rana return to her real family. If necessary, I'll get on my knees and beg him."

"When, and if, we reach the Dakota Territory, promise you'll let me handle everything. Promise you won't interfere with whatever I say or do. Maybe we can come to some peaceful compromise."

"How soon can we leave?" Nathan questioned eagerly.

Travis reminded Nathan, "We're already running weeks behind on our spring roundup and cattle drive. I don't see how we can take off for the Oglala camp until we return from Sedalia. Say six to eight weeks. Then we should be able to reach the Dakota Territory within three or four weeks. If all goes well, we might have her home by mid-August."

"That's two or three months! If things are as bad as you said, Rana could be injured or killed before we reach her," Nathan protested.

"Soldiers wouldn't kill a beautiful white girl."

"Even if she behaves like a Sioux enemy?"

Travis dodged that question by focusing attention on another problem. "Have you forgotten that Harrison Caldwell is breathing fire on your neck? Last summer and winter were bad for us, Nate; we borrowed plenty of money to get through. If we don't get those cattle to

40

market soon, he'll force Mason's bank to call in your loans so he can buy them up. If we lose that sale or get there too late for good prices, we're in deep trouble. He's already found ways to take over nearly every neighboring spread and close us in on three sides. That only leaves us protected by the river and McFarland's spread. I don't like the idea of being surrounded by that snake. Do you want to lose the Rocking *C* Ranch to that rattler while we're off chasing a ghost? Patience, Nate, or you won't have a home to bring Rana back to. Not unless you don't mind my having to marry Clarissa Caldwell to get it back for us," he teased cunningly to relax Nathan's tension and concern.

"I'll thrash you with a leather strap if you ever seriously glance in that vixen's direction. You just keep leading her down a flowery trail to keep an eye on her old man. Harry will hang back as long as he thinks he can get hold of this ranch through you and his daughter." Nathan cautioned, "We'd best make sure he doesn't learn about Rana, or he might see her as a kink in his dirty plans. Just keep letting that pretty vulture believe she's got her talons wrapped tightly around you and we'll be fine." He chuckled. "Little Clarissa and her father won't be none too happy when they get a look at my beautiful granddaughter."

Both men's gazes went to the mantel to eye the girl mentioned. Travis grinned and devilishly agreed, "Nope, Miss Clarissa Caldwell won't take kindly to Rana Michaels's arrival at all. I wonder just how accurately Soaring Hawk named his adopted daughter. *Watogla Tate*, Wild Wind . . . Lordy, Nate, we might have us a tough taming job ahead."

Later, at supper, Travis's keen instincts were alert. He asked, "You've thought it over carefully and you're sure you want to do this?"

Nathan's blue eyes locked with the lively green ones of

41

the man who was like the son he had never had. He sighed deeply and nodded. Travis had given him back his spirit, his vitality, his pride; Travis had brought him happiness and a new reason for living. He knew something of the hardships, loneliness, anguish, and humiliation the younger man had endured. But those emotions and experiences had toughened Travis; they had made him nearly invincible; they had honed his talents, instincts, and body into a powerful force that few men rashly challenged. Over the years since coming here, Travis had lost much of his brittleness and wariness. Nathan knew that his love, acceptance, and help had changed that coldness and filled that emptiness. He knew he had done as much for Travis as Travis had done for him, and understood that Travis might be leery of returning to the people he had rejected for the whites.

Nathan asked soulfully, "What would you do if she were your flesh and blood, Travis? If she were your daughter or sister or wife? I owe her, son. I'm the reason she was born, and maybe the reason she was captured. If not for my self-righteousness and obstinancy, Marissa would be alive and Rana would be at home tonight. I should have found the courage to kill that bastard she married!" Nathan declared, some of his old guilt and rage returning to plague him.

"You've got to face reality, Nate. What if she isn't Rana? This trip will be long and dangerous. It could take weeks to locate Soaring Hawk's camp. We can't just ride in and demand her return. If we ask too many questions along the way, word will spread and they'll get suspicious. We could get killed before we reach her."

Nathan fused his worried gaze on the man who was half-Indian and a highly trained warrior—a fact known only in these parts by Nathan Crandall. Travis's knowledge of the Indians and their language could be vital to his success. Yet the search for Rana did not have

Nathan as concerned as asking Travis to return to the Dakota Territory with him, for Nathan suspected the emotional and physical agonies that this fearless man had experienced there. While doctoring Travis's muscular body years ago, Nathan had viewed the scars of the Sun Dance and those of a brutal torturing. To force Travis to enter that territory again might refresh those painful years, those horrible events, those traits that had taken Nathan a long time and a lot of love to alter. He asked himself if he dared risk losing Travis to death or to the "old ways," in order to rescue a girl who might not wish to be returned home. Yet, there was no one who could better understand and deal with this present Rana or the hazardous conditions in the Sioux territory than Travis "White Eagle" Kincade.

"There's only one way to find out if she is my granddaughter. Rana had an accident during her last visit here; that injury would have left a permanent scar on her left ankle. If she wasn't wearing those beaded leggings, I'd point it out to you. She also has a birthmark on the underside of her left arm." Nathan paused briefly before saying, "I have no right to ask you to go with me, Travis, but I wish you would. I can put Cody Slade in charge of the ranch and Mace Hunter in charge of the cattle drive to Sedalia. We won't tell anyone where we're going."

Travis loved and admired this older man and told him, "I don't want to see you hurt again, Nate. You know what you always tell me: don't climb on a wild mustang who's sure to buck you off and cripple you."

Nathan shook his graying blond head and smiled stubbornly. "We both have a gut feeling it's her, Travis. You know better than most what kind of existence that is for a captive female, especially with all this fighting between the whites and Indians. Can we allow Rana to be slaughtered during a cavalry raid on their camp? What do you think either a white or Indian captor would do with

43

such a beautiful girl? Make her his whore," Nathan declared with a sneer. "It's too dangerous for her to remain in the Dakota Territory, no matter what she says or thinks. I'll risk any danger or pay any price to get her back."

Travis knew why Nathan hesitated over asking him to go. His love and concern were obvious. Travis wondered how he would feel returning to his mother's lands and people after all these years, and if it would be safe for him to enter Hunkpapa territory. He wondered if he was emotionally strong enough to deal with the feelings and situations that could arise during this journey. He could feel a lingering bitterness rising within him. He had tried to come to terms with his past and thought he had, until this matter had come up today. He could now admit that the "evidence" against him had looked bad then, but the Hunkpapas should have trusted him, at least given him the chance to defend himself. He did not know if he could ever totally forgive them for that denial. Travis could not help but wonder, if he were to tell Nathan about his past, which life he would choose to protect—his or Rana's. No, Travis decided unselfishly, the truth would compel Nathan to make a distressing choice.

Besides, he hated to think of Nathan's granddaughter being captured, raped, or killed. There was something about this girl that pulled at him, something that no woman had been able to do before. If she was part of Nathan, she belonged here with them. And he wanted to meet her, even if she were not Rana Michaels. Nathan needed him, and perhaps the girl did too. Maybe she was not as happy or as free as she appeared. Maybe she was not like the other women he had known, the ones who had made him so cynical and wary. Like him, this girl was trapped between two warring peoples. She was part of Nathan's family, and the Lakotas should not be allowed to take anything else of real value from him. He owed Nathan, and he owed himself.

As he envisioned Wild Wind, Travis's green eyes brightened and he grinned. He stroked his stubbled jawline. "I haven't had a decent challenge in a long time, Nate. Rana or not, that ravishing creature will make for a stimulating quest. We'll get supplies ready tomorrow and leave at dawn Sunday." Travis mentally added, *May the Great Spirit help us if she's anything like Marissa or Raymond Michaels,* but Travis did not share with Nathan his overwhelming sense of foreboding . . .

Chapter Two

Dakota Territory
May 24, 1867

Wild Wind ceased her swimming, for it had failed to relax her taut body or distract her troubled mind. Time had escaped without giving her an answer to her dilemma. She left the still-chilly water to stretch out on the spring grass in a secluded area along the riverbank. She closed her eyes and allowed the afternoon sun to dry and warm her shapely body and fiery hair. Neither she nor Lone Wolf had mentioned their last quarrel of weeks ago. Yet each knew it weighed heavily on the other's mind, just as each wondered what the other would do. The Sun Dance ritual and buffalo feast were approaching rapidly. If she did not make her own decision soon, the problem would be settled for her.

Wild Wind sat up and crossed her feet. She absently scratched a white scar on her left ankle, which sometimes itched when she was angry or tense. Her arms encircled her legs and she rested her chin on one knee. She had not changed her mind about marriage, especially to Rides-Like-Thunder, who was always trying to steal kisses or put his hands where they should not touch. She was tired of being the butt of jokes and teased. How could she marry a man who did not take her seriously, a man who thought mastering her was an amusing game?

Wild Wind was not afraid of animals or wilderness dangers; she could protect herself with weapons and cunning. She would not starve, for she knew how to hunt and cook. But secretly she had witnessed evil deeds of the man-beast enemy, and this caused her to hesitate over leaving her camp and people. She could not live in the forest or mountains alone; and once she rejected her people's laws and departed, she could never return. Was there no answer other than a forced marriage?

She leapt to her feet and paced back and forth along the riverbank until her bare feet made a path through the supple blades of grass. Needing solitude to make a decision, she had been here since dawn, but she had not achieved success. How she wished these lovely surroundings would share part of their tranquillity with her. How she wished *Tunkansila* would hear her prayers and respond, for Grandfather was supposed to know all things and to have love and mercy for His people. She was so confused, so torn by what should be a simple and happy decision for an Indian maiden: the choosing of a mate and the settling down to married life. Why was she troubled by a terrible sense of foreboding? Why was she resisting and lingering here when she had only two choices: marry or leave?

Wild Wind inhaled deeply and loudly. Perhaps she was overly tired today, for she had slept little the night before. She sat on her drying blanket and stretched out once more. If any peril approached, *Mahpiya* would warn her. She glanced at the cherished white stallion whom she had named Cloud. The highly intelligent animal loved and obeyed only her. He was sleek and swift, and he responded instantly to the slightest hint of danger to her. She smiled, then closed her eyes.

Travis Kincade and Nathan Crandall had been waiting over an hour beside the coulee for the young brave to return with Chief Soaring Hawk or with a message from him. Nathan glanced at Travis and asked, "Do you think he'll come to parley, or send a war party to kill us?"

Travis did not pull his scanning gaze from the harsh landscape before him as he replied, "From what I can recall about Soaring Hawk, he's a man of great honor and courage. I doubt he would kill us before letting us speak our piece. 'Course, things and people have changed a great deal since I left. You heard what those soldiers at Fort Wallace had to say. The Army's got several bands of Oglalas and Hunkpapas givin' 'em hell. Captain Clardy at our last stop told me they've been sending replacements up this way for months to squash Red Cloud and his followers. He said Red Cloud has been able to keep that Boseman Trail through the Powder River country and most of their forts closed for over a year. You know that doesn't sit well with the Army. If those Yankees think they can whip the Lakotas like they did the Rebs, they're in for a rough awakening. One Lakota tribe is hard enough to conquer, but several tribes banded together . . . No way, Nate."

Nathan leaned against the same large rock as Travis. "From the way those soldiers were talking and preparing, these Sioux Indians have 'em plenty nervous. Afore this matter is settled, I'll wager the Army's gonna regret teaching the Indians about massacres and broken promises. Hell, it's only been five months since Crazy Horse wiped out Colonel Fetterman and his entire troop. If you ask me, Travis, that's one warrior the Cavalry had

49

better watch very closely."

"You're right, Nate. Crazy Horse is smart and fearless, and he's tired of watching the whites try to annihilate the Dakota Nation. He's a born warrior, the same age as me. Put him with Soaring Hawk, Red Cloud, Gall, and Sitting Bull, and those soldiers are as helpless as newborn pups in a blizzard. The Army's filling a powder keg on Indian lands, Nate, and we're smack in the middle of its explosion area."

Nathan looked tired and worried. "Maybe we shoulda just sneaked into their camp and snatched Rana. I bet these Indians don't trust any white man. Once he learns why we came here, you think he'll . . . ?"

Nathan fell silent as Travis straightened to full alert and reflexively checked the Remington Army .44 pistols that were strapped to his muscled thighs. Travis had selected these particular weapons because they were more accurate and sturdier than the Colt .44. His green eyes narrowed briefly as he forcibly relaxed his taut body, which had stiffened in a careless show of fear or uncertainty. "They're here, Nate. Stay calm and quiet. Try not to look nervous. Remember, no shouting or arguing."

Nathan's hands shook and he wiped his suddenly moist palms on his trouser legs. Nathan glanced around. "I'll let you handle everything like I promised. Where are they? I don't see or hear anything."

"I make out eight of them, two on each side of us. Soaring Hawk should arrive soon. Relax, Nate. If he wanted us killed or captured, we wouldn't be standing here right now." Travis's keen senses had detected the stealthy approach of the Oglala warriors. Alone, he could have taken on eight warriors and probably defeated them, but he had Nathan's life to protect. He had to handle himself and this matter gingerly and wisely. He knew

Indians liked to eye a situation before encountering it. His sharp senses did not perceive any immediate threat of danger; but if he was mistaken, he was prepared to deal with it. His Winchester .44 rifle, which fired seventeen rounds, was lying on the hard dirt before him in case he had to drop to the ground and seize it quickly. His pistols were ready for firing, and he carried two concealed knives, which he could use with lethal skill.

Travis cautioned the older man, "Keep your hands away from your weapons, Nate, unless I give the attack signal. Then hit the dirt and fire right and front. I'll take left and rear. Stand here while I make contact. I need to let 'em know what we want." Travis stepped away from the gulch where their horses and supplies were waiting. He lifted his hands and gave the sign for "peace," his hands before his chest, the left palm turned upward and the right hand grasping the left one snugly.

Travis knew he had to depend on his skill in sign language to get his points across to the concealed warriors. He lifted his right hand to shoulder level. With the index and middle fingers extended upward and held together and with the other fingers and thumb closed toward the palm, he gave the sign for *kola*, "friend." He continued his mute one-sided conversation by giving the signs that he had come to make a trade for one of their white captives, the granddaughter of the man who was waiting with him. Travis silently entreated Chief Soaring Hawk to come and bargain with him for the girl's release. To show the warriors he knew of their arrival and their locations, he faced the other three directions and repeated his message. The sable-haired man waited a few minutes, but no one responded to his claims or his summons.

Travis knew his patience and courage were being tested, so he made certain his expression remained calm and his stance remained poised. Travis decided to reveal his Indian identity to Soaring Hawk and his band, for tribes rarely related the humiliating and painful news of a warrior's betrayal and punishment to outsiders. Unless the traitor posed a threat to allied tribes, the personal and embarrassing matter was usually kept private. And since all those involved in that treachery had been slain or driven far away, there would have been no remaining danger to the Hunkpapas or their Lakota brothers. Travis hoped that some of these warriors who were closing in on him might recall the famed and fearless half-blooded warrior, White Eagle. What he had to do was recover Rana, then get them out of this area before the Hunkpapas heard of his return and labeled him a threat to their Lakota brothers, as well as unfinished business for them.

Travis gave the sign for "color" by rubbing the fingertips of his right hand in a circular pattern on the back of his left hand. Then his hands formed the signs for *wanmbli* and *ska,* indicating his name of White Eagle. Lastly, Travis revealed he was part Lakota by giving the signs for "half-Indian" and "Sioux" with the "throat-cutter" movement, then signaled his bond to the Hunkpapa tribe. Again he motioned that he had come in peace to bargain with Soaring Hawk.

It was only moments before a lone Indian approached him on a brown and white Appaloosa whose painted markings exposed the numerous and daring exploits of his bronze skinned master. The man proudly carried a *coup* lance with feathers attached from one end to the other, a counting stick for his many deeds. A bow and quiver of arrows were hanging over his broad back, and a war shield was clutched securely in his left hand. A leather sheath that held a buffalo jaw hunting knife was secured at the right side of his waist. The markings on the arrow quiver, buffalo shield, knife sheath, and horse's rump worried Travis. They were symbols of the Black

War Bonnet Society and boldly announced his membership in that fierce and determined "war medicine" brotherhood. Clearly this was a man of great prowess and high rank.

The Indian, who appeared to be in his mid-twenties, did not dismount or speak. A long mane of shiny black hair settled around the warrior's brawny shoulders, and a beaded headband with geometric designs kept it from falling into his ruggedly handsome face and piercing eyes. The Indian's pleasant features were strongly defined. He was dressed in a breechclout and low-cut moccasins, leaving most of his well-developed body in view. His dark skin revealed white scars here and there, signs of past battle wounds and the Sun Dance. Around his neck there was a *wanapin*, an amulet in the shape of a wolf's head, with bared teeth, keen eyes, and ears erect and alert. Around his large biceps were secured arm bands with special *coups* colorfully etched on them and from which beaded thongs and feathers dangled.

"*Hau*," Travis greeted the warrior genially, fearlessly. The amulet implied that the warrior was Lone Wolf, and Travis assumed he had been sent to investigate this matter for his father. As Travis eyed the striking man who possessed Wild Wind, incredible jealousy sparked within him until he reminded himself that she was living as the Indian's sister.

Eyes the color of greased coal roamed the full length of Travis's body and settled on his face. The Oglala warrior asked, "*Nituwe hwo? Taku ca yacin hwo?*" It meant "Who are you? What do you want?"

Travis easily responded in the Lakota tongue of his mother's people, saying, "We have come to bargain with Chief Soaring Hawk for the release of a white captive. By the whites I am called Travis Kincade and by my Hunkpapa people I am known as White Eagle. Soaring Hawk, Chief of the Oglalas, is called a man of great

53

courage and cunning. Why does he send another warrior to speak and stand in his place?"

Lone Wolf stared at the man with intensely green eyes, deep golden skin, and nearly black hair. The white man's expression and stance told Lone Wolf that he was a man of great physical and mental prowess. Black eyes lingered for a moment on the red cloth band that was secured around Travis's forehead in the Apache style. He noticed that the man was clad in fringed buckskin shirt and pants and was wearing knee moccasins. Something was suspended on a leather thong around his neck, but it was hidden beneath his sienna-colored shirt. *"Iyeciciye sni yelo,"* the warrior remarked, telling Travis that he had not recognized him. He continued in his tongue, "Many times Mother Earth has renewed her face since I heard Hunkpapa tales of the half-white warrior with fire in his heart and head. My own eyes witnessed his skills and courage when our tribes camped together for the buffalo feast and trading season. You have been gone many winters, White Eagle. Why do you return this sun to seek words with my father?"

Travis said, *"Nawin Upizata he kci wowaglaka,"* telling the intrepid warrior that he wished to speak with Soaring Hawk. *"Tokiyaya hwo?"* the ranch foreman continued, asking where he was.

The warrior replied in Oglala in a tone of confidence, "My father lives with the Great Spirit. His life was stolen by the burning ball of a bluecoat's firestick. I am Lone Wolf, son of Soaring Hawk, chief of the Oglalas. Many changes have come to our lands, White Eagle, since you vanished. I believed you dead these many seasons. Oglalas joined the Black War Bonnet Society. Oglalas carry the signs of death and danger. Oglalas speak and wear war medicine. Many of our Dakota brothers have made treaty with the white dogs and have given away their lands and freedoms to end the white man's war, to

54

save their people. Surrender did not stop the white man's war. The white-eyes seek defeat of all Dakota tribes and conquest of all Indian lands."

Lone Wolf watched Travis intently. "Oglalas say, 'What is life without freedom, sacred lands, and honor?' But the white-eyes come swiftly and heavily as the winter snows. Many Lakotas are too old and weary to fight. Many have no warriors or weapons to battle our foes. Many have no place to run or horses to carry them. Soldiers attacked and burned many camps in the winter past; many starved and many died from the cold. The soldiers give little time to gather medicine herbs and to make weapons and to hunt game. They are sly and vicious as the badger. Many Lakotas live inside the fences that the whites called reservations!" he stated with repulsion, his eyes flickering with black fires of hatred and anger. Quickly he mastered his display of emotion.

"It is not so with the Oglalas and Hunkpapas. We fight our white and Indian enemies. Those who refuse to sign the white man's treaties are called renegades, hostiles, savages! The white man seeks to defeat them and slay them. To stand against the bluecoats becomes a challenge to destroy us. They declare war on those who will not yield their freedoms and lands to greedy whites. Many soldiers and weapons have been sent to this land to conquer the Lakotas. We have painted death on our shields and robes, and we paint the mark of the Black War Bonnet Society on our faces when we ride to battle our white foes. The Hunkpapas join with the Oglalas to fight this white enemy, to drive him from our lands. White Eagle has not been in our lands and battles for many seasons. You dress and speak as white, the path you have chosen to walk. Gall is war chief of the Hunkpapas; he is the adopted brother of the medicine chief, Sitting Bull. Sitting Bull draws all Lakotas together with his words. Grandfather gave him the power to see beyond

55

this sun to those to come. When he speaks, all Lakotas listen and obey, as you once did, White Eagle."

Knowing it was a show of bad manners to interrupt a warrior when he was talking, Travis remained silent and attentive as Lone Wolf spoke. "Red Cloud, Crazy Horse, and Lone Wolf of the Oglalas defeat more of the whites than all other tribes together. The soldiers fear us and wish us dead. We cannot drive them from the lands they have taken from our brothers, for they are many and they carry magic weapons. But we will fight to hold our lands until no Oglala or Hunkpapa warrior is alive. Our Cheyenne brothers fight beside us. No white-eyes is safe in our lands. Your white blood has chosen the white man's world. Go, and do not return while you side with our enemies."

Realizing that Lone Wolf was unaware of the dark secret that had driven him from these lands years ago, Travis relaxed slightly. "I do not side or fight with the white soldiers, Lone Wolf. I left our lands to find peace and acceptance in another place many suns' ride from our sacred Black Hills, a place where I am not forced to take my father's or my mother's side in a cruel war. I did not choose to be born with warring bloods. I rode from these lands to seek a place where the fires within my heart and head could cool. Seven winters past I found my place of honor and happiness with the white man who travels with me. I live on his ranch on the lands that once belonged to the Kiowas and Comanches. We come to claim his granddaughter and take her home with us. She was taken captive by your tribe many winters past. She is white, so she is not safe in your lands. Your tongue has spoken the many reasons why she must be sent home to her family. Hear my words of truth, Lone Wolf, and release her to us, for she is loved by you and your people and you wish no harm to come to her."

The warrior's stoic expression did not change. Travis

continued, "Your people need supplies for survival and defense, Lone Wolf; the man called Nathan Crandall will give you much money for her return to buy those supplies: food, blankets, knives, guns," he offered temptingly. "We come in peace. Let us sit and make trade." When Lone Wolf did not react, Travis reasoned, "What is the value of one white captive in exchange for needed supplies and weapons? You are chief. How will you help your people survive without food and weapons?"

"How much of the white-eyes money do you offer for one white captive? What is the girl's value to White Eagle and his friend?"

"Her value is as large as the heaven, Lone Wolf, but we do not have enough money to fill it. His reward to the Oglalas for rescuing his granddaughter and caring for her will buy many supplies."

The warrior did not glance at Nathan during this talk. "How can Lone Wolf buy supplies from white-eyes? Trading posts are guarded. Do you speak false, White Eagle? Do you set a trap for the Lakotas?"

Anger flared briefly in Travis's leafy green eyes, but he quickly suppressed it. "I am half Lakota, Lone Wolf. I do not wish to see my mother's people massacred. The whites are wrong to take Indian lands and lives. Many whites and bluecoats are bad; they seek to kill any Indian, even women and children and the old ones. The whites are countless, Lone Wolf, and I see great suffering and death for many Lakotas. The bluecoat war chiefs and soldiers battled another white enemy with numbers and weapons greater than those the Lakotas possess, and they won a painful victory. They are powerful warriors, Lone Wolf. They carry hatred for the Indian and hunger for his lands in their hearts and minds. As a stormy river, they cannot be halted or controlled. If you cannot make honorable peace, you must have weapons for your battles and hunts so your people can live. The old ones must not suffer in their last days or die on land far from the sacred hills. The women must not mourn the deaths of sons and husbands who are defenseless against the soldiers' fire sticks and longknives or be left to the charity of others who have little themselves. And what of the children? Must they suffer or grow under the shadow of white fear or be denied their lands and heritage? Must they be raised as slaves of the white-eyes?"

Travis fused his gaze to Lone Wolf's so the warrior could read his honesty and sincerity, praying that Lone Wolf did not know of his dishonor long ago. "I will help you get the supplies to make this war even. This very sun, many supply wagons are unloading at the Chambers Trading Post, two days' ride from your camp. We saw this with our metal eyes but did not ride close, for we wished no whites to learn of our journey to the Oglala camp. Nate and I will ride there with the money. The white traders are greedy. If they ask why we buy the supplies, we will tell them for friends to defend their lives and lands. Since we are white, they will not suspect that we buy them for your people. You must use them to fight soldiers, Lone Wolf, not innocent whites who have been tricked into coming here. Defeat the soldiers and make it impossible for settlers to exist on your lands, and they will return to theirs or push further west. Prove you are a man of honor and mercy by driving whites from your lands alive."

"I am to trust you with such a deed and plan?" Lone Wolf asked.

"As I trusted you with my life this sun. Send a band of your best warriors to guard us with the money and to guard the supplies after we purchase them. When we bring them to your camp, you will give the white captive to her grandfather. Do we make trade?" the green-eyed man asked. Travis knew about the 1830 Indian Removal

Act, the 1851 Indian Appropriation Act, the numerous worthless treaties, and the many brutal massacres of Indian camps, so he knew why Lone Wolf was reluctant to trust him or any white man, even if he did have a past reputation and identity as a renowned warrior.

The Sioux chief was intrigued. "Tell me of the white captive you risked your life and honor to seek. How do you know we have her?"

Without his awareness, Lone Wolf's expression responded to the shocking words of Travis Kincade as he related the tale of the Kiowa capture of Rana Michaels eleven years ago and revealed the details of the enlightening visit and the paintings of artist Thomas Mallory. "She lives with the Oglala people as the adopted daughter of Soaring Hawk. She is called Wild Wind," he explained. Motioning to Nathan, Travis said, "Her grandfather has come to bargain for her release. She is of his blood and belongs with him."

Lone Wolf said with a sneer, "You wish Lone Wolf to sell his own sister? What trick is this? The fires in White Eagle's head and heart now burn with the black fires of evil and betrayal. My sister belongs with her people. She is to join with Rides-Like-Thunder of the Cheyenne. Why do you seek to help the bluecoats buy her? What do they want with Wild Wind? I should slay you where you stand."

Travis was relieved when Lone Wolf did not mention his traitorous father, for he felt only shame and disgust for Jeremy Kincade's betrayal of his mother, Pretty Bird Woman, and her people. Travis had been ensnared and dishonored by his father's treachery, for he had ridden innocently with him that black day that had ended so tragically for his mother and many Hunkpapas. For a long time he had carried the bitterness, cynicism, and stigma of his father's actions. If a man could not trust, respect, and love his own father, how could he inspire such feelings in other men? he had wondered. But Nathan had taught him how to deal with those destructive emotions. Returning to these lands placed his life in peril, for the Hunkpapas would influence the Oglalas not to trust the son of Jeremy Kincade and would probably seek to slay him. Years ago he had tried in vain to clear his name and had barely escaped with his life. That burden still rode with him; yet there was no way to wash the black stain from his face, for all of the guilty ones no longer existed.

Travis replied in a measured tone that concealed his anger, "No, Lone Wolf, she is not your sister. Nathan wishes to have returned to him what is his, what Soaring Hawk took from the Kiowas and the Kiowas took from my friend, Nathan Crandall, who saved my life and has been as a father to me for seven winters. There is no deceit in our hearts and words. His heart filled with joy when he looked upon her painted face. I have seen the face of his daughter, Marissa; it is as Wild Wind's reflection on the surface of the water. I speak true; she is his granddaughter. He begged me to come to speak with my Lakota brothers for him. We come in peace, Lone Wolf. We have no quarrel with my Oglala brothers. We do not seek to trick or endanger Wild Wind or your people. She is the child of Nathan's daughter who was slain by the Kiowas. His heart burns only with love and hunger for her."

When the warrior remained quiet, Travis continued, "The bluecoats do not know of our visit to the Oglalas. He has come prepared to reward the Oglalas for their kind treatment and acceptance of his granddaughter and for her rescue from the Kiowas. If you love Wild Wind as we have been told, you will desire only her happiness and safety. We have seen and heard of the increased hostilities between the white man and all Indians, and you have spoken of them. Wild Wind is white. She is not safe here." Travis then recounted the many perils that could befall Rana from the whites and the Indians. "You are chief and your people are at war. Who will protect your sister if you are slain? Would she be safe here or in the Cheyenne camp? No. Let her return to her home and family, Lone Wolf. We will protect her and love her."

"How can you know my sister is the female you seek?"

Travis explained about the scar on Rana's ankle and the birthmark on her left arm. He pointed out the girls' matching histories, ages, and looks. "You know she is Rana Michaels," Travis stated firmly. "Just as you knew she must leave your people and lands one day," he added to test a suspicion of his. "That day has come."

Lone Wolf eyed the mixed-blooded male with renewed interest. The man's eyes and statements were startingly direct and confident. There was an air about Travis that could cause other men to be consumed with fear or to feel challenged. Yet Lone Wolf was not a man of fear or rashness. Seemingly without trying, the white man had used a tone of voice that suggested he was capable of challenging and defeating almost any foe or peril. Lone Wolf's mind filled with respect for the other man. Yes, he recalled this half-white warrior and his legendary prowess. He knew Travis was speaking the truth and was offering him a tempting path to help his people. Was this the path of destiny that had been calling to his sister for many years? Should he force her feet upon it? He glanced at Nathan Crandall and requested, *"Lel usi yo."*

Travis told Nathan, "He wants you to come over here. Don't worry, Nate; he can be trusted. Nothing's settled yet, but he's willing to discuss a trade." Travis quickly revealed the warrior's identity, his rank, and the fact that Soaring Hawk was dead. Nathan stepped forward to join them. The two white men stood side by side eyeing the powerful chief.

Lone Wolf slipped from his horse's back. To convince

61

his warriors that there was no danger and to express his lack of fear to the white men, he rested his lance and shield on a nearby rock, then removed his bow and quiver to place them with his discarded weapons. He faced them and, as he did so, instantly decided that his sister favored the older man, especially in the coloring of the eyes. In fluent English, Lone Wolf inquired casually, "What will you do if I refuse to bargain with my sister's freedom? Our peoples are at war."

"If you do not accept our offer in exchange for Rana, I will try to steal her from your tepee. If I fail, her grandfather will bargain with the Army to fight for her release. Do not force me to battle my brothers for what we know is right for all concerned."

"What if I order my warriors to slay you and your father friend? Why do you not challenge for Wild Wind in the Lakota way?"

Travis gently seized Nathan's arm and shook his head in warning when the older man started to interrupt. He smiled affectionately and encouragingly at him, then answered the warrior in Oglala for privacy. "My friend's protection and happiness come first in my heart, for he has given me love and acceptance as no other has. I am as his son. It would pain him deeply to cause my death while seeking the return of his loved one. He is getting old and needs me at his side. If I challenge for her, then she is mine, not her grandfather's. I seek to marry no woman until love is a strong bond between us. We came under truce. If you slay us, your face would be stained with dishonor. If I challenge for Wild Wind, her bargain price and all it buys will be lost to you and your people. Accept our offer, Lone Wolf, for we will not leave the Dakota Territory without her. You must trust me. If I were a man of lost honor and hate, I would have entrapped and slain you and your warriors."

Lone Wolf grinned, for he knew Travis could have and

would have done exactly as he had said, and probably would have succeeded. The warrior was cunning and astute. He knew Travis's words were not a threat; they were a sincere warning, a statement of fact. He could tell that the two white men were determined to regain the white girl who had lived as his sister for ten winters. Lone Wolf knew he could refuse Nathan's and Travis's demands and offers, that he could slay both men. But these were men of courage and honor, despite their white skin, and they were offering something his people needed desperately.

Lone Wolf sat and crossed his legs. He had many responsibilities on his shoulders. He needed a clear head for planning their defense against the awesome white attack that was sure to come soon. Worries over his sister constantly clouded his reason and provoked his anger and impatience. He needed the weapons, supplies, and money that Nathan was offering for her recovery. He needed Wild Wind's future settled. Undeniably, Wild Wind was Rana Michaels, and Rana was white. Perhaps she belonged with her true family, away from these conflicts between the Indian and white man. Perhaps the Great Spirit had sent this solution to him, for White Eagle had lived in both worlds and could help his sister adjust to her old life. Lone Wolf could not help but wonder what Wild Wind would say and do. Perhaps, he mused, it would be best for all if White Eagle and Wild Wind were joined . . .

Travis sat down before Lone Wolf. Black eyes locked with green ones. Travis could tell that the warrior was considering his offer seriously. Yet an air of mystery and a hint of amusement exuded from the warrior, which he tried to comprehend. Travis pressed his advantage by reiterating why Rana should be sent home and why Lone Wolf needed to accept their bargain. Recalling a fact mentioned earlier, he inquired, "Has the joining ceremony been announced for Rana and Rides-Like-Thunder? Is that why you hesitate or refuse to bargain?"

The chief answered candidly, "Many have asked for Wild Wind, but she has rejected all warriors. She threatens to leave our camp if I force her to join on the full moon. She bluffs Lone Wolf; she has no place to go that offers safety and happiness, and she is too proud to disobey before the eyes of our people. She is to choose her mate or leave by the Sun Dance, or I will bind her to my Cheyenne friend. What if my sister refuses to go with her grandfather? What if she chooses Rides-Like-Thunder or another warrior over him?"

Travis smiled at the amusing and strangely pleasing revelations. "She has been raised Oglala, Lone Wolf; she will obey the commands of her chief and brother. Do not give her a choice. Order her to return home with Nathan. Explain the bargain to her; ask her to sacrifice herself for the survival of her Oglala brother and people." Lone Wolf winced and frowned noticeably. "Such a brave and unselfish deed should make her proud and happy, perhaps earn her a tribal feast and *coup*, perhaps a special medicine wheel for her fiery hair," Travis suggested cleverly.

Lone Wolf laughed. He recalled how she had earned her last one by defiantly trailing a hunting party, then warning them of a white ambush in time to crush their foes. "White Eagle has not forgotten the ways of the fox," the warrior remarked, complimenting his cunning. He liked this half-white male, who he was beginning to think might make a good match for his sister. "Wild Wind was raised Oglala, but she carries white blood that makes her stubborn and defiant, as White Eagle was long ago. You have changed, my Hunkpapa friend. You have found peace and honor and acceptance in your new life. Would it be the same for my sister? Can you make her white again? Can I force her to obey me in this? Many times her Indian heart wars with her white skin. If she does not remember her grandfather, she will not wish to return to him. She might fear leaving with strangers to go far from the people she knows and loves. In truth, she desires to be a warrior, not a woman. If I agree to your trade, White Eagle, do you have the strength, cunning, and patience to tame a wild wind for her grandfather?"

Travis scowled in annoyance, dreading to learn if Rana had inherited any of her mother's bad traits or if she were anything like the twenty-eight-year-old Clarissa Caldwell, who could pass for twenty-three. Considering their personalities, it was no wonder those two Texas vixens had become close friends during Marissa's last few visits home, even though Marissa had been ten years older than Clarissa. Lordy, even their names rhymed! he reflected sardonically. It still surprised Travis that Harrison Caldwell's daughter had not persuaded Marissa to stay home and get rid of Raymond Michaels. From what Nathan had told him, the two women had stuck together during that last visit like a tick to a calf's ear. No doubt Rana and Clarissa would take to each other just as rapidly and tightly. His mind ceased its foolish ramblings. "I was afraid she was named accurately. It sounds to me like I'll be taking a problem off your hands. If you release her to us, I'll do whatever is necessary to get her home and get rid of that rebellious streak. Perhaps a good spanking will work magic on her. That's one white man's custom I heartily approve of."

Lone Wolf shook his dark head. "If she leaves with you, you must be kind and patient with her, White Eagle. Have you forgotten how hard it was for you to leave and to change?" he reminded Travis knowingly. "She is my sister and she is Oglala. I must speak with my council before I give you my answer. Come, you will wait and sleep in my tepee. Do not speak of this matter to my sister or to others. She will feel betrayed by our exchange. She does not agree with trading for another person as is done with wives and captives. If we vote to keep her, you must leave in peace as you came. Do not force us to slay good white men, for they are few and we count them friends."

"I cannot agree to leave without her, Lone Wolf, for I have given my promise to return her to her home and grandfather. Do not force me to battle for her. All Oglala warriors and their brave chief are needed to fight a real enemy, not their friend White Eagle."

Lone Wolf pictured himself addressing his council on this matter. He would explain his warring emotions and predicament to the wise and heroic men who sometimes made him feel too young and ignorant to be sitting around the same council fire with them. But he could not make such a crucial and troubling decision by himself. He would ask for the opinions and reactions of each member. He would listen carefully to each reply, then allow each member to cast a vote on whether or not to accept White Eagle's offer. With wry amusement he reflected that the council discussion and vote would be different if the young, unmated warriors of the tribe were deliberating and deciding Wild Wind's fate. He was glad he had not mentioned his imminent decision about enforced marriage to his Cheyenne friend and relieved that Soaring Hawk was not alive to confront his heartrending dilemma. If the vote went as he expected, he would have to convince his sister of his love for her and his desire to do what was best for all concerned, including her.

No one spoke as Lone Wolf continued his silent study of the situation. The Oglala chief concluded that perhaps it was an ironic form of justice that a white man's money and help would clear the tangled path to survival for his people. But there were dangers and obstacles to consider. The council might believe this was a bluecoat trick and order White Eagle and his friend put to death. The council could vote to keep Wild Wind or to allow her to make her own choice. The council could vote to torture the white men until they turned over the much-needed money for supplies and weapons. Or the council could vote to trick White Eagle into getting the supplies and weapons before slaying them. Even as chief, once he went before the council, he could not go against their vote.

To prevent Nathan from hearing his words, Lone Wolf responded in his native tongue. "If the council votes against you, then we will speak of such matters. Come to my camp, I will call the council together. My head and heart belong to this problem and it confuses them. Others must help make this decision. Tell White Eagle's friend to camp here with my warriors until the new sun glows in the sky. He does not know our ways and might interfere or offend. He is eager and afraid; he may speak words I do not wish others to hear. He is white. His words and presence could endanger two lives and our bargain."

After Travis nodded understanding and agreement, Lone Wolf advised, "There is danger for you and your friend, White Eagle, if the council thinks you speak or act falsely. Do not enter my camp if you are afraid to face death or cannot keep your word. You know our ways; the council's word is law even for their chief."

"I fear no one and nothing except dishonor, Lone Wolf."

"Speak to your friend; then we ride for my camp."

Travis sat in Lone Wolf's tepee awaiting the outcome of the council meeting, which had been going on for over an hour. It was near the eating time and Wild Wind had not appeared to prepare her brother's meal. Travis wondered if Lone Wolf had ordered her to stay out of the tepee until his return. He was edgy, for there had been an undercurrent in Lone Wolf's voice and manner that he had been unable to grasp. Yet he did not feel as if the warrior would deceive or betray him. He only wished he felt the same way about his council and tribe.

Time dragged on and Travis's tension mounted. Lone Wolf had not confined him to this tepee, but he wanted to be here when the girl arrived. He wanted to study her privately, to see what he and Nathan would be in for if they secured her release. He was annoyed by his anxiety and lack of patience. Had he forgotten that part of his Indian upbringing? Evidently Wild Wind had, for it was her duty to care for her brother's tepee and needs, and those of his guests.

The village noises became muffled by the buffalo hides forming the Oglala dwellings, for most had gone inside their tepees for the evening meal. Eating at this early hour would allow time for final chores before darkness claimed the settlement.

For the countless time, Travis glanced at the closed flap of the tepee, unaware that his impatience actually had to do with wanting to meet Rana Michaels before Lone Wolf's return. He had not been able to get her image out of his mind since his eyes had touched on it. If she did not come home soon, the fading light would deny him a good look at her, for it was too warm to build a fire inside the tepee this early.

Travis decided to take a short walk to the nearby river to freshen up and to revive himself. Just as he reached the tepee entrance, the flap was thrown aside and Wild Wind ducked to rush inside, slamming her head into Travis's hard chest. Both were caught off balance and tumbled to the ground with exclamations of surprise. Wild Wind landed atop the man in buckskins who was struggling to keep her from being injured from the ramming and fall. An abundance of fiery hair spilled over Travis's face and chest like soft hay falling from a loft and covering him. His senses went spinning at her nearness and her fragrance.

Wild Wind instantly realized it was not her brother she had bumped into and landed upon. She lifted her head and stared at the grinning man beneath her. The smoothly tan face that filled her vision was breathtakingly handsome. In a flurry of observations she noticed the red band secured across his forehead and the wisps of deep brown hair playing over it, which danced in the breeze of her rapid respiration. Her eyes took in his full lips, the tiny cleft in the center of his chin, the strength of his stubbled jawline, those incredibly green eyes that sparkled as they watched her, and teeth that flashed shockingly white against his darkly tanned features. She noted that a *wanapin* with Lakota markings had slipped from beneath his clean, chamois-colored shirt and now rested near the hollow of his throat.

While Wild Wind was studying Travis, he was doing the same to her. From viewing her portraits, he had expected her to have great beauty and allure, but nothing as potent as what he was now observing. All suspicious twinges about women vanished from his entranced mind. She radiated an awesome attraction that set his heart pounding and her scent reminded him of a meadow of flowers on a dew-fresh morning. There was an untamed wildness and earthy sensuality about her, which seemed to convey a powerful yet hazardous magic. Her eyes were large and magnetic, and he felt as if he were being drawn into a blue-gray whirlpool. Lashes and brows of dark auburn set off those arresting eyes perfectly. Her unmarred complexion was smooth and golden, which was unusual for a redhead, though not so the light sprinkling of pale freckles across a dainty nose and cotton-soft cheeks. Her lips were pink and full—the kind that pouted prettily and would kiss delightfully, he mused. From her length against his body, he guessed her height at five feet three or four. Her weight could not be much more than two sacks of grain, he estimated; perhaps a shave over one hundred pounds. With it resting on him, he could tell it was enticingly placed to tempt a man to boldness. His large hands wrapped completely around her slender arms. Compared to his six-feet-four frame, hers seemed tiny and fragile.

Travis sensed that this girl knew what she wanted from life and would risk anything to obtain her desires. Yet there was a compelling aura of softness with her strength, a warmth and vulnerability that her mother had lacked. This girl had a naturalness that other women would envy. He was certain that Lone Wolf had spoken truthfully when he had told him that many men desired her and had made large offers for her. And he was just as certain that this girl could pick from the best warriors and wrap her choice around her finger like a supple blade of spring grass. Thomas Mallory had not exaggerated her beauty. There had been no artistic misinterpretation or tricks of lighting. If anything, she was even more beautiful than her portraits. Mallory had been right; who could forget or ignore this ravishing and radiant creature?

In Oglala, Travis hinted mirthfully, "You must be Wild Wind. Perhaps Lone Wolf should rename you Whirlwind. Do you always make your guests prepare their own meals while you spin around?" he teased.

Wild Wind's cheeks pinkened, first from embarrassment and then from anger. How dare this white man touch her and insult her, compare her to a flighty *wamniomni! "Nanpi yuze sni yo!"* she demanded unflinchingly, ordering him to take his hands off her. He was so tall and strong, and so infuriatingly appealing. She was apprehensive about his curious effect on her, though she attempted to conceal her feelings. *"Nituwe he?"* She asked him who he was, questioning his presence and the freedom he was enjoying in her tepee.

Travis could not suppress his unintentionally provoking chuckles as he sat up, easily taking her along with him and setting her beside him on the ground. He had never met a woman who ignited such fierce passions within him. He suddenly felt relaxed; he felt alive and daring. *"Kopegla sni yo, Watogla Tate. Wanmbli Ska kola."* He shifted to an Indian sitting position and grinned at her.

She glared at him, for he seemed to be making fun of her or perhaps was challenging her to battle him or cry out for help. Though he seemed fearless and powerful, she met his challenge with a proud and willful jut to her chin and a pretty pout on her lips. She held herself straight and still, expressing confidence and self-control as she responded tartly, "I am afraid of nothing and no one. What do you want? A despicable white man can be no friend to my brother and the Oglalas! It matters not if you speak our tongue and give yourself an Indian name. The white soldiers killed my father and attack all Lakotas. My people make war against them. We will drive all whites from our lands, or they will die."

She looked him over for weapons and was surprised to see none. She wondered why he was calmly sitting here unarmed. He did not appear to be a fool or a reckless man, for his eyes and demeanor suggested intelligence and prowess. To test his reaction, she warned, "You steal into the wrong tepee, white dog. When my brother returns, he will capture you and slay you. He is chief of the Red Arrow Band. When he has taken his revenge, there will be nothing left of your body for the wolf or vulture." As she stared into his sparkling eyes and genial expression, she found that such an idea oddly pained her. His gaze was as soft as a feather but as strong as wet rawhide. His eyes made no secret of the fact that he found her beautiful and desirable. She could only hope that her eyes did not mirror those matching feelings, for they

71

surged madly through her mind and body. It felt good to touch him, to look upon him. She suddenly and absurdly wished he would escape unharmed. This was a man who would never need the help of the Elk Dreamer's love medicine to obtain or to hold onto his chosen woman. He could steal any careless maiden's heart and honor easily. Quickly she suppressed such strange thoughts and reactions.

Travis understood her anger and waxed serious. "I am half Lakota, Wild Wind. I offer no danger to Wild Wind or your people. I wait for Lone Wolf to return from the council. We are friends. I came in peace to offer help to your people against the bluecoats. I was born and lived in the camp of the Hunkpapas until seven winters past. I carry two bloods. My father was white and my mother Hunkpapa. Both are dead. I was named White Eagle by our medicine chief, Sitting Bull."

Travis lifted his fringed shirt to expose the scars on his chest muscles. "I was a warrior. Twice I offered my life to Grandfather in the Sun Dance; twice He spared it and honored me with many victories. I am sorry your father, Soaring Hawk, was slain; he was a man of great courage and honor. Lone Wolf fills his moccasins and tepee with the same measure of honor and courage. I live twenty moons of fast riding from your camp, in the land between the waking and sleeping of the sun. Lone Wolf brought me to his camp and tepee. When he returns, he will tell you I am his friend and guest. Are you injured?" he asked when she rubbed the top of her head.

She retorted, "When my brother returns, I will learn if you speak with a split tongue. If your heart is as hard as your body, you will die, White Eagle. You are part white, and I trust no white-eyes."

"Wild Wind is all white. Should a man of Lakota blood not trust her? It is wrong to hate all whites for the evil of some. Tell me how you came to be Oglala, the daughter of

72

Soaring Hawk," he asked politely.

"Only my skin is white; my life and heart are Lakota. We will speak no more until my brother returns and calls you friend or foe. What help did you come to offer my people? You are only one man, a half-white man. How can you help? Why did you leave the Hunkpapas?"

Travis smiled and shook his head of nape-grazing sable hair. "We will speak no more until your brother returns and calls me friend," he playfully retorted to intrigue her. "I did not mean to tease you earlier. My body was restless and my stomach is empty; they clouded my reason. Does Wild Wind know how to gather firewood and cook?" he mischievously teased, though he had just finished apologizing for doing so earlier.

In spite of her resolve to remain poised, Wild Wind narrowed her eyes and clenched her teeth. "Why do you insult Lone Wolf's sister?"

"Why does Lone Wolf's sister treat his guest so badly? It is past the eating time and White Eagle hears thunder in his belly. Do you wish me to hunt and roast my own rabbit?"

"You dare to shame and correct Wild Wind?" she demanded.

"You shame yourself with defiance, unless there is a reason why you come home late and do not prepare food for Lone Wolf's tepee. Perhaps Wild Wind has more than white skin to master."

"I will explain nothing to you, half-breed!" she exclaimed, panting.

"You will explain your lack of manners and disobedience to your brother and chief when he returns to a dark tepee and hungry guest. I was told of Wild Wind's bad ways, but I did not believe one so beautiful and smart could behave so shamefully and defiantly. I see the words and jokes of others hold much truth. It is wrong for a sister to bring such dishonor and unhappiness to her

73

brother and chief. I will seek food and warmth in another tepee until Lone Wolf returns."

Wild Wind frowned in dismay. This arrogant, insufferable man was going to get her into more trouble with her brother and people! As much as it hurt, she held her tongue and forced her manners to surface. "A smart man does not accept the foolish words of loose tongues, White Eagle. I have good reason to be late. My brother will understand and forgive me. I did not expect to find a white man in our tepee, one who tries to cut Wild Wind with his sharp, cruel words. I will return soon with hot food to quiet your rumbling belly and loud manner. I will build a fire to lighten the darkness in our tepee and in your head. You are Lone Wolf's guest and I will treat you as such. But do not speak to me again. Anger and hatred for you fill my heart."

Wild Wind arose gracefully. She brushed off her garments, then checked her hair with quivering fingers. Her stormy blue eyes flashing insults at him, she turned and left quickly. She would go to Myeerah's tepee to obtain food for her brother's insolent guest and information about him. Before the council meeting ended, Lone Wolf's tepee would have a cheery fire and hot food. Then she would see if the half-white man exposed her misbehavior to her brother. If he did, he would be sorry! So would Lone Wolf if he dared to reprimand her before that nettling creature with the devilish grin and mocking eyes!

Yet, as she walked toward Myeerah's tepee, she glanced over her shoulder several times to see if the stranger was watching her retreat; she found herself annoyed that he was not. Much as she tried not to be, she was impressed by him and she quivered strangely. He had a smile that brightened his handsome face and eyes like a fiery sunset. His body and grip told her he was powerful; his movements and responses told her he was agile and alert. He was a superior male and doubtlessly had been a superior warrior. His wit was quick and amusing, even if it had been directed at her. Surely he was a man of many sides and traits, and all seemed most appealing. If only he was not half white, she mused dreamily as she called his image and voice to mind. Suddenly a voice inside her head replied, But you are white too . . .

Chapter Three

As Travis Kincade built a small fire in the center of the tepee, he questioned his behavior toward Nathan's misplaced granddaughter. It was not right to view or to judge Rana in the same light as he did other women, or to treat her so rudely. His initial motives had been to test her character and to see if he could control her with cunning. He had thought that if he made her angry and defensive now, she would comply with his demands later, just to prove that his insulting accusations about her had been false, or at least exaggerated. If he were lucky, she would meet his challenge and would expose her mettle and suppress her disruptive ways. Hopefully she would think twice before "shaming" her brother and herself by being unwilling to accept her new fate or by refusing to behave like a proper Indian maiden of high standing.

Maybe she would use extra effort to impress him, for her initial study of him had been one of appreciation, and he knew women went after things that caught their eyes. She was accustomed to men pursuing her, just as he was used to women desiring and chasing him.

But this girl had been raised differently, raised as he had been, and hopefully without learning dirty, greedy feminine tricks. If he showed little or no interest in such an untamed minx, she might be intrigued into mellowing in order to entice him. One thing he knew for sure was that the girl had spunk. She was proud, and pride might aid his cause if she were led to believe that her departure would be a heroic and unselfish act. No matter what she might say or do to soften him, he would have to stand firm and blind to it, for he felt certain she would yield better and more quickly to a show of strength and persistence, or a display of scorn if she were to conduct herself badly. Perhaps her brother's leniency was the root of Lone Wolf's trouble with her, he mused. Travis felt he had to let this girl know immediately who was boss. He had to weaken her rebellious streak, make her defensive and compliant. Though they might be dirty tricks to play on her, it looked as if she would demand such deception and harshness to master her.

The kindling caught and Travis gradually added small pieces of wood. He sat near the blaze, feeding it when necessary and reflecting on Wild Wind. What an independent and ornery little cuss she was, as Nathan would say. She was going to be one bag of trouble, that mule-headed and irritating vixen . . . that ravishing and arrogant creature who would no doubt use her wits and charms to battle or disarm him. Lordy, this trip home was going to be long and rough! he told himself. Especially if Nathan became enchanted by her and interfered with his lessons and discipline. Without a doubt she would try to escape them at least once, just to annoy him with a display of her unusual skills. So Wild Wind wanted to be a fighter, did she? He would watch her every minute and mile during their trek home.

Travis envisioned her challenging expression and smug air; they reminded him of his own attitude long ago, before Nathan had taken him under his wing. Sakes alive, how he had changed over the past few years! People who had met or had known him before Nathan Crandall would not recognize him now. The thought brought a roguish smile to the ranch foreman's lips and eyes. He recalled certain lessons Nathan had used with him. Nothing made a person do something or do it well quicker than to have another person tell him he couldn't do it or do it right. He couldn't count the times he had behaved himself or had learned something new and had made sure he had done it better than anyone else, only because Nathan had challenged him with clever words or cunning expressions. Sometimes it had been to prove Nathan and others wrong, and other times it had been to show Nathan that he had been right about a hot-tempered, sullen youth who had touched the old man's heart.

Travis wished Lone Wolf would settle this matter tonight, so he and Nathan could carry out their part of the bargain and be gone before any Hunkpapa warriors came to visit. Maybe he had been a fool to let Nathan come here with him, for Nathan could become entrapped along with him if things went badly. If Lone Wolf and the Oglalas discovered why he had left this territory years ago and what his—

"Loyacin sni he, Wanbli Ska?" Wild Wind breathily asked, inquiring if he were still hungry and startling the dreamy Travis into reflexive action.

In a blurred instant, Travis was on his feet, crouching and holding a knife that had appeared in his left hand seemingly from nowhere. Poised for an enemy's attack, he saw Wild Wind inhale sharply and back away, her alert eyes never leaving his and her stance preparing to defend herself. Travis instantly relaxed and smiled. He replaced the knife in its sheath beneath his left pant leg. "I did not hear you enter, Wild Wind. You move as silently as the stalking cat . . . or as nimbly as a skilled warrior. Your eyes and instincts are sharp. You have watched and trained well. No foe would be safe around you."

Wild Wind had observed how rapidly and agilely the man had moved. She had intentionally sneaked up on him and she now realized that if his instincts had not been dulled by deep worry over some matter, he would have detected her stealthy approach. She had been wrong earlier, for he was indeed armed. By not blindly lunging at her, which she had desired, he had revealed self-control and the ability to rapidly assess a situation. She had hoped he would react foolishly and cause her to drop the food he had demanded she get for him. Yet when their eyes had fused, she had unconsciously clutched the containers to avoid dropping them and looking clumsy. Reluctantly, she was impressed by his show of superior training and pleased by his flattering remarks. She knelt beside his fire without commenting, retrieved a small wooden platter, and served his food, then handed him a bag with fresh water.

"Pilamaya," he thanked her as he accepted the meal and drink.

"A warrior should not lower his guard so completely, White Eagle. If a lowly female can sneak up on you, how are you safe in the forests? Have you forgotten your warrior's training in the white man's world?"

Travis was amused by the heavy sweetness in her voice and expression. "I saw no need to be on guard in Lone Wolf's tepee and camp. Surely no enemy would dare invade them. As for you, Wild Wind," he ventured slowly and evocatively as his mocking gaze swept over her, "there is nothing lowly about the daughter of Soaring Hawk and the sister of Lone Wolf. You value yourself too little. You should work hard to prove that others are wrong about you," he mirthfully suggested, smugly assuming that his distracting thoughts had allowed her to sneak up on him.

"I can be nothing less than Wild Wind. If others think false thoughts of me, it is a flaw in their minds and hearts,

80

and Wild Wind will not waste time correcting foolish people. Perhaps White Eagle should work hard to prove that Wild Wind is wrong about him," she retorted slyly.

Disconcerting green eyes leveled on the girl who was sitting across the fire from him and waiting for him to complete his meal before she ate, as was the Indian custom. He continued to eat slowly, without taking his eyes from her face. He noticed her cheeks pinken, but she refused to lower her gaze demurely. Her eyes were bright and startlingly direct, as her words had been. In a lazy voice that carried undertones of mischief, he inquired, "What if Wild Wind is not wrong about me? And what if she receives only the actions she provokes?"

Still she refused to pull her stormy gaze from his taunting one. *"Ota wayata he? Inipi he?"* she asked as he halted to stare at her.

"Yes, I had enough to eat; and I am full," he roguishly replied. "It was very good. Please thank your friend for me. You did not answer before. Can Wild Wind cook and tend a tepee?"

Wild Wind glared at him. She was not hungry, but she ate to prevent him from thinking he had stolen her appetite. When she was finished, she cleared their platters and washed them. She wondered why this disconcerting man vacillated back and forth between insults and apologies. What crafty game was he playing with her? She set the earthenware bowl containing Lone Wolf's meal on the flat rocks that encased the fire. She hung the water bag on a side pole. To dispel the unnerving silence in the tepee, she remarked as she worked, "The council meeting runs long. What news did you bring to my people? Why did you not attend?"

"You know it is not permitted for a guest to sit in Oglala council. I promised your brother I would not speak of such matters to anyone. We must wait to hear their vote, and obey it with honor."

Wild Wind observed Travis Kincade. If he had lived in this area, she would have heard of him or seen him before. If he were a friend, why had he never visited them? she wondered. He knew the Lakota customs and laws, and he spoke of them with respect and loyalty. Yet he looked and sounded concerned by the length of the meeting. "Is it good or bad that the council talks long?" she probed curiously.

Travis glanced over at her and shrugged. "*Slolwaye sni,*" he admitted, telling her he did not know. "*Unkomani kte,*" he added, asking her to take a walk.

"Tell me why you come and worry, White Eagle, and I will go."

Travis chuckled and shook his head before remarking, "You are too clever and perceptive for such a young woman, Wild Wind. I worry because the council's decision is important to many people. Ask me nothing more. Soon you will know all."

She did not heed his request. "Important to White Eagle?"

"Yes, because it is important to someone I love and respect, and to the survival of my Lakota people," he responded mysteriously. "Do you know anything about the white man's guns?" he questioned as he pointed to his pistols and rifle on a buffalo mat. When she shook her head, he commanded sternly, "Then do not touch them. They are dangerous. They can injure or slay a careless or nosy whirlwind."

"Do they carry great magic like the warrior's weapons?" she asked, knowing it was wrong for a woman to touch a man's weapons and ceremonial items, especially during her monthly flow.

"Their magic lies in their owner's skill and use of them, nothing more. I will return later. I need fresh air and movement."

As Travis headed for the entrance, she called out, "Do

you wish me to go?" She wanted more information and decided that a woman's soft hand could pick him better than a wildcat's claws.

Travis glanced over his shoulder and replied, "If you like." He saw her expression change and knew that was not the right answer for this vixen. "It's nearly dark. As I look more white than Indian and many in your camp do not know of me, perhaps it is wiser and safer for Lone Wolf's guest if you walk beside him." He ducked and left, eager to see if she would swallow his bait and join him. Recognizing that there indeed was truth in his conniving words, he walked slowly and cautiously.

"The meeting lodge holds secrets and dangers this moon. The council speaks in whispers. It is not good," she concluded worriedly as she caught up with his lengthy strides.

Travis furtively eyed her. He could tell from her increased respiration and the tightness around her eyes that she felt intimidated by him and that meeting. She shuddered, suddenly looking very vulnerable and afraid. That unexpected insight warmed him. To distract her, he rashly questioned her past and memory. "Lone Wolf told me you have been his sister for ten winters. He did not explain how a captive white child became the honored daughter of Soaring Hawk."

Wild Wind halted and looked at him strangely. "Why would my brother speak of such matters to White Eagle? I do not know from where you ride or why I have not heard of you. Why do you question me?"

"Is there some evil secret to your capture and adoption?" His crafty response worked, for it kept the conversation on her. "Most prisoners hate their captors, but you do not hate the Oglalas. Why?"

"Oglalas did not murder my family and capture me," she swiftly defended them. Her gaze lifted to the moon, which would reach its fullness within a week, and that sight seemed to panic her. She began to talk dreamily, as if to force the alarm from her mind. "Kiowas killed my family and stole me. They were a cruel and fierce band and I hated them. I do not remember how long I was with them. Then, ten winters ago, Soaring Hawk raided the new Kiowa camp and rescued me. Soaring Hawk explained that the white man had driven the Kiowas from their lands and that the Kiowas were trying to invade Lakota lands. There was a violent storm and many whirlwinds filled the air with dirt. The Kiowas and their horses were blinded by the winds and sands and did not see the Oglalas attack until it was too late. The Oglalas knew of such storms and wore thin cloths over their faces. They could look out, but the sand could not come into their eyes and noses," she related proudly.

She looked and talked as if she had drifted into a trance. "I was frightened. I tried to hide, but the sand burned my eyes and I could not see to run. Soaring Hawk found me lost in the whirling storm and took care of me. That is why he named me Wild Wind. He said the Great Spirit had come to him in a vision and had told him to take me as his daughter. His wife lived with the Great Spirit and his heart was full of sadness and pain. He ordered two Indian captives to care for Wild Wind, Lone Wolf and himself. When my father died, Lone Wolf sold the captives and Wild Wind now cares for his tepee. He is chief now and must take a wife. Soaring Hawk is gone and things are chang— Enough words of Wild Wind. Speak of White Eagle and his mission."

Travis knew the meaning of her incomplete sentence. He pressed, "Do you remember your white family, Ra . . . Wild Wind? Do you know where your real mother and father lived before your capture?"

Wild Wind became nervous and angry. To stop this distressing talk, she lied, "No, I was a small child. Speak of other things. I do not wish to remember those dark suns and moons." She lapsed into pensive silence. Many times in her sleeping and waking dreams she had seen a strange and wicked white man who terrified and injured her. She could hear him shouting awful words at her and see him striking her, his pale face distorted by evil and cruelty, his black hair flying wildly as he jerked his head and body about in fits of pure rage. She had heard herself sobbing and pleading to go home, but he had beaten her and called her filthy names. She had heard his icy laughter fill her ears and she had covered them to close out the wicked sounds. They had to be bad dreams, not memories, for she always saw herself as a grown woman, not as a child. Those terrible dreams were so strange, for she was always wearing white man's garments and her fiery hair was not long and thick as it was in real life and was worn differently. Many times the dreams were petrifying, for her lovely face would be swollen and bruised and bleeding. The older she became, the less the dreams filled her mind. Yet whenever she thought or spoke of the Kiowas, the bad dreams would return for many moons to torment her.

"What frightens you, Wild Wind?" Travis asked in concern.

She glared at him for his painful intrusion. "Go away. White Eagle is mean and bad." She whirled and raced back to her tepee.

Travis waited a short time before returning to the tepee to find her sitting on her sleeping mat, pretending to be beading a pair of moccasins. When he heard a quiet sniffle and saw her inhale raggedly, he walked to her and dropped to his knees. Lifting her chin, he stared into misty blue eyes filled with anguish. As a tear escaped to roll down one cheek, she tried to free herself from his firm but gentle grasp. He could tell she did not like exposing such deep feelings or a loss of control. He wanted to hold her in his arms and comfort her, then cover her face with kisses. He wanted to make love to this half-wild vixen, this part-woman, part-child creature, yet he dared not respond to such tempting hunger. "Do not cry, Wild Wind. I will speak no more of such days of pain and fear. You are very brave and special. Your people must love and respect you greatly. Do not be sad," he entreated, for her pain had had an overwhelming effect on him.

She watched him master the urge to lean forward to kiss her, and oddly she was sorry he had found the strength to do so. He was a man of many emotions and sides, a man of great prowess. Only a man of enormous strength would have the power and courage to reveal tenderness, as tenderness was a strength of its own that few men possessed. She could tell that it was difficult for him to expose such feelings, for the look in his grass green eyes told her that he had once known much suffering. As an Indian, he had been raised to master his emotions and to depend on himself for survival. Obviously he had left the Lakota world, and she wondered when and why. He was a new man, but the old one had not died easily or fully. She wondered which part of him he wished to slay, the Indian or the white, for surely those bloods warred fiercely within him, as they did with her sometimes. It was terrible to be torn between two lands and two peoples, to be neither accepted nor rejected by either. Her gaze seemed to mesmerize him. He appeared capable of experiencing powerful emotions and seemed vulnerable to certain forces, though it was obvious he fought to conceal and control such traits. She liked these impressions, and she liked him when he was this man.

"Tanyan amaye, Wanbli Ska. Pilamaya." She softly explained that she felt better and surprisingly thanked him as if it were because of him.

He smiled. *"Ohan."* He went to the buffalo mat she had

spread out for him, for it was very late, and mused silently, Yes, it was "good" . . .

Wild Wind watched him lie down in his garments and moccasins, his back to her because of the angle at which she had placed his mat. Putting aside her beading, she checked the fire. She added small hunks of wood, mostly knots, for they would burn slowly and give off enough light to chase the darkness and ghosts from the tepee. Then she removed her moccasins and, leaving on her garments, reclined on her sleeping mat. She closed her eyes to envision White Eagle's face, in order to study and admire it. Gradually she allowed herself to drift into light slumber.

Within the hour, Wild Wind was tossing restlessly and mumbling words that Travis could not grasp. She began to whimper and moan, and her head and body thrashed upon the sleeping mat. Travis eased over to awaken her from her nightmare. From the few words that came out clearly, he assumed she was dreaming about the Kiowas, whom he had recalled to her mind. He gently shook her and called her name.

In the horrifying dream, she saw her flaming-haired image fleeing the night-haired white man as she screamed for rescue. The evil man captured her by long curls of fire and jerked her to her knees. Large blue eyes and a muffled voice pleaded with him to let her go free, to stop hurting her. He sent forth chilling laughter and started pounding her with his fists. She could hear him shouting, "You little bitch! If you try to leave me again, I'll beat you and your sniveling brat senseless. I got you out of a nasty mess, so you owe me plenty, slut. You don't want me to tell your pa the truth about his whoring daughter before I put a bullet in his head, do you? I'm warning you, harlot, the next time you go against me in any way, they're both dead, and you too."

"Please, let us go home. I can't do this anymore."

"We got us a deal—silence for money. If you can't get it from your loving pa, earn it on your back, just like you earned your trouble. I'm broke, so shuck those clothes and git your pretty ass to work. You ain't gonna cost me my next stake by refusing to let Fargo poke you good. He's your best customer. You don't want me telling nobody the truth about you and that brat, so git in there and—" Suddenly the door crashed aside and White Eagle's towering body filled the opening. He called her name, but the brown-eyed enemy held her shoulder tightly and warned, "I'll never let you go; you're my gold mine."

Travis was shocked when she called his Indian name and begged for help. He seized her in his arms and shook her roughly as he told her to awaken: *"Kikta yo, Watogla Tate!"* She fought him and confused him with her Oglala words: "He will slay us if we disobey. He torments us and hurts us. Help us, White Eagle. Make the pain and blood go away. Kill him! Kill him . . ." She began sobbing against his chest.

His arms held her tightly and his voice spoke comforting words. "Do not cry or be afraid, Wild Wind. I will protect you from all evil. Come with me and trust me. No one will hurt you again," he promised in her tongue as he stroked her hair and placed kisses over her face. At last he had met a rare creature, a woman with real feelings, a woman like him, a woman who needed and wanted the same things he did.

Wild Wind reached out to his touch and comforting voice. She clung to his shirt and nestled her face against his. Her lips instinctively and hungrily sought and found his. As they sank to her mat, her arms encircled his body and she greedily feasted at his mouth. Her senses went spinning when his lips tried to kiss each spot on her face and neck. A curious warmth and trembling attacked her passion-inflamed senses. Suddenly he pulled away from her, and she felt lost and scared. Her whirling wits cleared as she watched him sit up and try to slow his rapid breathing. He wiped moisture from his face and turned his back to her.

After a minute, Travis said, "I was not fully awake when I tried to free you from your bad dreams, Wild Wind. I must not touch the dau . . . sister of my friend, Lone Wolf, in this way. Go back to sleep. I will be here to guard you from all evil."

Before he could return to his mat, she caught his arm to stay him and asked, *"Taku eniciyapi wasicun he? Waniyetu nitona he? Nicinca tonapi he? Tohan kin yagli kta watohanl he?"*

Travis half turned and gazed at her, wary of the power of those bewitching eyes and sultry lips. He answered her first three questions in order. "The whites call me Travis Kincade. I'm twenty-seven winters old. I have no children, for I have taken no mate." Not because Nathan had not tried to get him to marry and have children, but because he had not found any woman worthy of those roles. He replied to her last question with a question, "Do you wish me to return here one day?"

"Slolwaye sni," she replied honestly, pulling her gaze from his.

"Why do you not know your thoughts and feelings?" He lifted her flushed face, locking his probing gaze to her wary one. They stared into each other's eyes for a lengthy time and desire flamed between them. He tenderly caressed her cheek and stroked her mussed hair. "Do not fear me, Wild Wind; I bring you no harm. Why do you quiver?"

"Because there is something about you that troubles me. You are a man of many secrets and dangers, a stranger. I do not know why you came to our camp, but I do not think my people will trust you. There is too much hostility between the Indians and whites."

89

"If they do not trust me, the Oglalas might not survive this war with the white man. The whites are many and powerful, Wild Wind. I fear they are one enemy the Lakotas cannot defeat, and that pains me. If my blood were all Lakota, I would ride into battle with my people. But a warrior cannot fight the white man while he fights the half-breed disease. I am accepted in the white lands, for they do not know I am half Indian, but I am scorned in Indian lands, for they can see I am half white and it stirs their blood to hatred and cruelty. I wish it were not so. I wish I could share both lands and peoples, for I have missed my Lakota people since I rode far away. Neither side will allow it. Once long ago I was forced to travel a path from my mother's lands. I had to learn many new things and make many changes. It was hard, but a man of honor endures his suffering silently and bravely."

As he continued, his left forefinger absently pushed silky strands of golden-red hair from her face, and his eyes gazed more and more deeply into hers. Her magnetism was a tangible force and caused his voice to become husky. "When Grandfather changes our paths in life, we must not refuse to travel them or many will suffer for our selfishness and blindness. When I return to my wooden tepee in the white man's territory, I will never return to the land of the Dakotas, but I will pray to Grandfather to save His children and sacred lands from total destruction, and I will do the only thing I can to help them."

"White Eagle, tell me why you came to our camp," she urged and found herself wishing he would repy, "For you." She wanted to snuggle into his arms, to feel his touch and to touch him, to share kisses.

"Lone Wolf has my word of honor to hold silent. Go to sleep, Wild Wind. The new sun could bring many dangers for all in this camp. I will allow no harm to come to you and I will awaken you if the bad dreams return. I must leave when the sun rises in the heaven." Travis knew his last statement was not a lie. He would depart to buy the weapons or he would leave with her; and if not with her, then to return later to abduct her. He had promised Nathan he could get her back, and, after meeting her, he was more determined than ever.

Lone Wolf moved away from his tepee as silently as a shadow. He had been listening to and watching Travis and his sister since their walk. Lone Wolf turned and walked toward his tepee, intentionally making enough sound to be heard by the sharp ears of the half-white warrior lying inside his dwelling. He quietly lifted the flap and tossed a small rock on Travis's chest to obtain his attention. When Travis glanced in Lone Wolf's direction, the chief used sign language to command him to silence and to follow him outside for a private talk.

Travis obeyed without alerting Wild Wind to his departure and absence. The two men walked to the nearby river and sat on blankets. Travis tried to conceal his impatience, but he knew he must let the chief speak first.

"The council voted to give White Eagle a chance to prove his words and honor, if we agree to make trade. White Eagle and his friend Nathan will ride to the white man's trading post to buy weapons and supplies. My warriors will ride behind you to protect you and the trade goods. When the weapons and supplies rest in Oglala hands, Lone Wolf will tell his sister that White Eagle has made trade for her. Lone Wolf will command his sister to go with White Eagle. You must leave quickly after I speak words of farewell to her. If she battles my words, White Eagle must tie her hands and take her by force. She is a wild creature, and Lone Wolf has not tamed her

91

with words or punishments."

When Travis grinned in amusement, Lone Wolf warned, "Do not smile quickly, White Eagle. Soon you will feel the sting of her words and endure the troubles of her defiance. She is clever and daring; do not take your eyes or ears from her. If you earn her hatred and anger, do not turn your back to her; she is as skilled as my warriors. I pray Wild Wind will allow White Eagle to be gentle with her. When you return from the trading post, her grandfather must camp where he sleeps this moon. The council refuses to let him enter our camp and interfere with Wild Wind's farewell ceremony. He is old, and blind to our ways. He will not understand how White Eagle will be forced to treat his granddaughter. If he weakens and interferes, the matter will be hard for all concerned."

"It is agreed, Lone Wolf," Travis declared, accepting the exchange terms.

"There is more to hear before you answer, White Eagle."

His smile faded as he eyed Lone Wolf's expression. "Speak it."

"The council says that when you return to our camp White Eagle must join to Wild Wind before you leave with her. She will not be told of her grandfather and our exchange until you are many suns' ride from our camp and lands. She will follow her mate, but she might refuse to return to the land of the whites with strangers. Her mind and heart are troubled and she will think we trick her with claims of family. She thinks I wish to be rid of her and she will doubt our words." When Travis started to argue this astounding term, Lone Wolf held up his hand and cautioned, "Do not speak until I finish. You will join Wild Wind under Oglala law. Oglala laws do not matter to the white man. Rana Michaels and Travis Kincade are white; they will live in white lands, under

92

white laws. Once you leave our lands, the marriage will not be binding. It is a trick for my sister's obedience and to prevent trouble with the other warriors who have asked to make trade for her. No warrior can offer more than White Eagle's supplies and weapons. The exchange will not be questioned or criticized. The council demands that she leave joined to you. If you refuse to make trade and to join to her, she will be guarded until she is bound to Rides-Like-Thunder and sleeps on his Cheyenne marriage mat. Once her body is mated to his, she will never leave him. Join her and leave in honor, or she is lost to you."

A false marriage . . . Travis raged silently, cursing his bad luck. He knew as well as Lone Wolf that he was trapped, and traps and deceptions riled him. "What if she refuses when I ask her to join to me?"

Lone Wolf chuckled. "Do not play word games with me, White Eagle," he teased mirthfully. "There is no asking in Indian lands, only trading and telling. If she is defiant, she will be bound during the joining ceremony. When you are far away, you can say you pretended to join to her to get her away peacefully to return her to her grandfather. You must tell her the Oglala joining ceremony is not binding in the white man's world. Such words should make her happy, for she has refused to join to any man. But I warn you now, if you sleep upon the marriage mat with my sister, you must promise to join to her under the white man's laws. You must not dishonor Wild Wind or bring pain to her heart. How can she be sad or angry? She will have freedom and her people will be saved by her trade goods. Is it agreed?"

"What if Nathan doesn't agree to these terms? It seems cruel and dishonorable to trick her this way."

"I know Wild Wind, my Hunkpapa brother. If you buy her with trade goods and try to take her away with the truth, my sister will battle you fiercely. She has been

93

raised as Oglala, to hate and mistrust whites. She will fear your claims and she will try to flee them. It is dangerous and foolish to chase an escaped rabbit when the white wolves are running free and hungry. Take her away quickly and safely. Let her ride with White Eagle and her grandfather for many suns so that she might learn to trust and share friendship. When you speak words of truth many moons away, they will touch her ears softly and gently. Do not challenge her to accept strangers and hard words at the same time. Such words will come more easily from trusted friends. Do you know a better way to win my sister's freedom? Does my Hunkpapa brother lack the skills to entice my sister into leaving peacefully with him?"

Travis frowned at the grinning warrior. Lordy, he had never suspected he would be forced to marry the rebellious vixen to buy her freedom! He remembered what had happened when a white woman and her father had tried to force him to marry her. And he recalled the time when an Indian maiden's dreams of having him had provoked the Hunkpapas' rejection and had nearly gotten him killed . . . He forced thoughts of those treacherous days from his mind, for this situation was different; this marriage would not be real or a matter of his survival. Lone Wolf was right about his needing to get out of this territory as quickly and as safely as possible, but not for the reasons he had mentioned.

Travis considered the matter carefully and gave Lone Wolf the only decision he could make. The men talked for awhile, then headed for Lone Wolf's tepee. Travis realized that when dawn appeared and he rode out of camp, it would be too late to change his mind about this matter. He would explain the council's terms to Nathan, and his friend would have to understand the situation.

Lone Wolf strode along the path in front of Travis Kincade and, as the Oglala chief reflected on what had passed between his sister and the half-white warrior earlier, a mischievous smile slowly crossed his lips.

In his office on the Circle *C* Ranch near Fort Worth, lawyer and landowner Harrison Caldwell was speaking with his burly foreman, Silas Stern. "I don't know how you found those new men, Silas, but I like them," he remarked, then laughed wickedly, for Harrison recognized men with cold, evil hearts like his own. "You said they're real handy with those guns and rifles and aren't afraid to follow orders? Any orders?"

Silas's brown eyes sparkled with pleasure and arrogance as he grinned at his employer, a man whom Silas was careful never to cross. He knew how greedy and cruel Harrison Caldwell could be, for he had witnessed the man's evil and had obeyed orders that had sometimes curdled his blood. He had seen how Harrison had shrewdly used his power and reach to punish men who opposed or challenged him and how he had widely opened his cash box to or had bestowed favors on those who obeyed him or aided his cause. "I found 'em drinking in the saloon and I knew they weren't lying or spinning tales of past days. I watched and listened close for hours afore I hired 'em. I thought we could use two quick guns and stone nerves since McFarland ain't moving out fast enough; then we got Crandall to deal with soon. They rode with Quantrill during the war; they were in on them bloody raids in Missouri and Kansas. Wes said Jesse James helped 'em half the time. It bother you that Wes and Jack were in on that Lawrence massacre or that fight over in Baxter Springs?"

The ranch owner and lawyer recalled the bloodbath in Kansas that had claimed the lives of one hundred and fifty men, women, and children in August of 1863 as well as the slaying of over one hundred Union soldiers near

Baxter Springs. He had been a Southerner to the bone, so what did he care if Union soldiers and sympathizers had been slain during that recent war. Served them right, he decided coldly. "Nope, Silas. Fact is, Wes Monroe and Jackson Hayes did us all a big favor years ago. Those Yankees shouldn't have been so far from their beloved Union. I need men who obey orders for a price and without questions, men who aren't afraid to shed blood or go against the law, or die for their boss if it comes to that. Quantrill trained his men well, and I can use them. Still it wouldn't hurt to keep a sharp eye on them. I'm too close to success to have anyone muddy my waters. Crandall and McFarland are the only holdouts against my controlling this entire area. Once McFarland is sent on his way, I'll own every inch of land surrounding Crandall's ranch, and I plan to squeeze him until it hurts too bad to stay around for winter. Did you learn anything about where he and that Kincade went? It's been weeks, and Cody Slade is still running things over there. He refuses to tell Clarissa anything. Strange they would sneak off during the spring cattle drive . . ."

"All I could get out of his hands is what we already know. Cody's in charge and Mace Hunter took the cattle to market. If'n they knows, ain't nobody saying where they rode off to. You want me to sic Wes and Jack on some of 'em and see what they can learn?"

"No. Right now I have other plans for Monroe and Hayes. Just make sure our boys keep stealing and rebranding as many of the Rocking *C* calves and horses as possible before Nate returns. That was real obliging of him to get a brand that I can alter so easily. Tell them to make certain they aren't caught, or they're dead men. What I want Monroe and Hayes to do for me is to make sure McFarland gets on his way as soon as possible, any way necessary. In a few weeks, I'll let them make sure the money from Nate's cattle sale comes to me, not him.

When he can't repay the bank, I'll force good ole Wilber Mason to take over his ranch, real legal like. When she goes up for public auction, Monroe and Hayes can make sure nobody bids against me. If anything goes wrong, I have other plans in motion. Of course, they'll have to take care of Kincade before we can run off Nate."

Silas scratched his head of unruly black hair. "Miss Clarissa ain't gonna like that, sir. She's had her eye set on Travis for years."

Harrison chuckled. "Then she had best have his ring on her finger and have him working for me real soon, hadn't she?" he jested calmly, even though he knew he could never trust a man like Travis Kincade, who had been under the influence of Nathan Crandall too long. "She's only got herself to blame. It's her fault she didn't get any information out of that traveling painter when he did her portrait. She said he didn't know anything about Nate's sudden trip. If you ask me, I think the timing of Mallory's visit and Nate's rush is a little tight to be coincidental. I should have set the boys on him before he left."

As Harrison poured himself a whiskey, Silas frowned. He did not like the idea of tangling with Travis Kincade, or of killing him. Still, he would never interfere with his employer's desires. As for that dark-eyed, dark-haired daughter of his, Clarissa had been trying to snare the handsome foreman since his arrival, and she had not taken kindly to his resistance. That woman could be a real bitch, in actions and in character, he mused wryly. Every time Travis spurned or denied her, she came home and took it out on everyone present, including the lucky cowhand she chose to release her fiery frustrations on. Of course, none of the boys who rolled in the hay with her would boast on it. If one did, he was dead. Strange, her papa didn't care what she did, as long as she obeyed him and kept her doings secret from the town and their

97

neighbors. Silas admitted he might feel differently about her if she would rub that soft body against him a few times, or just once, in fact. He had seen how she had eyed Wes and Jackson up and down yesterday, and he had refused to warn her to steer clear of those dangerous men, men who were used to taking a woman, whether she said yes or no. Yep, those men were dangerous, but they seemed to have a curious sense of loyalty to whoever hired them. Even bold gunslingers like Wes and Jackson were not fool enough to go against a powerful man like Harrison Caldwell.

"That's all for tonight, Silas," Harrison said and watched the man leave. He wished his daughter could find a man like himself to marry, for he was weary of dealing with the crude Silas Stern. Yet he knew he could trust Silas completely, and he needed him a while longer. But as soon as he had the Rocking C Ranch under his control, Silas would not trouble him further. In fact, he was planning a lethal surprise for all of the men who knew his secret dealings . . .

Harrison sat at his desk and gazed into his whiskey. He was on the verge of possessing a vast and powerful Texas empire, and he would allow no one to stand in his way, including his daughter! When he had everything he wanted, he would govern his only child more rigidly. She would marry and settle down respectably with the man of his choosing or, as with Marissa Crandall, she would be sent into the world on her own. And he never doubted that the she-cat would land on her clawed feet. He was angry with her for failing him with Thomas Mallory. He did not like situations and people whom he could not control. Actually he did not like Clarissa and despised the thought of her inheriting his massive and lucrative spread, but she was the only seed of his loins. A devilish smile curled one corner of his broad lips. Maybe it was not too late to find himself another wife who could bear him a son. After all, he was only fifty-six and still virile. If he worked hard and fast, he could have him a son in a year or so and could rid himself of his spoiled, loose-thighed daughter! Too bad Nathan only had one daughter and she was dead. Marriage to Nathan's heir could have solved all of his problems quickly and simply, after Nathan's death.

"Little Marissa Crandall, what a fiery body and greedy appetite you had," he murmured dreamily, then rubbed the rapidly stiffening effect her memory created. "I wonder what your pa would say if he knew how many times you had climbed into bed with me."

Laughter filled the room as he recalled the things he had taught Marissa before she had suddenly run off with that fancy gambler. It did not matter to Harrison that he had gotten her drunk one afternoon and had taken advantage of her. For six months he had enchanted the vixen into sneaking into his bed at every available instance. He smiled wickedly as he trailed his fingertips up and down his hard member and slowly sipped on his whiskey, reflecting on those stimulating days.

He remembered how Marissa had been enamored of him, secretly eyeing him and flirting with him. He had done the same with her, for the seventeen-and-a-half-year-old innocent had been thrilled by the attentions of a handsome, rich, thirty-five-year-old lawyer and rancher. Their first encounter had taken place unexpectedly, when Marissa had ridden to his ranch to deliver a message while her father was away. He had enticed her to linger and to sample forbidden champagne. The daring, impulsive girl had agreed eagerly. Once her wits had been dulled, he had worked skillfully at seducing her, making sure she enjoyed their afternoon together. At first he had pretended to blackmail her with exposure to entice more visits, until the hot-blooded vixen had admitted how much she enjoyed their wanton bouts; he had always been careful to please her in order to keep her coming back for more, and gradually she had lost all inhibitions.

Marissa had sneaked over while his daughter was at school. He had sent his housekeeper away on errands or had given her time off for her own family. Sometimes, before he and Nathan had become enemies, Marissa had come over under the pretense of tutoring Clarissa or staying with her when his housekeeper supposedly could not. During those times, Clarissa had been locked in her room to keep her ignorant of their liaison. Some nights, Marissa would work him into a heavy sweat and would not let him sleep until the cock crowed. She had wanted to learn everything about men and sexual pleasures. Naturally he had been delighted to be her teacher and her pupil. He had waited for her eighteenth birthday to marry her, but Marissa had refused his proposal, claiming she wanted to enjoy her freedom a while longer. She began seeing other men, younger men, but swore she never slept with any of them. She loved to flirt and tease and bewitch them all. Finally, when she was nineteen, he had demanded they marry and halt this secret affair of one-and-a-half years. She had humiliated and pained him deeply by telling him that his size and stamina and appetite were too small for her, and she had ceased her visits, vowing to claim rape if he came near her again or tried to expose their lengthy, wanton affair. When he had traveled back East on business for several months, she had eloped.

Fury filled him at the memory of her casual dismissal, then sadistic pleasure washed over him as he recalled her brutal demise. He wondered if the Indians had enjoyed her before killing her, and he vengefully hoped they had. At least he had obtained his revenge on her last trip home. Secretly he had sent Clarissa to visit a friend one night, then had cleverly summoned Marissa to the Circle C Ranch with a forged note from his daughter, for the two had become friends, despite their different personalities. He trembled with ecstasy as he remembered that last night with Marissa tied to his bedposts and him feeding his savage hungers with her tasty body. He had learned the truth from his man Fargo about how she was being forced by Raymond to whore for her family's support, and he had given her no choice but to endure whatever he chose to do to her. He had threatened to expose their past affair and her current demeaning situation to her beloved father. After all, if she could sell it to strangers to stake her fancy gambler, he had reasoned, then, after what they had shared and she had done to him, she could certainly give him all he wanted or needed. Poor little Marissa; she had really changed, for the girl he had known would not have allowed anyone to use her, and it had seemed she no longer enjoyed sex. He had not cared, as long as she could sate his needs as only she had been able to do. Damn her, he mentally cursed. She had haunted him for years, and still did so on occasion. He shuddered now as he mentally relived that night of bliss and domination.

Perhaps he was the only one who had known why Marissa had run off a few days later with that no-good husband of hers. Besides being tied by the mysterious and powerful hold that Raymond Michaels had over her, she had had the knowledge of what her fate would have been at Harrison's hands—or at least what she had thought it would be. Actually he had intended to slay Raymond Michaels and marry his widow, for even then he had still yearned to possess her. Too bad he had forgotten to reveal his plans to Marissa while he was having the best night of his life. The truth was, Marissa Crandall Michaels had been terrified of her husband, and with just cause, from his reports.

Harrison still remembered the look on Marissa's face when he had boasted of supplying the money every time his man Fargo had copulated with her while seeking information for him. He had laughed at her for not having the guts to leave or to kill Raymond Michaels. Clearly she despised her husband and his cruelties, but the man had had some petrifying hold over her that she had been afraid to break or challenge. How he wished he had guessed their secret. Harrison knew that if he had offered her marriage and protection, she would be lying in his bed this very night, waiting to ease the aching in his loins, and the Rocking *C* would now be a part of his kingdom.

If only he had known Raymond Michaels would show up early . . . He had wanted to punish Marissa and play with her a few days before changing her life completely. When he discovered that Michaels had taken her away, he had planned to go after her, get rid of Michaels, and marry Marissa. The Kiowas had ended that dream. Too bad, he decided, for Marissa could have given him a handsome son and her father's ranch.

Soon he should begin looking for a wife, an innocent, beautiful young thing like Marissa had been, a girl he could train to his liking and needs. This time, he would not make the mistake of letting her know how pleasurable and rewarding sex could be!

Chapter Four

At dawn, Nathan Crandall stared at his ranch foreman as Travis revealed the unexpected terms for his granddaughter's exchange and his agreement with Lone Wolf. "That's a low-down trick, son, and I don't like it," Nathan declared angrily after learning of the deceitful marriage stipulation and the demand for Rana's ignorance of the truth until they were far away. As he listened, the older man jerked his head around to glare at the band of warriors who were waiting patiently for the two white men to ride out before them, and, as he did so, a silvery blond lock of hair fell over his forehead. His faded blue eyes narrowed and sparked with warring emotions as he absently brushed it aside and put on his hat.

Travis shrugged and frowned. "I know, but we have no choice. The joining won't be legal, so Rana can select her own husband when the time comes. You know I wouldn't take advantage of your granddaughter, even if she is the most beautiful female I've ever seen," he added with a roguish grin. "She's one headstrong filly, Nate. Looked and sounded to me as if she's carrying plenty of Crandall blood and spirit."

As the two men packed their camping gear and Nathan saddled his horse, Travis related his talks with and impressions of Rana and Lone Wolf. "She was one lucky girl to be taken in by Soaring Hawk and his people. But if I've pegged her right, she'll give us trouble just to show her mettle. Lone Wolf has enough problems without adding Rana's defiance or creating dissension amongst the other warriors who have their hearts set on marrying her. I must admit, she's a woman who could blind a man to duty and caution if she had a mind to. If she learned about our deal, she would choose an Oglala warrior to marry just to stir up things. The way me and Lone Wolf plan to handle matters, she won't have time to think or react badly. We have to be strong, Nate, or we'll never get her back to Texas. You have to remember she's been raised to hate and suspect whites since she was a child. If we don't follow White Eagle's suggestions, we're in for a long, rough ride home."

"Sounds crafty, but I still don't like it," he admitted, then asked worriedly, "What happens if we can't get the guns and supplies?"

"First we have to recover the money from where we hid it. Just follow my lead," Travis cautioned, then explained his plan. Next he walked to the Oglala band and gave them their final instructions. Then he mounted, took the reins of the four borrowed packhorses, and rode away with Nathan beside him and the Indians trailing at a safe distance.

Wild Wind awoke with a start and glanced toward the sleeping mat where the bedeviling stranger had slept the night before. She was disappointed to find it empty and felt he had intentionally left before seeing her, a fact she found vexing. She waited for Lone Wolf to awaken so she could question him about the enticing and infuriating stranger.

The young chief smiled and said guardedly, "Do not

trouble your spirit, little sister; he will return before the full moon. He rides with Oglalas to buy weapons and supplies for our people's survival."

"I do not understand, my brother. Why does White Eagle side with us against his own people? Can he be trusted?" she inquired.

The astute warrior recognized this opportunity for pushing his sister toward the man she would be ordered to marry. He responded cunningly, "Do you not know that White Eagle is half Lakota? He was born and lived under Grandfather's eyes for twenty winters in the camp of our Hunkpapa brothers. He trained as a warrior and many times I have heard of and witnessed his great prowess. He chooses to side with his mother's people because he feels the whites are wrong to invade our lands and to kill Lakotas. He is a man of great honor and courage. I call him friend and helper. He returned to our lands to obey the words of Grandfather. He has ridden many moons on a mission, and I must help him fulfill it. You must say and do nothing to dishonor him. In his hands is the power to save our people. His heart is good, Wild Wind. Do not hurt him or shame him."

She was surprised by his mysterious words and appealing tone. "What is the meaning of your strange words, my brother?"

"White Eagle has known much pain and sadness from his mixed bloods. Many times he has been rejected and scorned. He covers his heart to prevent more pain and rejection, and he hides his gentleness, for many foolishly think that such behavior reveals weakness. When he fulfills Grandfather's command, he will return to his home. I wish him to leave our camp with happy thoughts and feelings. Do not treat him as you do other warriors, for you have touched his heart and warmed it. Soon he will leave our lands forever. Do not send him away in coldness."

Astonishment widened her blue-gray eyes. Her heart began to pound heavily with excitement and her gaze mellowed dreamily. She had been touched and warmed by White Eagle. She hated to think of his departure, to think she would never be allowed to explore these feelings he inspired within her. "He spoke of me?" she asked eagerly.

Lone Wolf grinned and nodded, then cleverly changed the subject. "The full moon nears, little sister. Black Hawk and Prairie Dog have asked to make trade for you. Do you wish me to say you are promised to Rides-Like-Thunder? Or do you desire another warrior as mate?"

Wild Wind bristled and her cheeks flushed with annoyance. "I desire no man as mate, my selfish brother. Do not rush me. Who will care for Lone Wolf if he sends his sister away?"

"I will make trade for Myeerah," he calmly announced. He added pointedly, "After my tepee has privacy for a first night of mating."

Wild Wind's cheeks grew redder and she briefly lowered her gaze. She thought about her best friend, with her large brown eyes and silky black hair. Myeerah had been in love with Lone Wolf for years. She was smart and genial, the perfect choice for her Indian brother. "Myeerah will make you a good wife, my brother and chief. We have been friends for many winters and she speaks of you each sun."

"That is why my sister should have her own mate before I bring Myeerah to my tepee. It would be hard for her to become a wife and mother while her friend sleeps nearby. Childhood must be put behind her. If Wild Wind remains in our tepee, she would remain a girl. I do not wish her to see and hear how Wild Wind disobeys her brother and chief. It will be good for Wild Wind and Lone Wolf to take mates together on the full moon. We will join, feast, and enter separate tepees."

Her heart lurched in panic, for it seemed that freedom was swiftly deserting her. It would serve him right if she married a white man and moved far away where he could never see her again! That thought jolted her, for she knew who had inspired it. But how could the daughter of Soaring Hawk join to a half-blooded male, one who provoked her to anger and rashness? He was a stranger, and her time was short. No doubt he could have any woman he desired—if he even wanted to take a wife.

Wild Wind placed her back to Lone Wolf to ponder her troubling thoughts and her situation. She did not want to marry any warrior she knew, or one she did not know. Travis's image continued to appear before her mind's eye, warming her more each time. She remembered his stirring touch, his sensual smile, his tenderness, his entreating eyes, and his stimulating kisses. How could she despise his half-white blood and skin when she was all white? Time was her enemy. There was no time or chance to observe him. According to Lone Wolf's words, White Eagle would return the day before or the day of the full moon, when she was to give her promise and her body to her new mate. She inhaled loudly. She had been taught that whites were evil. This half-white male had inspired more bad dreams and rankling fears. Their lives were far apart. It was foolish to dream of him!

Wild Wind faced Lone Wolf. "I will obey, my brother and chief. I grow weary of our quarrels. I ask one thing; let me speak the name of my chosen mate on the sun of our joining day in six moons. I wish to be certain Black Hawk is the best choice for Wild Wind. Do not tell him or others I think on him," she insisted in order to stall for additional time.

Lone Wolf could hardly believe she was yielding, and so easily. He prayed he was not wrong about the reason behind her hesitation to announce Black Hawk as her choice, just as he prayed Travis Kincade would return on *or before the full moon, the time of her decision . . .*

"You Claude Chambers?" Travis asked the man behind the counter in the sturdily constructed trading post that was two days' ride from the Oglala camp, and three days' return ride with supplies.

The man looked Travis over, then did the same with Nathan. "Yep, that's me, owner of Chambers Trading Post, biggest and best post in these parts. What you fellers be needing today?"

"I'm Bill Saunders and this here is my friend, Thomas Clardy," Travis replied smoothly. "I just took over a wagon train whose scout got itchy feet after a few Injun attacks and run out on 'em. Got me about a hundred wagons of green easterners who don't know the difference between a man's gun and boy's peashooter. I left 'em camped about forty miles south of here while I try to round up some proper weapons and ammunition. I'm surprised the fools got this far alive. How are you set for rifles—Henry .44's and Winchester .44's?"

A broad smile crossed Chambers's face. The idea of a big sale caused his eyes to gleam. In eagerness he rubbed his hands together as he boasted, "I got all the guns you need, mister, and plenty of ammunition and supplies. Folks sure need protection with these renegades running loose, terrorizing and burning ever'thing in sight. How many you looking to buy? Where are your wagons heading?"

"Right into the hands of the Modocs and Shoshones. I tried to get 'em to settle around here, but they're determined it's Oregon. Best I can do for 'em is get 'em proper weapons and teach 'em how to use 'em. As for me and Tom here, we're heading on down to California soon as we get them settlers to the end of their trail. I got me about eighty men and boys who need good rifles and

108

enough ammunition to see us there—about forty boxes should do it. I'll also be needing . . . say fifty knives. Wouldn't hurt 'em none to learn how to fight hand to hand. Let's see," he murmured as if recalling his list of needs. "Them women are complaining about cold nights. You got around forty or fifty blankets? And I need four sacks of cornmeal; some got busted a ways back. What kinds of prices you asking?"

Chambers took a slate and a piece of chalk and began to figure his profit. Travis eyed him and the amount skeptically and shook his head. "I came here 'cause we heard you was an honest man, Chambers. Where's the next trading post? Maybe we can deal better there."

"Hold yer pants. I'll see if I can refigure. You don't know how hard and dangerous it is to get these supplies out this far. A man has to earn something for his troubles. Seventy-five dollars is a good price for a rifle like that." He suggested a slightly lower price for the items.

Travis looked over the list and the addition, then shook his head. "Still too high. I know what I need and how much money I got. I'll have to find me a place where my needs and money match. See ya," he said cordially and turned to leave.

"Then make me a decent offer," the owner challenged hungrily.

Travis returned to the counter and picked up the slate and chalk. After rubbing it clean, he spoke aloud as he wrote and figured. "Forty boxes of ammunition at five dollars each, fifty knives at three dollars each, fifty blankets at ten dollars each, four sacks of cornmeal at fifteen each, eighty rifles or carbines at fifty dollars each, and ninety dollars in sewing supplies, jerky, and coffee for five thousand dollars in U.S. money and gold. Plus I'll need to borrow one of your wagons to get it back to camp. Tom will return it in a few days. Is it a bargain,

Chambers?" Travis had added the last three items to prevent suspicion and hoped that his ploy would work.

"You're robbing me blind," Chambers accused deceitfully, knowing Travis's offer was a fair one. He himself was never fair unless he was forced to be. He grinned. "You're a smart feller, Bill Saunders. Them folks are lucky you signed on as scout. I'll let you have everything today except the knives. When your friend returns with my wagon, he can pick up the knives. Might say I have to protect myself in case my wagon don't come home again."

Travis had prepared for this demand. "Ninety dollars is more than enough proof against your wagon not returning. Tom and the others will retrieve the jerky, coffee, and sewing supplies when your wagon comes home. Those items will fit better on packhorses than a crate of knives. And don't go suggesting I leave the cornmeal, 'cause I don't want more sacks busted by bouncing them around on horseback for days. You write out a paper saying them supplies are paid for, just in case you ain't around when your wagon comes home."

"Let's go in the back room so you can look over the rifles," Chambers slyly suggested before Travis could. He led the way into the adjoining room and pried open five oblong crates containing fifteen rifles each, stacked in five rows of three weapons. He placed five carbines across the top of the first one and began stacking boxes of ammunition nearby.

Travis lifted and examined each of the five Winchester .44 carbines, which would fire thirteen rounds before reloading. In the first three crates of Winchester .44's, which would fire seventeen rounds before reloading, he examined a different row of rifles in each wooden box. In the fourth crate, he examined every rifle, as he did with the fifth crate of Henry .44 rifles. He was satisfied with his purchase, knowing his random search would have exposed any deception on Chambers's part.

"Harvey, nail them crates while Mister Saunders checks over this ammunition," Chambers ordered pleasantly.

Travis quickly and sporadically examined boxes of ammunition, then asked to see the knives and blankets. He followed Chambers into another room and waited for the man to count out fifty of each to be checked. Twice Chambers lost his count and had to restart it. As with the other items, Travis randomly selected knives and blankets to study for quality. "I'm going to trust you on the cornmeal. But if I find it bad when it's dumped into barrels at camp, I'm sending it back with the wagon. You set our other supplies aside to be picked up in a few days."

When Travis and Chambers had gone into the other room, Harvey sent Nathan to harness the team and wagon and to bring it around to the back door. When Travis returned to the first room, Nathan was watching Harvey and another man load gun crates. Afterward the ammunition, knives, blankets, and cornmeal were loaded by the two men while Travis paid Chambers and waited for a receipt for the goods that supposedly would be picked up later when the wagon was returned.

"You sure it's safe to go riding out with such a valuable shipment and only two guards?" Chambers inquired as he watched the two men climb aboard the wagon and take their seats.

Travis smiled. "I got me ten men waiting nearby in case of trouble. Only a fool would travel alone with that much money or this many supplies. They were to ride in if we didn't show ourselves soon."

Chambers laughed. "Like I said, Saunders, you're a smart man. Been a pleasure doing business with you and Tom."

As the wagon vanished behind a hill, Harvey joined

Claude Chambers, who was grinning broadly. "You get them crates swapped?"

"Yep. Good thing we'll be long gone before that Saunders finds out won't more than twenty of them rifles work and most of that ammunition ain't worth as much as this dirt," he said, kicking the sand beneath his filthy boots. "You sure pulled a sly one on him. Like he said, his friend shoulda stayed with us all the time as ordered. Made it real easy."

Between wicked chuckles, Chambers concurred, "Yessirree, the new owner will take over in two days and we can be on our merry way. I sure am glad I didn't have time to return that bad lot of guns and ammunition. Gave me a chance to sell 'em twice and avoid any problems."

"Saunders ain't gonna be none too happy when he gets past the top row in each of them crates. You sure he won't stop and check 'em?"

"He examined them real careful inside and he don't know you and Slim were given time to swap the crates. If they use any of them blankets or knives or cornmeal tonight or pull out any of them top rifles, they'll be fooled by good stuff. He won't discover his mistake for days, and then it'll be too late. We'll be heading for St. Louis."

"Them folks who wants them guns and ammunition ain't gonna be happy with them two scouts. They might even think them scouts are trickin' 'em. Hell, they might even kill 'em. Ain't that a shame?"

"Yep," Chambers agreed. "A cryin' shame. That Saunders thinks he's real clever, but ain't no man been born who can outwit me."

It was the morning of the full moon and Wild Wind was very much aware of the significance of this day in her life. She apprehensively carried out her last chores in Lone Wolf's tepee. Before this sun passed, her life would

112

change drastically. She could not stop her cold hands from shaking or her mind from drifting constantly to the half-blooded man who had failed to return before this awesome moment of decision had arrived. She had been haunted by her strange enchantment by him. She had thought about him and dreamed about him for days. At last a real man had entered her life and she worried that perhaps it was too late to study him and the potent attraction between them, though she believed he had felt it too. She knew he had been told of her "bad ways," and she realized that he might have been merely showing kindness to Lone Wolf's sister. After all, he could be so arrogant and infuriating! How could she reveal this pull she felt toward a white man? How could she reject her Oglala role? She had promised Lone Wolf and herself that she would relent to her destiny, and she dreaded it.

For the past few days, she had encountered curious stares and tension-building silence that had bewildered her, actions she could not understand because she had been on her best behavior. As soon as her Indian brother returned from his latest council meeting, she would have to relate her choice to him. Her heart pounded in panic and dismay. Then suddenly unusual noises captured her attention and set her pulse racing in suspense. He had returned! She put aside her task and went to investigate.

Travis Kincade halted the loaded wagon before the ceremonial lodge and jumped to the ground. The warriors who had traveled with him dismounted and awaited the approach of the chief and the council. Travis and Lone Wolf exchanged smiles and grasped forearms in greeting. A few words passed between them. Sighting her, Lone Wolf called Wild Wind to join them and to share this joyous moment.

Suddenly her feet seemed as heavy as large rocks and

her legs as stiff as posts. Anxiety rushed through her. She chided herself for her cowardice. Swallowing with difficulty, she ordered her body to obey the summons. She walked forward and halted at Lone Wolf's side, affectionately gazing at him and ignoring Travis's intimidating presence. She dared not look at him, fearing her expression would reveal her turmoil. She was glad she had scrubbed her hair and taken care with her appearance.

In Oglala, the chief announced to everyone, "Our Hunkpapa brother, White Eagle, has returned with many weapons and supplies for the defense and survival of our people. He has shown much courage, cunning, and generosity. As chief of the Oglalas and friend to White Eagle, I say he has earned a *coup* feather for his deed. What say the Oglalas?" he cleverly asked, initiating his ploy to release Wild Wind.

Sounds of agreement and praise filled the air. Lone Wolf placed the *coup* feather in Travis's headband as he stated, "White Eagle will be our honored guest this moon when your chief takes his first wife."

Wild Wind observed the proceedings, appearing proud and calm before the green gaze that watched her intently and obviously. She was glad she did not tremble and her cheeks did not glow like the fire. She sensed that something was about to happen, but she did not realize what. She was too ensnared by thoughts of how to stall her joining tonight. If only White Eagle had visited her camp sooner!

As he had planned, Lone Wolf queried, "What can Lone Wolf and the Oglalas do to reward my friend and brother for saving our people?"

In an unwavering tone, Travis casually replied, "I desire to join with Wild Wind this sun. I offer all you see in trade for her," he stated, motioning toward the wagon filled with weapons and supplies.

Wild Wind's mouth fell open and her eyes widened in astonishment as she whirled to stare into Travis's unreadable face. When Travis's gaze shifted to hers, he smiled confidently and enticingly. Before she could gather her wits and force her tongue to respond, Lone Wolf had accepted the bargain and everyone around them began cheering. Wild Wind's gaze raced to her brother's grinning face, then moved to the beaming ones of those around them. She did not know what to think or feel at this unexpected turn of events.

Black Hawk instantly stepped forward and declared, "I have spoken for Wild Wind. The daughter of Soaring Hawk must not join to a half-breed."

Silence fell over the assembled group at the insulting claim. Lone Wolf focused angry eyes on the belligerent warrior. "I am chief. White Eagle is called friend and brother. Your words shame you. Lone Wolf did not accept Black Hawk's offer; it was not enough for Wild Wind. Do you offer more than White Eagle for her trade?"

Black Hawk's gaze slipped over the heavily loaded wagon, then he eyed Travis with contempt and hatred. "It is wrong to send the daughter of Soaring Hawk and sister of Lone Wolf away with a half-white man. He lives in the white lands, in the white ways," he argued.

"His heart is Lakota; his deed is Lakota. His honor and courage are high. He is a good mate for the sister of your chief. Why do you dishonor Black Hawk and his people with dark words and feelings?"

"Wild Wind belongs with her people," the warrior continued offensively, trying to prevent his loss of the flaming-haired beauty.

Lone Wolf glanced at each council member and asked, "Is there one among you who agrees with Black Hawk?" Because they were all part of this ploy, each man shook his head. Lone Wolf looked at Black Hawk and stated,

"Wild Wind will join to the man who brings deliverance from our enemies."

"It is wrong, Lone Wolf. She does not wish to join him and travel away from our lands," the jealous warrior reasoned frantically.

"The sister of Lone Wolf will obey her brother and chief and the Oglala council. She has much courage and honor. She would not refuse to join the man who saves her people and lands. I will speak with my sister and hear her words. Come, Wild Wind," he commanded, taking her arm and leading her inside the ceremonial lodge to talk.

Lone Wolf walked to the center of the large tepee and sat on a buffalo hide. Wild Wind followed his lead. She looked into his entreating gaze and questioned, "Do you truly wish me to marry him and leave our people and lands? I have been raised Indian; I know nothing of the white world. White Eagle is a stranger to me." Even as she argued, she was filled with stirring anticipation. She had wanted time to get to know him, but she had never suspected he would ask for her in joining. He had seemed the kind of man who enjoyed his freedom. He wanted her, and today! But his smile had been mischievous and his look smug. Did she dare relent to her wild desires and his control?

"This is the sun of our joining, my sister. Is there a man with more honor and courage to choose, a man who offers more for Wild Wind and her people? Do you seek to insult White Eagle and dishonor your brother and chief by refusing to join to him?"

She was dismayed and hurt by the seeming ease with which he was bargaining and sacrificing her. "Do you seek to punish me for behaving badly many times? For not choosing Rides-Like-Thunder?"

"No, my sister. I do what is best for you and our people. War covers our lands as the spring grasses. Far

116

away with White Eagle, the sister of Lone Wolf will find safety and happiness. Do you forget that your skin and blood are white? There is no dishonor in joining to White Eagle. Think of your people, my sister, not of Wild Wind."

If only she knew White Eagle and grasped his motives for this unexpected demand, she reflected frantically. He had such a potent effect on her, and she feared losing herself in him. If only he did not insist they join and leave today! Thoughts of being alone with him both alarmed and excited her. "Lone Wolf said that Wild Wind could choose her mate this sun."

"The sun is high and no choice has been spoken. Before the eyes of White Eagle and our tribe I have accepted trade for you. Will you shame me and hurt me with defiance on our last sun together? Do you fear White Eagle?" he shrewdly inquired. "Do you wish him to ask for another in joining? Who can match the beauty and skills of my sister? Who is more worthy to walk at the side of White Eagle?"

"He is white, my brother, and lives far from our lands. He seizes me too quickly. You cannot force me to join to him and leave. Will he refuse to give our people the weapons if I refuse to join to him? Can you not take the weapons from him? Do you fear his power?" she inquired, wondering why this demand for her had not come as a surprise to her brother and why he was so eager to comply. Had this intriguing man asked for her before leaving camp? she mused. After all, they had been powerfully drawn to each other from the beginning.

"Lone Wolf will not answer such wicked questions. Many times you have shamed and angered Lone Wolf and his people. Many times his heart has known great pain and sadness over Wild Wind's deeds. If your heart is Oglala and honor lives within you, you will obey my words. It is the vote and will of our council. Do you

117

refuse him?"

It was not Travis she was refusing; it was his intimidating rush. She felt trapped, helpless; others were ruling and controlling her life. "He will carry me far from my brother and people," she fretted, recalling her fears over her dark dreams and dreading this white challenge. There seemed to be too many changes to accept at the same time.

"Hear my words, sister, for Lone Wolf does not speak falsely of Grandfather's visions." He slowly related his past dreams about her departure and why he had taught her to defend herself. He spoke of his fears for her survival during this war with the whites and for the survival of his people. "The moon Grandfather revealed to me in dreams has come. It is time for my sister to tame the wild winds that blow through her head and heart. Grandfather has chosen your path and you must walk it with pride and courage. Far away with White Eagle, Wild Wind will become the woman warrior she hungers to be."

"I do not wish to become white again," she protested in dread, apprehensive about the shadows that surrounded her past and uncertain about Travis. She wanted more time with him, more time to explore her feelings.

"You are white, little sister," he gently reminded. "Go in peace to seek your new destiny and tame it bravely as I have taught you."

Outside, Travis tried not to appear worried or tense, but he was both. He sensed what was taking place inside the lodge and wondered how he and Lone Wolf would be forced to deal with it. He had to entice her to accept him so they could depart quickly before trouble struck. He wished his offer could have been more than a trick, for he truly wanted her. His gaze shifted to Black Hawk's, whose expression was cold and taunting.

Suddenly the tepee flap was thrown aside. Lone Wolf

approached the group awaiting him, pulling the obviously reluctant girl along with him. He placed Wild Wind's hand on Travis's arm. "Lone Wolf accepts the offer of White Eagle and will give his sister in joining."

Immediately Wild Wind pushed past Travis and the others to head for her tepee without speaking or looking at her intended mate or their audience. Although well acquainted with their customs, she felt betrayed by this "exchange," which made her the possession of another. She angrily suspected that the two men had plotted secretly. Her life was changing, and she felt helpless. She was confused by her warring emotions and embarrassed by the degrading situation.

Watching her flight, Travis said, "The joining must take place soon, Lone Wolf. The ride is long and hard and we have been away from our lands many suns. White Eagle and his friend must return home to protect them."

Lone Wolf thought he understood why the man was in such a hurry to claim his adopted sister and be on his way: he did not want to give Wild Wind time to change her mind or to flee and cause trouble. He smiled. "We will prepare for the joining," he announced happily.

Within ten minutes, Travis and Wild Wind were standing before the ceremonial chief and listening to his Oglala words of joining. At the proper time, Travis turned to the silent girl and lifted the edges of the joining robe, which Lone Wolf had lent him. He tensed again as Wild Wind hesitated briefly before stepping to him so he could wrap the feathered cloak around her body to seal their joining. He could feel her slight trembling and she refused to look up at him. Clearly she did not want to marry him or leave these people. He was baffled by her compliance. No doubt her sharp mind was plotting his defeat and her escape this very minute, neither of which he could allow. A few more words were spoken, then the ceremony ended.

The quicker they left, the sooner she could learn the truth and be free of this farce, he mused dourly. Him, too, for his crazy feelings for her scared the hell out of him. Evidently he had misjudged her attraction to him, and that conclusion did not sit well. "Get your belongings and say your farewells, Wild Wind. We must leave," he told her, unaware that his voice and gaze appeared chilly to her.

She looked up at him, her stare challenging and her chin held high. She did not like being forced to comply with a demand that would alter her entire life. She feared his magic and her impending return to the white world. He owned her, and he was being the man she did not like again! The least he could have done was ask her first, or warn her! She whispered angrily, "Do not give Wild Wind orders. You have not taken me from my lands and people yet. I only obey the council's command to save my people and to punish my brother for selling me to a half-breed. I wished to join to Black Hawk or Rides-Like-Thunder; you have ruined all. Perhaps you will be sorry for forcing me to become your mate. Perhaps I will not fit in your white world."

Travis concealed his anger as he grinned and nodded. Perhaps, thinking he would be gone soon, she had been having fun with him. Perhaps she had used him to make Black Hawk jealous. Either she did not like being forced to marry and leave or she had been using her wits and charms to get her way; in either case, she had lost.

"White Eagle has many bad traits. Perhaps trading is the only way White Eagle could obtain a mate," she scoffed insultingly. Why wasn't a man like him joined? she wondered silently. Because he was viewed as a "despicable half-breed"? Did he need a mate and feel she was a good choice because she was white and would not expose his Indian heritage?

"Wild Wind has many bad traits. Perhaps slyly trading

120

her to a stranger was the only way Lone Wolf could be free of her cutting tongue and wild ways," he taunted devilishly. "Perhaps I can tame them before we reach home. Do not forget, your words and honor bind you to me. If you do forget, I will bind you with thongs or punish you."

Without replying, she turned and, with great dignity, walked to her tepee. She was distracted as she collected her possessions and stuffed them into several *parfleches*.

Myeerah entered the tepee and found her immersed in packing. "I wish you did not have to leave," her lovely friend told her.

Wild Wind did not want to dampen her friend's happy joining day or leave in such gloomy spirits. She would not give the other girls reason to pity or ridicule her. Her self-sacrifice must be carried out bravely and unselfishly, or at least appear so. She could not help but recall Lone Wolf's words in the ceremonial lodge. Having been raised by Indians who were firm believers in and followers of visions and dreams, she felt this was the Great Spirit's will, or His test of her courage and obedience. Perhaps some exciting challenge lay before her, even at the side of that mysterious and vexing male. Perhaps her separation from the Oglalas would not be forever. She smiled and artfully replied, "Do not worry, Myeerah. He is very handsome and brave. I must not show eagerness and joy at his trade, for his pride would grow too great. Wild Wind must force him to seek her heart gently and patiently. As the doe, I will dart and run and hide, and he must chase me. He will not tame the wild wind; she will tame a mighty eagle," she teased. "White Eagle does me great honor to choose the sister of Lone Wolf and to offer so many trade goods. But you must tell no one of my secret."

The girl was fooled, and delighted. "My heart is happy that he pleases my friend. His face is handsome and his

121

body virile. He is strong and cunning. If Lone Wolf did not cause fires in Myeerah, her eyes would settle on White Eagle," she confessed with laughter.

"Be happy with my brother. One sun, Wild Wind will return to visit. I wish to find many children and great joy in this tepee."

Myeerah left to retrieve a parting gift for her best friend and Wild Wind knelt on a buffalo mat as she continued her packing. Her back to the entrance, she allowed herself to become lost in deep thought. Her mind envisioned the evil white man of her nightmares and she murmured, "No white dog will ever harm me or own me."

Her thoughts drifted to Travis. She was nervous about leaving with him. He had not revealed her bad behavior of that first night. He had made her relax and talk freely. But still she wondered, Had he asked for her because she had rashly inflamed his body? Did he need a strong woman of courage, daring, and wits? A white woman to conceal his dark past? "I must not be afraid or bad," she declared aloud as she completed her packing and shifted to sit on the buffalo mat to await her friend's return.

Suddenly her line of vision was filled by the towering physique of her new husband, whose gaze seemed to encompass her. She failed to notice that he had closed the tepee flap to assure their privacy.

Travis came forward and hunkered down before her. His intention in visiting her had been to offer encouragement and to lessen her tension during this difficult period, but this was forgotten as he looked at her and drank in her stimulating presence. Unable to master his feelings and thoughts, he allowed his smoldering gaze to engulf her exquisite features, which set his body aflame with desire for her. It was obvious that he had trouble swallowing as he tried to clear his throat to speak to her. He was quivering with tightly leashed passion and straining to keep himself under control. His respiration became shallow and rapid. All he could think for a time was, She's my wife and I want her. He was sorry he had been rude and harsh, and he was determined to win her approval and help.

Wild Wind's body and emotions reacted to his presence instantly. Her gaze fused with his and she was unable to think clearly. He seemed to dominate her entire world and all sights and sounds of other things were lost to her. Her tongue refused to speak and her body had the urge to fling itself into his arms. Her lips craved a melting against his and her mind begged to let her senses soar like his Indian name. She felt charged with anticipation and energy, yet held fast by weakness and apprehension. She felt bold and brave, yet hesitation and cowardice sneaked into her mind to prevent her from rising, walking to him, and surrendering eagerly to his allure. The drums had never beat more swiftly than her heart at this moment. She did not know what to say or do, or even if she could compel her body to obey her. She was flustered and enraptured, and her reaction annoyed her.

Slowly Travis's body drifted forward until his knees touched the ground and brushed lightly against hers. His shaky hands slipped into her hair on either side of her head, and he looked deeply and longingly into her expressive gaze, which sent forth messages of a matching hunger. Nothing and no one, including himself, could have halted him from touching her and savoring her lips. He lowered his head and brought his mouth down to hers, evoking a shudder from each at the blissful contact. The kiss was tender and exploratory, but gradually it deepened to reveal mutual desire. Travis's strong arms closed around her body and drew her up to lock her possessively within his embrace. His lips skillfully claimed hers and sent their senses spinning.

Wild Wind's hands moved up his hard chest to ease

around his neck. Without hesitation or inhibition, she pressed her body against his in a manner that exposed her desire and announced her surrender. An August day could not have warmed her body more than his nearness and passion. She was trembling with feverishly awakened needs. At that moment, she wanted him urgently and was willing to yield without reservation, to follow him wherever he led. He was the only man to claim her heart, her love, her desire, her life, her all.

Abruptly Travis's lips left hers and he pushed their bodies apart. Both were flushed and breathing heavily. She eyed him inquisitively and tried to reclaim her stirring place in his arms. Then she understood the reason for his withdrawal as Lone Wolf's voice called out to him more sternly, "Come, White Eagle, we must complete our trade. This is not the time to begin your life with my sister."

Travis glanced at her as if guilty of some misdeed. His embarrassment and dismay were obvious, and they cooled her ardor. He mastered his respiration, then replied, "I will join you soon, Lone Wolf."

The chief did not enter the tepee or leave his position outside the closed flap. Lone Wolf's sharp instincts and keen senses had absorbed enough to know he should separate them quickly; yet he was tempted to allow Travis and Wild Wind to make this joining a real marriage by sealing their vows with their passion and commitment. He decided it was too soon. "The sun passes swiftly, White Eagle. We must hurry."

"I am coming," Travis answered, then gently caressed her cheek and smiled apologetically. In a few more minutes she would have been his completely. He was shocked by the power of his attraction to her, but he knew she was also taken by him. "I must go. I came to tell you not to fear me or leaving your people. Prepare to ride, and I will come for you soon. Do not allow anger and

124

false pride to spoil your departure. We will speak later."
He paused. "Surely what has just passed between us
proves that it is I, not Black Hawk, you crave."

Wild Wind watched him rise and leave, closing the flap
behind him. She wished her brother had not interrupted
them, and she wondered if he and others had guessed
what was happening inside this tepee. She blushed and
tried to calm herself but found it difficult. His kisses and
touches had created a fierce aching within her, an aching
she knew only he could appease. There was a magic
between them, and she was delighted by it. Now she was
ready to leave with him. But then his last words echoed
through her mind. Had he been trying to enchant and
control her? Trying to ensnare her with her own
feelings?

The wagon had been unloaded and Travis was opening
the crates to show the warriors how to use the different
weapons. "I'm glad this matter has been settled
peacefully and quickly, Lone Wolf," Travis remarked.
Yet he was uncomfortable. He did not like the way his
neck kept itching, a sure sign of trouble. He had not
trusted Claude Chambers; it had been the reason he had
ordered Nathan not to take his eyes from the crates for an
instant. Travis knew that if Chambers had a hundred
barrels of water, he could not trust the greedy man to
share even a dipper of it with a dying man. A cold shiver
ran over the Texan's body as he realized his keen
instincts and suspicions were about to be proven
accurate.

Lone Wolf noticed the man's reaction to the trade
goods just before Travis declared in vivid rage, "That
sorry bastard! He switched crates on us! These guns and
ammunition are useless. I'll kill the sneaky bastard."

"What troubles you, White Eagle?" the young chief
asked.

Travis explained the problem, knowing how the

125

deception would appear to the Oglalas. "We'll have to go back to the trading post. This time, Chambers will reward us with more than our fair share."

Black Hawk stepped forward and accused, "The white-dog lies. He seeks to trick us. He sets a trap for the Oglalas. He betrays us. I say kill him and the white-dog who waits nearby. The trade is no good. Seize him! I challenge for Wild Wind and his life."

Lone Wolf stared at the furious Travis, who was glaring at his hostile warrior. "What trick is this, White Eagle?" he demanded.

Travis met the dark gaze and replied, "I swear on my life and honor that the white trader will pay for this black deed. I will go after the guns and prove White Eagle did not betray the Oglalas."

"The white-dog has no honor or true words. He must die."

"Black Hawk speaks in anger with a swift tongue," he retorted. "The knives, blankets, and cornmeal are good. Many of the guns and bullets are good. I will return to the trading post to replace those that are bad. I will punish the white-eyes who tricked me. I must be allowed to prove my honor and words. Wild Wind is mine."

"No!" Black Hawk declared thunderously. "You must die." The warrior drew his knife and lunged at Travis. Buffalo Slayer and Two Ponies seized the warrior and restrained him until their chief spoke.

Prairie Dog rushed to Lone Wolf's tepee and explained the dangerous situation to Wild Wind and Myeerah. The women hurried to where the argument was taking place. Wild Wind keenly and fearfully observed the confrontation. This man was her husband, she reflected, perhaps her destiny . . .

"Hear me, Lone Wolf," Travis beseeched, "I did not lie or trick you. I demand the right to prove my innocence. I will ride to the trading post for more guns and ammunition. I will punish the trader."

Lone Wolf eyed the man critically, praying that Travis was speaking honestly and wanting to believe him, for he knew how much was at stake. "Buffalo Slayer, ride with Prairie Dog and Two Ponies and bring the other white man to our camp. We will hold White Eagle's father friend and wife until he returns with more guns. If he does not return, I will slay the white man and Wild Wind will join to Black Hawk."

A gasp of astonishment from the girl alerted the debating men to her presence. "Tell me what happens here, my brother," she coaxed.

Lone Wolf explained Travis's dilemma. Her gaze went to the man who was now her husband. Her probing eyes searched his face and observed his stance. No, she decided to herself, this man would not shame himself or risk the life of his friend by tricking her people. He was too clever to be unmasked this easily. It had to be a terrible mistake.

"If he has betrayed us, he must die," her brother told her.

Black Hawk said with a sneer, "I will slay the half-breed for fooling you and shaming you, Wild Wind. He cares not for Wild Wind. He only desires a wild spirit to master. He seeks our shame and deaths. In five moons, he will be dead and you will join to me."

Wild Wind was antagonized by the warrior's words. She was not a fool or a prize! She walked to Travis and studied him, all too aware of what had occurred between them a short time before. She knew that if a man tricked you in one way, he would trick you in others. Surely he could not cause her heart to soar and her senses to cloud if he was evil and deceitful. "Do you lie, White Eagle?" she asked softly.

Travis met her steady gaze and responded, "No. I was tricked. I must slay the man who betrayed and

127

dishonored me." Travis felt as if his personal history was almost repeating itself. Once more the Indians were accusing him of treachery, and again he was innocent. But this time there was more at stake than his life and honor. He inwardly raged against the false charges and his vulnerability, but he was touched by the lack of doubt in her eyes and voice.

When Travis repeated how he had checked the items, then explained that the trader had cheated him by switching them, she knew he was telling the truth. "I will ride with him, my brother. If he lies, I will slay him for my people." She watched the effect of her words on Travis.

Black Hawk shouted, "No! I will ride with the white dog and guard him. You are a woman. Do not seek to protect your new mate."

Wild Wind whirled and shouted back at the nettling warrior, "I am only a woman, but my arrow and knife find their targets more times than yours, Black Hawk! If he has shamed and tricked me and my people, it is my right to slay him. We are joined only in words, and false words can be broken. If you ride with him, I am sure he will not return alive. As does White Eagle, Wild Wind looks white. Only she can enter the white dog's trading post and watch him for tricks. My people need guns and supplies to battle the white-eyes. I joined to him to obtain them for my people. Now I must help him replace those stolen by the evil white dog. Until his words are proven good or bad, his mate lives under this shadow of suspicion with him."

"You cannot ride with me, Ra . . . Wild Wind. It is too dangerous. The trader will expect my return for justice. He will be waiting to trap me. I will need twenty warriors, Lone Wolf. Guard my father friend and wife carefully. I will return for them in five moons."

"Who is this father friend, and where does he camp?"

128

she asked.

Instead of replying, Lone Wolf ordered his braves to capture Nathan Crandall and to bring him to camp. He was not surprised when Travis warned them not to injure the old man. "He will be safe for five moons, White Eagle. On the sun of the sixth moon, he will die and my sister will join to Black Hawk, if you betray us again.

"No, my brother. If I am freed, I will join to Rides-Like-Thunder as you promised," Wild Wind announced, declaring her rejection of Black Hawk, whom she had rashly believed she could easily enchant and master. She was astonished at the clever way in which the warrior had concealed his dark side from them. If anything happened to her new husband, she would not remain here!

"So be it," Lone Wolf concurred, to Black Hawk's fury.

Wanting to give her courage and hope and having a desire to annoy Black Hawk, Travis ignored the eyes watching them as he took Wild Wind's hand and smiled at her. He entreated confidently, "Do not worry. I will prove my honor and words and return for you soon. You are my wife and you must trust me." She nodded and lowered her gaze, and he knew it was to shield her emotions from him and the others. Travis was not given time to await Nathan's arrival and speak with him. Instead he was soon riding off with the band of warriors to seek Chambers.

It had required enormous self-control for Wild Wind not to hug him and kiss him farewell. She had nodded understanding and her agreement with his words, then had squeezed his hand tightly to let him know she believed him and would be waiting eagerly for his return.

After watching Travis and the warriors ride away, everyone went back to their tasks but Wild Wind and Black Hawk, who remained where they were until the band was out of sight. The jealous warrior scoffed, "Be careful of the evil fires of love and passion, Wild Wind. If they burn too swiftly and wildly, they will leave nothing of you but blackened coals. You are a fool to trust him. He is bad, and he has gained control of your will and wits. If you are rash, the eagle's claws will tear your heart and life to pieces. He did not wish to join to you. Lone Wolf demanded that you leave as his mate, not his whore. What is an Indian wife to a white man? Only a lowly squaw to warm his mats until he grows weary of her."

She glared at him and retorted, "The only evil here is within you, Black Hawk. Think of your people, not your wicked desires. You make a fool of yourself before our people and you blacken your face with shame. I will wait for his return, then go where he commands. It is as I wish, and so it shall be. You will see," she declared smugly.

Near the trading post over two days later, Travis pointed to a lone cottonwood in the distance and told the leader of the band, "If I do not show my face by the time the sun reaches the top of that tree, you must attack the post and take the guns. If I am slain in the battle, tell Lone Wolf what happened. My friend will teach the Oglalas how to use the white man's firesticks. When the training is over, he is to release my friend and my wife to return home." He impulsively removed his *wanapin* and handed it to the silent warrior as he said, "Give this to Wild Wind . . . if I die."

Buffalo Slayer took the necklace and gazed at it. It was a circular medallion made of sacred red stone. Upon its surface was scratched a war eagle in flight, one talon clutching a thunderbolt and the other one tightly grasping two broken shafts of an arrow. Around the eagle's neck was suspended a smaller medallion with symbols of the War Bonnet Society. Buffalo Slayer lifted curious eyes as Travis snapped the reins of the harness and headed the wagon toward the trading post.

Once inside, Travis was angered to discover the extent of Claude Chambers's guile. He explained his problem to the new man in charge, who accepted no blame or responsibility for the treachery. And no amount of reasoning could sway the man's unfavorable decision. He would not even honor the receipt for the items already purchased. Travis did learn that Chambers and his two cohorts had not left the post until yesterday morning and were heading for St. Louis.

"Yore quarrel is with Chambers, son. I can't take my time and money to exchange damaged goods you bought from him."

Travis returned to where the Indians were waiting for him. "At dark, we go in and take what's ours. Post some guards, Buffalo Slayer," he gravely advised, hoping to avoid more trouble and another delay.

Travis began pacing with unnatural impatience, musing that darkness could not arrive quickly enough to suit him. He knew he had no choice but to steal the guns and ammunition, or Nathan would be dead and Rana would be lost to them.

Finally, when all seemed quiet in the small settlement near the trading post, Travis cautiously returned to the large, sturdy wooden structure.

"We're closed," a voice called out without opening the door. "Come back in the morning."

"It's Bill Saunders. I've got a deal for you, a thousand dollars."

The bolt was moved aside and the door opened slightly. "What's your deal, Saunders?" the man inquired eagerly.

Travis held out a leather pouch and shook it, making the emptied bullets sound like clinking coins. "A thousand and those useless guns until I can track down

131

Chambers and retrieve my money for the exchange. You'll have the money, plus those guns to exchange for another sale. I'll need twenty rifles to arm my men to go after him. Deal?"

The man pondered his offer and his blank expression. "And what's to keep you from not coming back after you catch Chambers, if you can?"

"The fact that I need eighty rifles more than I need the money Chambers swindled out of me. I've got a wagon train of green settlers sitting practically helpless three days' ride from here. The quicker I can track Chambers and get my money back, the sooner I can arm my people and be on our way to Oregon. You won't be sorry for helping us," he coaxed. "I'll pay you a hundred dollars for your help and trust."

The man seriously considered the lucrative deal. Finally he shook his head and replied, "Sorry, son, but it ain't wise to trust a desperate stranger with so much of my stock."

Travis sighed loudly and grimaced. "I was afraid you wouldn't be obliging." He drew his pistol before the man could slam and lock the door. Pushing the man inside, he bound and gagged him, then rendered him unconscious to prevent a witness to his actions. When a voice called out from the other room, Travis rapidly reacted. Without making a sound, he hurriedly concealed himself near the door to the adjoining storeroom. When the man entered the dim area to see why his boss had not answered him, Travis carefully struck him over the head and he too fell unconscious. Then he went to the door and gave his signal.

As quietly and swiftly as possible, the gun and ammunition crates were exchanged. When the warriors attempted to take more than Travis had purchased, he halted them, saying, "The man who cheated us left. Our battle is with him. We steal nothing from the innocent.

132

You must take the goods to Lone Wolf while I track and punish the man who betrayed me. I will return in a few moons."

"We are at war, White Eagle. We need many guns and bullets."

"If we take more than I paid for, Buffalo Slayer, the new trader will send the white soldiers after thieves. The wagon is heavy and must travel slowly. We do not have time or enough warriors to battle many soldiers. Even in war, men must have honor. If they come after thieves, we could lose everything."

The warrior gave Travis's words deep thought. He smiled and nodded. "We will do as White Eagle says. He is cunning."

Travis wrote a message on the slate, telling the owner he would return soon with the money to pay for the guns and ammunition. He placed the two men where they could not free themselves or send out an alarm for at least a day, then set the slate within the men's line of vision. All he could do was pray the owner would accept his claim.

As silently and stealthily as they had approached the secluded area, Travis and the warriors departed. At a safe distance, Travis advised the band's leader to cover their trail and be careful. He knew that the supplies in that wagon meant Nathan's life and Rana's freedom. Taking his *wanapin* from Buffalo Slayer, he smiled. "I will return to Lone Wolf's camp for my friend and wife after the white man is punished."

"What if the white man or soldiers capture or slay White Eagle?"

Travis inhaled deeply. He knew he was lingering in this perilous Hunkpapa area too long, but he could not allow Chambers to get away with his treachery. "If the Great Spirit does not protect me on this journey, do not let Wild Wind join to Black Hawk. Make sure Lone Wolf remembers his promise to release my friend and his . . . my wife."

"Buffalo Slayer will give White Eagle's words to our chief." The warrior smiled, for he comprehended this man's feelings for Wild Wind.

Travis watched the wagon and the warriors ride away into the darkness and prayed they would reach the Oglala camp within the time limit. As he galloped off in the other direction, visions of Rana filled his mind. He was sorry she was not his wife under the white law that ruled Nathan Crandall's life, for he knew that Nathan would not see their joining as a binding reality. Yet, if there was one truth he knew, it was that he wanted Wild Wind with all his heart and might, and he prayed she felt or would soon feel the same.

Chapter Five

Four days had passed and Wild Wind was becoming more edgy with each new sun. She was disappointed and annoyed that Lone Wolf had postponed his joining day until her predicament could be settled. Joining to a half-blooded stranger and traveling so far away from all she knew and loved was intimidating. She wondered, What if White Eagle were not pleased with his Indian-raised wife? What if she could not adapt to this new existence and people? What if something happened to him once they were far away? She hated doubting herself or him, but such feelings could not be suppressed. If only her suspicions would vanish. One more day, she thought anxiously, then quivered in anticipation.

She had not been allowed to visit the tepee where the man with silvery yellow hair and eyes the color of a stormy blue sky was being held prisoner. He was kept under guard but was treated gently. The way the white man watched her from a distance, she wondered if he blamed her for his friend's perils. She wished she could speak with him, to see if she could learn more about White Eagle and his lands. Sometimes his intense blue stare unnerved her; sometimes its tenderness reached out to her. Sometimes his face frightened her . . .

Wild Wind continued her chores, entrapped by deep thought, just as she was trapped by the unexpected events of the past few days. She knew Lone Wolf was hoping White Eagle could avenge himself and prove his words. She wished he would discuss the alarming matter with her, but he refused. At times he was stern and cool, and at other times he was very kind and warm. She sensed that his feelings were as confused and as tormented as hers. He had been offered a way to help his people, only to have the glorious near-victory threatened by betrayal. She could tell that Lone Wolf realized his leadership would be questioned because he had trusted the white man, that he would be humiliated for being fooled by him and for trading his sister for useless goods. She had grasped the heavy responsibility he carried, and it had mellowed her feelings toward her brother. She had tried her best not to upset him with words and actions. But this waiting and not knowing was eating at her poise and increasing her tension.

On the last moon, she had tried to convince Lone Wolf to carry out his joining to Myeerah, hoping her friend could distract her Indian brother and bring joy into his eyes once more. She had offered to stay with friends to give them privacy. Lone Wolf had told her he could not think of personal and selfish matters at such a critical time.

Whenever she observed Lone Wolf visting with the friend of the man who had made trade for her, she would discover herself praying that White Eagle would return and save his friend's life and her brother's honor. She had come to accept the reality of what the trade goods could do for her people. Yet she worried over the dreams her Indian brother had revealed to her, wondering where her new path would lead her if White Eagle returned alive. She recalled her own fearful dreams of the evil white man with dark hair and eyes, and she begged the

136

Great Spirit to make them only bad dreams and not visions of moons yet to be.

"Why did you marry me, White Eagle?" she murmured in confusion. "Will you take me far away, use me, and desert me? Will you allow the evil spirit who haunts my dreams to harm me? Why do I fear you and these powerful new feelings?"

Ever since White Eagle's departure, Black Hawk had stalked her everywhere she went. His igneous eyes had visually stripped her garments from her body, then brutally punished her with their fiery heat. He looked at her as if he despised her, yet craved her as well. "I will never let you have me. I will flee or die first," she vowed aloud as she recalled the persistent warrior.

The thought of mating with Black Hawk or Rides-Like-Thunder or any other man dismayed her now, after such close contact with Travis. She had happened upon lovers or animals mating in the forest, so she knew it was a natural part of life or loving. Vividly she remembered being in White Eagle's arms and tasting his kisses. She recalled his tenderness during her dark dreams and their walk. She could almost feel the fires that had inflamed her body at his touch, and the pleasure she had received from his gaze and nearness. Oddly she did not fear his sleeping mat.

Perhaps, she admitted, she had provoked his mischievous and taunting actions. Perhaps he had heard wicked tales of her misbehavior, as he had alleged. Yet he had chosen her and had made the largest trade offer any maiden had ever received. She helplessly questioned his feelings and motives. She did not want to be a tame-the-wild-wind game to him, a game about which she had so often been teased. And, if he had tried to fool her people, had he hoped to leave with her before they learned of his deceit—leave with the sister of Chief Lone Wolf as his hostage? If only she did not sense some great mystery and reluctance surrounding him.

She reflected on her taunts to him after their joining. He could have chosen any maiden, and won her. Why her, an Indian girl? Why had he returned to the land of his birth? Why help the Oglalas? "Who are you? What are you? Why do you ensnare me and trouble my spirit?" she asked aloud.

Surely he would return for his friend, but how would he feel about her and her people for doubting him, for threatening him and his friend? So many questions and mysteries, she concluded nervously, completing her chores and attempting to push her distressing thoughts aside, to no avail.

The morning of the fifth day arrived. Lone Wolf entered the tepee and announced that Wild Wind was to serve food to the white man. She looked at him quizzically, silently questioning his unusual order and his reasons.

In a rare moment of kindness, or weakness, Lone Wolf had yielded to Nathan Crandall's plea to meet his granddaughter once before he died, if it were to come to that today. Lone Wolf had secured the older man's promise to reveal nothing to her about her past or his reason for coming to the Oglala camp. He told Wild Wind now, "I wish him to see the reason why his friend will return to our camp. He is old and weak and afraid. He knows White Eagle has taken you as his mate. When his senses are filled with Wild Wind, he will trust his friend to return for one whose beauty is greater than Grandfather's flowers. If he must die, he will believe some evil kept his friend from returning. He is a good and gentle white man. He must not suffer for another's dark deed." He paused. "Do you wish me to send another with food and smiles?"

138

For the second time, Wild Wind felt that her brother was lying to her. Yet she did not expose her doubts and anguish. Another mystery, she concluded sadly. "I will go, my brother and chief."

She was not surprised when Lone Wolf accompanied her and remained at her side. She offered Nathan food and waited for him to consume it. He did so slowly, his eyes seeming to drink in her face and essence. He did not appear afraid, only sad, and seemed overly happy with her visit, as if she were warming sunshine on a cold winter day. Neither did he appear weak, in spirit or in body. This was a man who knew hard work, she realized, who knew courage, who loved and trusted his friend . . .

When Nathan could no longer stall his meal and her visit, he smiled and thanked her, and moisture filled his eyes. He removed a turquoise and silver pendant and handed it to her. It was a curious shape, as if it had once been a circle and someone had cut a small section from its top and sealed it in a point on its bottom. It looked old and precious. As she eyed the lovely treasure, a pain flashed inside her head and she rubbed her right temple to ease it. With quivering fingers, she held it out to him in polite refusal, for it frightened her.

Nathan closed his hand around hers and the pendant, indicating that he was insistent she keep it. Lone Wolf translated Nathan's emotion-hoarse words. "It belonged to his daughter. He wishes you to have it for your kindness. Do not offend a dying man by refusing his generosity." Lone Wolf had noticed her reaction, and he knew it had been the suppression of a memory.

Wild Wind met Nathan's gaze and probed it, learning nothing. She allowed the man to place the pendant around her neck. Again, she was baffled by the curious moisture that brightened his eyes. She could not explain why, but she felt drawn to this man. She smiled and

139

said, *"Pilamaya."*

"My sister thanks you and accepts your gift. If it pleases her, I will bring her with food before . . . the sun sleeps."

His hesitation was not lost on any of those present. If Travis and the guns did not return in the next few hours, Nathan would not live to eat another meal or to see the sun go to sleep. Lone Wolf had spoken, and he could not change his mind. He dared not tell Wild Wind who this endangered man was, nor did Nathan want her to know under these circumstances.

Anticipating her husband's return, Wild Wind left Nathan and her brother to wash her hair and body and dry herself in the afternoon sun in the company of some of her friends. Her garments and possessions were packed, and she felt a certain satisfaction that the other girls were envious of her and charmed by Travis. Her pride demanded that she appear trusting and confident around them as well as around her spurned suitors.

A few at a time, the other women left the river, their baths and washing completed. "Are you coming, Wild Wind?" Myeerah asked.

Wild Wind glanced at the sun. It was past the treetops, time to prepare her brother's evening meal. So little time left for White Eagle to return and the man called Nathan to live . . . Would time forever be her foe? she wondered. It always seemed to be battling her.

"Go along, Myeerah. I will return shortly." She needed to be alone, for it seemed the worst was about to happen. Clad in a drying blanket, she stood and began to walk along the riverbank to expend part of her tension. She tried not to think about her fate, yet her mind allowed her to think of nothing else. Time and distance passed unnoticed.

"He will not return, Wild Wind," a cold voice taunted nearby.

140

She glanced toward her right and her gaze fell on Black Hawk. Although her body was covered, she felt naked, and she was alarmed by his gaze. "Why," she asked angrily, "do you torment me, Black Hawk? Have you no pride and honor? White Eagle will return before dark."

The warrior laughed, and the sound of it was wintry and mocking. "Buffalo Slayer and his band have returned. They took many guns and bullets from the trader's wooden tepee. The white dog did not return with them. His friend will die, and you have no mate."

Wild Wind paled. "Was he slain in battle for the guns?"

The warrior laughed coldly once more. "Buffalo Slayer watched him ride away in the dark. Our warriors did not chase him; they rode swiftly to bring the guns to our camp before soldiers could pursue them. White Eagle is gone. I will demand to track him and slay him, and I will demand Wild Wind as my *coup*. I will not be denied."

"You lie," she accused boldly, her blue-gray eyes chilling.

"My words are true. I spoke against the white dog many times. I said he could not be trusted. I tried to save Wild Wind from his tricks. I must be rewarded for my words of warning. Wild Wind will be mine."

The aggressive warrior yanked her to his hard body and covered her mouth with his. Even when she struggled fiercely, he did not release her. Tightly banding her arms to her body, he clamped his hand over her mouth and dragged her into the concealing bushes, his abrupt movement deterring her from kicking. He fell to the ground with her and pinned her hands to her sides with his strong thighs. Withdrawing a wide rawhide strip from his waist, he secured it over her mouth to cut off her screams for help, then loosely bound her hands with another strip. She could hardly breathe from his heavy weight across her torso and could not wiggle free. His forearm across hers prevented her from striking out or battling him. He shifted to yank off her blanket, exposing her naked body to his crazed senses. His roughened hands moved over her breasts as his eyes grew wilder with lust and determination. When she continued her futile battle, he told her, "Once you are mine, Lone Wolf will be forced to give you to me in joining." His mouth fastened to one breast and he sucked greedily on it.

She freed her tied hands and, for a brief instant, pounded on his head and shoulders. Laughing, he seized them and pinned them to the ground above her head. His legs wrapped around hers to halt her kicks and thrashing. He gave his attention to the other breast, nursing hungrily like a baby starving for his mother's milk.

Suddenly Black Hawk was ripped from her helpless body. Wild Wind watched as her new husband beat her attacker as if he were as crazed by fury and jealousy as the warrior had been with lust. White Eagle showed the man no mercy; clearly he wanted and was trying to kill Black Hawk with his bare hands. Stunned by the warrior's attack and White Eagle's sudden rescue, she merely watched the action as if she were detached from her body. Her wits and control returned finally as the warrior drew his knife and lunged at White Eagle. Shaking violently, she came to her knees and sent forth a gag-muffled scream.

As suddenly as the battle had begun, it was over. The men fell to the ground and, during the scuffle, the knife was shoved forcefully into Black Hawk's chest.

With revulsion, Travis tossed the dead warrior aside and did not even glance at him. He went to Wild Wind and, drawing his own knife, cut her bonds. Before she could throw herself into his arms and thank him, he reached for the blanket and flung it at her, saying, "Cover yourself and return to camp. You should not place yourself in such peril. He was blinded by you. No

142

man takes what is mine and lives to enjoy it." He whirled then and left, heading in the direction of the settlement.

Wild Wind stared at his rapidly retreating back. He was in a great hurry. His face, which was dirty and sweaty, had not been shaven for many suns. His clothes were dusty and his hair tousled. She saw that he walked like a man consumed by fiery rage, one seeking some challenging prey to conquer and burn beyond life or recognition. Surely he did not blame her for Black Hawk's actions! She had done nothing wrong. On unsteady legs, she stood and tried to wrap the cover around her trembling body. It slipped from her grasp, and she cursed it and her weakness. Her reaction filled her with anger, and the anger instilled control.

She rushed past Black Hawk's body without looking at him. Seizing her garments, she yanked them on. Then, grabbing her other possessions, she hurried toward camp. She had to discover the truth, or the peril awaiting him.

Travis entered the camp, and with unsuppressed relief, noticed the wagon standing near the ceremonial lodge. He strode in that direction, scolding himself for cutting it too close for Nathan's and Wild Wind's safety. Lordy, he was too fatigued and worried to think straight! Wild Wind should not have been at the river alone; she was too trusting and tempting! She had this way of causing a man to lose his wits and his control. If he hadn't rushed off, he would have pulled that naked body into his arms and taken her in pure animal heat, right beside his dead enemy! She did crazy things to him, and he was in no shape to resist her.

The shouting of his name called Lone Wolf's attention to Travis's arrival. The chief smiled at him, then wondered at his stormy mood. Nathan, who was examining the guns, turned and saw Travis approaching them. Nathan winced, for he knew Travis's look and walk

143

meant trouble.

Travis greeted his friend with a bear hug and a forced smile. "Have they been treating you right, Nate?" he inquired needlessly as his keen gaze examined the older man's face and body.

"We did not expect White Eagle this moon. Buffalo Slayer told us you rode after the treacherous white dog," Lone Wolf remarked.

"I found the bastard and killed him," Travis informed the warrior as he withdrew a scalp lock from his pocket and handed it to him. "Put that on your *coup* stick for all to see what happens to those who trick or betray the Oglalas." He did not say how easy it had been to locate and battle Claude Chambers and his two hirelings, all of whom had been camped and getting drunk on whiskey purchased with his stolen money. He had ridden like a devil-pursued man to pay the new trading post owner, who had not concealed his astonishment at Travis's honesty. Then he had ridden like mad to make sure he arrived before this sun set, just in case the wagon was late. In five days, he had covered many miles, and most without food or sleep. "I rode like the storm clouds to make sure Lone Wolf did not make another mistake. You see I am a man of honor and truth," he stated coldly, pointing to the wagon and then flicking the small section of hair into the chief's grasp. "Not so, a warrior named Black Hawk. He lies dead near the river for trying to rape my wife." To avoid causing Nathan any further distress, Travis spoke in Lakota. After finishing his account, he ordered himself to calm down, for the dangers to Nathan and Wild Wind were past. He only wanted to get out of this territory before any Hunkpapa warriors passed this way and remembered him. Damn, he swore silently, feeling utterly fatigued, his nerves taut.

Nathan caught his arm and asked worriedly, "Son, you all right?"

144

"I will be as soon as we're heading home. I was in a little bit of a rush, so I haven't eaten or slept for days. I had forgotten why I left this bloodthirsty land. Seems I've regained some bad traits, which you'll just have to correct again," he stated jokingly to relax the man.

Travis turned to Lone Wolf. "Any more objections to our leaving as soon as we show you how to use those weapons?" he inquired sullenly.

Lone Wolf shook his head. "Where is my sister?"

"Here," Wild Wind answered, pushing her way to his side. She was miffed by White Eagle's coldness and refusal to comfort her at the river.

The young chief eyed her intently. Her hair was mussed, her cheeks were glowing, and signs of minor injuries were visible. "White Eagle says Black Hawk attacked you near the river," he probed.

"White Eagle speaks the truth. Black Hawk is dead and Wild Wind is safe," she responded, but her look at Travis was filled with tiny blades. "White Eagle had to battle Black Hawk to the death to rescue me."

"Is there more?" he questioned sternly.

"No," she replied and pulled her stormy gaze from Travis.

"Your husband needs food and sleep. Do you wish me to have another see to his needs while you recover from your struggle?"

"Yes," she stated, angry with Travis and wanting to avoid him. She left the group and went to Lone Wolf's tepee to lie down, assuming it was surely too late to begin their journey today.

Myeerah and her mother fed a hungry Travis before he went to the river to bathe and change clothes. While Nathan instructed the warriors on the use of the rifles and carbines, Travis collapsed on the sleeping mat rolled out beside Nathan's in the guest lodge. There being no need for him to remain alert and on guard in the safety of

145

the camp, Travis drifted into deep and much-needed slumber.

When Lone Wolf finally entered his tepee long after dark, Wild Wind gazed evocatively at him. He told her he had eaten with Myeerah and her family and would join to the lovely girl after his sister's departure in the morning. Lone Wolf did not offer any information about her missing husband, and Wild Wind was compelled to question his absence.

"He sleeps in the guest lodge with his friend. He will come for you when the new sun appears. He has kept his word and his bargain. You belong to White Eagle," he reminded her, noting her rebellious glare.

"Perhaps, like my brother, he wishes privacy on the first night with his mate," she speculated, then blushed at her bold words.

"I offered to sleep in the guest lodge with his friend. He was weary from his journey and said there will be other nights to claim his mate. He says White Eagle and Wild Wind are strangers, and strangers do not share a sleeping mat. Be happy he is a good and patient man."

Lone Wolf hoped his words would silence her probing questions and would end her curiosity. He claimed his sleeping mat and closed his eyes, aware that she was still gaping at him in astonishment. Soon she would learn that, as he had promised, White Eagle would not take her to his sleeping mat and would free her from her Indian joining vows, which held no power in the white world. Soon she would discover that it had been her grandfather who had desired her freedom. Eventually Lone Wolf's mind drifted to other matters: his joining with Myeerah on the next moon and the defense of his people with Travis's guns.

Wild Wind lay down in a huff. She was sleeping alone

on the first night she might have shared with her new husband. She would be humiliated and teased for her lack of appeal to him. How dare he ignore her! It was no excuse that he was exhausted! At least he could have slept in her tepee to prevent gossip. She had been desired by many warriors. They were joined, and joined couples slept together. He would pay for this insult, she vowed irritably.

Early the next morning, Wild Wind sought out Myeerah to help her prepare for her joining to Lone Wolf. The two girls went to a secluded spot near the river. As they bathed and dressed, Myeerah said, "The sun climbs high, Wild Wind. It is time for you to leave." The girl sensed that her friend was intentionally avoiding her new mate, was actually hiding from him. "Do you seek to make White Eagle angry?"

Wild Wind stiffened and her eyes glowed with intense emotion. "For many moons I waited for his return. He can wait one sun for Wild Wind. She must show no eagerness to leave with a stranger. He joined to me, then insulted me by sleeping in another tepee. If he is tired, he must rest before our long journey," she scoffed. "He makes fun of Wild Wind and pretends she is not desirable. If that is so, he should not have chosen her. Let him wait and worry. Let him see Wild Wind does not find him desirable as a mate."

"Do you fear him?"

"I fear nothing and I will not be shamed before my people. Perhaps he will grow weary of waiting and leave without Wild Wind."

Myeerah wisely suggested, "Let us return to camp."

"No. Sit, and Wild Wind will braid your hair. Your fingers are not working well on this happy day. I must see my friend and brother joined. The white man can do nothing to harm me in our camp."

Travis was pacing as he awaited Wild Wind's return to her tepee. He had assumed she was off somewhere preparing to leave or saying farewell to her friends and people. He glanced at Lone Wolf and remarked pointedly, "Wild Wind moves slowly this sun."

Lone Wolf motioned to her belongings, which were ready for the journey. "She will return soon, my friend. She was angry and confused when her mate slept in another lodge. She fears others will laugh and tease her for her husband's action. Let her head and spirit cool. She does not understand why you cannot take her to your mat."

"I gave Lone Wolf and her grandfather my word not to touch her. It's getting late. Where can I seek her hiding place," he questioned, wishing he could have spent the night with her.

"Be strong and patient, my friend. If you show anger, she will be happy for causing it. I must prepare my band. We ride with our Hunkpapa brothers this sun. Two Ponies tell me they come to hunt and feast with Lone Wolf. It is a good day for a joining."

His words struck Travis like a physical blow to an unprotected gut. Without showing any fear or tension, he would have to find Wild Wind and Nathan and ride out as fast as he could. He would claim he had to hurry home to defend his lands, an excuse Lone Wolf would understand. "I will be strong, Lone Wolf. I will find her and take her, by force if necessary. I must show Wild Wind she has to obey, to prevent trouble on the trail."

Lone Wolf shrugged and agreed. "Do as you must, White Eagle. I will not interfere. Her defiance must be tamed for your safety."

Travis went to speak with Nathan. "Listen to me

148

closely, Nate, because we don't have much time. I never told you why I left this area, because it was too painful and humiliating and I wanted to forget it. But it's past the time you heard the truth. My father, Jeremy Kincade, was a trapper and trader in these parts back in the days when Indians would accept and befriend a good and honest white man, or one who appeared to be one. One day he tangled with a pack of wolves and was rescued by a Hunkpapa hunting party. After they tended him, he took up with them and later married my mother, Pretty Bird Woman, daughter of their war chief."

The mention of his deceased mother brought anguish to Travis's eyes and voice. He cleared his throat and continued. "He stayed for years, then went off supposedly to check out the advancing white man. When he returned, I was thirteen, and he said it was high time I learned about my white blood and civilization. He was my father and I was curious, so I obeyed him. We traveled around for two years, but I didn't like what I was seeing and hearing. I was almost sixteen and I was taller and stronger than he was. After some arguing and a shooting in Kansas, we went back to my mother's camp. He trapped and sold furs until the Hunkpapas stopped him for killing too many animals just for their skins. One day he accidentally encroached on sacred burial ground and found gold. He started sneaking off to collect it and hide it. He planned to leave as soon as he had enough—if a greedy man ever has enough gold. Two of his trapper friends showed up and joined him, so he needed more gold for his partners.

"You know what happens when men get too greedy. Four braves caught them panning in the river on sacred land. They shot three of the braves and stabbed one. Jeremy figured it was time to get out quickly. He knew most of the warriors were out of camp, hunting and raiding. He sent his two friends to the nearest fort to tell the soldiers the Hunkpapas had twenty white captives they were torturing and killing; he thought that would keep the warriors busy while they made their escape with the gold. He returned to camp and calmly packed up his belongings and told us he was heading off for a few months. By then I was eighteen and loved being a hard-to-match warrior. He asked me to ride with him to the edge of the Hunkpapa territory to say good-bye. Maybe he was trying to save me from the attack, but it didn't matter to me then and it doesn't now. He was evil and worthless."

Travis inhaled before continuing as he forced the new anguish from his voice. "Like a trusting son, I mounted up and rode off with him to rendezvous with his cohorts. One of the wounded braves reached camp and exposed Jeremy Kincade's treachery. That warning gave the Hunkpapas time to send for their warriors and to summon help from our Blackfeet brothers. The soldiers were defeated, but many Hunkpapas were slain, including my mother." He breathed deeply and for a time cast a fixed stare on the distance.

"A war party was sent after us and pinned us down before they could recover the gold, or mention it to me. I had some rivals and enemies in camp, and I didn't know why we were being attacked; so, like a fool, I defended myself and my father. After his friends were slain, I tried talking to the warriors. They captured us under a false truce and we were dragged back to camp. Trouble was, the brave who had escaped death to warn them claimed I had been with my father, desecrating sacred land and taking part in the killings. Charge-A-Buffalo hated me because the girl he loved had had her evil heart set on me. I guess he figured he'd keep us apart by getting me killed. He died without clearing me. Jeremy tried to convince them I was innocent, but what was the word of a white enemy and half-breed traitor against a renowned warrior

150

who had endured agony to warn his people? They tortured Jeremy all day, then killed him. Before he died, he told me where they had hidden the gold, which was nothing more than yellow rock to the Indians. They didn't care about the gold or its recovery, only our alleged crimes."

He stated bitterly, "They wouldn't even allow me to fight a truth challenge. They tried to torture a confession from me and planned to kill me at dawn. After dark, Pretty Rabbit freed me. Hell, she owed it to me for causing Charge-A-Buffalo to hate me and lie about me. She had fueled his desire, jealousy, and desperation by always comparing him to me unfavorably. Plenty of times she told him if it hadn't been for me she would have loved and married him. She drove him wild with hunger and mad with frustration. Charge-A-Buffalo was clever and proud; he made sure nobody witnessed or learned about his shameful rivalry, so he wouldn't look foolish or bad. Pretty Rabbit wanted us to escape and marry, but she was killed before we got away. Lordy, Nate, wicked vixens have always gotten me into trouble! I'm telling you the truth. If Jeremy hadn't been slain, I would have battled him myself to prove his evil blood did not flow within me. He's responsible for my mother's death and my people's rejection; he didn't deserve to live."

When he paused, Nathan said, "I'm sorry, son. I know it must have been hard losing everything and everyone like that. Sometimes greed takes over and a man don't know what he's doing. I see why you had trouble talking about this or trusting anyone. A betrayal like that would make any man bitter and hostile, especially a boy. The Hunkpapas should have known you by then. It wasn't right to cast you out."

"With so many dead and Charge-A-Buffalo's words against mine, all they saw was my white skin and my father's treachery. Even those who believed me dared not

151

speak or act against the council's vote. There wasn't any way to prove my innocence, so I had to ride and keep on riding. For months I was dogged and attacked. The Hunkpapas won't ever forget what happened or forgive me. That's the problem, Nate.''

"What do you mean, son?" he inquired in confusion.

"The Hunkpapas are part of the Lakota Council Fires. Their camp is only a few days' ride from here. If they learn I'm nearby . . . I don't have to tell you what danger me and you would face. I'm sure they're still watching and waiting for me to return for that gold. We've got to get the hell out of here pronto. Lone Wolf says a Hunkpapa hunting party will arrive today. If the Oglalas hear the Hunkpapas' charges against me, they'll think I did try to fool them the other day and that I only replaced the damaged guns to save your hide and mine. It'll start all over again and we won't stand a chance of survival and escape, not with Rana. Besides, we've been gone for over a month. There's no telling what Caldwell is up to now. McFarland is getting on in years; he could get nervous over our lengthy absence.''

Nathan's expression revealed his grave concern. "Let's go."

"That's the other problem. Your defiant grand-daughter is off hiding somewhere. She's peeved because I spent the night with my friend instead of my wife. Something about feminine ego and pride. I'll explain what I have to do, Nate, and you can't interfere. We've got to ride, hard and fast. You get our horses saddled and ready to leave. I'm going to find Miss Rana Michaels, tie her up, and get us out of here before those Hunkpapas arrive.''

Nathan gasped in shock. "You can't treat her like that, son," he protested. "She'll be scared, and them Indians will be plenty mad.''

"Better her scared for awhile than us dead. Lone Wolf

152

gave his permission to use force to claim her. Don't forget, she's supposedly my wife now. Defiance can be dealt with harshly, and she does have a reputation for rebellion and stubbornness. Let me handle it my way. We can lose her and our lives if she balks and stalls our departure."

Nathan did not like the idea, but he realized from Travis's words and expression that he was genuinely worried, and when Travis Kincade was worried, he'd better worry too. "All right, son, but be gentle."

"That's up to your granddaughter, Nate."

As Travis and Nathan were leaving the tepee, Lone Wolf joined them. "Wild Wind is at the river with Myeerah. Come, we will get her. It is best for all if others do not see her battle you."

The horses were saddled and Wild Wind's possessions were collected. Then the three men headed for the river and quickly located the two women downstream by their voices. Lone Wolf wisely suggested, "Tell your father friend to wait here with the horses." Nathan obeyed.

Lone Wolf called out to alert the women before he and Travis approached. The warrior chief smiled at his beloved and frowned at his adopted sister.

"Have you lost all pride and courage, Wild Wind?" Travis asked. "You have stalled our departure long enough. We must go," he commanded firmly.

Wild Wind glared at White Eagle, then at Lone Wolf, who did not defend her against such treatment. "Wild Wind will leave when she is ready to leave. I will see my brother and friend joined first," she asserted. Startled that White Eagle had sought her out so boldly, she stared defiantly at the man before her line of vision, for his size and stature seemed to block out everything and everyone else. As her challenging gaze met his narrowed one, a strange warmth passed over her body and she found she was having difficulty thinking and breathing. She

153

realized that if ever a male was masterful in exerting his prowess and in controlling any situation, he stood before her now, and, indeed, he owned her. Yet she was still wary of this man who had so easily enchanted her and alarmed by the emotions he had brought to life. She would not let him think her a coward or a weakling—or his lowly squaw! she stubbornly decided.

When she tried to push past Travis, he captured her arm in a firm yet pain-free grip. "We ride, woman," he commanded sternly. "I have work to do and land to protect. You hide like a frightened rabbit."

"I will ride after Lone Wolf and Myeerah's joining," she replied. She yanked on her arm, but White Eagle would not release it. She scolded him in Sioux, and still he held her securely. A curious panic flooded her body, and her blue-gray eyes blazed with fury. Her other hand attempted to claw free the imprisoned one. White Eagle simply captured it and stared calmly at her, his green gaze mocking her helplessness.

Nettled, she called him names and fought him. Travis looked and behaved as if nothing unusual were taking place. He pulled a rawhide thong from over his pistol and bound her wrists. She was astonished when Lone Wolf did and said nothing to the brazen man with laughing eyes. "Release me, white dog!" she shrieked at him. She struggled fiercely, to no avail. At last she was rendered breathless from her exertions and protests and could do no more than shake with rage at his actions. To make matters worse, Travis lifted her and tossed her over his shoulder. Then he strolled to his waiting horse and stood her beside it.

Bewildered, Nathan asked, "What's going on, son? This can't be necessary."

Travis glanced at his friend and reminded, "Don't forget what I told you, Nate. We need to head for home and she's fighting me. She's demanding to hang around until tonight to watch her brother's joining. This little wildcat will settle down after we get away from here. Please let me handle her and get us on the trail pronto," he urged.

Wild Wind glared at Travis, then spewed forth insults and threats in the Indian tongue. When she added, "*Sunka ska, nanpi yuze sni yo! Mni kte sni yelo!*" Travis removed his bandanna and gagged her so that she would not draw the attention of others. He was glad Nathan could not understand his Oglala words as he refuted, "Yes, you will go with me. And if you call me a white dog one more time, I'll spank you. And I'll put my hands on you anywhere and any time I please, if I please."

Wild Wind soon realized that her Indian brother would make no attempt to come to her aid. But it also seemed obvious that the older white man was annoyed and distressed over her vile treatment. Yet, when her gaze sent an appeal to him for help, he winced and lowered his head as if hurt and embarrassed. Suddenly she twisted, ducked, and forcefully threw her shoulder into Travis's midsection.

He grunted and staggered slightly at the unexpected attack. Then he seized her by her forearms and shook her, warning, "Behave, woman, or I will punish you for acting like a fever-mad raccoon. You are a chief's daughter and sister, and my wife, not a wild she-bear who is wounded. You are making a fool of yourself and shaming all of us."

Nathan helplessly questioned, "Are the gag and bonds necessary? She's only a scared child, Travis. Don't be so rough and mean to her."

Travis Kincade drilled his leaf green eyes into her stormy blue ones. Then he grinned roguishly and quipped, "Damn right, they're necessary, Nate. This little viper would strike without warning if she had the chance. I'll release her when she learns and uses some

155

manners, or when she remembers she's a woman and not a little savage. And she had best learn quickly, 'cause my temper and patience are short. I plan to take real good care of . . . my defiant wife, if she lets me," he murmured, his smoldering gaze slipping over her face and body.

When Nathan started to debate Travis's words and actions, Travis cautioned, "Taking up for her only encourages her to act worse, Nate. We can't stay any longer, and she won't leave peacefully unless I use force. She's only trying to prove to herself and her friends that she can control me. We ain't got time for silly female games. Please, stay quiet."

Wild Wind was overjoyed when her flushed cheeks and flashing eyes did not expose her understanding of Travis's words. Rather, both men interpreted these signs as indications of her anger. As far as these white men would know, she had forgotten English, which could not be considered unusual for a girl captured as a small child who had heard and spoken only Sioux for years. She decided to encourage the older man's friendship and help, for she felt this would annoy her new husband. She would be clever and patient, she mentally plotted, until she could defeat him and escape. She would teach him about manners and kindness, and about Wild Wind.

Travis mounted agilely, then reached down to scoop her up in his powerful arms. When a resentful Wild Wind found herself on the same horse with her white tormentor, she sat rigidly before him, her chin held high and her gaze focused on the distance. Never had she been so humiliated or infuriated or mistreated. Knowing Lone Wolf and Myeerah were witnessing this degrading display, she ceased her struggles, vowing this white devil would pay dearly for shaming and abusing her.

After Travis and Lone Wolf had exchanged parting words, Lone Wolf touched her arm and advised her to be obedient to her new husband and happy in her new life. Wild Wind's gaze settled on the warrior. Her eyes told him she would never forgive him for this deed, even when he asked for her understanding and forgiveness. She shook her head and tore her misty gaze from his entreating face. She would not be forgiving or understanding while she was a humiliated captive who could neither speak nor move. Lone Wolf had the authority to order Travis to remove the bonds and gag so she could hug him and speak words of farewell. Since he made no attempt to do so, he did not deserve her forgiveness. Let him suffer, as she was suffering.

Travis was annoyed by her obstinancy and spitefulness. "Do not worry about her, Lone Wolf. I will make certain she is safe and happy. When her temper cools, she will be sorry she behaved so badly. You did right by trading her to me. I will take good care of her."

"You are a good and wise man, my friend. My sister is strong and proud. Give her time and patience. She will come to accept you and her new life. In time, understanding will fill her mind and heart."

"I wish happiness and long life for my Oglala brothers and Lone Wolf. May you find great success on the hunting grounds and in battle. May the Great Spirit ride with you and protect you from your enemies. Soaring Hawk is proud of his son, a wise, strong chief and a powerful, cunning warrior, as he was. May you find peace and joy with your new mate on this happy joining day. I am proud to call you friend."

Travis smiled when Lone Wolf responded with the heartfelt words, *"Pilamaya, Wanbli Ska. Wakan Tanka ni'ci un. Tanyan yaun nunwe, Watogla Tate. Icantewaste, mitanksi,"* which translated: "Thank you, White Eagle. May the Great Spirit go with you and guide you. Goodbye, Wild Wind. Be happy, my sister."

Travis knew their time was fleeing. He kneed his horse

and rode away. When they were almost out of sight of the settlement, the girl began to battle him like a snared badger. She wiggled and thrashed, threatening to send both of them to the hard ground. His horse was well trained, and he released the reins while he struggled to control her and their precarious position. His arms banded her body and he shouted at her, "Stop it, Wild Wind! You do not have to be afraid of me and Nate." When she did not relent, he commanded, "Be still, or you will make me hurt you. We must leave here—*now*," he stressed impatiently.

The realization of a permanent parting with her Indian brother and her friend Myeerah had struck her hard. Soon all she knew and loved would be lost to her forever. She did not wish to leave in this cold manner, with cruel words between them. She wanted to go back to say she was sorry, but she could not explain this to White Eagle through the gag. She hoped her actions would enlighten him and he would remove it, but all he did was threaten her and shake her. Her anger and desperation grew.

When she attempted to shift herself to peer around his broad chest, Travis saw her pleading gaze and understood her actions. He removed the gag and inquired, "Do you want to say something?"

"I must go back and speak with my brother and Myeerah," she coaxed. "It is wrong to leave this way," she informed him sullenly.

Travis knew he could not comply with her wishes. "There is no time, Wild Wind. The sun is high, and we should have been on the trail long ago. You should not have behaved so badly or wasted precious time trying to provoke me. Lone Wolf knows you are angry and hurt; it is natural. He will forgive you and forget your defiance and cruelty. The trail is filled with enemies. We must become friends or our lives will be in danger. For once, be a good girl," he commanded.

158

She glared at him, her look scorning his order and his refusal. *"Hiya kola! Wanbli Ska toka!"* she declared heatedly declining his offer of friendship and calling him her enemy. She asked to be untied, but he shook his head and unwisely grinned at her. "You are mean and evil; that is why I resisted leaving with you. I hate you. I will never yield to you. If you try to force me to sleep on your mat, I will claw out your eyes. I will escape and return to my people," she warned coldly.

Vexed at having to behave this way and knowing time was short before the Hunkpapas' arrival, Travis retorted, "If you try to escape or disobey, you will be sorry. When I take a woman to my sleeping mat, it will not be a hateful, defiant child. You are selfish and coldhearted, and you were mean and evil to your brother. Stay my enemy if it makes you feel better. I do not need your friendship or your body, only your obedience. I cannot see why any warrior would chase after a bag of trouble like you. Obviously the jokes about you are true. One of us will tame a wild wind; the choice of who does it is yours."

Incensed, she scoffed, "If you do not wish me as your mate, why did you make trade for me? Did you need a slave for your chores?"

"You are not my slave or prisoner," he replied too quickly. He sighed in annoyance at his slip and added, "Unless you behave like one."

"If I am of no value to you, release me," she responded.

"No. I made trade for you to help Lone Wolf and his people. I offered them many guns and supplies. In exchange, I had to ask for something they viewed as having great value. I could not ask for horses, because your people need them for fighting and hunting. I could not ask for furs, because it is wrong to slay so many animals. There was nothing else of value to ask for in trade. I believed taking Wild Wind as my wife would make the trade one of honor and fair exchange. You are a white woman, and you caused trouble many times for your brother and his people. He was about to trade you just to get rid of your sharp tongue and rebellious ways. You should be glad I rescued you from an enforced joining. Just do as you are told, and we will not have any problems."

He could tell she was getting more angry by the minute. He decided to try reasoning with her. "White women can do the things you desire, things that need to be done in our lands—hunting, riding, fighting, and protecting your family. We thought you would be happy with other whites, and safer during this war between our peoples. I did not choose an Oglala woman, because an Oglala would feel lost and frightened in my white world. Since you are white, you will fit in easily. If you escaped or I sent you home, you would live in shame and ridicule. You would no longer have trade value or pride. You would be dishonoring your chief and the trade that could save his people. I gave you the chance to do something good and unselfish for the people who raised you and loved you. I believed you had pride and courage. I thought you were smart and could relearn the white ways and accept them. You will go with me willingly or by force, but you will not cause trouble and dishonor. I have never raped any woman and I will not start with you, wife or no wife. You have more thorns than a wahoo tree, and I do not like getting pricked on my sleeping mat. Do the chores. I will ask nothing more."

Wild Wind recognized the truth in most of his words. Nothing was as important to an Indian as honor and the survival of his tribe and lands. If she rejected her appointed role in this intimidating episode, she would face shame and ridicule. He knew the Indian ways and the paths of cunning too well. His reasoning had been flawless, except for one point: his motive for claiming her in trade. She was neither blind nor a fool. She recalled that night in her tepee; he was a virile man and he had found her desirable. She was his wife now, and he would not ignore her for very long. Too, she questioned why he had made trade with the Oglalas instead of the Hunkpapas. Or perhaps, she decided, he had made trade with both. She was too angry and confused to be flattered by his compliments, which had been laced around insults or chiding, but she had caught them and now stored them away in her keen mind. She wondered if he would come after her if she were to escape, and she concluded that he would. The only honorable way she could return to the Oglala camp was through his death, and he was not a man who would die easily. She was trapped. "Then I am your captive and you are my enemy," she announced. "I will ride my own horse. I am not a child." For now, all she wanted was to put some distance between them.

Nathan turned back when he saw that Travis was making little progress in his argument with his granddaughter. He fretted over their conflict, asking, "What's wrong, Travis?"

"Just a battle of wits and wills, Nate. I'll explain later. Ride a little ahead and keep an eye out for visitors while I settle her down." He watched as Nathan reluctantly gave in to his order, which Travis knew would keep his older friend from making a slip. To Wild Wind, he said in Oglala, "We do not have time to exchange harsh words. You ride with me until I know you can be trusted."

"No," she protested, and tried to slip from his saddle and arms.

Travis hurriedly caught her, then placed her bound hands over his head and settled them around his waist. "Behave, or I will twist you over my knee and whip your fanny. Maybe that is what you need."

Wild Wind decided to test him and to get free of his

unsettling embrace and nearness. It was difficult to locate any extra flesh around his middle and to imprison it between her fingernails, but she worked until she was pinching him painfully. "I will ride Cloud or walk."

Travis grabbed her mischievous hands and held them away from his body, scowling at her. With her teeth, she caught the tender flesh at the function of his arm and chest. She bit him, then gradually increased her pressure as he struggled to break her tenacious hold with his other hand. Nothing seemed to encourage her to stop biting and resisting him. She wanted him to toss her to the ground or place her on Cloud's back, for she realized she did not enjoy his pain. Though she would not unclench her teeth, she added no more pressure.

Travis grimaced in discomfort, but he had endured more pain than she was giving him. He did not cry out or strike her. Instead he stared down into those turbulent blue-gray eyes. "How can someone so beautiful be so damned mean and savage? You're gonna force me to hurt you and cause more trouble between us," he mumbled to himself in English. In Lakota he stated, "Wild Wind, I will have to gag you again when I get that lovely mouth free. If you stop biting and behave, I will let you ride Cloud soon and I will untie you so you can signal your brother."

As he was speaking, he had grasped her head between his hands and indicated his resolve to obtain freedom at any risk or threat of pain. Given an opening, she ceased her reckless action. "Your word of honor?" she probed, implying that his offers were the reasons for her rapid release of his flesh.

Travis nodded, then whispered softly and gratefully, *"Pilamaya."* He tied the bandanna around his neck, showing her that he would not gag her again. "A truce, woman? Your word of honor to behave?" After she nodded, he pulled on the reins to turn around his horse.

As he sat her up straight before him and cut her bonds, he muttered in English, "So very beautiful and dangerous, and as cold and wild as a Texas blizzard. You're gonna be one tough and delightful vixen to tame, if any man has the cunning and strength to do it . . ."

Travis watched her use sign language to relate her love and farewell, and her hopes for Lone Wolf's happiness and survival. He watched her ask for forgiveness for her previous action and saw that Lone Wolf returned her signals in kind. Thoughtfully, he noticed that tears brightened her lovely eyes as he saw her send Lone Wolf one final smile and wave.

The flaming-haired beauty with steel blue eyes looked up at Travis and whispered softly, almost seductively, *"Pilamaya, mihigna."*

Travis smiled mysteriously as he responded in Oglala, "You are welcome, my wife. Remember your promise: no more fighting with words or hands. We go home . . . We should take care of that name right now," he suggested, as if an idea had just struck him. "You will need a white name to prevent any hostility toward you and any nosy questions. My name is Travis, Travis Kincade. Can you say it?"

"Travis, Travis Kincade," she repeated obediently.

"Very good," he remarked cheerfully. "I will call you Rana, a soft, beautiful name for a beautiful and hopefully gentle woman."

Rana shuddered as the vaguely familiar name rifled across her mind. She stiffened and paled. "I do not like that name. I am Wild Wind."

"You are my wife, and I am naming you Rana, Rana Michaels," he insisted, perceiving the effect of the name of her and observing her ensuing actions. He hoped that Nathan would not return now and interfere.

Rana unconsciously grasped the heart-shaped pendant that Nathan had given to her and toyed nervously with it.

163

She remembered where she had heard the strange name Rana and had viewed the *wanapin*—in her bad dreams. Or, she fearfully wondered, were they visions of horrible days to come? Suddenly she yanked the pendant from her neck, leaving a red scratch on her satiny flesh. As she started to fling the necklace away, Travis grabbed her hand and prevented her panicky behavior. "I do not like the white name Rana and I do not like the *wanapin;* both are evil. Grandfather sent me warnings about them in bad dreams. Now you, my husband, bring them to life. As I feared, I must not trust you. You have lied to Wild Wind and tricked her; this I know is true from my dark visions. Is this not so, Travis Kincade?"

Travis kept his expression closed to her probing gaze. He knew he could not reveal the truth, not when she was so suspicious of him. As Lone Wolf had said, she needed time to become friends with them before he related the story of her past to her. Evidently she was haunted by bad memories, which she considered dreams or visions. It would be unwise to admit he had lied and duped her. Instead he tried a different path. "I will keep the necklace for you until you realize that it comes from a good heart and not a bad vision. Grandfather was preparing you to face your new destiny, one where you must live as Rana Michaels. Do not resist His revelations and will, Rana. Do not fear the bad dreams or your new life far away. You are my wife, and I will protect you from all harm."

The nightmare she had experienced on the day of Travis's arrival filled her mind. She was confused and alarmed by the unknown, which seemed to be surrounding her. But the man who had rescued her in her dark dreams was now at her side, her husband. She had to be brave and cunning. "I will become your Rana as Grandfather commands," she told him, then pulled his head downward and fused their lips to test him in another way.

Taken unprepared for her action, his senses whirled madly as she greedily kissed and embraced him. His arms pulled her tightly against him and he seared his lips over hers. As his body flamed and tensed with desire, his tongue danced with hers and his fingers relished the feel of her thick hair. His lips moved over her face and he enjoyed its softness and sweet smell. He inhaled the freshness of her hair, then nibbled at her ear before his lips hungrily sought her mouth again. For a time, he was lost in the wonder of this newly discovered creature and ensnared by her potent magic.

"A storm is coming, my husband. We must return to camp and wait for it to pass," she suggested as loud thunder filled her ears and passion's flames licked at her body. It was no secret that she wanted this man as much as he wanted her. It was past time for them to taste the sweet pleasures of bodies joining in blissful rapture. Surely the fierce storm that was building within their bodies was as powerful as the one nature was threatening to unleash on the land. What better way to spend such an afternoon than in her husband's arms?

Her words enabled Travis to partially clear his wits. When he leaned back, both were flushed and breathless. His gaze locked with hers. "I see a wahoo can have precious treasures as well as prickly thorns," he murmured huskily as his thumb caressed her lips and his fingers gently held her chin. "Perhaps a few pricks and pains are worth enduring to pluck such lovely flowers and delicious fruits."

She hinted boldly, "Let us return to my brother's tepee before he has need of it after his joining. The storm will surround us soon."

Travis glanced above them, then twisted to check the sky in each direction. He frowned, for many reasons. He was sitting here dallying with a ravishing woman who believed she was his wife and was eagerly offering herself

165

to him, while dangers from foes and nature were closing in on them. This wit-stealing vixen was far too tempting to be ignored and nearly impossible to resist, Travis mused silently. He wanted her with every burning inch and tingling nerve of his susceptible body, yet he was going to have to refuse her, though it was as clear to him as a June day that if she were not Nathan Crandall's granddaughter, he would have unrolled his sleeping bag and taken her then and there. Travis was vexed for allowing himself to be talked into this false marriage with a wife who desired him and expected him to make love to her, a wife who would not understand his constant rejection of her many charms. He almost wished she had retained her fury and resistance, for her willingness to surrender to him was making it painfully hard to reject her. Of course, he admitted, her show of fiery passion could have been a cunning trick to captivate him in order to get her way. Whichever, there was only one way to cool her spirit and take the heat off him.

"Sorry, woman, but we have to ride, storm or no storm. You wasted too much time this morning with your silly games. Have you forgotten that you hate me and will never yield to me? Do not use your body and a false surrender to keep us from leaving today. A husband, not his wife, chooses when and where to unroll the sleeping mat, and I do not choose this time or place." Travis knew his words came out too harshly, punishingly, and he was instantly sorry, but he dared not apologize or explain. He had tried to come up with a clever reply that would keep her from tempting him again, for he doubted he could resist her time after time. It would not be wise for them to get too close this soon. When they reached Texas, she would have to be protected from the Caldwells and he would have to continue his fake attraction to Clarissa. Travis realized he should stop calling Rana his wife, for where they were heading, she would not be considered so. He would have to keep her away from him, even if he had to be cruel and deceitful to accomplish it.

Rana's cheeks glowed, this time with anger and humiliation. "You offer truce and friendship, then cruelly insult me," she scolded him defensively. "It is not wrong to wish to see my brother joined to my best friend. I know what I must do. I agreed to our joining to help my people and I will honor the terms of your bargain with my brother. I was not teasing you with a false surrender. My kiss was to thank you for your kindness and your vow of protection, and to seal our truce. You pretended to desire me, to choose this time and place. I did not resist your hunger, for you are my husband and I promised not to fight you again. Blame White Eagle for misleading Wild Wind with his false kisses and touches. Wild Wind will be happy if he never mates with her. But do not call her to you, then scold her for coming when it is her duty!"

Travis cursed softly through clenched teeth. He seemed to be doing everything wrong where she was concerned, and he was taking too much time trying to climb out of this bottomless pit he had dug for himself. He mumbled in English, "Hellfire, Rana, I can't tell you why I can't make love to you. It isn't right for me to touch you, and I was a damn fool to do so. Lordy, I hope you don't tempt me like that again. You don't know the truth about us."

He looked at her downcast head and sighed heavily. "Hear me, Rana," he said in Oglala. "I expect only friendship and obedience and respect from you. I will not . . . call you to me again."

She lifted her head and stared into his troubled gaze. "I do not understand, Travis Kincade. You do not want Wild . . . Rana to be your wife? You wish Rana to live as . . . as a sister to Travis?"

167

"Yes, I need you to behave like my sister," he agreed defensively, although his entreating gaze belied his stinging words. A sisterly relationship was the last thing he wanted, but it offered some measure of safety until such time as he could reveal the truth. "Truce?" he coaxed hoarsely.

"If you will trust me to ride on Cloud," she responded softly.

After giving her a long, searching look, he spurred his horse forward and they joined the curious and worried Nathan. Travis told the man he would explain matters later. Right now, he needed to put distance between his and Rana's responsive bodies. "Swear you will not try anything foolish," he demanded of her. "Promise you will obey me."

"White Eagle traded for Wild Wind. She belongs to him. She will become Rana. Rana will obey the orders of Travis Kincade." She watched the effect of her words on him, carefully concealing her emotions. As Travis spoke with Nathan, Rana mentally questioned his strange English words and his curious sadness, and his denial of their blazing passion. From what she could see and hear, a sister was not what he wanted her to be. She would not tell him she could speak and understand English, for she could learn more about him this way . . .

Chapter Six

"I hear congratulations are in order, Papa," Clarissa Caldwell stated sweetly as she entered her father's office. "It seems you finally squeezed out Mister McFarland. Now you own every spread that surrounds the Rocking *C* Ranch. Once you take it from Nathan, we'll have the largest cattle empire that ever existed. Isn't it exciting? How do you plan to root out old Crandall? He seems dug in for life."

Harrison Caldwell looked at his nefarious daughter. He admitted that Clarissa was a beautiful and seductive woman, but he knew she was also selfish and vain, and often too wild and reckless. The greedy Clarissa did not care about their ranch or property, except for the prestige, power, and wealth they represented. She did not concern herself with how her father made money, as long as she had plenty to spend. She rarely inquired about the methods her father used to deal with people, but she made certain that no one doubted or challenged the power and influence that spilled over from him to her. He wondered if Clarissa ever worried about her advancing age, for she was still unwed at twenty-eight. His gaze traveled over her ebony hair, dusky complexion, and deep brown eyes. Several times he had instructed her to use her seductive talents or devious skills to aid his plots against his enemies, or to entangle those who stood in the way of his having what he wanted. Clarissa had always enjoyed those little "assignments." She had done everything he had asked of her, except win Travis Kincade over to their side, or make Caldwell a proud father. No, he could never love or be proud of this conniving and lecherous little bitch. No doubt she would slit his throat if it suited her purposes! he mused in disgust. It was a shame a man could not trust his own child, and she could not trust him . . .

"Papa, are you listening?" she inquired, peeved at his lack of attention and affection. No matter what she did to please him or to win his approval, or what she did to annoy or to punish him, she could not elicit the desired response from this man who had sired her.

"I was thinking about roots, Clarissa. We both know Nate's going to hand his ranch over to Travis. If you would put down a few roots with Kincade, I could kill Nathan and be done with all these tricky games and dangerous gunslingers. I want you to keep an eye on those last two Silas hired; they could be trouble if not handled properly."

"How close do you want me to watch them, Papa?" she asked with deceptive calm. Carrying out his little deceits meant nothing to her, but she hated him for uncaringly asking her to whore for him. If he were truly so strong and smart, he wouldn't need her! The only reasons she had done such things for him had been to exercise her power over men and to prove she could outwit them. Each assignment had taught her more about men and her father, lessons she needed in order to learn to compete in this "man's world." One day, she vowed coldly, he would pay for his vile treatment and lack of love.

"Close enough to make sure they don't interfere with our plans, girl. As soon as we're done with Crandall, we'll have everything we want. I'm going to strangle him out before winter."

Yes, Clarissa thought dreamily, she would have everything she wanted by winter. As soon as her despicable father created one of the most powerful and lucrative spreads in the West, she would get rid of the old bastard, take over the Caldwell empire, and marry Travis Kincade. This was everything she had dreamed of, and she would do anything necessary to make it a reality. She knew her father's evil secrets, past and present, for she had spied on him since the age of eight. If she had desired, she could have destroyed him with the truth, but that would have cost her her dream. She also knew Marissa's dark secrets, all of them, even one that neither of their fathers knew: the secret that Raymond had used against her dead friend . . .

A knock sounded on the door. Wes Monroe and Jackson Hayes were invited inside and Clarissa was dismissed. Harrison shook each man's hand, slapped each on the back, and complimented them on their defeat of James McFarland. "You boys did a fine job of running him out. Now, the Flying *M* Ranch is mine. The timing was perfect; nobody around to outbid me for it. I've got you boys a little bonus for working so fast and without any trouble. I like a good, clean job." He handed each man a packet of money. He had been careful to be very generous, to retain their loyalty and interest. "I want you boys to hang low for awhile. Make sure you stay out of trouble. I got one more matter for you to take care of for me; I want you to run out Nathan Crandall as soon as he gits back from some secret trip he's making." While he was speaking, Harrison tried to remind himself not to use language that might be over the heads of these crude men, for he had found that educated speech often caused envy and dislike. He knew it was better to stay close to their level of understanding or education to avoid

171

resentment; "working in the gully," as he called it.

"I'll pay you ten times what's in them packets," he offered, planning to get rid of these dangerous men as soon as Nathan and Travis were dead. "Just make sure you don't catch the sheriff's or U.S. Marshal's eye. I don't want anybody connecting you boys to these crimes, since you work for me. I want this matter to look real legal."

"Whatever you say, Mr. Caldwell," Wes Monroe remarked genially. "Me and Jack could use us a little rest and fun. McFarland was harder to discourage than we thought. We was trying not to damage property which would soon belong to our boss. Hell, we didn't have to kill more'n three men and forty steers. All you have to do is scare women and kids, and their men are forced to move on. When a rancher ain't got no hands, he can't run his ranch."

After the meeting, as Wes and Jackson were leaning against the hitching post outside Harrison Caldwell's office, Wes Monroe scoffed, "That old coot didn't even ask how we scared them women and kids and got their men to running off like crazy. I ain't had me that much fun since we rode with Cap'n Quantrill."

Jackson Hayes teased, "Stop bulling, Wes, you just like to rape and kill. If'n I knows you, you got plans for robbin' Caldwell and poking that bitch of a daughter. What'chu waitin' on?"

"This plan he's got going for Nathan Crandall. He'll have lots of money in his safe to buy off that ranch after he does in Crandall. We'll let him get his money together, then we'll relieve him of it. He thinks he's so damn smart and walking high over us. He's mine, Jack. I'm gonna peel him like a juicy apple, and take ever'thing he's got."

"What about that gal of his'n? Can I have her afore we move on?" his partner wheedled, for West was the brains of their outfit.

172

"Just make sure you leave me a little piece this time."

"I'll try, Wes. I just get so excited, I lose control."

"I know, Jack. I've had to clean up some of your bloody messes. Just give me a spit of time with her before you have your fun. I been watching them skirttails swish for weeks while she's walking away from me. That little bitch is coming down a few notches afore we leave."

Wes looked down the dirt street and grinned wickedly as he watched Clarissa enter a mercantile store. He was tired of moving from place to place, one hitching post away from the hangman's noose, with never enough whiskey and money and women to last long. And he was tired of taking orders from arrogant bastards like Harrison Caldwell. And he was tired of being strapped to a stupid partner like Jackson Hayes. He liked this town, and the Circle C Ranch. Maybe he would hang around a long time. Maybe he would kill Caldwell and Jackson, and marry Caldwell's daughter. Being a rich, powerful rancher with a beautiful, helpless wife sounded mighty fine to him. He had too much on Caldwell and his little brat for her to go screaming to the sheriff. Yep, he decided with a satanic grin, he just might take Caldwell's place in this area . . .

Travis, Rana, and Nathan had ridden for hours and had managed to avoid the violent storm that was currently attacking the Oglala camp. Travis kept glancing to their rear, praying that the storm would not shift and head in their direction and force them to halt their journey. He wanted as much distance as possible between them and the approaching Hunkpapa band. With luck, the storm would have delayed the hunting party's arrival. He could not imagine what would happen if the Oglalas learned the truth about his past, but he knew what the Hunkpapas would do. The sooner they were out of Lakota territory and their reach, the better.

Travis and Nathan were glad that Rana had not given them any trouble so far. Without a cross word or hesitation, she had ridden between them and had kept up with ease, making Travis proud of her. Earlier Travis had cautioned Nathan not to divulge any secrets around Rana, for a person often understood another language even if he could not speak it. He also warned himself to hold silent around her.

Rana had not spoken to either man since beginning the journey. She knew Travis was watching her with eagle eyes, ready to snatch her to his lap the moment she made a false move. She would prove how obedient and intelligent she could be, until it suited her to behave otherwise. She was aware of how often the older man's gaze slipped to her and of the warmth that filled his eyes. He seemed such a strong, gentle man. Whenever she looked his way, he would smile encouragingly. Perhaps his presence was the reason why her husband refused to touch her. No, she quickly answered herself, her husband was in a hurry. The question was why. She had noticed Travis watching their backs and saw that his body was still tense. There was an air of apprehension and mystery about him; she could sense his deep concern.

Rana did not understand this handsome male, but she knew she was strongly attracted to him, and he to her. Her emotions were in turmoil. One minute she told herself she despised him and would battle him all the way to her new home. The next, she wanted to make love to him, and was determined to do so or be told the reason why she could not. She did not like the way he could so easily control his emotions and hers. Other men had always found her beautiful and desirable, and had had to struggle inwardly to keep their hands off her; some had found they could not until she prevented them. How strange and infuriating that this half-blooded man had to be the one to stir her passions to life. How strange to want to possess and reject the same man at nearly the same time. Maybe he felt the same way, she ventured. Even if he was her husband, she could not allow him to play games with her feelings. Yet, as they rode swiftly, Rana plotted how to entice Travis while pretending to spurn him.

It was mid-afternoon when they stopped to rest and water the horses. Rana patted Cloud's forehead, then hugged him. She looked at Travis and said casually, "I will return soon." She headed into the trees, delighted that he did not stop her or question her.

"You don't think she'll try to escape, do you?" Nathan probed anxiously when she was out of hearing range and sight.

Travis removed his hat, wiped the moisture from his forehead, and replaced it. As he began unpacking something for them to eat, he replied in a playful tone, "For some curious reason, Nate, I don't think she'll try anything foolish, at least not yet. Right now, she's more concerned about disappointing her people and shaming herself than she's scared of us. If we can stay calm and friendly, maybe she will too. At least we've gotten her to accept the name Rana."

Nathan helped Travis with their light meal. "That was a sly trick, son. How long should we wait before telling her the truth? She seems like a smart girl and not one to take kindly to deceit."

"I'd say give her a week or so to get used to us before dropping it on her. That'll give her plenty of time to adjust to the news before we reach home. We're too close to the camp and she's still a little peeved with me right now. If we get her dander up, she could go hightailing it back to her brother to find out why he tricked her."

Travis explained how she had reacted to her mother's

175

necklace and the name Rana Michaels, and he told Nathan about the nightmare she had experienced that first night. "The truth might confuse her and frighten her. We're still strangers. We've got to give her time and patience."

"You think she remembers part of the past?"

"My guess is yes. But something back there has her scared, Nate, so she doesn't want to remember it. Lone Wolf told me she used to have those bad dreams lots of times. Maybe it's nothing more than that she can't allow herself to recall the good without recalling the bad. That's how it was with me. I found it was better not to think about the past at all. Hell, you can't change it, so why keep it on your mind and let it rub you raw inside?" he declared bitterly.

"She's beautiful, isn't she?" Nathan murmured, locking his softened gaze on the girl who was approaching them slowly. Nathan did not notice when Travis absently agreed and forced his longing gaze away from the fetching sight. "She's got her mother's spirit. She's impulsive and daring, and she's tough. I won't let happen to her what happened to my Marissa. I'll kill any man who goes near her."

"Love isn't something you can control, Nate. All you can do is pray she doesn't meet another Raymond Michaels. But if you start pushing her and bossing her, I can promise you she's going to rebel. That little vixen is the most willful and infuriating creature I've ever met."

Nathan chuckled. "That sounds just like somebody I used to know," he teased, his blue eyes sparkling with mischief.

"With luck, you'll be just as successful at taming her as you were with me." Travis grinned and winked at Nathan.

"Who said I was finished with you, son?" Nathan retorted. "For a man who's down on women, love, and marriage, you sure do seem to know a lot about 'em. Shame you've never met a good woman."

Rana watched the two men teasing and laughing, and it made her feel good to see how close they were. She walked past them to the stream to wash her face and hands. She turned when Travis called her name but did not respond when he asked in English if she were hungry.

"*Loyacin hwo*, Rana?" he repeated.

"*Han,*" she replied, then joined the two men. She thanked Travis for the food he handed her, then wondered why he did not scold her for not handling this female chore. She ate slowly and daintily as she watched Cloud nibble on grass nearby.

Travis asked suspiciously, "Have you finished yet?" When Rana did not react to his words, he inquired in Oglala, "*Wanna lustan hwo?*"

She glanced at him, praising herself for her quick and clever mind. "*Han,* Travis Kincade."

The three packed their supplies and mounted, ready to continue their long journey. They rode silently and swiftly until dusk. When Travis located a spot in which he felt it was safe to camp, he told them, "We'll stay here tonight, then leave early in the morning."

Travis was pleased when Rana willingly helped gather wood and prepared their evening meal. When everything had been cleared away, the two men placed their sleeping rolls near the fire, then Travis unrolled Rana's buffalo mat between them. He even smiled when he told her to go to sleep and explained that they would have a hard day's ride ahead. He stretched out on his bedroll, knowing from past observation that Rana slept on her right side which would compel her to face him. He watched her surreptitiously.

Rana took her appointed place between the two men, lying on her back and staring at the star-sprinkled sky overhead. For a long time, she and Travis did not sleep.

177

She was very much aware of the ever-increasing distance between her and the Oglala camp, and how each day brought her nearer to her new destiny, one that she could not envision. She recalled Lone Wolf's words: "You have trained and waited for the Great Spirit to return you to your destined path. Do not cower in fear or doubt and refuse to walk it." She shuddered with apprehension.

"Are you cold, Rana?" he inquired softly in Oglala, noting that the weary Nathan was slumbering peacefully.

"No," she responded in Oglala. "How far is it to your home?"

"Wikcemna nunpa nais wikcemna yamni anpetu," he replied, giving her a time of twenty to thirty days.

As she turned her head and looked at him, their eyes fused. "There is much to learn. What if your people do not accept me?"

Travis's gaze roamed her exquisite features and flaming hair. She looked so vulnerable and insecure. He realized how intimidating this sudden change must be to her. Lone Wolf had told him she had sworn never to allow anyone to hurt her again. Like him, she had become defensive and wary. She wanted to appear tough and hard, but she was a compelling contrast of strength and softness. He smiled and reached out to caress her cheek. He said tenderly, "You are very smart, Rana. You will learn everything quickly and easily. Do not worry; everyone will like you and accept you. Go to sleep. It is late."

She smiled, her expression softening with the gentle gesture. "Is that why you chose Wild Wind?" she inquired seriously.

He chuckled. "I chose Rana because she was the woman of most beauty and value in the Oglala camp. Was it not a great honor to help your people? Do not fear me and your new life."

"Was White Eagle afraid of this new life when he left

178

the Hunkpapa camp long ago?" she questioned curiously.

Travis rolled to his back and inhaled deeply. He wanted to continue talking pleasantly with her, but he did not like the direction the conversation was taking. "I will explain those past moons another time. I was young and bitter, and my leaving was not as yours. My mother and father were killed in battle, and speaking of such times brings pain and sadness. Is it not the same with you?" he asked pointedly.

Rana eyed him intently. She was filled with an urge to embrace him and comfort him. His tone and look had exposed such anguish, such resentment. Clearly those "past moons" had been tormenting and difficult times for this man. Perhaps that was why he had trouble revealing deep emotions and why he continually tried to avoid or to master them. He liked to be in control of himself and the situation, and emotional turmoil prevented it, or so he believed. This was a man who had been hurt deeply and who now lived too much within himself. She liked this sensitive, vulnerable, gentle side of her new husband. Suddenly she wondered if he had had a lover or a wife who had been slain in that same battle and if that were the reason he had left the Lakota lands and was reluctant to reach out to her. That speculation caused jealousy to flood her body. She had so many doubts and questions about this man.

"Yes," she admitted softly, "the past can be painful."

"One day, will you tell me what you remember of your past?" he asked gingerly, and watched her stiffen in panic.

"I wish to forget it. Do not ask," she beseeched him. "When the sun has gone to sleep on a day, it cannot be recalled or changed."

"Things that happen because of events of a past sun can be changed," he gently corrected. "Mistakes or evil

179

deeds can be made right and old enemies can become new friends," he clarified.

"It is a mistake to leave when my people are at war."

"I cannot save the Oglalas, Rana, but I can save you. You are not deserting your people by returning to where you belong. If you stay, you can do nothing to halt their destiny, but only bring about your own suffering and death. To yield or change is not a defeat or self-betrayal."

Rana did not want to question his disquieting words. "Tell me about your home and lands," she entreated to distract him.

Travis glanced at her and grinned. "Another day, Rana. We must sleep. We have a long ride ahead. Are you restless tonight?" She sighed and nodded. He asked, "Does your heart quiver with fear?"

Rana's expression became one of annoyance. "I do not quiver in fear. I am tired. I will sleep now." She turned her back to him, rankled by his insinuation of cowardice, and she vowed to prove him wrong.

Travis knew he had said the wrong thing; he had meant "anticipation," not "fear." The problem was that often a meaning was lost through a difficulty in translation. He was sharp enough not to chuckle at her amusing reaction. "Good night, Rana. Sleep well." Travis closed his eyes, but his keen instincts remained alert through the night.

Rana did not sleep well and was irritable when Travis aroused her the following morning when dawn was barely a reality. Travis had already gathered wood, built a fire, and prepared coffee. She seized a blanket and headed downstream to bathe. When the dark-haired man questioned her obvious intentions, she sullenly replied, "Yuzaza wacin."

"Hurry, and do not go far. Enemies could be nearby."

"I can defend myself," she tartly informed him. "I am not a child or a frightened girl. Will you return my knife and sheath?"

Travis studied her for a moment, then retrieved the items from his saddlebag. He handed them to her and warned, "Use it only for defense, or I will take it away. Do not anger me with silly games."

"I will use my knife to defend Wi . . . Rana against all dangers. I am smart. A weapon is not for play. Your warning insults me."

"Your behavior this morning insults me and you," he retorted. "A person should not be angry without reason. And when a person does not feel well, he should not blame or annoy others for his bad feelings. Go, bathe, and return quickly. We must eat and ride."

She started to quarrel with him, then changed her mind. It was a waste of time and energy to exchange bitter words with him. She glanced at the older man, who was watching them intently. When Nathan smiled at her, she did not respond. "I will hurry, my husband," she stated sarcastically, then glowered at him.

Travis scowled, then shook his head as he watched her departure. His troubled gaze wandered over her gently swaying hips and hair. One look into that stunning face had been enough to set his body aflame for her. He swore under his breath in Lakota as he tossed the saddlebag to the ground and reached for the coffeepot and a tin cup.

"Trouble between you two again?" Nathan inquired as he held out his cup for a refill, his gaze going from one to the other.

"Nothing I can't handle, Nate. She's in a bad mood this morning. I think she was too nervous to sleep. She realizes this trade is for real and that she's getting farther away from the Oglala camp. She's having trouble understanding a new husband who doesn't touch his wife."

"Maybe you should tell her the marriage isn't real, so she can stop worrying about becoming a wife," Nathan suggested.

"Isn't real, Nate?" he repeated skeptically. "To her, it's very real. She's been raised under Indian laws and customs. She believes in them and follows them, just like you with your white religion. Telling her our marriage isn't binding or real is like telling you there isn't a God. Or telling you your American laws aren't legal or binding, that it's all right to murder and steal. This was a crazy idea and I shouldn't have gone along with it. She's going to be furious when she discovers how we've lied to her. And she's going to be hurt."

Nathan did not know what to say or do. He could tell Travis was upset. He knew that Travis, like his granddaughter, had been raised as an Indian, raised to honor and accept Indian laws and customs. Nathan wondered if that was the problem that seemed to be harassing and confusing the young man who was like a son to him. Maybe it had been a big oversight on Travis's part; maybe he had not realized he would feel as if they were legally married inside his head and his heart. Perhaps Travis was still bound emotionally to his Indian heritage. To Nathan, the Oglala joining ceremony had merely been meaningless words. Yet he realized he would have to face the reality that it had not been viewed in that same light by Rana and Travis. And though he could not be sure, Nathan had a strong suspicion that he was right in these assumptions and speculations.

Travis's return to this area and the Lakota people had sparked old feelings and thoughts. For awhile he had become Indian again, and he had enjoyed it. Long ago he had been forced to give up this kind of life, and it had been unwise of him to confront it again. Perhaps he was still more Lakota than he had realized. His heart had surged with joy and excitement, almost as if he had been coming home and the white world was far away. No matter how much Travis told himself the marriage was not legal or binding under the white laws of his chosen people, he could not forget or ignore his Indian upbringing. Part of him said they were truly joined, and part of him said they were not. Part of him said he wanted this marriage, and part of him said he did not. He cursed his recklessness, for now he was trapped between his friend Nathan and his wife, Wild Wind. There was nothing he could do until he either convinced Nathan that the marriage was binding or convinced Rana that it was not.

While growing up in the Hunkpapa camp, Travis had witnessed many joining ceremonies. He recalled his own, envisioning Rana's touch and willingness to marry him and remembering the words and seriousness of the occasion. He recalled how he and Rana had pledged themselves to each other beneath the eyes of *Wakan Tanka,* who was the same as God to him. He remembered opening the marriage cape, her stepping inside, and his closing it around them to bind them for life. He still believed in the Great Spirit and the Indian way of life, through which he had been wed to this unique woman who trusted him. Were the Indian law and religion any less binding or sacred than the white man's? If he stood in a white man's church and repeated those same words in English, would it be any different to him, for him? He did not like being troubled by his conscience, a conscience that had been born during his years with Nathan. Now he had to think about more than himself, yet he knew that if it had not been Nathan and his granddaughter involved—

Nathan interrupted his train of thought. "You did the right thing, son. It was the only way we could rescue her. Those Indians didn't give us any choice. She'll understand once we explain everything to her."

"Do you forgive and forget when someone makes a fool of you? I know I've never forgotten or forgiven what Jeremy Kincade or Beth Lowry or Pretty Rabbit did to me

183

and others. Just like I can't overlook what Harrison and Clarissa Caldwell are trying to do to us. Maybe you were right; we should have told Rana the truth from the beginning. She'll despise me. Who knows? Maybe she'll be delighted she isn't really tied to me. Let's drop it, Nate. Here she comes."

"You look as pretty as a field of flowers, Rana," Nathan stated, appreciatively eyeing her as Travis translated his compliment. She was wearing a clean buckskin dress with beaded designs, and her thick red hair was neatly braided and secured with decorative rosettes. Her eyes were large and bright, and her skin appeared smooth and flawless. Nathan smiled as he noticed her bare feet. He saw why Travis was attracted to this woman he had vowed to ignore. Maybe—

"*Pilamaya*, Nate," she responded, deceptively appearing calm.

After they had eaten, Travis announced that it was time to mount and ride. Rana sat down to pull on her moccasins. She was mildly surprised when Travis extended his hand to help her rise, then lifted her to Cloud's back with an ease that revealed his strength and agility. She stated mischievously, "*Pilamaya, mihigna.*"

Travis sent her a look that told her he wished he could yank her off Cloud's back and kiss her soundly. She had not missed the way his hands had lingered on her waist, or the way one had leisurely slid down her left leg, or the way his gaze had feasted on her features. Maybe it would be wise to keep touching him, she mused, and reminding him he was *mihigna*, her husband . . .

They rode for hours with Rana between them, their fast pace and the noise of the horses' hooves preventing any conversation. When they halted for the midday meal, Travis told Rana to stay with Nathan while he did some scouting.

"Do you expect trouble, my husband?" she asked

worriedly, her entreating gaze meeting his intense stare.

A warm flush passed over his body. "Just being careful. I need to conceal our trail. We have been leaving one a child could follow."

"I do not understand. Do you think my people will come after you? You do not trust them?" Her large, blue-gray eyes searched his.

"You left many hungry, angry men behind," he teased roguishly. "When Rides-Like-Thunder discovers you are gone, he might come after you. If I am slain, you are free to join to another."

"Do not make jokes with me, Travis Kincade," she scolded.

"That is true, Rana, but I seek to hide our trail from enemies—soldiers and renegades," he replied honestly. "If the soldiers learn that I purchased the guns for warriors and killed the white man who tricked me, they will come after us. As soon as we can, we need to find you some clothes. Those Indian garments stand out like a dark sky. We do not need to arouse any suspicion this close to your camp. I doubt your identity is unknown to the whites and soldiers or to enemy tribes, a beautiful white girl with big blue eyes and flaming hair . . ."

"You think they would try to capture me and harm me?"

"For one reason or another," he answered vaguely. "Promise me you will stay here with Nathan and behave yourself."

"You do not trust your wife?" she probed.

Travis knew he would be gone for awhile, and he did not want to bind her and cause more trouble between them. He was afraid Nathan would not be able to handle this willful, clever female, for his friend underestimated her cunning, her daring, and her apprehension. If he used clever words and expressed faith in her, he might win her trust and obedience. "Lone Wolf told me you are as well trained as his warriors. I need you to protect Nathan. He is not as young or as quick as you are. You could flee and hide, or defend yourself. Stay alert so you can warn him of danger. But do not take any foolish chances. I love him more than my own life. Will you do this for me, Rana?"

Rana could not suppress her smile at his beseeching words and his look of concern for her safety. "I will do as you say. Be careful," she added, then hurriedly glanced away to prevent him from reading her expression. She wanted and needed to understand this man who had become such a big part of her life. She wanted to learn what he expected, and desired, from her. And she wanted to test her feelings as well as his.

"Your courage and honor are matchless. I am pleased with you."

Travis approached Nathan and related his plans. He whispered, "Keep an eye on her, Nate, and don't say anything around her."

"You watch yourself, son."

"If there's any trouble, ride fast and I'll catch up with you." He called Rana over to them and said, "Stay close and ready to leave."

Rana and Nathan watched Travis ride off into the trees. As instructed, they tended the horses and ate a light meal. When all was prepared, they sat down to await Travis's return.

"I wish you remembered English, Rana, so we could talk. Me and Travis will have to start teaching it to you before we get home. I don't want anybody giving you trouble, and I'll kill anyone who does. Lordy, we were lucky to find you. You don't know how much I love you, girl. You're going to be happy once I get you home. I won't ever let anybody harm you again. Damn them Kiowas for stealing you!"

Rana stared at him quizzically. Nathan assumed her

186

curious look was because he was speaking English and she could not understand him. He touched her arm and smiled. "Don't worry, child. Everything will be fine just as soon as Travis explains everything to you."

A lengthy time passed and both Nathan and Rana became worried about Travis. Rana stood and walked around to master her tension. She noticed that Nathan was eyeing her as if he expected her to run off at any second. Realizing she was making the older man nervous, she took a seat near him. Her ears were straining for any noise, any indication that Travis was returning. She suddenly wondered what she would do and how she would feel if Travis were slain. They had been joined for eight suns and had not shared a sleeping mat. Maybe he was not pleased with her. Maybe he thought she was still a foolish girl. Surely he had a good reason for refusing to share a sleeping mat.

Nathan captured her hand in his and patted it with the other one. "He'll be all right, Rana. He's too smart to get into danger. I just wish he wasn't so troubled about you. It ain't good to be so distracted in enemy territory. I tried to warn him."

Rana had to grit her teeth to keep from asking, Warn him about what? And to ask why and how he was troubled over her. Maybe pretending not to understand them had been a mistake, because she could not ask questions. With Travis gone, she was missing the perfect time to obtain information from this older man who seemed to like her very much, who had eyes almost the same color as hers. She was glad Nathan was so gentle and nice, and she liked him. He vaguely reminded her of someone she could not remember, someone special who had warmed her heart. There was something about his face and voice that reached out to her. Perhaps Grandfather had put him in her dreams or visions long ago. If only she could recall them clearly, but she did not want to push herself, for too many of those dreams had been bad ones.

Travis appeared as if from nowhere, astonishing both Nathan and Rana with his skillful stealth. He frowned at them and scolded lightly, "If I had been an enemy, you two would be in deep trouble."

Rana's half-smile faded instantly, but she knew he was right. She suspected that Travis had intentionally sneaked up on them. She told him she would be ready to ride soon, then vanished into the trees.

"She been behaving?" Travis questioned anxiously.

"Not a peep out of her. We need to teach her some English, son, so I can talk to her. Any signs of danger out there?"

"Nope. I covered our trail and made a false one in another direction. I don't like it, Nate; things are too quiet. We've got us a storm brewing, and I don't mean the weather." Travis decided it was best not to tell Nathan that three of Lone Wolf's braves had been trailing them until this morning, probably for Rana's protection.

"You said Crazy Horse and his Big Bellies have been lying low for awhile. It's been months since he massacred Captain Fetterman over at Lodge Trail Ridge. And Red Cloud hasn't moved his Bad Faces Band out of the Powder River area, has he?"

"We don't have to worry about Red Cloud; he's set on keeping that Bozemen Trail closed. They're riding between the Black Hills and Little Bighorn. But you can bet Sitting Bull and his Strong Heart Society aren't sitting around doing nothing. What we have to worry about is Crazy Horse banding together those Lakotas and Cheyenne. Lone Wolf told me he's been plotting against Fort Kearny and C. F. Smith all winter. He's planning on striking at them soon. After what he did to Fetterman, the Army is ready and waiting to retaliate. It'll be a bloodbath."

"Is Crazy Horse crazy like his name?" Nathan inquired.

"That's a mistake in translation, Nate. Our word is "crazy"; theirs is "enchanted"; and believe me, he's got more magic and appeal than those soldiers can imagine. He doesn't take scalps or count *coup*, and he rides in front of his band. He's totally fearless, Nate. I doubt the Union Army has any leader as cunning and daring, and we're heading near his target area. Let's get moving," he announced, not wanting to take time to eat or rest. "Rana! *Inankni yo!*" he called loudly, telling her to hurry.

Rana appeared soon and mounted her beloved white stallion. As they rode off, she took a place at Nathan's right side, putting the older man between her and Travis. Travis did not bother to shift her, for he knew he had singed her ego and pride again.

It was past dusk when Travis called a halt to their day's ride, which had left all three of them tired and tense. While Travis thoroughly scouted the area and tended the horses, Rana helped Nathan gather firewood and prepare their meal. When the food was ready, Nathan called Travis to join them. Discarding the Indian custom for the white one, Travis instructed Rana to eat with them, not after them, and she enjoyed being treated and viewed as an equal. Travis ate silently and quickly, then unrolled the sleeping mats. Nathan wished them good night, then took his place and was soon dozing.

Rana sat staring into the fire as she brushed her hair. She was neither sad nor happy. When she took a blanket and headed for the river, Travis went after her and asked where she was going. "*Wanuwan wacin,*" she replied without losing a step.

"It is too late to go swimming and the water is too cool. Lie down on your mat and go to sleep," he ordered moodily. Travis knew he possessed the brute strength to control the stirring minx, but he had little desire to tangle with her. She provoked and enchanted him at every turn. In spite of his past female trouble and his current obligations to Nathan, he was being drawn closer to her with every passing hour.

She halted and looked at him, protesting, "I am dusty and tired. I wish to bathe before sleeping. You hurry me in the morning."

"I just want to get us safely out of this area. Several tribes are painting up for war with the soldiers, and other tribes are going to join them. I do not want us caught in the middle."

"Why do you give Indians guns, then refuse to fight with them?"

"This is not my war, Rana. I cannot take sides. I only helped your people even the odds by giving them a fighting chance for survival. I am half Indian and you have been raised by them. Soldiers would not be too friendly toward us, and neither would the Indians because we are white. You have been in that Oglala camp too long. You do not know what it is like to be trapped between warring sides, belonging to neither. I must get you out of those Indian garments and out of this Indian territory before someone guesses who you are. You do not want the soldiers using you to obtain Lone Wolf's surrender, do you?"

"No," she hastily responded. "But why did you not warn my people?"

"I did. That is why Lone Wolf traded you so readily." Knowing he had spoken rashly, he tried to cover himself. "He knew this war was heating up fast and he did not want you getting hurt by it. He loves you, Rana, but you are white. You could be a threat to them. He wants you to be safe and happy. He did what was best for everyone. Can you understand and accept that?"

"If I did not accept it, I would not be here with you.

190

Why must you be so cold and angry with me, Travis Kincade? It is hard to leave my people and make the changes you demand. It makes me sad and angry that you do not trust me or like me." With this, she raced off toward the river, wondering how her words would affect him.

She hurriedly yanked off her moccasins and dress and tossed them aside. As she loosened the ties on her breechclout, Travis walked over to her. He seized her chin and lifted her head, intending to debate her mistaken impressions. Tears sparkled on her thick lashes and her wide eyes were somber. Her long, wavy hair settled wildly about her shoulders and reflected the moonlight, giving her a sensual aura. As she clenched her teeth, her lips formed a natural and seductive pout. She allowed the breechclout to slip from her fingers and fall to the ground, making no attempt to shield her nude body from Travis's gaze. This attractive, stimulating man was her husband, and she wanted him.

The flesh beneath Travis's light grasp was as soft and slick as an expensive satin ribbon. Her body was lithe and shapely. Where she was tanned, her skin was as golden as honey and as creamy as its texture. Where her tan stopped, her skin was as white as a fluffy cloud and as soft as freshly picked cotton. He knew he should not allow his gaze to roam her ravishing face and stunning figure, but he could not stop himself. Every inch of her seemed to call out for tender, loving caresses. She was so sleek and exquisite. Never had he viewed a more perfect woman. He yearned to let his hands explore her body, to allow his lips to follow that same trail. His respiration became ragged and his grip on her tightened slightly. His green gaze glowed with unrestrained desire. "Lordy, you're beautiful," he murmured. He was losing himself in those magnetic blue-gray eyes, and for a time he did not care. As with aged whiskey, she was utterly intoxicating. All of the times he had taken women in the past, it had been for physical release, to appease his sexual urges. It was not like that with Rana; his entire being craved her. The other women he had wanted only for a night of pleasure. But Rana he wanted completely, permanently!

Rana boldly stepped closer to him and drew his head down to hers, fusing their lips as she mesmerized Travis with her gaze. A groan escaped his lips and his arms encircled her body to mold it tightly against his. He kissed her fiercely, ravenously. His fingers tangled in her silky hair as he pressed her head to his, allowing his eager mouth to explore hers leisurely. He could feel the stimulating warmth of her body through his shirt. His hands slid down her back and, grasping her buttocks, he drew her to him. The intimate contact staggered his senses and inflamed him dangerously. He groaned again, unable to hide his rapidly fleeing restraint and mounting desire. He had craved this provocative vixen since first sighting her, and he wanted her beyond control or reason.

"Come, lie with me, my husband," she whispered seductively, pulling the captivated Travis down to the discarded blanket with her. She fastened her lips to his and feasted greedily. Her arms went under his and around his firm, supple body to stroke his muscular back. As his lips seared over her face, down her neck, and to her breasts, she writhed and caressed his lower body with her own. His actions brought her sheer bliss. While he savored one brown peak and then the other, her fingers played in his sable hair. She loved these wild, wonderful feelings he evoked and yielded eagerly to them.

All Travis could think about was possessing this enticing creature who was driving him wild with hunger for her. Never before had a woman stolen his wits and control, until Rana. He wanted to take her swiftly, and yet with maddening leisure, for she belonged to him by

Indian law and by right of rescue and conquest. Desire for her had been driving him crazy for days, and he wanted to enjoy every second of this first joining of their bodies. His deft hand wandered down her supple frame, caressing and tantalizing each area as it traveled toward her unprotected womanhood, which radiated a heat in which he desperately wanted to warm himself. Lordy, he had never desired a woman so strongly or felt so possessive of one. His restraint was rapidly disappearing and he knew he could wait no longer to take her. He had to—

"Travis! Travis, where are you, son?" Nathan called loudly, his voice coming from a distance.

Travis went rigid as reality slammed hard into his gut. He leaned away from Rana, breathing heavily. "What the hell am I doing?" he murmured in disbelief. "I can't make love to you. Why did I let you tempt me like this again? You've got powerful magic."

Knowing that Nathan would continue to call and seek them, Travis stood up and straightened his shirt. He tried to master his respiration and douse his fiery passion before calling out, "Be there in a minute, Nate. Everything's fine. Rana wanted a bath, so I'm standing guard." He pulled the naked girl to her feet and whispered in her ear, "Get bathed and get back to camp as quickly as you can."

The astonished Rana gaped at her husband when he left her to join his friend as if nothing had been going on between them. Anger, embarrassment, and frustration consumed her. She could not imagine why a husband would behave as hers did. He had acted as if there were something wrong with his desiring her and with their making love. There was nothing shameful about love or sex. He had responded to her, had been hungry to possess her, even willing to do so until his friend had awakened him from his dreamy world. Travis was not a coward, she

193

knew, so what had frightened him and quelled his passion a second time?

She eased into the chilly water to cool her own passions, but her temper remained heated. She raged aloud as she bathed roughly, "Why do you kill such good feelings and douse such wild flames of desire? Do you belong to another woman, or to her dead spirit? You are 'angry without good reason,'" she charged, using his own words. "You blazed with anger when Black Hawk tried to take what was yours, yet you refuse it. You have hurt me and shamed me deeply."

When Rana finally returned to the campfire, Nathan was dozing again and Travis was lying on his back, his hat resting over his eyes. She snatched up her sleeping mat and spread it out on the other side of the fire, away from the two men. Sullenly, she lay down and tossed a thin blanket over her trembling frame. As she was settling herself, her gaze drifted across the fire to observe Travis propped on one elbow, watching her intently. She glared coldly at him, then turned away, vowing never to allow him to treat her that way again. It was surprising how swiftly sleep came to her, despite her fury and tension.

As Travis watched her sleeping form, he realized that Rana was slowly chiseling away at his stony heart. Each day he was finding it harder to be tough and resistant. Taming her was like trying to master a wild mustang without breaking its spirit. It was like tampering with another's destiny or trying to leash pure spirit and energy, like trying to control the very essence of life itself. He asked himself, how did one capture sunshine in his hand?

He remembered how Elizabeth Lowry and Clarissa Caldwell had tried to ensnare him with their feminine wiles, and how Rana's own mother had toyed with susceptible men, if he could believe the stories he had heard about Marissa Crandall Michaels. Women's desires could prove treacherous to an unsuspecting man, as Pretty Rabbit's had been.

To make White Eagle jealous and to snare his attention, Pretty Rabbit had used Charge-A-Buffalo; she had driven him wild with desire and frustration. The warrior had loved her and had wanted her as his mate, but she had toyed with him to get at White Eagle. After she had cruelly rejected the warrior and had told him he was nothing compared to White Eagle, the warrior had been consumed by hatred and anguish. To revenge himself on White Eagle and to punish Pretty Rabbit, the warrior had lied about White Eagle's involvement with his father's evil deeds. Charge-A-Buffalo had wanted to make certain that if he could not have Pretty Rabbit, White Eagle would never have her and she would never have White Eagle. When he had been captured, falsely accused, tortured, and scheduled for death, Pretty Rabbit had viewed his perilous predicament as the means to finally win him. But though she had died trying to help him escape, her evil scheming had kept Travis from feeling any remorse over her death.

Yet, over the years since that tragic incident, he had thought a great deal about the Hunkpapas' actions and in a way had come to understand and forgive them. His father had been a malicious enemy, and he had been a half-breed. He had left the Hunkpapas to travel with his father for two years in the white world, and perhaps they had thought he had been tainted by it. He had been at his father's side when Jeremy had been captured following his vile treachery. A courageous, renowned warrior had made charges against him, one whose hatred and feelings of rivalry were unknown to their people. He had begun to realize that with such "evidence" against him, perhaps their behavior had been logical and natural. Maybe he would have done and felt the same if the charges had been against another half-breed or white man.

195

Before going to sleep, Travis admitted to himself that he had learned one thing: hatred and bitterness could be a ravenously devouring disease. With Nathan's help and love, he had conquered the worst of it; and no matter what the Indians had said or might believe about him, he could face the Great Spirit with a clear conscience and an innocent heart.

...

Chapter Seven

For two days, the small group continued their journey at the grueling pace that Travis had set for them after his frustrating encounter with Rana. When they stopped to camp that second night, Travis moodily went about his tasks while Rana disappeared to bathe. He made no attempt to question her or to stop her, and Rana did not ask permission to leave camp. During the past two days Rana had been riding next to Nathan and sleeping away from the two men. It had become clear to Nathan that the two were ignoring and avoiding each other, and this behavior intrigued and worried the observant rancher. Too, he was becoming flustered by his obligatory silence, for he knew the best way to solve a problem was to meet it head-on.

Nathan now inquired seriously of Travis, "Don't you think it's about time you tell me what's bothering you, son? You've been pushing us close to exhaustion for days. There ain't no way we can stay alert and strong at this killing pace, and you haven't even tried to cover our trail. What's wrong, son? You're running like a dog with his tail afire. The same goes for Rana. You two have hardly spoken or looked at each other in two days. You've been letting her come and go as she pleases, like you don't even care if she tries to escape. I feel like I've been riding between two fierce enemies traveling under a bitter truce. Is there something you haven't told me about Rana or our situation?"

Travis tensed in dread. He should have known his actions would call Nathan's attention to him. How could he explain the truth to his best friend without increasing his worries? "I told you, Nate, I want to get us out of this territory pronto, at least past Forts Kearny and Smith. We're only two days' ride from Fort Laramie, and we'll be crossing over the Mormon and Oregon Trails on Sunday. The Indians could be watching them for wagon trains or troop movements, and the soldiers at those forts are getting plenty nervous. They're in a mood to shoot first and check around later. Our best strategy is to head overland and stay clear of forts and villages until we're out of Nebraska. I'm trying to protect you and Rana. I'll ease up in three or four days, as soon as we make Kansas. I know what I'm doing, Nate."

Nathan eyed the younger man. "Do you, Travis? Talk to me, son," he urged gravely, indicating that he did not accept his foreman's explanation.

Travis did not like deceiving the older man. Except for keeping the reasons for his originally leaving this territory a secret, he had always been open and honest with Nathan Crandall. Anguish and shame had caused him to keep silent about his father's treachery, but far different emotions were keeping him silent about this present complicated matter. By now Nathan thought he knew all about the younger man, yet Travis realized he did not even know himself where Rana was concerned.

"What's gotten into you, son?" Nathan persisted gently.

Travis inhaled deeply, feeling like his neck was in a tight noose. "All right, Nate, if you want the truth. I'll give it to you. Your granddaughter is a beautiful, desirable woman. She's trying her damnedest to become my wife in every way possible, and sometimes I have a hell of a time remembering who she is and what the real situation is between us. The faster we ride and the farther away we get from here, the sooner I can explain things to her and stop all this temptation. By the time we reach Kansas, it'll be too late for her to try anything rash or foolish. We can tell her who she is and why we came after her; then maybe we can all have some peace. But frankly I don't think she's going to understand why I married her or why the council demanded that we join."

Travis leaned against a tree as if needing its support. "It sounded like a clever idea back in the Oglala camp, like the easiest and quickest way to handle her, but I don't think so anymore. There are too many complications and feelings involved. Rana had a rough, frightening childhood, traveling from one saloon to another, watching her parents being slaughtered, enduring captivity by the Kiowas. Once she got settled in with the Oglalas and was treated like a princess for years, she became spoiled. We might as well face it, Nate; she's impetuous and stubborn, and she's too damn proud for her own good. She's been living wild and free in the forest and plains. She's been taught Lakota laws and customs. She's been taught to depend on her wits and courage—to depend on herself, Nate. Her skin is white and she's your flesh and blood, but her heart and life are Indian. She's used to sidestepping her brother to get her way, and she's had countless warriors begging for her. When she finally obeys her brother and marries a man, he doesn't come near her. It doesn't sit well with her that I'm not behaving like a husband. This situation has got to be as confusing and embarrassing for her as it is for me. It's got her ego in an uproar. Since she was seven, this is all she's known and loved. Then we walk in and make demands on her, force her to leave and change, to become civilized. It doesn't seem fair. But you're right, Nate; things can't go on this way. I've got to settle down or I could endanger all of us."

Travis straightened and rested his hands on his gun butts. Clenching his teeth, he declared sullenly, "Hell, Nate, I've never been in this kind of predicament before and I don't know how to handle it. It's got me plenty worried, and even a little scared," he admitted. "You're depending on me, Nate, and I don't want to fail you."

Nathan touched his shoulder affectionately. "You won't fail me, son, and you never have. My life was nothing but hard work and bare existence until you came along, Travis. You don't know how much you mean to me, son. I know this must be hard on you and Rana, but everything will iron out as soon as we can explain matters to her."

Travis shook his head and frowned. "I'm not so sure that won't make matters worse, Nate. She loves her brother and trusts him, and he's let her down. And we let her down. We made it look as if she didn't have enough sense or honor to understand the truth or have any say about her life. We treated her like a child or someone who couldn't think for herself, as if she didn't have any feelings or didn't deserve to know the truth. We bought her like a piece of property. We didn't ask for her understanding or cooperation. We all tricked her. And she's going to be mad at us, Nate. I know how I felt when I discovered my father's treachery. All I knew was that he had lied to me and used me. Once she hears the truth, how can she trust us and accept us? We simply expect her to take our word that we did it all for her own good? Hell, we're strangers to her!"

"I'm her grandfather, Travis," he argued sadly. "I had to get her back. I couldn't just leave her there to get tangled up in that war."

"I know, Nate, but we're asking a lot from her. She's

hardly more than a child. I think the best thing for me to do is to apologize to Rana and start being nicer and easier on her. I can't blame her for acting on a lie I created. Until I can tell her the truth, I need to go along with it, at least halfway. As soon as we finish eating, I'll ask her to take a walk—see if I can't straighten things out a little bit."

"What are you going to tell her?"

"I don't know, but I have to tell her something. The longer I let her stay mad, the more she's going to be tempted to run off just to get back at me. If there's one thing I've learned, Nate, it's that women can be spiteful and selfish. They'll go to any lengths to get their wishes, or make you sorry they didn't . . . Tell me about that necklace you gave her. It seemed to make her nervous," he remarked carefully.

"I gave it to Marissa on her last visit. She wore it every day. Sometimes, when she was rocking Rana to sleep after a bad dream, Rana would hold it and rub it. It always seemed to calm her down, so I was planning to buy her one. I never got the chance. After Marissa was killed, the housekeeper found it and a doll I had given to Rana in the bottom drawer in Marissa's bedroom. I guess she left them behind so Raymond wouldn't take 'em and sell 'em for a poker stake." He paused for a moment, then continued. "Marissa and Rana both became edgy after he showed up at the ranch. What was I supposed to do, Travis? The law is on the husband's side, and she was willing to leave with him. If she had said one word against him, I wouldn't have let him take them away. I had this gut feeling she was planning to come back home. She never had a chance, but now we're giving Rana one. I kept that necklace all these years and gave it to Rana while you were gone. You think she remembers it?"

Travis replied candidly, "I think she doesn't want to remember it, or anything else about her past."

201

"Does that include me, son? I know she only saw me a few times, but I was hoping . . ." Nathan did not finish his wistful thought.

"You said she was happy at the ranch. Maybe it will spur her memory. One thing for certain, you need to get as close to her as possible before we reveal the truth to her. I think I'll speak to her before supper, then maybe we can all eat better. I'll return soon."

At a secluded area near the stream, Rana was also thinking and planning. She finally understood that there would be no going back to her old life and that she would have to make the best of this baffling situation. For two days she had been thinking about her new life and Travis. Somewhere out there a new destiny awaited her, and it included her mysterious husband. To keep from making herself and the others unhappy, she would have to accept the way Travis wanted things, or seemed to want them. She would have to show complete control and patience, and behave like a woman, not a child or a wild vixen. She was tired of her cold, self-imposed silence. It was making her miserable and tense, when all she wanted was to smile and be happy again. She yearned for him to like her and accept her, to be proud of her and his choice. She hated the way Travis was treating her and the way he was pushing them. His troubled spirit seemed to be driving him and she had no doubt that she was somehow to blame. Maybe she had said or done something to offend him or displease him. Maybe he believed those ugly stories about her. Maybe he doubted her reactions to him. If only he could explain his feelings and his reasons for rejecting her, perhaps they could come to some understanding.

Rana was terribly bewildered. She recalled the few stirring moments of closeness they had shared: the incident in her tepee, the kiss at the beginning of their journey, and their passionate embrace near the river. Each time, things had gone well between them until she had yielded to passion or had tried to inflame him. For some inexplicable reason, feeling desire for her angered him and caused him to lash out cruelly at her. If there were to be peace between them, she would have to keep her distance from him; she would have to live as his sister, as he had so contradictorily requested. Perhaps if she showed him her best face and ceased "tempting" him, he would settle down so they could get closer. One day she might even convince him to take her as his wife in the true sense.

With this enticing thought in mind, Rana completed her bath. Wrapping herself in a drying blanket, she washed her soiled dress so that it could dry during the warm night. Afterward, she slipped into her white garment, which she knew was her most flattering dress. She brushed her hair and allowed it to hang free down her back. Above her left ear, she secured the tiny medicine wheel made from quills in the sacred colors of blue, yellow, white, red, and black with a breath feather attached to its center. Seeing that it was nearly dark, she collected her possessions and headed toward the camp to join the men.

As she made her way back, she was surprised to find Travis waiting for her in the shadows of a tall tree. She halted before him to view his expression and to learn what he wanted. He did not look angry, only tired and troubled. She observed the way his gaze slipped over her from her head to her bare feet and she watched his troubled look increase; suddenly she regretted dressing so prettily to catch his eye and to soften his anger.

When he did not speak, she eyed him quizzically. He seemed to be having difficulty finding words, or perhaps, she mused, only the right ones. Apprehension filled her.

He was so handsome and virile, and she longed to enjoy his lips and arms. At times such as this, he made her feel so unsure of herself, so vulnerable and helpless. His mere presence caused her body to warm strangely and to quiver. His look caused all thoughts to rush from her head except those of him, and it inspired her heart to beat as swiftly and forcefully as the drums during the Victory Dance. He even affected her breathing and the moisture in her mouth. As if that were not enough, he also made her legs go weak and refuse to move. No man had made her feel this way before, so weak and compliant. It was alarming, and yet very pleasant. Taking a deep breath, she looked into his eyes and waited.

"Lordy, woman, you're not going to make this easy for me, are you?" he mumbled. "How do I explain myself without making you furious with me?" He half turned and pounded his fist on the tree, for he had never before explained himself to a woman.

Rana softly replied in fluent English, "Say what is in your heart, my . . . Travis. I do not wish to cause you such pain and trouble. It is not good for us to behave as fierce enemies. What does Rana do wrong? Are you sorry you chose me? Do you wish to send me away?"

Travis faced her and stared into that upturned face with its innocent, appealing expression. Damn women for having and using such potent wiles! he cursed silently, then said aloud, "So, you do remember English. I thought as much. You're one clever and stubborn girl, Rana Michaels."

"My people did not like to hear the white man's tongue, so I did not speak it unless my brother asked it of me to question captives. Does it not please you that I can speak with you? Where we go, will you not wish me to keep the Oglala tongue a secret?"

"From now on, speak English. Why did you trick me?"

"Trick you? You did not ask if I could speak your

204

tongue, and you did not order me to speak it. Is it strange for a white girl to speak the white tongue? Did my brother not tell you?"

"No, he didn't, and I was under the impression that you had forgotten it. You were captured as a small child and you've only heard Oglala for years. But I suspected you understood more than you let on. But that isn't what I wanted to discuss," he declared, changing the subject before he could become angered by her deceit. He had no right, he knew, for his duplicity was worse.

"Discuss?" she repeated the unfamiliar word, knowing he had a right to be angry with her for withholding her knowledge of English from him.

"Talk about," he clarified. "These last few days we've . . . I've been acting badly. I wanted to tell you I'm sorry for being so mean and hard on you. I know this change in your life must be confusing and frightening, and I haven't been making it any easier for you. I want you to undertand some things about me and our marriage," Travis ventured, wanting to stay as close to the truth as possible. He had to get this particular matter straight between them, for both their sakes.

"I didn't come here looking for a wife, and I'm a little confused about finding one. You know it's the custom to choose something of great value in exchange for the guns and supplies I gave to your people. Since you were white and the war was heating up, I thought it would be a good idea to get you out of Indian territory. If what I heard was true, you were having problems in the camp. I had already asked for you in trade when they said I would have to marry you before you could leave with me. It would have been an insult to refuse to marry the sister of Chief Lone Wolf when I had been willing to trade for her. I'm not used to having a woman around, Rana, so you'll have to give me time to get adjusted to the idea. If you weren't so innocent and special, I could toss you on my

205

sleeping mat and think nothing about it. But you are special, Rana, and I don't want to take advantage of a situation you were forced to accept. I promise you that Nate and I will do all we can to make you happy and safe. He likes you and feels drawn to you, Rana, so please be kind to him. His only daughter was killed years ago, and she looked a lot like you. That was her necklace he gave to you. For now, let's just become friends and get to know each other. Will you try to be patient and understanding? Can we have a real truce?" he inquired earnestly.

"Do you have a wife waiting for you?" she queried anxiously, aware that warriors often took more than one mate and knowing she could never share a husband, especially this rare man standing before her.

"No. You see, Rana, we're both white. We'll be living on white lands, under white laws and customs. The Oglala laws and customs are not accepted, or even recognized, by the white man. Our marriage is binding only in Indian territory and under Indian law, but we're not Indian and we won't be living here. You'll be like my sister. You'll be free. Do you understand what I'm saying?" he asked nervously.

Consternation flooded her features. She moved a few steps away from him and drifted into deep thought. Finally she turned and looked at him. "We are not joined in your eyes? You do not want me?"

Travis responded carefully, "We're not joined in the eyes and laws of the whites, and we'll be living as whites. We must obey their laws and customs. That's why it's wrong for me to make love to you. I want you to be free and happy and safe, Rana."

She realized that he had cleverly avoided her question. "You are half Indian, White Eagle. Is that half not joined to Wild Wind? Do the laws of Grandfather and your mother's people mean nothing to you? Have you forgotten all you were and knew?"

"No, Rana, I haven't forgotten. I love my people and believe in Grandfather. But I've chosen the white world and must live by its laws and ways. It troubled my spirit to join to you falsely, but I believed I was doing what was good for you. When war comes to your camp, no white girl will be safe there, from whites or Indians. I couldn't let you be killed or placed on a reservation, or worse. In war, men are evil and fierce. And I couldn't rescue you without following the wishes of your adopted people. You're very beautiful and tempting, and it's hard to remember you're not my wife. Unless we're married by white law, Rana, we can't share a sleeping mat. You're returning to the white world, so you must accept this. I can't dishonor you or use you selfishly. You have the right to choose who and what you want."

"Is there a woman you love in this land you call Texas? Is she why you hurry home and do not take Wild Wind as promised?"

He grinned at her jealous look and tone. "I have no wife, or a woman close to my heart. Come home peacefully with me, Rana. Let me . . . teach you to find your new destiny. I promise you this is how it should be. You will be able to come and go as you please. You'll be free and happy with us. Don't fight Grandfather's will," he urged.

Rana smiled, for now she understood his dilemma: he was being torn between two bloods and peoples. One law said they were not joined, and the other said they were. Was this the "truth" that had tortured him? she wondered, knowing there was a simple way to end his suffering, though it was too soon to mention it. *Oh, my love,* she thought dreamily, *you are far more Indian than you realize, and you do not wish me to be your sister!* She had wanted happiness and freedom once, but now she wanted Travis more. She had not wanted to marry and he had told her that according to white law they had not, yet

207

she had been extremely pleased by their joining. She had wanted desperately to be allowed to be herself, yet now all she wanted was to be his!

"I do not like battling you with words each day, Travis Kincade. I promised my people I would go with you, and I will keep my word of honor." Words she had spoken to Black Hawk returned to haunt her and she repeated them hoarsely: "We are joined only in words, and false words can be broken. I will be your sister and friend. I will try to accept your ways and be happy in your lands. If it is not so by winter, you must promise to return me to my people. Do you agree?"

Travis sighed loudly in relief and smiled broadly, for he knew she would adjust. "That seems fair enough. It's a deal, Miss Rana Michaels. Let's go eat and get some sleep. I'm starving and exhausted," he announced cheerfully, holding out his hand in invitation.

Rana glanced at it, laughed softly, and teased, "Do sisters and brothers touch in this tempting manner?"

"Maybe you're right. No need to add fuel to a fire that should be left to smolder for now. Come along, sister. It's late."

As Rana followed Travis to camp, she boldly reflected, *The sun will set on your resistance sooner than you think, my love, because we are joined in the eyes of* Wakan Tanka *and in our own eyes . . .*

As the two entered the small area where they were camping for the night, Nathan instantly detected the change between them. Both were smiling and appeared lighthearted. They looked comfortable side by side and a pleasant warmth seemed to surround them. Nathan relaxed, deciding all would be fine now. He listened intently as Travis hurriedly related the essentials of his talk with Rana. He was astonished to learn that his granddaughter could speak English, but unlike Travis, he

208

did not try to recall what he had said around her. He was too excited by the news.

Nathan smiled and laughed at the same time. Clasping Rana's hand between his, he stated exuberantly, "I'm so glad we can talk, Rana. This is going to make things so much easier for all of us. I've got so much to tell you. You're going home and—"

"Nate," Travis called to him to halt his rapid and thoughtless flow of words, "we've got plenty of time to tell Rana about her new home. It's late and we're all tired. Now I understand why Rana kept quiet about speaking English; she didn't want us to talk her ears off."

Nathan caught the hint and tried to master his rampant emotions. He was pleased with the way Travis was handling the matter, letting the facts trickle out a few at a time to keep from drowning Rana in a river of truth. "Old men do have this tendency to babble, don't they, son? Travis here doesn't do much talking, but I do. I'm real proud of him, Rana. He takes good care of me and our lands. A man couldn't ask for a better son or grandson," he stated affectionately, unwittingly misleading Rana about their relationship.

"His eyes say he has much pride and love for you, Nate. It is good for families to be close to each other. I will be happy and honored to live in your home."

"We're the ones who are happy and honored to have you join our family, Rana," Travis told her. "Now that we have a peaceful camp, why don't we all get busy with supper? Rana, I was telling Nate that it looks like there's going to be trouble in this area soon between Crazy Horse's band and the soldiers at Fort Kearny. I would like to be long gone before they start battling each other again. Do you mind riding fast and hard for a few days?"

"I understand, Travis. I will ride fast and hard at your side."

"Good," he murmured, smiling at her.

The following morning, Travis, Rana, and Nathan were in high spirits and smiled frequently at each other as they hurriedly ate and packed to leave. As Travis had requested, the small group traveled quickly, taking only short rest breaks for the horses and themselves. At one point they all burst into laughter as a herd of deer bolted across their path and startled their horses as well as the deer.

His shiny eyes revealing his genuine happiness, Nathan shouted to Rana, "Wait until you see how many we have on our ranch."

Rana had shouted back, "How big is your ranch?"

Nathan beamed with joy and pride as he replied, "A hundred and fifty thousand acres of prime grazing land. You'll love it there."

Rana instantly concluded that he was right. Excitement surged through her as the lovely scenery moved swiftly past, taking her further from the Dakota Territory and closer to Texas. Each time she glanced at the man riding to her right and slightly ahead of her, tremors of anticipation and desire assailed her. Today she felt at ease with these men; she began to believe that her new destiny held great things for her. Gone were her bitterness and anger; they had been replaced by joy and hope.

As the fast-paced journey continued, there was little conversation, for neither Rana nor Nathan wanted to distract Travis from his intense alertness. Nearing dusk, Travis rode ahead to scout the area he had selected for their camp. It was obvious to his companions that he remembered this area well, for he always seemed to know where to find water and lush grass for the animals.

As they gathered firewood and prepared their evening meal, Nathan described his ranch and home for Rana.

When he told her she would have her own room and could come and go as she pleased, Rana was amazed, for she had never known such privacy and freedom before. She was also astonished by the large amount of cattle and horses Nathan owned, for it was more than those owned by several tribes combined. She decided these men must be strong and clever to control so much land and to own so many animals. She could tell that both men had deep love and respect for their land, which caused her to feel a similar respect for their great skill and success.

Nathan told Rana about the neighboring ranchers and towns, explaining as he did so about raising cattle and horses and selling them. He related colorful tales about the history of Texas and his homesteading days, and finally he told her about his wife, Ruth, and a little about his daughter, Marissa.

"Marissa . . . ," she echoed the vaguely familiar name. "It is beautiful, soft like music or the spring rain. You miss her now that she lives with the Great Spirit. It is sad to lose those we love and need. My father, Soaring Hawk, lives with *Tunkansila*. He was a great warrior and chief. My brother, Lone Wolf, walks closely in his tracks." She wanted to ask more questions about his daughter, but she sensed that the topic was painful to the old man, and to her, too, for some unknown reason.

"I know you'll miss them, Rana, but don't be angry because we're taking you home where you belong."

She looked over at Nathan and smiled. She was glad he felt she belonged with them. "I willingly go where the Great Spirit leads."

When Travis joined them to eat, he teased, "I see Nate's been talking your ears off again. He's just excited about having a woman in the house again. I think he's forgotten how much trouble they can be."

"Women give trouble only when they must," she retorted.

211

"To get their own ways," Travis slyly came back at her, then grinned devilishly. He sipped his coffee, eyeing her over the cup's rim.

"Do you not use clever words and deeds to get your way?"

Nathan chuckled. "She's got you there, son. This girl is smart and quick. She's going to keep us on our toes."

Travis sighed dramatically. "I'm sure of that, Nate."

When Rana excused herself to prepare for bed, Travis cautioned, "Watch what you say about Marissa, and don't mention the Kiowa attack. She could panic and bolt. Just a few more days, and I'll tell her everything."

"I'll be careful, son, but I sure am eager for her to learn she's my granddaughter. She's really settled down, hasn't she?"

"Yep, and I hate to have to upset her again." Travis did not tell Nathan that he hoped it was not an act on her part to disarm them. He knew what wily deceivers and artful pretenders women could be.

The following morning, Travis ordered Nathan and Rana to hang back while he checked the area where they would cross the Mormon Trail. As far as he could see in any direction, there was no one in sight. Satisfied, he rode back for Rana and Nathan. They were forced to go several miles out of the way to skirt a large lake and to find a place to ford the North Platte River. After riding on for miles and fording the South Platte River, they eventually came to the Oregon Trail. Again Travis told them to wait for his signal as he rode away to scout the area.

This time, Travis was gone for over an hour, causing Nathan and Rana concern over his safety. When he did return, they openly showed their relief, then noted that he was carrying several items of interest. Travis dismounted and dropped his findings on the ground. Rana and Nathan came forward to question him, curiously looking at the strange pile of possessions.

"There was trouble over there and not too long ago from the look of things. Four wagons were attacked by Cheyenne warriors. They were chased off by soldiers, probably from Fort Smith. They all left in a big hurry 'cause there wasn't any burial detail around and the Indians didn't recover their dead. They don't need these things anymore, so I took them. Rana, see if any of the clothes will fit you. If we meet up with other soldiers, it'll be best if you aren't dressed like that. Might inspire too many questions and too much time to answer them."

Rana sank to her knees while she and Travis looked through the dresses, shirts, pants, and shoes he had taken from three of the wagons. When they found several garments that seemed to be close to her size, Travis told her to change into them while he packed the others.

"She might have need of these pants and shirt later, so we'll keep them. You take these, Nate. Extra weapons might come in handy if one of ours breaks or we need some trade goods."

Nathan placed a pistol and ammunition in his saddle-bag, Travis concealed another knife in his right boot, and each secured a rifle to his saddle.

When Rana returned, her nose was crinkled in dismay and she was walking clumsily.

"What's wrong?" Travis inquired.

"The dress is fine, but the moccasins do not feel good."

"Shoes, Rana," he gently corrected her. "Let me check them." He looked and felt around each one, determining that they were slightly large. "Sit down," he instructed, then wrapped torn strips of material around her feet before putting on the shoes again. "That'll have to do until I can buy you a better pair. You said you could

213

use a bow and arrows, didn't you?" When she nodded, he handed them to her and said, "Keep these in case you need them later. Take this too," he added, handing her a larger knife in a fancily carved sheath. "When we get time, I'll teach you how to handle a gun and you can have the one I just gave Nate." He ripped off a ribbon from a dress that was too large for her and cut it in half. "Here. Tie your braids with these. Soldiers might wonder about those Lakota rosettes. Better hide that *wanapin* too. Let's get moving before those Cheyenne or the soldiers return." He packed the few supplies he had taken, then they mounted and rode away, leaving the discarded items behind.

Each day the weather became warmer and the days longer. When they camped on June ninth, Travis scouted the area thoroughly, then remained on full alert. Twice he left camp just to "take one more look around."

During the next two days, Travis ordered a more cautious pace, knowing they were only a few days' ride from Fort Kearny, the object of Crazy Horse's destructive design. They were too far out for hay gatherers or woodcutters from the fort, but not for patrols, especially during such intimidating times. Having learned that the Sioux and Cheyenne were determined to recover this area from the soldiers and homesteaders had made Travis wary and tense. He knew he could defend himself and escape danger, but he had Nathan and Rana to protect. He felt as if he were escorting them through a prairie fire with so much smoke that he could not accurately and swiftly determine which trail would lead to safety.

Sensing his concern as they sat around the fire that night, Rana coaxed, "Do not worry. We will reach home safety." Then, before she could stop herself, she asked, "Why did you leave your mother's camp and people? Did your heart feel strange stirrings returning to these lands?"

Travis focused his keen gaze across the river and nodded. Tomorrow they would be in Kansas, a day closer to the truth. "I know how much the Lakotas want to drive the white man from their lands. It cannot be, Rana, for they are strong and many and they have weapons that can slay a whole tribe or destroy an entire camp in a few hours." He did not tell her how the soldiers were using the six-year-old Gatling Gun, powerful cannons from the recent war, and dynamite, a new weapon that had been discovered last year, in order to drive the Indians off their ancestral lands and kill any resistors.

"I've lived with the white man and I know his power and greed. These lands must be shared, or the Lakotas will be pushed aside or killed. My mother's people have hunted on these lands for more winters than I can count. Her father, and her father's father, and his father have fought and died here; they are buried on the sacred mountain. Children have played and learned here. Victories have been celebrated. Enemies have been conquered and driven away. Laughter and songs have filled the air. This land is the Lakotas', and that too must pass. Once Grandfather smiled on his children; He gave us plenty to eat and protected us. Many times I rode into battle and returned with great honor. Then the white man came and wanted what was ours. Now the Lakotas must relent and change, or die. My words and fighting would change nothing, so it would be foolish to sacrifice my life for a battle already lost when the white man first set his eyes and heart on this land. My sons must be born free, where they can claim land to hunt and raise children and die in peace, a land where they will not be shamed for their mixed blood."

When he glanced at her, she was watching him with a tender expression that charged through him like a bolt of lightning. There was a deep, dreamy stare in her eyes that said she would withhold nothing from him. "I'll go check on the horses," he stated quickly, wondering why he was pouring out such private feelings and thoughts to her.

Rana grasped his arm to halt him. "Do not pull within yourself, Travis. How can I know you if you shield such feelings from me? You keep much a prisoner inside when there is comforting freedom outside. Is it wrong to share such feelings with your . . . sister?"

"Not wrong, Rana, just hard. I've never talked with anyone like this except Nate. Get some rest; it's late."

Rana watched Travis's defensive retreat, then turned to Nathan. "He carries much pain and many secrets inside his heart. Why did he leave his mother's people? Why did she marry a white-eyes?"

"I think it would be best if Travis answered those questions, Rana. The Indians gave him a hard time because he was a half-breed. That boy was hurt deeply and it isn't easy for him to talk about the past. If those Hunkpapas hadn't rejected him, he would still be a warrior. I'm glad they did, 'cause he would be fighting a losing battle. That's why we couldn't leave you there. If them Indians don't make truce with the white man, it's over for them, and Travis said they won't."

Lines of sadness marked her face. "He spoke the truth, Nate. My people will die before they yield their lands to the white-eyes."

"Your people are white, Rana," he gently reminded her.

"Only by birth. The Oglalas raised me and loved me, and my heart belongs with them. I was taught to hate and mistrust white-eyes, but I do not feel this way about you and Travis. I do not understand this, but I accept it. Where we go, are the white-eyes as you are?"

"It's like with Lone Wolf and Black Hawk, Rana; there're good and bad whites, like good and bad Indians.

216

But don't you worry none. You got me and Travis to take care of you. We'll be a family again."

Rana looked off toward the woods into which Travis had vanished. She went over his words and Nathan's as she drifted off to sleep. Sometimes she had trouble understanding their meanings, as when Nathan had spoken of "a family again." She knew she would have to listen carefully and work hard on her English before she reached their home.

Rana realized now how fortunate she had been that Soaring Hawk had captured and for several years had enslaved a white school teacher. She had been a spirited, resilient woman who had taught Rana many things, including the importance of having an independent, bold nature, which had proven so vexing to the men in her life. For now, she would not reveal the extent of her knowledge, for she felt she could learn a great deal about Travis and Nathan as they attempted to teach her what they thought she should know.

The next morning, they resumed a similar travel pattern. Just before their noon break to rest and eat, Travis detected signs that seized his attention. He moved off to have a closer look, leaving Rana and Nathan camped near Beaver Creek. He had chosen a spot where the creek grew wide and deep and was banked heavily on one side by trees, which would provide cover during his absence. He knew the Indian tracks he had spotted were fresh, and he wanted to trail the party for awhile to make certain they had not stopped nearby or were doubling back. Less than thirty minutes after Travis's departure, trouble struck.

Rana had been about to excuse herself when, through the underbrush, she saw the band of crudely dressed soldiers dismounting and making signals about surrounding their camp. Her heart pounded in fear, for she realized that soldiers would not attack other whites unless they were evil men bent on evil deeds. Evidently they had either sighted them farther back and had trailed them here or they had discovered their fresh trail and had tracked them to this point.

She hurried back to where Nathan was sipping his coffee and shook his arm frantically.

"Bad men come, Nate. We must prepare to fight. They sneak around us in the trees. This many," she told him, holding up seven fingers. "They carry short and long guns. I believe they plan to attack us."

Nathan tossed the cup aside and grabbed his rifle and ammunition from his horse. "Get behind those rocks and stay down," he ordered as he led his horse around the rocks to drop his reins near the creek bank.

Rana did the same with her beloved Cloud, then seized her bow and arrows before concealing herself. The large creek was at their backs, but trees that could offer the villains cover grew before and on either side of them. Anxiously she waited with Nathan.

A voice called out, "Just give us what money and valuables you have, then we'll be on our way. Ain't no need to fight and die here."

Nathan caught glimpses of dirty uniforms as the men fanned out before them, and he realized they were probably deserters. He knew the Army ranks were filled with men who were dodging justice, men who sought vengeance for the outcome of Mister Lincoln's war, and men who had been toughened by frontier perils and hardships and were conscience dead from years of fighting and killing. Still, he had to try to bluff them. He shouted in return, "You best git, boys. Soldiers will be here any minute now, and you don't want them to find you attacking and robbing innocent folks. Besides, we ain't got no money to give you."

"Then we'll take your horses and guns," the voice responded.

"And leave us afoot and weaponless in Injun territory? No way."

"Then we'll have to come and take 'em," the voice replied smugly.

"Then, by God, you try it!" Nathan called out bravely, knowing it was fight or die, or worse for his grand-daughter once these men got a look at her. He prayed Travis would return soon but knew he couldn't count on it. He glanced at Rana, who had dumped the arrows from the quiver and now had one poised for release. She smiled at him, warming his heart with her show of confidence and courage. "You know how to use it?" he asked.

"I can outshoot most warriors. I will help you battle them. We must fight or die. The Great Spirit will protect us and guide our aim."

Nathan grinned, for her words did not sound boastful, just honest. "Then let's give 'em a fight they'll remember."

When Nathan spotted movement to his side, he aimed and fired, winging and angering one of the men. Gunshots came from several directions at once. Nathan and Rana ducked their heads and waited for it to cease or slacken. The bullets glanced off the rocks with "pings" and "zings," sending broken chips flying here and there.

Rana peered around one rock, took aim, and caught her target in the center of his chest. She quickly seized another arrow and placed its nock on the bowstring. Since she had only six arrows, she would have to make each one count. She cautioned herself to be patient and alert. When she saw a man racing from one tree to another, she dropped to one knee beside the rock and fired at him, then swiftly flung herself behind the rock before the rapid firing of more bullets could strike her. From the man's scream of pain, she knew she had at least

219

wounded him. She laughed happily, then reminded herself that this was not a game she played.

Nathan warned, "Don't take chances like that, girl."

"We must get many of them before they rush us, Nate. When their courage or anger mounts, they will charge like furious buffalo. We cannot shoot that fast; they would capture us. We must show them we lack all fear and are skilled fighters."

"Darnit, Rana, you're just a young girl," he reasoned.

"Today, I am a warrior," she refuted, then grinned. She readied another arrow and peered around the rock. A burst of gunfire greeted her curiosity. This time when it lessened, she bounded to her feet and fired at the man wiggling toward them on his belly. He howled and rolled over as the arrow embedded itself in his neck.

At that same moment, Nathan fired several times but missed the swiftly moving target that changed positions as the man worked his way closer to them.

For a time, both sides held their fire and the silence grew loud around them. Rana strained her ears to hear every noise, knowing the silence meant danger. Suddenly gunfire came from both sides, causing Rana and Nathan to turn back to back to answer it. Nathan's horse panicked and raced off, but Rana's loyal steed held his ground, moving about nervously as he sensed the danger. Nathan experienced a surge of fear for the safety of his granddaughter and fired wildly into the trees. Rana released two arrows and one lethally found its target in the man whom she had wounded earlier. She withdrew her knife from its sheath then and placed it nearby, for she had only one arrow left.

Another burst of gunfire captured their attention, preventing them from seeing the man who had slipped into the creek and was working his way below bank level to flank them. Slowly and silently he crawled on his stomach up the bank and inched his way toward Rana,

220

knowing the old man, whom he assumed was her father or grandfather, would surrender once he grabbed the girl and put a knife to her throat. As the man neared Rana, something happened that he had not anticipated; Cloud reared, whinnied, and attacked him, for Rana's horse had been trained to defend her from peril.

Confusion broke out. The other men rushed them as Rana had predicted. Nathan fired, killing another one of their attackers just as he made a grab for Rana's arm. Rana accidentally discharged her last arrow when the man had grabbed her arm. Quickly she flung the useless bow aside, scrambled for her knife, and immediately engaged herself in a scuffle with the man who was being nipped by Cloud. During their fierce struggle, the knife was kicked out of her reach.

Several shots rang out and suddenly her beloved Cloud fell dead, his red blood standing out boldly against his white hide. For a time, Rana was frozen with shock and anguish, but she was spurred into action again when the dripping man lunged at her, sneering, "I'll get you, you little bitch."

Nathan's gun was empty and there was no time to reload. He grabbed the man as he shouted, "Run, Rana! Hide till Travis returns."

Rana knew the only way she could help Nathan and save herself was by securing another weapon. With men closing in on them from three sides, all she could do was fling herself over the rocks and make a dash for the weapon on the man who had fallen in the clearing. Nathan delivered a stunning blow into a wounded man's abdomen and quickly raced around the rocks to defend Rana's back and aid her escape. The three remaining men instantly pursued them.

"Back to back!" she called out to Nathan, tightly grasping the knife she had yanked from the dead man's sheath.

Nathan drew his own blade as he followed her clever suggestion, for flight had become impossible. The slender girl pressed her shoulders against Nathan's, standing poised for an attack that she thought would come quickly, though it did not. Her dress had been ripped and dirtied, and wisps of fiery hair had escaped her braids. To the men, she was a wild, stunning creature who provoked heady lust as they appreciatively and lewdly eyed her up and down, then grinned at each other.

"Well, well," the leader of the outlaw band murmured as he licked his lips in anticipation of having this entrancing vixen. "Looks like you got something more valuable than money or horses, old man. You two might as well give up, 'cause we ain't."

"*Sunka ska!*" Rana shouted, called him a white dog, then spat on the ground to show her contempt for them. She narrowed her wintry blue eyes to expose her determination to stand her ground and battle them. Surprise registered on the leader's face and he studied her once more.

"A white girl who speaks Sioux and uses a bow like that?" the second man called Curly queried suspiciously. "You men know what that means. Girl, if you weren't such a looker, we wouldn't touch none of them Sioux's leavings. How long was you their captive? You two escape them Injuns, or did the old man here trade for you?"

"You lay one finger on my granddaughter and I'll cut off your hand," Nathan threatened rashly, but Rana was too alarmed by their peril to take his slip seriously. "You boys best git while you can. When my grandson gets back with those soldiers, you'll be in deep trouble."

"You sure do talk big when the odds ain't in your favor, old man."

"What we jawin' and waitin' for? Let's take 'em. I got me a bad itch what needs scratchin'," announced the third man, named Buck.

"Me too," Curly agreed readily.

"Curly, you and Buck slow down. We ain't had this much fun in a long time. They can't stand there all day like that." The three men began to slowly, playfully circle Nathan and Rana, laughing and grinning and eyeing them like helpless prey in a steel trap.

Buck did not follow Fess's advice. "Come on, girly, let's me and you get to know each other better," he said and reached for her.

In the blink of an eye, Rana had reacted skillfully by cutting a long gash on Buck's arm. He howled in pain and retreated a few steps, glaring at Rana in disbelief. "You little savage," he sneered as he yanked his bandanna from his neck to wrap it around the gaping wound.

When Curly lunged forward Rana brought up her foot and kicked her new attacker in the groin. Almost with the same movement, she scooped up a handful of dirt and flung it into Buck's eyes. For a time, both men were disabled.

Nathan reacted spontaneously by throwing his knife into Fess's chest. Then he sprang forward to yank the blade from the man's body and stab him again. Enraged by Nathan's assault and his agony, Fess battled him with all his strength. Bloody blows were exchanged, and the men fell to the earth to continue their desperate struggle.

Before Curly could recover from the nauseating kick to his privates, Rana seized the dead man's rifle and delivered a staggering blow to Curly's jaw with the wooden butt. She heard bone and teeth shatter as the man fell backwards, trying to decide which injury to hold.

Buck had cleared his eyes enough to focus on the girl who was fighting them like a skilled soldier or a highly trained warrior. He grabbed her from behind and shook her back and forth as she kicked at his shins and clawed at his hands. "You dadburn wildcat. You're gonna be plenty sorry afore I finish with you." He whirled her around and landed a forceful slap across her flushed face, sending her staggering backward and to the ground. Buck made a diving leap on her before she could roll free, straddled her, and pinned her shoulders to the ground. He cursed as he tried to control the thrashing female.

Fess vowed coldly, "I'm gonna kill you, old man, after you watch what we're gonna do to that little bitch of yours."

Curly's head cleared and he ignored his pain in his attempt to get at Rana. He knocked Buck aside, shouting, "This gal is mine! She'll wish she'd stayed with them savages afore I let her loose," he threatened ominously as he flung himself on her. He imprisoned her hands beneath his legs and started slapping her and pulling her hair as he cursed her vulgarly.

Buck grabbed Curly's right arm and yelled, "Don't kill 'er afore we get to use her! You can punish her later. Let's git that dress off and git at 'er. She owes us plenty."

As Curly eased the pressure on her arms, Rana jerked them free and slammed her head into his broken jaw. In torment, Curly fell to his back and rolled wildly as his hands gripped his battered face.

Before Buck could seize Rana, Travis suddenly appeared behind him. He yanked him around and pounded him violently with both fists. Rana tried to stand to locate a weapon, but Curly's hands went around one ankle and impeded her search. Though she stomped on his arm and kicked his ribs, Curly held on tightly.

Travis hastily drew a knife from his boot and ended Buck's threat to anyone. As he moved to assist Rana, his keen eye caught Nathan's greater peril. Fess was hovering over the older man with a knife poised and ready to take Nathan's life. In what appeared to be one fluid movement, Travis dropped to one knee, drew his pistol, shot Fess, whirled on the ground, changed knees, yanked the second knife from his other boot, and threw it forcefully, striking Curly in the middle of his back before he could hit Rana again.

Except for the erratic respiration of the three weary survivors, deathly silence filled the clearing. Travis hurried over to Rana and asked, "Are you hurt?" His green gaze roamed her dirtied, bruised face, and he berated himself harshly for allowing such danger to befall her and Nathan.

Now that the threat had passed, reality set in on Rana. Her wide eyes scanned the area, taking in the death that surrounded them, death for which she was partly responsible. She had never killed anyone until today, and that realization staggered her senses. She looked at her bloody hands and ruined dress. Her face was sore and her body ached. She knew she looked terrible. The after-effects of facing such grim hostility and near-death struck her deeply. She was so far from home, in a land where evil whites lived and preyed on innocent people, and she was heading for a land where her new destiny loomed as a dark shadow over her head. Her control was sorely strained and she trembled and wanted to weep, but she hated to expose such fear and weakness. Without answering Travis, she walked around the rocks and stared at Cloud's body before sinking to the ground beside it. She stroked his head and neck as tears ran down her cheeks. *"Mahpiya, Mahpiya,"* she murmured in anguish, dropping her forehead to his neck to sob.

Travis and Nathan followed her and observed the tormenting scene. Travis fell to one knee beside her and gently stroked her hair as he said tenderly, "Come away from him, Rana. Don't punish yourself this way." He tried to pull her into his arms to comfort her. "I'm sorry, *micante*. I should have . . ."

Enveloped in anguish and consumed by belated shock,

225

Rana lifted a tear-streaked face and glared at him. Why was he always so loving and enticing at the wrong times? she wondered irrationally. She was not "his heart," for he had rejected her! She interrupted him coldly, "You should have protected us. Or returned to help us. *Mahpiya* is dead. I hate all white-eyes! Do not touch me again, half-breed!"

Chapter Eight

Travis winced from what seemed to him a just attack. He too felt he was to blame for permitting her injuries, for endangering her life and Nathan's, and for getting Cloud killed. Sadness and remorse etched lines into his darkly tanned face and dulled his emerald eyes. When Nathan gently grasped his shoulder and wisely suggested, "Leave her be awhile, son," Travis looked up at him and nodded.

The two men walked away to talk privately. Nathan recounted their fierce struggle, telling Travis how bravely and cunningly Rana had fought. "I have to confess, son, I was plenty scared for us."

Together they checked the area and found seven men dead, three by Rana's hand, which did not include the injuries she had inflicted on two of the last attackers. Travis knew she was experiencing shock from the encounter and grief over her loss, but still her sharp words had cut him deeply. He understood how she must be feeling and he longed to comfort her. If she had not been trained to defend herself by Lone Wolf . . . He shuddered, refusing to complete that horrifying thought.

"We'd better get this mess cleared away, Nate, and move on. We can't let nervous soldiers find Indian

227

arrows in these stinking deserters and blame the wrong side. I don't want innocent Cheyenne attacked because of these scum. You get cleaned up and pack your gear. You aren't hurt, are you?"

Nathan smiled warmly. "I'm fine, son. A little bruise here and there, but nothing to keep me down or still. You should have seen her in action, Travis. She put me to shame," he declared proudly.

"I saw part of it and my heart nearly stopped. When I heard gunshots, I couldn't get here fast enough. Then I didn't know who to help first. I didn't have much choice when I saw that knife gleaming over your head. I shouldn't have been gone so long."

"You can't be everywhere and do everything, son. If it weren't for Rana and you, I would be dead, so don't be so hard on yourself."

"If it weren't for you, Nate, I would have been dead seven years ago," Travis responded. "Nothing excuses my carelessness today. I knew how dangerous this area was, and I shouldn't have left you two alone. Evidently my instincts aren't as sharp as they used to be. There was a time when no man could sneak up on me," he stated in disgust.

Nathan examined Travis closely, for something was eating at the younger man. "You're bleeding, son. Let me bind that cut before we get busy."

Travis glanced absently at the wound, having forgotten about it. He knew it needed tending, so he did not reject Nathan's assistance. He removed his shirt and sat on a rock, his mind on the suffering girl.

"This isn't a knife cut, Travis. How did you get this wound? Nobody fired a gun except you," Nathan probed, suspicious.

"Like I said, Nate, my instincts are off these days. I caught up with those renegades, but they had doubled back on me. I was hit and lying on the ground before I

228

knew they were behind me. That's what took me so long to return."

Nathan realized that Travis's survival and return meant that he had fought and overcome his red-skinned assailants. "You're lucky you weren't killed. That proves you haven't lost anything. Except maybe a little pride," the older man added, chuckling.

"You always did think I was better than I am," Travis teased.

"Nope," Nathan argued earnestly. "You always think you're less than you are. You've got to remember, son, no man is perfect, but you're as close as they come to it. Not counting a few minor injuries, we're all safe and alive, and we have Rana with us."

"I suppose you aren't counting your . . . Rana's horse. She loved that animal, Nate. We'll have to take one of those men's."

"What about the rest of their horses?"

"We'll release them. We don't want to take anything branded or marked as property of the U.S. Army. When we reach the next fort, we'll tell them what happened and make an offer to buy the horse. At least we won't have to worry about Rana anymore. She's tougher and braver than I realized." While Nathan bandaged his arm, Travis closed his eyes and envisioned her valiant struggle against the two deserters.

When Nathan finished, Travis stood and tossed his shirt on the rock to allow the blood to dry. Then he began removing the telltale arrows from the men's bodies. He searched until he was holding the six he originally had given her. After replacing them in the quiver, he looked over at Rana, who had not moved from her prior position though she had ceased her crying. She was so still and quiet that she appeared to be sleeping; yet Travis knew she was not. "Rana, you need to choose another mount from those men's horses so I can saddle him and load

229

your gear. I'm sorry, but we have to leave quickly."

Rana pushed herself from Cloud's body and took one last look at him before standing to face Travis. "I wish to take back my cruel words to you. I spoke them when I was not myself. They were mean, and untrue. You are a skilled warrior of much honor and prowess. You have done all to protect us, and you saved our lives. I am ashamed for behaving as a hurt child. I ask forgiveness and understanding."

Relief filled Travis. "Thank you, Rana. That makes me feel better, but your words were true. I promised to keep you safe and happy. I failed. I was gone when you needed me and now your heart bleeds over *Mahpiya*'s loss. When we get home, I'll find you another special horse to take his place. Are you hurt anywhere?"

Her eyes grew misty at his soft words and sensitivity. She shook her head. "As with my brother, you carry a heavy burden to protect your family. It was wrong for me to add foolish weight to it. Do not be angry with me," she coaxed as her gaze went to his bandage and bloody arm. Concern darkened her eyes. "You are injured."

"It's fine. Nate took care of it. Do you want to wash and change clothes first or pick a horse to use?"

Rana checked her appearance. "I will choose the horse first," she replied reluctantly, wanting that necessary chore done quickly.

Rana and Travis walked to where the deserters had left their horses tethered. She looked at each of the seven mounts, then selected the best one. Travis grinned. "You'll make a good rancher 'cause you sure know good horseflesh. You constantly amaze me, woman."

Travis unsaddled the horse and led him to where Nathan was waiting. "I'll round up your horse while you and Rana get ready to ride. I doubt he ran far with his reins down."

After Travis left, Nathan turned his back while his

granddaughter bathed and pulled on another dress. Rana decided that it was not the time to question Nathan about the scars on Travis's chest and back or the Lakota *wanapin* around his neck. As she was brushing and braiding her hair, Nathan explained why Travis had been delayed and how he had been wounded. Rana was glad she had apologized before learning such facts, for her apology would mean more to Travis. She was beginning to understand why the man had such a disquieting effect on her and caused her to behave so impulsively . . .

Back in the Oglala camp, Chief Lone Wolf was meeting with several Hunkpapa leaders and warriors. His dark eyes slipped around the circle to halt briefly on Sitting Bull, Gall, and Dream Hunter. When news had reached their camp about the joining of Wild Wind to a half-blooded man named White Eagle/Travis Kincade, the Hunkpapas had ridden swiftly to confer with their Oglala brothers about this man. Lone Wolf had described Travis's visit in detail and had sat stoically as the war chief, Gall, had revealed White Eagle's past to him.

"You say White Eagle claimed innocence in his father's treachery. I say his actions in my camp prove he has no hatred for the Lakotas. Many winters passed that he did not return for the yellow rocks. I say Grandfather spared his life to help us this full moon. I saw only a man of great courage and prowess, a man of complete honor and truth. Grandfather sent him to the wooden tepee of my sister's people and brought him back to our lands to claim her as his wife. It is as it should be."

"His father's blood runs in his body, Lone Wolf. He has tricked you and betrayed you as his father did your Lakota brothers. Many died long ago. We must ride after him and punish him."

"His mother's blood also runs in his body, Gall. My

231

warriors rode with White Eagle to buy the guns, and they spoke of his courage and cunning. Others trailed him in secret when he rode from our camp. My warriors returned to say that he spoke to no enemy. He honored his words and bargain. He travels fast to return to his lands. I see why he was eager to ride like the wind; his Hunkpapa brothers wish to slay him for a black deed he did not do. Look into your hearts, my brothers. He lived and fought at your sides for eighteen winters. All tribes knew of his prowess and victories. Why did you turn your hearts against him? He has suffered much because you rejected him. I saw sadness in his eyes, then his joy to be in these lands once more, and finally there was new sadness that he could not remain. He was and is a good man. Grandfather protects him. Let this past evil die."

Dream Hunter nodded and concurred. "I say Lone Wolf speaks wisely and true. No warrior was braver than White Eagle. His *coups* were many and his heart strong and true. I say he was tricked by his father as the Hunkpapas were tricked. Many spoke against White Eagle while the pain of lost loved ones and the anger of his father's treachery burned fresh in their hearts and minds. I say that the heart of Charge-A-Buffalo and his words to White Eagle were evil. We must bury this deed."

Sitting Bull listened intently to each man before speaking. "A strange darkness seeks to cover the sky to keep sunshine from Grandfather's children and creatures. Evil rides behind this darkness, but its source is not White Eagle. White Eagle was touched by Grandfather. He has been sent to help his people and to show forgiveness for their blindness long ago. White Eagle was not our enemy then; he is not our enemy this moon. I gave White Eagle his name and *wanapin* when he returned to our camp when he was ten and six winters old. Even as a boy, he caused strange stirrings in my heart and visions in my head."

Sitting Bull drew on his redstone pipe before continuing. "When I had walked the face of Mother Earth twenty-five winters, I saw him in my visions as a mighty eagle who was forced to fly each sun and moon without rest. I saw a broken arrow, for he was of two warring bloods and could never know peace in our lands. When his father and people dishonored and betrayed him, he broke the war arrow and sought peace far away. In a later vision I saw the white eagle capture a thunderbolt with his talon, for his skill and courage were great. Around the eagle's neck I saw the *wanapin* of the War Bonnet Society. My visions have come to pass. White Eagle has found peace in another land. He returned when our Lakota brothers were painted with the War Bonnet markings. He gave them guns and supplies for defense and survival. As the thunderbolt, he has shown much power and magic. For his deeds, he earned a special *coup:* the sister of Lone Wolf, granddaughter to the man he now calls father and friend. Life is a mysterious circle like the sacred medicine wheel, my brothers. It was broken many winters past. It is whole again. We must leave White Eagle to his own destiny," Sitting Bull concluded with a wisdom that exceeded his thirty-six years.

Lone Wolf closed his eyes in relief, for Travis Kincade's destiny was now shared by his sister. He recalled the night he had revealed the joining demand to Travis and how the man had accepted the term with very little protest. He remembered the way Travis and Wild Wind had reacted to each other. Yes, he decided happily, all was as it should be. Suddenly sadness washed over him, for he knew then that he would never see Wild Wind again. He thanked the Great Spirit for the love and days they had shared. *Be free and happy, my little wildfire,* he prayed.

*   *   *

Travis, Rana, and Nathan rode over undulating prairie land that had been shaped by nature and held fast by endless miles of grass upon which buffalo and wild game grazed. They traveled over plains broken by occasional valleys or rolling hills. Sometimes they would not see enough trees to conceal one horse and rider, much less three of each. Other times they would ride past or through a heavy covering of them. The sky above remained a tranquil blue and the weather was glorious.

Nathan and Rana were cheerful and relaxed, having been drawn closer by their shared brush with danger and death. Rana tried not to think about the fate of her cherished white stallion, for his death meant one less bond with the Oglala people and her past life. She wondered if the Great Spirit was cutting all ties one by one as she rode toward her new life. She was dressed in white garments, riding a white man's horse, speaking the white man's tongue, living with two white men, and wearing her hair in one heavy braid down her back instead of two in the Indian style. Except for the possessions hidden in her saddlebag and the feelings in her heart, there was nothing left of her life in the Kiowa and Oglala camps. Already that world seemed so far away and long ago.

Each time their pace slowed, Nathan and Rana exchanged words quickly. Nathan had already begun to help her with English words and numbers, which he mistakenly believed she had forgotten over the years in the Indian camps. Each time they halted for a rest break or for Travis to dismount and look around, Nathan would drill Rana on what he had told her during their previous stops. Rana allowed the mostly unnecessary lessons to continue because Nathan was experiencing such pride in teaching her. She savored his patience and affection, and she enjoyed the way he bragged about her intelligence and determination to Travis, for impressing her husband thrilled her.

Nathan and Rana knew that Travis was still upset about what had happened to them the morning before. Both knew he expected a lot, perhaps too much, from himself, and they felt it would be best to leave him alone to work through his feelings.

Travis was tense and quiet, but not for the reasons they believed. His keen eyes cautiously scanned their surroundings, and he allowed nothing to distract his intense concentration today. His astute senses were constantly gathering information, studying it, sorting it, and remembering it. His entire body felt on edge, every nerve on full alert. Even his skin seemed to prickle in warning, as if everything he was or had learned was warning him of the presence of evil. His perceptions were so forceful that his body remained constantly taut, his eyes narrowed, and his teeth clenched. Anyone who knew anything about this area and its people would recognize signs of impending peril along the way, signs— both Indian and white—he had been sighting and reading all day.

Travis hoped that Nathan and Rana did not realize how worried he was, even though he had cautioned them to stay close to him and ready to respond to his orders rapidly. He had been taught trail signs and the language of blankets and feathers, and he had not forgotten them. No one could make nature speak as clearly or as loudly as the Indians. He could tell the tribe an Indian was from simply by looking at his moccasin print. He knew how to read markings, attachments, and positions of feathers to learn how a warrior had earned his *coups* and how he was ranked. He could send or interpret smoke signals. But today, it was the trail signs that disquieted him.

From the signs left behind with artfully arranged stones, deftly bound bunches of grass and carefully positioned sticks and cuttings on tree bark, Travis knew

235

where the Indians were going, when they had passed this area, how many were in the hunting or raiding parties, and what their intentions were. It looked as if Kansas would be more dangerous traveling than either Dakota or Nebraska.

When they camped for the night, Travis waited for Rana to excuse herself before telling Nathan, "We'll make Fort Wallace a little past noon tomorrow. I want you and Rana to camp near the fort while I do some checking around. Try to discourage anybody from approaching and talking to you two. But if you get visitors, make sure she understands that everyone will be told you're my father and she's my wife. I don't want any contradictions or slipups." To make sure they each told the same story, Travis went over the details once more.

"There's been a lot of fighting going on in this area for the past year, Nate, and it's going to get worse during the summer. While you and Rana get some rest, I'll nose around the fort and see what I can learn. With any luck, I can trade that Army horse for another one and pick up a few supplies. Try to keep Rana hidden as much as possible. She's a beautiful and tempting female, and some of these men haven't seen or had a woman in ages. We don't want anybody dogging us when we leave Fort Wallace."

Rana awoke several times during the night to find Travis's bedroll empty more often than not. When she stirred at dawn, it was empty once more. She quietly slipped from her sleeping mat and went to seek him. By then, it was obvious to her that Travis had been constantly scouting the area. She remembered his fierce concentration during the last day and a half, recalling how many times he had dismounted to study the trail. She had been distracted by her grief over Cloud's loss and her learning games with Nathan, which had revealed the older man's kindness, admiration, and patience. From

236

now on, she would pay closer attention to the trail and to Travis's grave concern, for she already knew most of the things Nathan was trying to teach her. She reasoned that when a man of great courage and prowess became quiet and alert, it could only mean trouble or danger.

Rana was slipping through the trees, looking right and left for a sign of Travis. When she halted to listen for a clue to his location, she heard nothing. As she turned to head back for camp, she was confronted by a broad chest. Inhaling sharply, she stepped backward in astonishment as she found Travis standing within inches of her. "You drift as silently as a shadow and as secretly as a calm wind. I did not hear you move or breathe. I am happy you are not an enemy, for my hunting skills have dulled."

Travis grinned as he told her, "If you could hear me and see me, then you would be the better hunter and warrior. Is it not best for me to have keener instincts and skills? You have proven yourself in battle, but I have no *coup* feathers to give you." He eased out of the Indian speaking style when he murmured, "I'm proud of you, Rana. Every place has its bad men and perils, including Texas; so I'm relieved you know how to defend yourself and can fight with us. It's good to find a woman who has a generous heart and a smart mind. Most of the ones I've met are deceitful, selfish bi . . . women who only think about themselves and couldn't fight their way out of an empty barn. You're very special, and I hope you stay that way."

Rana wondered if there were clues in his insults about women that might explain his continued distance from her. If so, she decided, this was not the time to explore them. She tucked away that piece of information, declaring, "I am glad I do not displease you, Travis Kincade. In time we will come to know each other, for you are unlike other men I have known. It is good to find a man with a strong heart who thinks of others before himself and is unafraid to show gentleness when others need it. I was seeking you to ask questions. Why do you fear for our safety? Do the marks on the trail worry you? What do they say?"

"I'll explain tonight. When we reach Fort Wallace after the sun is high, I'm going to speak with the soldiers. I don't want you to be afraid, but you must be careful. When I return, I'll explain our situation. Promise me you'll stay with Nate and obey him."

"But the bluecoats are enemies," she protested fearfully.

"Not anymore, Rana. You're part of the white world again. Unless we're careless, nobody will discover our secrets. Most people think I'm half-Spanish, not Indian."

"What is Spanish?" she inquired.

"You know how the Lakotas look and speak and act different from the Mandans or Arikaras or other Indian nations. The Spanish are one of the white nations. Texas has plenty of Spanish or half-Spanish people. I blend in without any trouble. You will too if you don't do or say anything to expose your past."

"Will the whites despise me for living with the Indians?"

"Most whites would rather see a woman die than become an Indian captive. They wouldn't understand or believe your situation, so keep quiet about it," he advised seriously.

"I will do as you say, but it will be hard. For many winters I was taught to hate and mistrust whites. I have forgotten what it is to live or be white. You and Nate must teach me such things again."

"We will, Rana," he promised, then smiled at her. "Let's get back or Nate will start to worry about us," he suggested, wary of the enticing solitude and her compelling nearness.

Later, as they neared the fort, they met several

238

scouting and working details, which they passed without any problems. Travis was glad he had told Rana to dress in the pants and an over-sized shirt and to trap her flaming hair beneath a floppy hat. But these devices only concealed part of her beauty and shapely figure. He could not help but notice how the men who came close to them eyed her with looks of intrigue and admiration. Twinges of jealousy and possessiveness assailed him once more.

Travis halted and suggested they make camp within sight of Fort Wallace, assuming it would be safe to leave them alone this close to the voice of white authority and power. Before riding off, he reminded Nathan and Rana of their instructions, then led Rana's borrowed horse after him to explain why they had it. He hoped the commanding officer would feel obligated to let them keep it or to replace it.

Upon reaching the fort he dismounted and tied both sets of reins to a hitching post, then walked to the officer's quarters. Once inside, Travis learned that the commanding officer was at Fort Harker at a meeting with other post commanders. To the officer left in charge, he explained the trouble on the trail and turned over the personal possessions of their attackers to provide clues to the deserters' identities. The man was annoyed by the purpose of Travis's visit, for it meant reports to officials and letters to the deserters' homes. He called in one of his men, a corporal, and told him to locate a horse that Travis could buy at a reasonable price. Then he thanked Travis insincerely and dismissed him. As Travis left with the dusty corporal, he heard the officer in charge grumbling to himself about too much work, not enough pay, and several other disadvantages to Army life in the West.

The man led Travis to a small corral and told him to take his pick of the aging beasts for ten dollars. Travis glanced at the animals and scowled.

"The stallion one of your men shot was worth more

239

than every horse you have on this fort. There isn't a mount in this corral that would last three days. You find me a decent horse and I'll pay you twenty dollars and throw in a rifle for your trouble. It's a long way to Texas, and I don't want my wife walking or riding double. I hold the Army to blame for our problem and I expect you to handle it fairly."

The offer of ten extra dollars and a rifle caught the man's interest. He thought about some horses that had been delivered two days ago but had not been branded "U.S. Army" yet. Smiling greedily, he told Travis to follow him to another corral. As they were walking, the brawny corporal began to talk freely and genially to this man who was going to help him exist more comfortably until the next payday.

"I hear you boys been having lots of Indian trouble over this way," Travis remarked evocatively.

"Yep," the man replied as he rolled a wad of chewing tobacco around before settling it on the left side of his mouth. "Them Dog Soldiers and Sioux been giving us fits since last summer. If you ask me, they're trying to take back Kansas and Colorado. Shame we can't set 'em to fighting themselves like we did those Cheyenne and Pawnee. Long as they're fighting each other, they can't fight us."

"How did you pull a trick like that?" Travis inquired with a grin.

"The Army's been giving the Cheyenne guns to make raids on the Pawnee camps. Soon as they kill 'em off, we'll light into the Cheyenne. Hell, if we could get rid of Tall Bull and Roman Nose, them Cheyenne wouldn't know how to plan an attack. General Sheridan's planning a big campaign to settle ever'body's troubles out here. He's got us guarding the settlements and roads till he gets his strategy together. After what he did to the South a few years back, ain't no doubt he'll have these savages under

240

control by spring."

"If you have enough men left to fight by the time he gets here," Travis added, then chuckled deceptively. "From the way it sounds, you've been losing a lot of men, to Indians and deserting."

"I guess you heard about Fetterman and his defeat. Lost over eighty men in that battle. That don't include two whole detachments wiped out this past winter. When Colonel Custer passed through here not two weeks past, he found eleven cavalrymen slaughtered less than twenty miles from the fort. Circling buzzards lead 'im to the bodies. Weren't no pretty sight neither." The corporal went on to describe in detail the incident that inspired the warning, "Save the last bullet for yourself."

"Custer? Is he fighting in these parts?" Travis questioned, having heard colorful war tales about that particular man. Travis himself had not fought in a war that had had nothing to do with him.

"Yep. Seems like the Army is sending every ex-Union officer it can find out here. I suppose they think they can tame the West like they did the South. 'Course Custer's in a might of trouble these days. These last months he's been ripping up and down the Republican River trying to whip them savages or send 'em running. Guess he found out them Injuns fight harder and dirtier than them Rebs. Once he got into Colorado near them gold mines, he had men deserting in packs like hungry wolves. He was so mad he sent troops after 'em, and he caught some of 'em. We wuz told he made his regiment march a hundred and fifty miles in less than three days, hardly givin' 'em time to take a piss. Word is he's been placed under arrest for a list of charges long as my johns. I don't know if he's the biggest fool or the bravest man I ever met."

They reached the corral and Travis smiled as he eyed these new mounts. "Take your pick," the corporal offered. "Where you heading in Texas?"

241

"Pa and me got a ranch near Fort Worth. My brother was serving in the Army up in the Dakota Territory and got himself killed by a Sioux named Crazy Horse. Me and pa went up to fetch his widow. She was so pretty that I married her before we left the fort."

"That's what I call taking care of your family real proper. Good thing she was willing, weren't it?" the man teased, then winked.

"With no money or family, she didn't have much choice. Besides, I can be mighty persuasive when need be," he replied mirthfully.

The corporal laughed heartily. They talked on for a time as Travis craftily enticed more news from the corporal. After the deal was struck, Travis walked to the sutler's post for a drink and to see if he could pick up more information. He also wanted to buy Rana a pair of shoes.

As he was leaving, the corporal told him, "You head straight for Fort Dodge, then Fort Cobb, and you should miss them Cheyenne and Pawnee bickerings around Fort Larned. Them commissioners are trying to work out a treaty at Medicine Lodge and Fort Laramie. They're just wasting their time; ain't no treaty with savages gonna last."

Travis thought to himself that it wasn't any wonder, considering the massacres taking place at innocent, helpless villages like the one at Sand Creek, which was less than seventy miles from Fort Wallace. The Indians had been given no reason to trust the white man or to believe his paper treaties. At least the Indian "Dog Soldiers" were raiding and fighting northeast of them, for they were the ones Travis wanted to avoid the most.

Quickly returning to camp, Travis related the news to Rana and Nathan, withholding only tragic or alarming facts. "Nate, I think it would be best if we kept a guard posted tonight. I wouldn't put it past those Indians to

242

send a few scouts to this area. This fort is almost sitting in the middle of nowhere, in the middle of their territory. Rana, why don't you keep a sharp eye while Nate and me take a nap. Nate can take the first night watch and I'll take over at midnight. Then we'll all have enough rest to be able to head out at first light."

Rana was delighted to be a part of Travis's plans, and she was pleased that he thought so highly of her skills. Before he could lie down, she insisted on checking and rebandaging his injury. She was pleased to find that the flesh wound was healing quickly, just as she was pleased by the brown ankle boots in soft leather that he had purchased for her.

Fortunately the night passed without any problems and at dawn they were already heading south. Travis kept on constant alert and set their pace accordingly. They covered a lengthy distance that day, halting to camp near Ladder Creek just as dusk dropped its shadows over the land. As he and Nathan had previously agreed, this would be the night of truth for Rana.

While Nathan and Rana set up the camp and prepared their meal, Travis scouted the area in all directions. Satisfied that it was safe, he returned to camp to sit quietly and apprehensively.

When everything had been cleared away and the three were sitting on mats near the campfire, Travis ventured hoarsely, "Rana, Nate and I have a few things to tell you. I'm not sure where to begin, so I'll let Nate start by telling you about his daughter, Marissa. Please, just hear us out and stay calm," he advised mysteriously.

Rana looked from one man to the other, then settled her quizzical gaze on Travis. "I do not understand. What troubles you?"

"Please, this is important to all of us. Listen to Nate's words and trust us," Travis coaxed worriedly, dreading her reaction.

243

Rana focused her attention on Nathan. Slowly and painfully he described his daughter's past: Marissa's years on the ranch, her wild and impetuous ways, her willful marriage to Raymond Michaels, what Nathan knew of their life together, and her last visit home. As he told her of Marissa's child, Rana began to fidget and breathe erratically, but still she held silent. He told Rana how Marissa and Raymond Michaels had been murdered and how his granddaughter had been kidnapped by the Kiowas. He told how he had looked for her for years, and finally had been forced to give up his futile search. He related the details of Thomas Mallory's visit and its enlightening results. He described Rana's birthmark and the scar she had received while visiting his ranch. "I'm your grandfather, Rana. My daughter, Marissa Crandall, was your mother. You used to play with that necklace when you were a little girl," he remarked when he noticed her rubbing it nervously between her fingers as she had done so long ago. He was glad Travis had repaired it and that she had agreed to wear it again. "Your mother left it at the ranch before she died. All these years I've hoped and prayed you were alive somewhere and that I would find you again. When I saw the painting of you, I cried with joy. Travis and I couldn't leave Texas fast enough. We came to the Oglala camp to find you and to bring you home where you belong. You're safe now, Rana. No one will ever hurt you again. Isn't that right, son?"

Rana whirled to look at Travis as he urged her to accept Nathan's shocking words. Many thoughts and images filled her head and conflicting emotions assailed her. They had lied to her and tricked her! This older man was her grandfather by blood and birth . . . Travis was his "son"? No, that was only an affectionate name, she decided. Travis was a Kincade, part Indian from the Lakota lands. She eyed him intently, for his part in her life intrigued her most. She was his "mission?" All along he had come after her . . . She remembered his starting to call her Rana several times and the way he had attempted to question her about her past and memory. He had told her that "mistakes and evil deeds" could be changed or corrected. Were they telling her the truth? How could this be happening after all these years?

Nathan described Marissa and stressed how much Rana favored her deceased mother. "You're my flesh and blood, Rana. How could I not come after you and do anything necessary to get you back? It was too dangerous for you to live there. You don't belong with Indians."

These revelations stunned her, and her heart drummed rapidly. She tried to resist the unexpected news. She was being taken away from all she had known and loved; and now he was telling her incredible things that denied even that reality. According to his words, she was not heading for a new destiny; she was returning to an old one that strangely frightened her, though she could not remember why. "Did you tell Lone Wolf these lies? Is that why he gave me to you? You tricked me," she accused.

Travis tried to explain his talk with Lone Wolf and their decisions, but as he had suspected, they did not sound logical or reasonable now. "We did what we had to do to get you free, Rana. Your grandfather loves you. He wants you to be safe and happy. Please understand."

Just like that, they had ridden into her life and were trying to change all she knew and was! Why would they speak such false tales? she wondered. "I do not understand. How can he love me? We are strangers. I am not his Rana Michaels. I am Wild Wind. I will return to my people."

"I can't let you do that, Rana. As with the other tribes, the Oglalas will soon be herded like cattle onto reservations where freedom and privacy don't exist but

245

poverty and disease do. Oglala spirit will die in captivity. That's no life for you. How long do you think it would take before soldiers or Indian agents found a way to get at you? They would force you to do whatever they wanted, and you'd have to do it to protect your people. If the Oglalas did resist reservation life or rebel against it later, all they would be able to do would be run and hide or fight and be killed. I've been on the run before; it's nothing but hardship, pain, and death. We didn't want that kind of misery and peril for you. Search your heart and head, and you'll know Nate speaks the truth. Don't be afraid to trust us and accept us. You belong on the ranch with us."

She glared at Travis. "You did not come to help my people. You came to steal me. You lied. You tricked me and betrayed me."

"Only because the Oglalas made it necessary. They said we could not trade for you and take you away unless I joined to you. It was to keep the other warriors who wanted you from challenging our rightful claim on you. You are Rana Michaels! You're white, and Nate is your grandfather!" he stormed forcefully at her.

"What coward lurks inside your body, White Eagle? Why do you wait until this moon to tell me such things, if they are true?"

"Because we knew how you would react, just like you're doing. We wanted to be far away from the camp so you wouldn't try anything crazy like escaping. And we wanted to give you time to get close to us so you wouldn't be afraid. How can you be angry because your family has finally found you and you're going home? You should be happy about this news. I know it was wrong to trick you, and I'm sorry. It just sounded right and easy at the time," he admitted.

"That's why you gave my people those guns and supplies? That's why you asked for me in trade and joined to me falsely? Your words and deeds do not match, coward with a dark heart!"

Her words rankled and he scoffed, "Wild Wind was known for her disobedience and stubbornness. I did it so we could get you free and take you home with the least amount of trouble and time. There's a bloody war going on in that area, and we have a ranch to take care of. I wanted to get you and Nate out quickly and safely. And I didn't marry you falsely, because our joining isn't legal to whites, and we're white. When you want to marry, you can choose your own husband, not be traded to a man like a possession. You're free, Rana. Just like your mother, you can come and go as you please, and probably will."

"You did not like my mother?" she probed defensively.

"I never knew your mother. I've only seen her portrait."

"I do not understand. Nate calls you son," she pressed hesitantly.

Her words and expression surprised Travis, who stared at her oddly. Suddenly he grinned roguishly as he shook his head and responded, "No, Rana, I'm not your uncle by blood, but I am by law. Nate adopted me as his son years ago, like Soaring Hawk adopted you as his daughter. My legal name is Travis Kincade Crandall, but most people know me as Travis Kincade. Your mother, Marissa, was Nate's only child. During the first year after we met, Nate and I became best friends; we're like a real family now. I've been living with him for seven years and working on his ranch as his foreman. I helped him get you back because I love him and I thought I was doing the right thing for him and for you. You're smart enough to understand what we're telling you; open your heart and accept the truth. All we're asking for is a chance to correct the past. You have a home and a family. We risked our lives to claim you. Is this news so offensive?"

"Travis is like a real son to me, Rana. I begged him to

247

help me get you back. I'm sorry we all tricked you. Travis didn't want to lie to you or marry you falsely; he did it for me and for you. The Indians made those demands and we didn't have time to argue. We were forced to go along or they wouldn't have let us have you. I was planning to give Travis my ranch until I discovered you were still alive. With Marissa dead, you two are all the family I have. When I die, I want the two of you to share the ranch. Will you come home with us? Will you give us a chance to make you happy? Will you try to understand and forgive us? All we wanted was you, my little Rana."

Rana watched the older man as he spoke. Had she discovered who she was at last, and where she had come from? she asked herself, wondering what these changes would mean to her. Nathan had touched and warmed her heart with his tale of suffering and dreams, but anger and fear had lodged there too. She thought about Travis, in light of this revelation. If she was Nathan's granddaughter, and she suspected she was, it would explain why Travis had refused to touch her, despite the fact that he desired her and felt married to her in his Indian heart. No doubt, after hearing those awful tales about her, he had expected to dislike her and to find her easy to resist. He had planned to ride in, make a trade for her, then hand her over to her grandfather. The situation had turned on him because of Lone Wolf's terms, and this intrigued her. Now Travis was caught in a painful trap—which served him right for deceiving her, she decided. He had teased her and tempted her with his kisses and gazes; now she could do the same to punish him, for he had no hold or power over her. Perhaps he too should be forced to learn a few things and to make a few changes . . .

"I will think on your words and deeds before I speak what is in my heart. This should not have been kept secret from me," she declared aloud.

Travis quickly concurred. "You're right, Rana, but

248

that can't be helped now. We made a mistake. We've apologized and explained, so there's little more we can do. I know you've endured many dangers and changes lately, and you've been facing them bravely and with skill. We're very proud of you. But I wonder how much you learned from the Oglalas. Did you learn about patience and self-control? Are you smart enough to understand more than you can see? Or brave enough to face a new life? You've proven you have the courage and cunning to fight like a warrior, but can you behave like a woman? Can you feel and show love and kindness? Are you wise enough to accept what you know is true? And generous enough to offer us a truce and understanding? I said you were very special. I hope I wasn't wrong."

Chapter Nine

For the next few days, Travis watched the trail signs closely to keep them away from peril and people. From the evidence he found along the way, it seemed the Cheyenne and Pawnee were fighting bitterly over the land that had not as yet fallen under the control of the settlers or soldiers. He wished the Indians knew how the whites were duping them into killing off each other, for this was not the time for intertribal wars; this was a time to declare a truce in order to battle the more lethal enemy of both tribes. While the Indians were becoming fewer and weaker, the whites were increasing their numbers and strengths. Each year, more forts were being constructed on the Great Plains, more soldiers were being sent, and more settlers were arriving.

After crossing the Sante Fe Trail and the Arkansas River, they skirted Dodge City and Fort Dodge because Travis had no idea how Rana would act among people, and he did not trust her to be left alone with Nathan. As he had been with Marissa, Nathan was becoming too lenient with Rana, for he was blinded by his feelings for her. Nathan did not believe she could do anything wrong, and he would never have corrected her if she had because he was too happy to have recovered her and feared losing her again. He had become totally enchanted by his granddaughter, and Travis prayed this girl would not hurt Nathan as her mother had.

They passed near the Crooked Creek battle site and, on June twentieth, camped just inside what was now called Indian Territory, which would one day become the state of Oklahoma. It had been forty-seven days since they had left Texas, twenty-three days since the joining ceremony, seventeen days since they had left the Oglala camp, and five days since Rana had been told the truth about herself.

Travis did not know what to think about the exquisite redhead with steely blue eyes, for she had been behaving in a most unexpected manner, like a perfect lady or a misplaced angel. Having been told of Wild Wind's turbulent past by Lone Wolf and having witnessed her temper and willfulness in action, Travis was now suspicious of her sunny attitude and obedient demeanor, though he was pleased by her friendliness and compliance where Nathan was concerned. He found himself watching her furtively, day and night, as if she were a hot kettle that was simmering cleverly without giving off alerting steam, a kettle that he knew could burn one badly if it were touched in the wrong place. Travis felt that it would be very much in character for Rana to seek punishment or revenge—however small—for the trick they had played on her, a trick for which he seemed to be taking the brunt of the blame rather than being able to share it with Nathan and Lone Wolf. If this little wildcat were as conniving as most women he had met, he mused, she would bide her time until the right moment presented itself. He had advised, almost demanded, that she trust them; yet he did not fully trust her, for it did not seem to be Wild Wind's nature to allow herself to be tamed so quickly or easily.

Each day Travis had waited for the ground to slip from

beneath him but he could do nothing more than speculate on the type of retaliation she might take. He wished he could detect some hint of a scheme so he would be better prepared to thwart her. In about eight or ten days, they would reach the Rocking *C* Ranch. Between here and there, they would cross more plains and prairies, an occasional rocky slope, rolling hills, several rivers, and vast Indian lands. It was these Indian lands to which Travis's attention and thoughts were drawn now as they made camp for the night.

Indian Territory had been chosen long ago as the relocation sight for the "Five Civilized Nations" from the South: the Cherokee, Creek, Choctaw, Seminole, and Chickasaw. In 1834, this entire region had been divided among these tribes, and each tribe had been assured of its ownership and authority over a certain portion of the area. During the recent North/South war, most of these tribes had sided with the Confederacy because so many of them owned slaves. Afterward, in 1866, the Government began forcing new treaties on the five nations, compelling them to cede parts of their assigned territories to the United States to be used as homes for other Indians they planned to relocate, as if their objective were to bunch all Indians into one area where they could be watched and controlled carefully and easily. The Government was, perhaps intentionally, overlooking one major problem: the Plains Indians did not like other Indians claiming their ancestral territories, especially with the help of the whites.

Travis had decided that maybe it was all a clever plot to reduce the numbers of Indians and their tribes by placing them in bloody conflict with one another, for the woodland Indians from the South had no training against the awesome skills and prowess of the Plains warriors, who were determined to hold on to their sacred lands and hunting grounds. He wondered how long it would take before everyone, Indian and white, realized that re-located Southern tribes could not coexist peacefully with the fierce Plains tribes of the Kiowa, Cheyenne, Arapaho, Comanche, and Apache Nations. He felt certain the U.S. Government would never honor the treaty they were offering the Sioux, which promised to transform most of Dakota into the Great Sioux Reservation, for that area was too rich in grazing lands and gold. The Medicine Lodge Treaty Council was scheduled to be held in Kansas within a few weeks and the Fort Laramie Peace Talks were to take place in Wyoming in the spring; Travis won-dered how much, if any, difference those papers and promises would make, for he was very much aware that flowery words seldom changed ingrained feelings.

Because the Cheyenne were longtime friends and allies of the Lakotas, Travis often thought about the Cheyenne leaders he had met and had ridden with, some before he had left the Hunkpapas and some afterward. During this present journey, he had learned many new things about these men. He knew that Tall Bull and Black Kettle wanted peace with the whites and survival for their people, as did so many Indians these days. Unlike many of the "Dog Soldiers," as the whites called members of the Cheyenne Dog Men Society who were some of the most highly trained and skilled warriors who had ever existed, Chief Black Kettle was willing to accept the white man's peace treaty and go to a reservation. The leaders of the Dog Soldiers—Tall Bull, White Horse, and Bull Bear—only wanted peace; they were proud men who would never sacrifice their freedom and honor; they were not men who could laze around a reservation. No, Travis reflected, like the Lakota branch of the Sioux Nation, the Cheyenne Dog Soldiers would battle Indian and white to retain their lands and dignity. Travis felt that these Cheyenne leaders were too smart and honorable to kill off the Pawnee for the devious white man and, he decided, if he were given the opportunity to see them, he would tell them so!

During the next few days they would be traveling through the area that had been given to the Creeks, with whom the whites had made a strong treaty. Therefore Travis assumed they would not be facing any problems. If everything went as he planned, they should reach the Fort Cobb Agency within the next few days.

Travis sat near the campfire and sipped his coffee while pretending to ignore Rana, who was talking and laughing with Nathan. Every time they had stopped to rest or camp for the night, Rana and Nathan had worked together on chores or her education. The older man was teaching her about English words and numbers and had promised to teach her to read, spell, and write when they reached home. He also told her he would explain about money and shopping and would take her into town to let her practice her new skills. They used sticks, rocks, or knives and the ground to write their "lessons." When they were not studying, Nathan would relate facts about the ranch and hired hands, Fort Worth, their neighbors, her parents, Rana's childhood, and her visits to the Rocking C Ranch. Gradually Rana was able to associate her captive teacher's lessons with those Nathan provided and she began to be amazed at how much she was remembering and learning. And as Rana's knowledge and determination increased, both she and Nathan seemed to enjoy themselves more and draw ever closer.

Travis secretly observed the vivacious creature whose laughter and voice sent tremors over his weary body and called every nerve to attention. He noticed the way her grayish blue eyes sparkled with life and excitement, and the way the corners of her mouth curled playfully when she smiled. In the firelight, her skin reflected a vibrant, healthy glow, as did her long curls. He wanted to bury his hands in that thick mane of golden-red hair and tease strands of it beneath his nose. He wanted to feel her cotton-soft lips against his. His eager gaze savored them for a moment before traveling lower. Evidence of her battle with the deserters had vanished. Her lithe arms and legs, which appeared sleek and golden in the flickering light, were revealed to his scrutiny from her careless position on her furry mat. He yearned to let his hands wander over them with his eyes closed and his senses unrestricted. But his hands and lips craved more; they itched to explore every inch of her enticing body. Damn, what potent magic and temptation was sitting only a few feet from him! he cursed in frustration as he shifted from a position that was becoming uncomfortable. It was reckless to sit there watching her and hungering for her until his body ached for hers!

Travis attempted a casualness he did not feel as he left his sleeping roll and headed toward the surrounding trees. He walked to the nearby Cimarron River, yanked off his clothes, and slipped into the water. The weather was warm, but the water was still cool, especially at this late hour. He thought to himself that, with luck, maybe it would chill his passions and cool his temper. He needed to relax, and to get Rana Michaels off his mind. He had done his part to help her and Nathan; the rest was up to them. Maybe he was feeling a little jealous and left out; those two were so wrapped up in each other that they hardly noticed he was around. It sounded crazy, but he felt lonesome even in their presence! He dared not join them for fear of offending Rana and causing her to pull back from her grandfather while trying to avoid him. She had barely looked at him or spoken to him since they had had that enlightening talk with her. Funny, but he missed the way things had been going between them. The more he was around her, the more he wanted to get to know her, the more he wanted her.

Travis eyed the faint glow of their campfire, confident that he had made certain no one was around to spot it. He swam downriver then, into the shadows near the other bank, and nonchalantly draped his arms over a fallen tree. He envisioned Rana lying in the glow of dying flames, the colorful light dancing mischievously on her flesh and hair. He closed his eyes and fantasized about her beckoning him with a sensual glance and parted lips. He would leisurely remove her garments and lower his naked body to hers. His lips would drift playfully over her eyes and ears before slipping down her throat and . . . His body began to respond to his provocative thoughts. But it did not matter how much he desired her, he told himself, because she was Nathan's granddaughter. Perhaps it was her resemblance to Nathan that had touched him and softened him. With Nathan's looks and blood, surely she could not be wicked. Yet Marissa had been, his keen mind debated.

Hellfire, what did he know about women, he fumed, except bad things? After his problems with Elizabeth Lowry and Pretty Rabbit and Clarissa Caldwell's grasping pursuit, the last thing he needed was more female trouble. As with the selfish and conniving Indian maiden, the perfidious and vindictive Elizabeth Lowry had nearly gotten him killed, and the avaricious Clarissa Caldwell wanted the Rocking C Ranch as much as—if not more than—she wanted him. Then there was all that nasty gossip about Marissa . . . Were all women vain, selfish, deceitful, insensitive bitches? he wondered sullenly.

Considering the bad blood she might have inherited from her parents, Rana could be similar to the others. But if that assumption were accurate, he too could have been poisoned by his father's evil blood. If only he could understand Rana or see what was lurking inside that clever head. If only he knew how much like Elizabeth, Clarissa, Pretty Rabbit, and Marissa she was . . .

Rana looked at the deeply slumbering Nathan and

257

smiled. He appeared so kind and loving, asleep or awake, and she was learning so much about him, from him. He was a giving, generous person. Over the years since her mother's murder and her abduction, this man must have suffered terribly, she thought compassionately. Not knowing a loved one's fate would surely be sheer agony. Her grandfather had had no way of knowing how lucky she had been after her second capture. While she had been living happily and freely with the Oglalas, her dear grandfather had been existing on torment and loneliness and fear, at least until Travis Kincade had entered his life. She could not truly imagine the anguish her grandfather had endured long ago, and she could not bring herself to cause him more pain and sadness now. In fact, he wanted to do everything she could to make up for those lost years.

Rana knew Nathan had spoken the truth about her identity and the past. She believed he sincerely loved her and wanted her to return home with him. She could see it in his eyes, hear it in his voice, and perceive it from his spirit. Though she was still annoyed and hurt over their deceit, she was trying to accept their motives. As Travis had claimed, they had risked their lives to "rescue" her, and they had found a peaceful way to reclaim her. She would never have accepted or forgiven them if they had used soldiers to take her from the Oglalas.

It also vexed her that Travis thought he had done the right thing, especially since his tactics had included beguiling her. She became angry each time she wondered if he had actually believed those awful stories about her. She could not deny that Nathan had justified Travis's role in this scheme to reclaim her. Still, she did not like the way he had played his part, marrying her falsely and allowing her to be tempted by him. He had led her to believe she was bravely and honorably sacrificing herself to him to help her people. He had pretended she was worth a great price to him and had expected that she would be thrilled to be chosen by him. He had played with her vulnerable and naive emotions to keep his game a secret. He had made a fool of her, and she of herself, before her people. She asked herself if it mattered that he had been forced by Lone Wolf and persuaded by her grandfather to deceive her. Yes! she decided in annoyance. Yes, that irresistible rogue needed to be taught a lesson too, so he would never try to fool her again!

Rana's thoughts drifted to her Indian brother, Lone Wolf. She prayed that he and Myeerah would share a long and happy life, and she hoped to be able to visit them again one day. She thought of everything Soaring Hawk, Lone Wolf, and the Oglalas had done for her over the years. She prayed that they knew how much she loved them and appreciated their acceptance. She prayed urgently for their survival and peace.

She wondered why Lone Wolf had insisted that Travis marry her, for he had known that the union would not be consummated or considered real where they were going. Had he done it to make Travis feel responsible for her safety and happiness, particularly if something were to happen to Nathan? Or had he sensed the strong attraction between them and feared they would yield to it without being joined? Lone Wolf was perceptive and cunning, so there would have had to have been a good reason for his curious term.

Rana dreamily recalled the days since she had ridden away from the Oglala camp. She had always wanted the chance to prove herself and her skills. She had wanted to do exciting things, share dangerous adventures, help her people, and remain free. And yes, to live "wild" when the mood struck her! She had to admit that Travis and Nathan were providing her with the opportunities for which she had longed and had battled Lone Wolf to obtain. They were allowing her to help them in every way, to be like their partner on the trail. She had been given weapons and was expected to fight if necessary. They had permitted her to stand guard on several occasions. She knew she already possessed the "patience and self-control" Travis had questioned, for she had been forced to use them and hone them of late, though sometimes it had chafed her to practice them. Yet during the past few days she had come to realize that it was foolish to continue fighting what had been, what was, and what would be.

Rana stood up and stretched her fatigued body. She had hoped Travis would have returned to camp by now so she could go refresh herself in the nearby river. Maybe she was being too hard on him, she mused. Maybe it was time to relent slightly, for if she did not, he might lose all interest in her, and she did not want that. She knew from the sly way he had been watching her that she had him worried. She frowned, realizing that it was not good for their scout to be distracted, especially by unfavorable thoughts of her. If she were careful and wily, by the time they reached the ranch she might have him wishing they were married under the white law . . .

Rana smiled devilishly as she gathered her things. She concentrated on bringing Travis's face to mind, a face that she could have stared at all day and all night, a face on which every feature was shaped and colored perfectly. There was so much beauty and strength of character revealed in his stunning features. His expressions always imprisoned so much emotion, emotion that was tightly controlled but straining for release. How she loved to see those leaf green eyes sparkle with mischief or glow with desire or darken with vexation, for they exposed how deeply and passionately he could feel. When they were riding swiftly, the wind would blow through his dark hair and arrange it in roguish waves, as if the wind were some playful female spirit who was enchanted by him and could not resist touching him. As a doeskin drawn snugly over a tanning frame, his golden brown flesh was stretched tightly over his muscular body. She longed to run her fingers over him from head to foot and enjoy that stirring blend of softness and firmness. He was every inch the stimulating and superior warrior.

She remembered how his mouth had melted against hers and their tongues had danced together joyfully. She recalled how her body had reacted to the way his hands had moved over it. She wanted to experience those thrilling sensations again, for they had made her feel wild and free yet all the while a willing captive in his arms and under his control. If any man could tame Wild Wind, it would be Travis Kincade, for she was eager to surrender to his masterful touch.

Rana had noted that Travis had disappeared amongst the trees to the left of their camp, so she now headed toward the right. She walked to what she considered a safe distance, knowing she should not stray far even for privacy. Laying her possessions aside, she leisurely undressed, for she doubted anyone would be sneaking about at such a late hour.

Recalling the night she and Travis had touched passionately near a river, she stood on the bank for a few moments, stretching and flexing her body as sweet memories filled her mind. She inhaled the mingled fragrances nature provided and smiled dreamily, as if totally pleased with her life and her feelings. Rana braided her hair and, using a rawhide thong, secured the heavy plait to her head to avoid getting her hair soaked. Taking a cloth and soap Travis had bought for her at Fort Wallace, she gingerly made her way down the bank and into the water. She muffled a squeal as she discovered that the water was much cooler than she had imagined. She bravely splashed it on her quivering flesh, then hurriedly lathered from neck to knees. Lifting them one at a time, she soaped each leg and foot. Then she lathered her hands before tossing the cloth and soap on the bank. After washing and rinsing her face, she made her way into the deeper water to rinse off. In no hurry now, she swam around for awhile to exercise her stiff body and to warm herself.

When Rana finally returned to the bank, she could not locate her drying blanket and garments. She glanced to her right and left to see where she had placed them, but she sighted nothing. Her wet body glistened in the moonlight, and she shuddered as a breeze swept over it. Surely she had not swum that far from where she had left her possessions and entered the water! She searched the area again, mumbling curses to herself.

"Osniyelo, Watogla Tate? Tokel oniglakin kta hwo?" a mellow voice asked from nearby. Travis chuckled as she whirled and, blushing, tried futilely to escape the perusal of the man leaning against a tree.

His amusement did not anger her, and he sensed this. She replied in English, "Yes, I am cold, White Eagle. I have nothing to say for myself. I have done no wrong. I stayed near camp, and you always camp where it is safe. My blanket, please." She smiled as she held out her hand, trying to look calm despite the awkward circumstances. She alertly noticed that he had spoken in Lakota and had used her Oglala name. She wondered if he were feeling and thinking Indian tonight . . .

"It's 'I have done nothing wrong' or "I have not done anything wrong,'" he mildly corrected, then grinned. "What if I had been an enemy? You would have a serious problem about now," he teased as he dangled the blanket from one finger and her garments from the others. "And I don't always choose safe places to camp. Remember those deserters."

She retorted confidently, "You would not make the same mistake two times. I have no problem; you are my . . . grandfather's friend. I am safe." She made no attempt to reach for the blanket as she watched his eyes sparkle with mischief, and rapidly mounting desire. She casually removed her headband, unbraided her hair, and shook it loose to fall around her shoulders. Her eyes never left him. His sable hair was damp and wisps clung to his face and neck. His shirt was missing and his hard torso was moist; she noticed that there were wet spots on his pants and that his feet were bare, as if he had left the water quickly and recently. He seemed such a splendid, enticing male animal as he stood before her. Her heart was thudding so fiercely that simple breathing was becoming difficult.

Travis knew she was accustomed to bathing outside and around others, but, he wondered, did she feel no modesty around him? No, he told himself; it was stiff resolve and courage that kept her from fleeing or protesting over his bold intrusion. He was impressed by the way she was handling the situation. "I am your grandfather's friend, but not yours?" he questioned in amusement, potently stimulated by her naked beauty, her close proximity, and her evocative stare.

"That is your choice, Travis Kincade. You have apologized and explained your deceit. I must try to accept your words, or I must return to my . . . the Oglalas. I believe that I am Rana Michaels and that Nathan Crandall is my grandfather, as Lone Wolf believed; otherwise he would not have sent me away with you. Nate must not be hurt or made sad again. If it will make him happy, I will return to his home and learn to be white once more, as I was long ago where my memory does not reach . . . The river is cold this moo . . . tonight. It was not wise to bathe so late." She shuddered as another breeze passed over her wet flesh.

Dropping her garments, Travis stepped forward and wrapped the blanket around her, clasping the edges

263

tightly in his balled hands just beneath her chin. As she looked into his eyes, he remarked, "No, it wasn't wise to bathe tonight. I was swimming over there," he informed her, pointing to a fallen tree that was half submerged in water.

"Why did you say nothing to stop me?" she asked softly.

"Because I didn't want to startle you and have you wake Nate with screams. Both of us swimming without clothes might have looked suspicious to him. Besides, I was enjoying myself too much," he added, grinning. "If you hadn't been so distracted by such deep thoughts, your sharp instincts would have felt my presence. With your training and skill, I'm surprised I got past you, even underwater. You are one beautiful, tempting creature, Rana Michaels. If you weren't Nate's granddaughter, I would take you here and now."

Rana laughed seductively as she placed her hands on his chest and leaned closer to him to share his body heat. "If I were not Rana, Travis Kincade would not have ridden into the Oglala camp and made trade for me and joined to me with false promises. If I were not Nate's granddaughter, I would not be here with you tonight."

In a voice that had grown husky Travis refuted smoothly, "Even if you weren't Rana Michaels, I still would have traded for you, but you would be sharing my sleeping mat now instead of having your own. Frankly, I'm almost sorry I have a new sister instead of a lovely wife." His gaze probed hers to judge how his provocative words had struck her. Her eyes were like liquid pools of blue magic that summoned him to drown in them.

"We are joined in the eyes of the Great Spirit. If you desire me so fiercely, why do you want me to be your sister and not your wife?" she reasoned bravely as her tantalizing gaze remained fused to his.

"Because I love and respect Nathan Crandall too much

to seduce his granddaughter. He would despise me for taking advantage of you. I've told you, Rana, our marriage isn't legal for whites."

Rana had questioned the meaning of "legal" before; now she asked the meaning of "seduce." When Travis explained in a mixture of Oglala and English, she tried to suppress her mirthful laughter.

"What's so funny?" he asked, his brows knit in confusion.

"Did you tell my grandfather I tried to seduce you the night he called to us by the river? Is that why you were frightened and left me?"

"I was upset because I let things go too far between us that night and I left because I couldn't have resisted you if I had stayed. That wasn't the time or place for us to . . . get together, if we do. Now I understand why so many warriors were battling over you. You have powerful magic, woman, and you should learn when and where to use it. You're a cunning thief who steals a man's wisdom and control."

"How can I steal what should be mine by law and by your word of honor? Our hearts are Indian. We are joined by Indian law. If White Eagle takes Wild Wind to his sleeping mat, Rana will not tell her grandfather," she cunningly promised. She lifted one hand to move her forefinger over his lips. "If he discovers the truth, tell my grandfather I have powerful magic and I seduced you," she teased playfully.

Travis frowned in dismay. He captured her enticing hand to halt its action and argued, "*I* would know the truth. I cannot lie to him and deceive him, Rana. To him, we are not married. He trusts me, and loves me, and needs me. He has been closer to me than my own father was. You are like his own child. Taking you could destroy the bond between us and hurt him deeply. Nothing is worth that."

Rana smiled happily, for she saw he was a man of immeasurable honor. "I understand. I am pleased you love my grandfather so much. You are his true and loyal friend. I will do nothing to break the bond between you and Nate; it is special and rare. You must teach me all you have learned since leaving your mother's people. I want my grandfather to be proud of me, as he is of you. Will you be my friend and help me?"

"I've never had a female friend before. That might prove interesting. The fact is, my luck with females has been mostly bad."

"You tease me," she accused merrily as she quivered with excitement. "How can a man of White Eagle's looks and prowess not have many women chasing him? Are there some you wish me to fight off?" she jested. Snuggling closer, she murmured, "It is cold tonight. Share your warmth with me while we talk. There is much for me to learn."

Travis shook his head to prevent himself from being mesmerized by her incredible eyes. He was all too aware of the danger in standing here with her like this. "You should dry off and get dressed. You're cold, and it's too late to teach you anything tonight. We don't want Nate wondering where we are and looking for us again. He might not understand this."

"You are afraid to be alone with your sister friend?"

"Yep," he confessed between hearty chuckles.

"You are right. There is a pull between us that should not be between brother and sister. Return to camp. I will follow soon."

"Is that what you told Lone Wolf?" he questioned suddenly.

Baffled, she looked up at him. "I do not understand."

"Did you tell Lone Wolf we were drawn to each other? Is that why he demanded we marry before you could leave with me?"

"I did not speak of such things with my brother. I do not know why he forced you to join to me. You should not have agreed. He is wise and kind; he would have released me without the joining. I could not believe my ears when you asked to make trade for me and be joined to me. You forget, I did not know it was a trick until five moo . . . days ago."

He tapped her on the nose as he replied, "I think he wanted to make sure I would feel responsible for you. Then again, he could have seen or heard us and thought it would be wise to bind us together just in case we lost our heads one night by a river." His eyes twinkled roguishly.

"My brother knew you were a man of honor and control. He knew the truth about me. He knew you would not touch me. There was a reason for his demand, but I do not know it."

"One day you'll be glad you aren't bound to a rogue like me. You're free to choose your own husband, not forced to accept a stranger. I want you to be careful when we get home, Rana. You're a beautiful woman, and you'll be a rich one. Men will be chasing you."

After Travis explained the meaning of "rich," Rana told him, "I cannot choose to marry another man until I no longer feel joined to White Eagle. I was raised Indian. I do not think and feel white."

Travis stared at her regretfully. "I'm sorry I've made you so confused. In time you'll accept the way things are in the white world."

Rana had been trying to point out the fact that if he desired her so much he could marry her under white law and thereby have her without hurting Nathan. She suddenly realized that he might not want to marry her, might be glad, in fact, that the Indian ceremony was not binding. She knew it was possible for a man to desire and take a woman without loving her or wanting her as his mate. Perhaps she was reading his feelings wrong. He was

267

always talking about her choosing and marrying another man. Maybe he did not think she was good enough for him or was the right woman for him. Nathan had said that Travis had not wanted to marry her, that he had only done so because Lone Wolf had demanded it. A painful suspicion began to gnaw at her, a suspicion that it was Nathan who wanted her, not Travis. She realized she should not be chasing him so boldly, and that realization saddened her. Quietly she informed him, "You are right, Travis Kincade. I must change or others will suffer." She stepped away from him, gathered her things, and moved into the concealing shadows.

Travis caught the change in her mood. He wished he could admit that he felt joined to her too, but he knew it would be wrong to confuse her even more. She needed time and clarity of mind to discover who she was and to adjust to her new existence. After all, he would be close at hand at all times. Besides, the ravishing vixen just might be toying with him, trying to lead him on for tricking her! He knew about the little games women played with men, games several had tried to play on him. They used their bodies like weapons, with skills to match those of the most cunning warrior. They teased, enticed, rewarded, or punished a man if he didn't follow their rules. They wanted to own a man and control him. They wanted him running after them as if he couldn't survive without them. They wanted him to pet them and spoil them. They wanted him to sacrifice everything to prove his feelings and receive their attentions only. They used him to make other men jealous, or used other men to make him jealous and nervous. They wanted him to think with his loins instead of his heart or head. They could be so selfish, so predatory, so eager to possess and consume, and so damned insidious!

He knew that women like Clarissa, Pretty Rabbit, Elizabeth, and Marissa would do anything to get their way. They did not care whom they hurt or used. Maybe Marissa's daughter was just like her mother and the others. Plenty of worthy warriors had tried to win Wild Wind as a mate, but she had rejected each of them. So why would she cast her sights on the stranger who had deceived her and had refused to acknowledge her surrender? Unless she wanted to teach him a lesson! No, he could not permit this untamed creature to come between him and Nathan. He could not allow himself to be hurt again, for he knew from experience that physical pain was nothing compared to emotional agony. No matter what Rana's motives might be, he would have to resist her.

He would never forget his near-fatal experience with Elizabeth Lowry because he had scars to remind him. That treacherous viper had pretended to be so sweet and innocent while all the while she had been trying to snare him. He had been working for her father in St. Louis and had learned by then to be nice and polite to ladies and especially to bosses' daughters. Beth had enticed and encouraged him for weeks before he finally agreed to partake of her charms, and she had had plenty of them. Thinking back, he realized his emotional wounds from the past had been too fresh during her siege. It had been twenty-two months since his torture and rejection by the Hunkpapas, which had come hard upon his father's betrayal and death and his mother's death. Maybe that nineteen-year-old, bitter, lonely, arrogant youth had needed someone to love him, to need him, to make him feel he was the most special male alive; and Beth had been an expert at such pretenses. He had been searching for something and—even knowing Beth was not it—had allowed her to distract him. Hellfire, what had really happened was he had gotten tired of making excuses not to take what she had been forcing on him!

After escaping the Hunkpapa camp, he had gone from

place to place, working all kinds of jobs as he learned his way around in the white world, but never staying anywhere more than three months. He had always been careful to keep his identity and past a secret from everyone, for he knew how people felt about half-breeds. After the Hunkpapas had stopped sending warriors after him, he had slowed his pace, but he had then discovered he was merely existing from day to day. Without a home, family, identity, and purpose in life, he felt lost. Riding with a band of outlaws, he committed crimes but never got caught. As a U.S. Marshal, he fought and killed men legally. He scouted for the Army for awhile. He escorted a wagon train through Indian lands and briefly rode with fierce and cunning Apaches. He worked on a ranch, then was a bank guard for two weeks. Still he missed that sense of belonging, that feeling of pride, the stimulating adventure and thrill of being a warrior. Despite his efforts, he had been unable to find anything or anyone to fill that nagging void; and he had been unable to forget the stain on his face and honor. His father's crimes and his own rejection had eaten away at him.

Beth had entered his life at a time when he was willing to allow himself to be used, maybe as punishment. At that time, life and people meant little to him; he was just passing the days until his head cleared and his heart stopped hurting and yearning. He had taken Indian and white women in the Hunkpapa camp, but it had always been for the purpose of assuaging his lust, or as a learning experience. He had not loved Beth or desired anything permanent with her, but she had been insistent about sharing herself completely with him. And men did have their needs, he had told himself then. Even when their brief affair first began, it had not been because he had wanted her or had pursued her.

After a barn dance and a few drinks one night, Beth

had sneaked into his room and had practiced her numerous skills on him; and she hadn't been a virgin. For a week, he had allowed her to share his bed, but he soon realized he was making a foolish mistake. He quickly became tired of her grasping ways and sorry attitudes, and finally he refused to see her again. He was willing to risk getting fired if keeping the job meant keeping the boss's daughter happy as well.

For weeks, Beth was furious, then suddenly she mellowed. He discovered that she was using other men to make him jealous. Beth should have known it wouldn't work, he reflected now, because he had had no feelings for her, not good ones anyway. As he continued to watch her use her wiles, sensual skills, wealth, beauty, and position, he discovered the real Beth, and he lost all respect for her. When she allowed him to find her with a man, his indifference turned to disgust. Despite what Pretty Rabbit had done to him nearly two years earlier, he had not expected Elizabeth Lowry to have such a vengeful and utterly evil streak.

One night an Indian girl who worked in the Lowry home came to him and revealed the details of Beth's scheme to entrap him. It seemed that Beth had told her father he had seduced her and she had become pregnant, though she had neglected to mention that she had also slept with many other men before and since her week with him. She was demanding that her father force Travis to marry her immediately. The Indian girl told him that Beth's accusation was a lie; she knew that Beth had twice experienced her monthly flow since he had stopped seeing her. The girl then warned him to flee St. Louis. But, like a fool, he did the same thing he had done once before, after his father's exposure; he remained to prove his innocence and courage, vowing he would not run like a guilty coward.

Beth's father would not listen to him and threatened to

271

hang him if he did not marry his daughter. Enraged, he shouted out the names of countless men who had enjoyed Beth's charms, especially those who had taken her since him. He then challenged Beth's father to question those men or to prove his guilt, and he vowed to seek the help of the authorities in his defense. That had been another mistake. Lowry immediately ordered his daughter to pack her belongings and announced he was sending her back East to a school for girls that sounded like a prison.

As for him, Lowry hired two gunslingers to torture him and kill him, not only to prevent the Lowry name from being smeared but because Lowry wanted revenge for having his child's evil exposed to him so blatantly.

Travis vividly recalled how the ruffians had lured him into a trap with a faked note from the Indian girl who worked for Lowry, a note pleading for Travis's help. He had gone to her aid and instead had been thoroughly beaten by the two ruffians, who had then left him to die in the wilderness after stealing nearly all of his possessions. As for the Indian girl, her help in warning him about Beth's scheme had gotten her raped and murdered right before his eyes as he was losing consciousness.

But Nathan Crandall had come along, found him, and adopted him, so to speak. It had taken him months to heal, and when he had gone looking for the Lowrys, he had learned they had been robbed and slain by bandits. He had never found the two bastards who had nearly beaten him to death, but he believed that one day they would cross his path again.

Nathan had been having trouble with rustlers and renegades and had begged him to return to the ranch after his search, so he had returned and stayed to help the man who had saved his life. Time had passed, his ability to feel had slowly increased, and he had never left Nathan Crandall's side again. From the day Nathan had found him to this one, whenever he had needed a woman, he had paid for one in town.

Travis's thoughts turned to Clarissa Caldwell. Just like Beth, that little vixen had pursued him for years. But he had learned his lesson, and he had never done more than tease her with lips and hands when it had suited his purpose to taunt her or to pull information from her. Besides, he did not want to give Harrison Caldwell anything he could use to harm Nathan, or do anything that might be used to force him to leave the ranch and the man who was his best friend. He knew how much like Beth Clarissa was, and he was not about to be ensnared by the same trick twice. Just like Rana had said, he never made the same mistake two times . . .

Rana . . . Rana was nothing like those vindictive bitches who had schemed against him and had made him so cynical. He remembered how she had felt in his arms and how she had wanted him as fiercely as he had wanted her. He recalled how Black Hawk had tried to attack her, and he suddenly realized that she might turn to another man eventually if he kept pushing her away. Her expression of moments ago flashed before his mind's eye and his heart lurched wildly with desire and panic. *By damn, you're mine, Rana Michaels*, he vowed and rushed off to see what was keeping her so long.

Travis found her resting her forehead against a tree while she cried softly, her body still clad in the drying blanket and her other possessions carelessly lying on the ground. He realized how deeply he was confusing and hurting her with his contradictory words and actions. "Please don't cry, Rana," he entreated. "I really got us into a terrible mess, didn't I? Don't hate me. I didn't mean to hurt you."

"Hate you?" she echoed, lifting her head and gazing into his troubled eyes. She leaned against the tree. "That is not true. So much is happening around me and inside me. Why do you fear me and reject me and race from my

273

side each time we touch with deep feelings?"

Travis looked at her and replied honestly, "It isn't you I fear, Rana; it's my loss of control that scares me. When there's nobody around like Nate or Lone Wolf, I can't stay clearheaded or restrained. We're too attracted to each other to be alone. Lordy, woman, you make me think and feel crazy things. No one has ever tempted me or affected me like you do. Staying around you is like tossing a match on a dry haystack and hoping it won't catch fire. You make me feel weak and reckless. I tried to return to camp to avoid more temptation, but I was worried about you." His respiration had altered noticeably and he was staring at her with intense longing, though he was afraid to touch her. He desperately wanted to yank her into his arms and kiss her again and again, yet he was frightened by what such contact would lead to. His hands were shaking and he was beginning to feel tense and damp all over from the strain on his self-control and from his burning desire for her. He warned himself to return to camp immediately, but he could not force his legs to obey his conscience's precautionary message.

Rana understood his dilemma, for she shared his feelings. They both wanted each other, needed each other, and she felt they should surrender to the battle that was raging within them. She knew how close they were to the yielding point and had already decided which path she wanted to take. Their bodies, and even the air surrounding them, were charged with emotion. Surely this was meant to be, she told herself, refusing to stop her hand from reaching up to caress his taut jawline yet knowing what such physical contact would do to both of them. It seemed as if the Great Spirit had entrapped them together, as if He had created this unique moment just for them to discover each other, as if He had lowered some magical flap for privacy to this lover's tepee of nature's construction. Travis's pull on her was too great and she could not resist it, did not want to resist it. Her instincts told her that as surely as Mother Earth was fated to change her face with each season, they were fated to change their lives and hearts this season. In a tone just above a silky whisper, she told him, "There is no reason for your fear and control. I yield to you by my choice, for I desire you. It is sad and painful to deny such needs. Is it not better to walk a path of truth and happiness? How can I remain near you if I cannot have you? Your rejections cut my heart too deeply. If your feelings match mine, why must we remain apart and in torment? How can this beautiful and powerful thing between us be evil or wrong?"

Her words, expression, tone, and nearness prevented him from retreating or protesting. He was intoxicated and utterly entranced by her. Travis grasped the hands caressing his cheeks and pressed them to his lips. As his gaze remained fused to hers and he absorbed her presence, his lips and tongue played sensuously in her palms. When she moved closer to him, his arms slipped around her body and his lips seared over her right ear. As they drifted down her throat, she trembled and swayed against him, enslaving his senses. His mouth brushed over her bare shoulder and traveled back to the hollow of her neck and up to her ear to nibble there. When Rana's arm encircled his waist and she arched her body against his, Travis's hands slipped into her cascading tresses; they cupped her head and lifted it. His eyes held hers for a heart-stopping instant before his lips captured hers in a fiery kiss that ignited their smoldering passions into a roaring blaze of urgency and reality-consuming force.

One kiss blended into another, leaving them breathless and increasing their cravings. As Travis's hands wandered over her shoulders and back, the drying blanket glided to the ground. The feel of her succulent flesh against his greedy hands drove him wild with desire. As his fingers moved over her soft curves to caress her buttocks and upward to rove over her tempting breasts, he shuddered with rising need.

Rana shifted sideways to give him more freedom to explore her aching body. He cradled her in the curve of his right arm as his mouth feasted at hers and his left hand closed over a firm breast. When its peak instantly responded and became taut with desire, his mouth was enticed to drift over her chin and down her throat to capture it, leaving behind a tingling trail of kisses. The bud danced joyfully with his lips and tongue until she urged him to share this new bliss with the other brown peak.

She was astonished by how his actions affected her from head to foot; even her tummy quivered in anticipation and delight and her legs grew weak. Her entire body was alive and aflame, as was his. Passion's fires burned brighter each moment. His mouth returned to hers and they kissed feverishly. They wanted each other instantly, fiercely, but each instinctively knew their joining should not be rushed, even if control was becoming impossible.

Travis's left hand moved past her abdomen, enticingly stroking her flesh along the way, and boldly entered the auburn forest between her sleek thighs. As it labored skillfully, eagerly, gently, his mouth worked on hers until she was limp and breathless. "Take me, Travis," she urged hoarsely, "for I burn for you."

His mouth seared over hers in a blaze of passion and he held her tightly, possessively, against his body. Suddenly an owl screeched loudly overhead, startling him and alerting him to their dangerous surroundings. "We can't, *micante*, not here, not now," he told her painfully. "Nate would be furious and hurt if he discovered my betrayal. I promised him and Lone

Wolf I wouldn't do this, because of our false marriage. Besides, this place isn't safe with my senses so dulled and my mind so distracted. I want you like I've never wanted any woman, but we shouldn't have to rush our first union, or fear discovery by Nate or some enemy, or feel as if we're doing something wrong. There's a lot to be settled between us before we go any further, and we need a special time and place to come together. Lordy, you do steal my wits and control!"

Rana grasped his head between her hands and forced him to meet her compelling gaze. "We can and we must, Travis. You are mine, and I need you, as you need me. I do not care if we are not joined under the white law. You are not seducing me, or taking advantage of me, or betraying Nathan Crandall. You must not think and feel this way. This matter is between White Eagle and Wild Wind—no one else. Do not leave us burning for each other again."

Travis listened to her arguments and observed her expressions. She was being truthful with him, and with herself. He knew there would be no turning back this time, for it really didn't matter that this wasn't the best place to make love for the first time, or even that they would have to rush and remain alert.

He released her to remove his pants and drop them beside her belongings. Then he bent over and spread the drying blanket at the foot of the tree. "I can't resist you any longer, Rana. Hunger for you is eating me alive inside. Right or wrong, I must have you tonight."

They sank to the blanket together and, as they lay down, he warned, "I have never desired anything or anyone as I crave you. Once you are mine, no man will take you from me and I will never release you. The burning of flesh is nothing compared to the burning of a heart. If both do not blaze fiercely for me alone, Wild

277

Wind, do not yield."

She clasped his face and drew it close to hers. "If yours do not burn for me alone, White Eagle, do not take me, for, in doing so, you pledge your heart, life, and honor to me." She paused for a moment to look deeply into his eyes. "But if they do burn as fiercely as mine do, you must claim me tonight, for it is torment to be near you and be denied you. Did we both not know this time would come when our eyes and bodies touched in Lone Wolf's tepee? We can no longer resist what must be between us."

Their eyes locked as each sought the other's pledge in the glowing moonlight, then both smiled. Travis lay half atop her and, for awhile, they were content to look into each other's eyes and caress lightly, lovingly. Both knew time could be short, but they savored each moment. They nibbled on each other's chins, savored each other's lips, shared warm respiration, and drowned in pools that reflected love and desire. It was a time to move with tenderness, to explore emotions as well as passions, to allow spirits to mingle as well as fiery bodies. It was a time to tame the fears and doubts that had enveloped and restrained them; it was a time to surrender to the wild winds of sweet ecstasy. It was a time for sweet, savage hearts to fuse and become one for all days.

Travis stroked her mischievous curls and teased fingers over her features as if he had been a blind man studying them. "My heart is beating loud and heavily, *micante*. I've never felt this way before, wanting a woman with more than my manhood, and it's frightening. I knew this union would come to pass the moment my eyes touched on your painted image, for I desired you even then. Yet I can hardly believe you're real, or you're here in my life, and in my arms tonight. I was afraid to reach out to you, afraid you could never feel this way about me. And I'm not a man used to experiencing or admitting fear. I've always had bad luck with women, so I've never liked or trusted many. You're so different, and that worries me. I need to know you better so I can understand what I'm thinking and feeling. Giving and sharing come hard for me."

Rana's finger teased along his neck and shoulder as she replied, "I too feared the strange feelings that attacked me. Each time you left camp, I prayed for your return. Your face gave joy to my heart and your voice stirred my soul. Lone Wolf was forcing me to join, and I was afraid to refuse. How could I explain that I desired a stranger? I have wanted you and this moment since the first night you came to my brother's tepee. When I awoke to find you gone, I feared I would not be allowed time to know you. Each time you turned away from me, it confused and pained me deeply, for I did not understand many things. Each time we touched, I knew why I had refused to join to another. In my heart, I was waiting for you, Travis Kincade, and I must have you for my life-circle to be complete and happy. This is as it should be for us."

Travis leaned forward and sealed her lips with his. They kissed and caressed until the flames of heady desire raged within their minds as well as their bodies. Very gently Travis entered her receptive womanhood, holding her possessively and fusing their lips in that special moment. He hesitated briefly to master his throbbing manhood and to allow her time to adjust to their physical bond. She had not cried out, and he assumed that her active life had allowed her to embrace this moment with little discomfort. He had known that a virgin would experience less pain if the man were gentle and patient, and he had tried to be both.

Softly he whispered, "You are mine now, *micante,* and I am yours. We have become a circle that must remain joined forever." His body shuddered then with enormous need and from the wonder of her total surrender. His sexual pleasure had never reached such heights before. He labored lovingly, carefully, until she was matching his rhythm and their bodies were working feverishly as one. Both could feel the heady tension building within and between them, building to a pitch that beat as forcefully as war drums.

Eagerly, rapidly, they climbed passion's spiral until they swayed sensuously on the precipice of victory, overcoming all doubts and hesitations, then flinging themselves over the edge of control. When her rapturous release came, her mouth and body clung to his, extracting every instant of the glorious experience and telling him to cast his own caution aside. As he seized blissful ecstasy, he murmured against her lips, "You are mine, Wild Wind, forever mine. Let no man or thing come between us. We are one now."

They lay nestled together on the thin blanket, aglow in the warmth of sated passion. Contentedly they listened to their joyous heartbeats and to the harmonious blending of music sounds created by nocturnal creatures, birds, and insects. Moonlight made its way through the trees into the small clearing and splashed across their entwined bodies. A hint of a breeze tried to rustle the leaves and branches, but they were too supple with new life to comply. The fragrance of wildflowers and the heady smell of pine teased at their noses. Serenity surrounded and pervaded them.

As the night air became cooler, they snuggled closer together, not wanting the moment or their contact to end. But they were in enemy territory and Nathan was sleeping not far away. Though neither felt tired or drowsy, both knew they needed rest and sleep for their journey.

Travis propped himself up on his elbow and gazed down at Rana. He watched how the moonlight gleamed on her shiny hair and was reflected in her entrancing eyes. His heart fluttered. He wished they could make love all night, but the hour was late and the idea dangerous, especially when he considered his reckless seduction and his rash confessions.

She smiled and asked, "Do you know how rare you are? I am glad you belong to me." She pulled his head to hers and kissed him.

"I've made plenty of mistakes, Rana, but I don't guess I turned out too badly, did I?" he jested, teasing his fingertips along her spine. He knew it was time they returned to reality, but he dreaded it. There were things he did not want to do or say, things he did not want to face.

"I would trade nothing and no one for you, Travis Kincade."

He kissed the tip of her nose. "I sure am glad I traded something for you, woman. Do you know how hard it's been to resist you? Or how hard it will be for us to avoid each other until our lives are settled?"

Rana's heart was too full of love and happiness to comprehend his last words. A dreamy haze still enveloped her. "I am glad White Eagle defeated Travis Kincade in this battle. We cannot change what is meant to be, and it hurts us and others to try."

"But sometimes we hurt others if we don't try, *micante*. Like Nate, when he discovers what happened between us tonight. I'll have to find the right words to explain our feelings and behavior to him. He trusted me to keep my word to stay clear of you. I have proven myself a man of little honor, a man of weakness."

She scolded him angrily, "Do not speak such false words! You are not to blame because we could not resist the fires that burned between us. Our Indian souls are bound as one; it was our Indian bodies that yielded. We are not children, and we cannot be forced to reveal our actions and feelings to anyone, including our family.

281

Speak no evil of yourself. You have more strength and honor than any man I have known. Some things must be held secret; a moment such as we shared is one of those things. If you tell my grandfather, it will spoil it for us. Please, let White Eagle belong to Wild Wind in silence until the moo . . . day when Rana and Travis can share their secret. Wild Wind and White Eagle are joined and have done nothing wrong. Rana and Travis must find themselves and each other if they wish to share our life-circle."

Rana loved him, but she did not want Nathan to force Travis to marry her under the white law. She felt it was important that they share this special secret and intimacy, for she hoped it would bind them together in both worlds. She wanted him to learn to love her and trust her above anyone else, including her grandfather. She wanted him to ask her to marry him again, but this time of his own free will, not because of force or guilt. He needed the freedom to decide that he did not want freedom from her.

"Your words are true and wise, *micante* . . ." Travis began, about to ask her to marry him under the white law. But unwillingly he recalled the many problems and perils he faced, perils that could endanger Rana if he staked his claim on her too soon. He knew he would have to overcome them first; only then could he take her as his wife for a second time. For now, they needed to explore feelings: their own and each other's. They needed to learn to trust and to share completely. This thing between them was more than physical; it had to be given time and effort so that it could be allowed to flourish. He just wished he felt less guilt over duping Nathan. "I don't want anything to stain this special moment. For now, it will remain between us. We will allow Travis and Rana to seek themselves and each other, but Wild Wind will always belong to White Eagle alone."

Rana caught his hesitation and realized that something had stopped him from speaking everything that was in his heart. That aura of mystery surrounded him again, this time arriving unbidden. Though she knew that these new feelings and the situation were difficult for him, she sensed she had won him, and the thought made her smile happily. When the time came—and it would—he would explain everything to her. Until then, she would give him her love and her trust, and she would teach him to do the same with her. There was still so much they had to learn about each other and about the life they would share, she mused as she kissed him hungrily and embraced him. In Oglala, she murmured seductively, "Tonight, I am Wild Wind and you are White Eagle. When *Wi* returns with a new day, we will become Rana and Travis again."

Chapter Ten

The following morning, while Nathan was away from camp, Rana stopped her chores to ask Travis in a rush of words, "Were you angry with me because you thought I asked Lone Wolf to force you to marry me? Do you think I used the Elk Dreamer's love medicine to snare you? Did the wicked tales about Wild Wind cause you to mistrust me?" She had decided it was time for openness and honesty between them, for she knew it was the only way they could grow closer. She had come to understand that it was not enough to love and desire a person; friendship, loyalty, trust, and respect were also vital. She knew this attraction between them was far more than physical. But did he? He seemed slightly withdrawn this morning, a little nervous, even a little guilty and embarrassed. Perhaps it was the reality of a total commitment that frightened him, for he had always appeared so independent. Or perhaps he was overly concerned about Nathan's reaction to their intimacy. Men viewed such things so differently from women. In the wilderness, life was precious and often too short, and she believed it should be lived to the fullest. She didn't want him to worry or pull back into himself, for she truly believed they had been made for each other.

Travis looked into the arresting face of the woman who had blinded him to everything except her the night before. It was intimidating to be so enthralled by another person, another power. There were so few people he admired, respected, trusted. If Rana's feelings and dreams did not match his . . . He wanted to trust her totally, but he was afraid, for he remembered the defiant, arrogant, disobedient vixen she had been, the kind of woman her mother had been, the kind most women were. And how could she love him and desire him after his deceit, with his half-blooded heritage? How could she, a beautiful, ravishing woman, want nothing from him except his love? He had always lived by his instincts, and they told him now to be wary of this bewitching woman, wary of his hunger and weakness for her. Like her, he needed time to adjust to this complicated situation and to these often alarming and novel emotions he felt. Yet, having realized all this, he still could not force himself to hold back from her completely. He stopped in the midst of saddling the horses to respond. "I wasn't mad at you, Rana. I know you didn't have anything to do with Lone Wolf's joining demand; he made it before you saw him or spoke to him after my arrival. I'm partly worried about the ranch. We've been gone a long time. Besides, you have more magic than any Elk Dreamer, *micante*, and it's driving me crazy trying to keep a cool head."

Rana smiled. "I know this magic between us is hard for you and we must travel this new path slowly and carefully. We stood beneath the eyes of the Great Spirit and spoke joining words, but the whites say they mean nothing. It is painful and confusing when the head and heart think and feel differently, or when others control your words and feelings. I was raised to accept and to honor Oglala laws and customs, to believe in *Wakan Tanka*. My head hears your white words, but my Oglala heart battles them. It is like saying to the whites the sky is

286

green and the grass is blue when I have been taught otherwise by the Indians, as have you, White Eagle. For years I was Indian, but now I am white and must yield to the laws and customs that control my new life. You and my grandfather have asked me to make many changes quickly. Have you forgotten how it was when you left the Hunkpapas? Did your heart and life change as soon as you left your mother's lands? Was it easy and painless for you?"

He responded instantly, "No, it wasn't easy or painless, Rana. In fact, it hurt like hell and I battled those changes for two years. I didn't know where I was heading or what I was going to do. If it hadn't been for your grandfather, I would still be a hostile, bitter loner, drifting from place to place, fighting and rebelling and searching for myself—if I were still alive, that is. I was forced to leave my home; my family was dead. You're lucky; you're returning to your home and a family. Just the same, it won't be easy in the beginning. But you have people who love you and want you, people who'll help you adjust. At least you won't be alone in a world you don't understand, as I was. My past damaged me, Rana. I need time and understanding."

Travis ran his fingers through his thick sable hair and adjusted his red headband. As he attempted to decide what to tell her about his experiences, his green eyes narrowed and his brows knit, causing tiny lines to form above his nose and creating a misleading frown. He gazed at her, his look direct but uncertain. "There's so much you don't know about me, or your new life." He glanced at the ground, allowed his eyes to dart from side to side, then looked back at her.

As she awaited his reply, her puzzled expression matched his perplexed one. She recalled what Nathan had said about the Hunkpapas "rejecting" him. "You said you were 'forced' to travel a path away from your

287

mother's lands. Will you explain your strange words? Where did you get the scars on your body? How, Travis?" She could tell he did not want to talk about his past, and probably had not revealed it to anyone but her grandfather. She was pleased he had told her this much and she hoped he would relate even more about himself, though she prayed he was not mourning a lost love. If he could be open and honest, it would mean he wanted her to understand and accept him. Yet his hesitation and tension indicated there were things he was not ready to face.

He sighed heavily. After last night, he owed her an explanation, though it would be hard to lower his guard and be candid. If he allowed her to get too close too quickly, it might impair his judgment. To relax himself, he joked, "I don't suppose you can think any worse of me than you already do. All right, Rana Michaels, I'll tell you what happened years ago in the Hunkpapa camp and why I was in such a hurry to get out of the Oglala camp and far away from Lakota lands."

Rana listened intently as Travis described his troubled past from his birth to his departure from the Hunkpapa village. He did not leave out his father's treachery or his mother's death or Pretty Rabbit's role, or how, after the Hunkpapas' torture, he had been forced to escape to avoid being executed for crimes he had not committed. His anguish and bitterness were evident to her. He had been betrayed and rejected by everyone and everything he had loved and respected. When he confessed he had been afraid the Hunkpapas would arrive and repeat the false tale to the Oglalas before he could recover her for Nathan—especially during the mix-up with the guns and the morning he had bound her and ridden off rapidly with her—she understood why he had been so aggressive and anxious to get her and Nathan out of that area with all speed. She surmised he had been right, for Indians

288

We've got your authors!

If you seek out the latest historical romances by today's bestselling authors, our new reader's service, KENSINGTON CHOICE, is the club for you.

KENSINGTON CHOICE is the only club where you can find authors like Janelle Taylor, Shannon Drake, Rosanne Bittner, Sylvie Sommerfield, Penelope Neri and Phoebe Conn all in one place...

...and the only service that will deliver their romances direct to your home as soon as they are published—even before they reach the bookstores.

KENSINGTON CHOICE is also the only service that will give you a substantial guaranteed discount off the publisher's prices on every one of those romances.

That's right: Every month, the Editors at Zebra and Pinnacle select four of the newest novels by our bestselling authors and rush them straight to you, usually *before they reach the bookstores*. The publisher's prices for these romances range from $4.99 to $5.99—but they are always yours for the guaranteed low price of just *$4.20!*

That means you'll always save over 20% off the publisher's prices on every shipment you get from KENSINGTON CHOICE!

All books are sent on a 10-day free examination basis, and there is no minimum number of books to buy. (A postage and handling charge of $1.50 is added to each shipment.)

As your introduction to the convenience and value of this new service, we invite you to accept

4 BOOKS FREE

The 4 books, worth up to $23.96, are our welcoming gift. You pay only $1 to help cover postage and handling.

To start your subscription to KENSINGTON CHOICE and receive your introductory package of 4 FREE romances, detach and mail the card at right *today*.

We have 4 FREE BOOKS for you
as your introduction to
KENSINGTON CHOICE
To get your FREE BOOKS, worth
up to $23.96, mail the card below.

FREE BOOK CERTIFICATE

As my introduction to your new KENSINGTON CHOICE reader's service, please send me 4 FREE historical romances (worth up to $23.96), billing me just $1 to help cover postage and handling. As a KENSINGTON CHOICE subscriber, I will then receive 4 brand-new romances to preview each month for 10 days FREE. I can return any books I decide not to keep and owe nothing. The publisher's prices for the KENSINGTON CHOICE romances range from $4.99 to $5.99, but as a subscriber I will be entitled to get them for just $4.20 per book or $16.80 for all four titles. There is no minimum number of books to buy, and I can cancel my subscription at any time. A $1.50 postage and handling charge is added to each shipment.

Name _____

Address _____ Apt. _____

City _____ State _____ Zip _____

Telephone (___) _____

Signature _____

(If under 18, parent or guardian must sign)

Subscription subject to acceptance. Terms and prices subject to change.

KC0795

We have
4
FREE
Historical
Romances
for you!

(worth up
to $23.96!)

Details inside!

rarely forgot or forgave a matter of broken honor. Yet she still sensed he was not telling her everything about his past.

"When I left the Lakota lands long ago, if you hadn't been a little girl I would have stolen you and taken you along with me," he teased to lighten the gloom around them. "You see, Miss Michaels, I've been nothing but trouble to myself and others since I was born. Now do you understand why I said you'd be glad you weren't joined to a jinxed renegade like me? If not for your grandfather, I'd be worse than I am. By now, the Hunkpapas have reached your camp and Lone Wolf has probably learned what he will believe to be the black truth about me. I wouldn't be surprised if he sends a band of warriors to hunt me down and rescue you. I was determined you were going home with Nate, even if I had to carry you hog-tied and screaming every mile of the way. That's where you belong for lots of reasons, including your survival. I swear I tried to honor my promise to Lone Wolf and Nate about you, but you found my weak spot and captivated me."

Travis waited for her to say something, but she just kept staring at him with those liquid blue eyes that he could not read. He prayed she wasn't sorry about last night. "I'll make a deal with you, Rana. If you decide to reject me for any reason, I'll leave the ranch and never come back, if that's what it'll take for you to remain with Nate. He turned my life around and gave me everything I needed. Seeing him happy means a lot to me. Adopted son or not, I swear I won't make any claim on the ranch. It's rightfully yours. I wouldn't want you to think I was trying to hold on to it by ensnaring you. I know I deceived you in the Oglala camp and I've broken my word about staying clear of you, so I guess you have little reason to trust me. But, please, make sure you know what you want and what you're doing."

Beyond Travis, Rana could see Nathan approaching and knew there would be no time or privacy to express her feelings. She realized how much Travis loved and respected Nathan. She was certain he had never begged anyone for anything before today, and his willingness to risk and sacrifice so much for Nathan touched her deeply. Travis had just shown her the path by which she could force him to marry her. It would be easy for her to demand that he marry her in order to be allowed to remain with Nathan and the ranch, but in her heart she knew she could not walk such a path. He had been tormented and betrayed too many times, and it would be a grave mistake for her to use any kind of coercion to win him. As he had said, he needed time and understanding. For Nathan's benefit, she declared aloud to Travis, "You said you would replace Cloud. Do you have a white stallion on the ranch?"

For a moment Travis was baffled by her question and behavior; then Nathan called out, "You two ready to ride?"

Rana smiled at her grandfather and nodded. "I'm eager to get home, Grandfather. I'm tired of riding and camping. Travis has promised to give me a horse as special as Cloud." Her gaze met Travis's as she spoke words that carried a dual meaning. "I will hold him to his words."

"If Travis said it, Rana, you can believe him. Sometimes he's a little hard to live with, but he's the best man I've ever met. I don't know what I would have done all those years if he hadn't been with me."

"You're biased, Nate," Travis teased in return, wondering which words she was going to hold him to. To Rana he said, "Let's go before he gets mushy on us." He grinned at her then, letting his eyes say far more to her than "thank-you" for the way she was treating Nathan.

*   *   *

When they reached the Fort Cobb Agency, again Travis left them camped nearby while he scouted the conditions in the area. He had not been gone ten minutes before Rana began questioning Nathan about this mysterious, enchanting man with whom she believed her destiny was entwined.

When Nathan discovered that Travis had divulged part of his past to Rana, he assumed it would be all right for him to reveal more facts to her. After all, he decided, they would be living together in the same house. Too, he had dreams of bringing these two young people together, for he could not imagine a better match for either one. He sensed they were being drawn to each other, and that pleased him, though he had no doubt their attraction intimidated the carefree Travis, who had a history of bad luck with women.

Nathan related what he knew about Travis's experiences with the Hunkpapas and described the incident that had brought him and Travis Kincade together, including details of Elizabeth Lowry's treacherous role in their meeting. He was not surprised when Rana asked for more information about the two women who had caused Travis to display such a grim attitude toward the female sex. As Travis had instructed, he avoided an explanation of Travis's relationship with Clarissa Caldwell, for Travis had felt she might drop innocent, though dangerous, clues to Harrison and his daughter when they eventually met.

Nathan and Rana discussed Travis's life in the Hunkpapa camp and on the ranch. Clearly she was fascinated by his adopted son. When finally they had exhausted the subject of Travis Kincade temporarily, Nathan saw the perfect opportunity to relate more information about Rana's father.

"Why did my mother marry such a wicked man?" she probed after listening intently to Nathan's words.

"I wish I knew, child. I guess love is one of those

mysteries of life. Sometimes we don't use wisdom to pick the person we love. I remember when I first saw my darling Ruth," he murmured dreamily. "She was the prettiest girl I had ever laid eyes on. I couldn't think about anything until she was mine. Whenever I left on a roundup or cattle drive, I couldn't wait to get back home to my Ruthie. I hated for us to be separated, especially for months at a time. I wish you could have known your grandmother, Rana. If she hadn't died so young, your mother would have had someone to keep her straight. I should have remarried, 'cause I didn't know much about raising little girls. Sometimes it's hard to believe they're both gone forever," he mused dejectedly.

As Rana touched his arm and smiled comfortingly at him, Nathan ventured, "Maybe how I felt about Ruthie was how my Marissa felt about your father. It's a shame he was so bad. All he wanted was my ranch and money; that's why he married her. Some men are just plain greedy and evil, and they'll do anything to innocent young girls to get what they want. I tried to keep her from marrying him. I begged her to marry Todd Raines; she had been seeing him for a few months and had seemed to like him. I guess I was wrong about their feelings. She told me she didn't want to marry a poor wrangler. She knew I would have made Todd my partner if they'd married, so that wasn't the real reason she refused his proposal. She just up and ran off with that fancy gambler and crushed poor Todd's heart. If she hadn't, she would be alive today. And if Travis hadn't come along, Todd would have his place in my life now. He's still real special to me." He paused for a moment, lost in thought. "If Travis had been around, Marissa wouldn't have looked at another man. 'Course the marriage wasn't all bad." Nathan beamed as his eyes washed over Rana. "They had you, my precious little Rana. Lord knows I wouldn't take anything for you. I'm so glad I got you back."

"So am I, Grandfather," she agreed, then kissed his cheek.

Nathan declared that it was time he took a nap in order to be ready for his guard duty later that night, and as he settled into sleep, Rana watched him with deep affection. She noticed the way the dappled sunlight filtered through the trees and illuminated his blond and silver hair. His skin was leathered and lined from age and exposure to the elements, but he was still a striking man. She recalled how his gray-blue eyes filled with warmth and love and glowed with happiness each time his gaze settled on her, and she was glad fate had returned her to her family. This older man needed her sunshine in his life, sunshine that she was determined to provide for the rest of his days.

Rana had come to realize that he and Travis were right about her having no future in the Oglala lands, but she ached over the hardships she knew her adopted people would endure. Yet, as Travis had told her, there was nothing she could do to keep the Lakotas from their destiny except suffer and die along with them, which would have been her fate if she had insisted on remaining in the Dakota Territory. She hoped she could return one day to visit them, especially Lone Wolf and Myeerah. She would pray for their survival and hope they could change with the times as she had, as she was determined she would.

She was looking forward to her new life on the ranch and to winning the heart of Travis Kincade, for he warmed her soul with a strange radiance that could only be love. As she considered Travis in this light, speculations about her parents invaded her thoughts. How she wished she had known them, or could remember them. Her lack or loss of memory made her feel that something special was missing from her life. But she knew that if she worked hard, Nathan Crandall and

Travis Kincade could fill the void.

Rana was giving Travis more thought than she had ever given anything in her life. She knew they could offer each other more than a physical attraction, and she prayed he would recognize that truth and surrender to it, as she was doing. They could make a good pair—fighting, working, living, and loving, side by side. She understood that his luck with women had been bad, but that could change if he would only allow it. He was skittish and wary. She needed to be patient with him, to show him she was not like those other women, who had used and hurt him. She didn't want him to feel trapped, or to claim her out of guilt.

She envisioned his handsome body, which had been scarred by so many troubles. Worse, his heart had been scarred deeply as well. His enticing body, though healed, would always carry reminders of those tragic events, but his heart could recover if he permitted her to tend it with the medicine of love. He had not expected to become entangled with her. She dreamily recalled their passionate night together, which had made her long to share many more. Perhaps he had confessed more than he had intended that night and now regretted his candor. At least she was confident that she was not in competition with another woman, dead or alive. But, she asked herself, which would be easier to battle, a real woman or painful ghosts from his past? Still, with these facts in her possession, she could understand him and better plan her winning strategy . . .

Later that night, while Travis was taking his watch, he attempted to force his thoughts from the girl who was sleeping by the campfire, for she was a powerful distraction. He could not forget how she had smiled at him upon his return that evening. She had laughed and chatted with Nathan, and with him. All afternoon he had been eager to get back to camp just to be near her, and his body had ached for hers then, as it did now. He truly enjoyed talking with her, looking at her. Her smile warmed him all over, and her voice made him quiver. He could think of nothing more pleasant than holding her in his arms while they shared their innermost secrets and desires, unless, of course, it was making love to her. Yet, he couldn't move too swiftly with her, or she might think he wanted more from her than her love. He had to be careful around her, for they couldn't carry on a secret affair under Nathan's nose; that would have been wrong.

He had never seriously considered marriage before meeting her; now he thought about it constantly. She was causing him to experience a wide range of emotions, filling his head with hopes and dreams. And it seemed he was having the same effect on her. Was she as scared as he was about making a permanent commitment to another person? Was she just as afraid to trust him completely and risk total surrender? Would it make a difference to her, now or later, that he was a "despicable half-breed"? What if she met and wanted another man after they reached home? What if she craved a wild life, as her mother had? That would break Nathan's heart, and his too, if he allowed it. He had been independent for so long before taking on the responsibility of Nathan Crandall; now he was seriously considering adding Rana Michaels to his list of priorities, if she permitted him to do so. First, he had to make certain that this was what he wanted and needed, and she would have to do the same. She could win any man she set her sights on, and he wanted her sights on him! Where was that willful, defiant, arrogant girl others had described? How had she changed so quickly, so completely? It had taken him years! Whatever decision he made about Nathan's granddaughter, it would be a permanent one, and he vowed it would be made wisely and cautiously, and with her agreement.

In less than a week they would reach home. He would have to give her time to adjust to her new life and to the people in it. He would have to let her find herself, and he prayed she would also come to understand him. He could not get it out of his mind that they were joined, yet he was very much aware that if he staked a claim on her, he would have to be ready to back it up with a white man's marriage. In her camp, she had not wanted to marry because the cost would have been her freedom, which she prized so highly. In her new life, she could have both, whether or not her choice of a mate included him. Lord help them all if she was only seeking amusement or revenge on him. No, he refuted mentally, his Rana would never do that.

Feeling somewhat more confident, he stood and stretched, then left the campfire to scout the surrounding area.

Rana rolled to her back and sighed restively as her talks with Nathan swirled inside her head to inspire bad dreams. The black-haired man was chasing her again and spewing forth threats and crude language. For a time, all she could do was watch the terrifying action, but suddenly his words became clear. He was shouting, "You're the lowest kind of woman alive! You didn't care whose bed you crawled into, just so you got yourself diddled good. I know all about that bastard and the woods colt he sired. You mess with me, woman, and I'll tell everyone your foul secret. That little piece of information is worth a fortune, and you're gonna get it for me. You don't want your pa or that kid learning what a wicked slut you are. If I told what I know, your old man wouldn't give you a nickel and he would take that kid away from you. You ain't fit for nothing but giving men pleasure and earning money to keep my mouth shut. You try anything foolish and it's all over."

Rana shifted to her side as she subconsciously tried to block out the painful scene, but another one quickly filled her mind: "This is your last chance. I ain't gonna have nobody ruining my plans. You fool, you know who Fargo works for and I know who you been dawdling with behind my back! He can't help you, girl. He only wants what you owe him . . . You're coming with me today, and if you open your mouth, I'll fill his ears and watch all of you suffer. He'll despise you, and you'll never get a cent from him. If I toss you out, how will you and that brat live? You'd best be glad you two got me to see after you. I could stomp the Crandall name into the mud if you give me a mind to. Get your things. If this visit didn't soften him up, nothing will. Just give him a month or two, then we'll . . ."

Rana squirmed to her other side and snuggled into the furry mat. She watched the flaming-haired girl with tear-filled eyes leave the room; yet she could still see and hear the frightening man with his narrowed brown eyes. She watched him stalk toward her and could feel herself backing away from him in panic. She hated him and feared him, for he was evil and cruel. He glared at her and ordered, "Get your things packed for the last time, girl. I've found me a way out of this mess. I'm gonna have it all, and then some. Yep, me and that little dark-haired vixen are gonna take it all. Yep, we're gonna have us a real spread with no problems to bother us. She's a greedy, wicked little bitch, but I can use her help." He laughed, then pointed to a small picture of someone who appeared very much like her. "One day you're gonna be prettier than she is, but you won't be no stupid whore. Yep, little brat, you're gonna get me everything I want from your pa. Maybe when you get a little older, I might want more, since you ain't . . ."

Rana almost whimpered in her sleep as she resisted the

dreams that seemed determined to haunt her. She could see this woman who looked so much like herself packing clothes in a box. For some reason she put a *wanapin* and a baby inside a tall wooden hole and closed it. Then she looked across the room and said, "No more fear or running. No more lies about me. No more degradation and threats. No matter what happens, it must end. I'm going to kill him; then we can be free and happy. I'll never let anyone or anything harm you again, my love. Once he's dead, the truth will be buried forever. I've been a coward too long and he's nearly destroyed me. Nothing can be worse than living this hell, not even the truth. God forgive me for what I've done, but it was a mistake, my love, a terrible mistake. Surely I've paid enough for it. Once it's done, I'll come home. Home . . ."

"Rana," Travis whispered as he shook her gently. "Rana, wake up." He watched her fight the nightmare, though she resisted awakening. He was baffled by the words he had overheard, yet he had a gut feeling that Rana was repeating words she had heard her mother say long ago. He wondered how she had remembered them so clearly and if she would recall them when she was awake. Evidently, if this was more than just a bad dream, he had been mistaken about Marissa Crandall Michaels. He wished he knew what the "lies, threats, and secrets" were. It seemed Raymond Michaels had had an awesome hold over Marissa if she had hated and feared him enough to plan his murder, one that fate had not allowed. Oddly, he felt sorry for Nathan's daughter, for something terrible had ruined her life. He wondered if anyone alive knew her secret.

Rana stirred and opened her eyes to look upon the smiling face of Travis. She was trembling and her eyes were moist. His gaze and touch were so tender, and she needed tenderness desperately. She refused to think about the dark dreams, which were becoming hazy now.

Instead her hands rose, encircled his neck, and pulled his head down to seal their lips. She allowed him to fill her senses, to chase away her fears. When their lips parted, she murmured, "I need you, Travis. Will you hold me?"

Something in her gaze and voice exposed the depth of her need at that moment. He lay down beside her, pulled her into his arms, and rested her head against his shoulder. Cradling her like a small child, he stroked her hair. She nestled closer to him and sighed peacefully. Travis held her until she was sleeping again, this time without dark dreams. Even then he did not want to release her. It all felt so right as he lay there beneath the stars with her in his arms and his friend Nathan slumbering nearby, as if he had everything of importance within his reach. He somehow knew no peril would befall them tonight, for *Wakan Tanka* had brought them together and was watching over them. He embraced her tenderly, closed his eyes, and drifted off to sleep.

Three days later, they approached the Red River, which separated Texas from Indian Territory. It was Thursday, the twenty-seventh of June, and they expected to arrive home by Saturday. Fortunately they had not encountered any problems in Indian Territory, and they shared the excitement and joy of reaching home within two days.

Travis instructed, "I want you two to stay here while I check the current and woods on the other side. When it's all clear, I'll signal you to follow. Take it slow and easy, 'cause the river's high and fast."

Travis urged his horse into the water until it was deep enough for the animal to swim. His gaze scanned the distant bank for any sign of danger. While Rana and Nathan watched and waited, Travis and his mount gradually made their way toward the other bank, angling downriver slightly because of the strong current. Just as they reached the other side, a man jumped from behind thick bushes and fired his rifle at Travis. The bullet struck him across the left temple. Rana screamed as Travis fell backward into the swirling water and briefly disappeared beneath its fast-moving surface. As his ambusher tried to seize the stallion's reins to steal him, the horse reared and pawed, knocking the villain to the ground. The highly trained beast trampled the man's legs and arms as he yelled and vainly attempted to scramble free.

Rana's gaze strained to locate Travis in the water. Finally she sighted him bobbing along with the swift current, dazed and helpless. She shouted to Nathan, "I'm going after him! Wait here and watch for more attackers." Before Nathan could react or speak, she kneed her horse into a rapid gallop along the riverbank to get ahead of Travis. When she had covered enough distance, she urged the animal into the water and guided him to the center, where Travis was being swept toward her. With skill and in desperation, she placed the horse in Travis's watery path. When he reached her, she grabbed his shirt and pulled on it with all of her strength. It was a fierce battle, for the current was powerful and greedy, wanting to keep the handsome treasure for itself. Her hand cramped, but she refused to release her grip. Pain shot through her fingers and up her arm at the strain. The water yanked at Travis's body and she feared she would not be able to hold on to him.

Rana prayed for the strength and skill to save this man she had come to need so desperately. Her horse was also panicking and she tried to comfort and steady him with soothing words. She could tell the animal was having a difficult time struggling against the river's pull and their combined weight. She had to maintain control of the animal and her seating because she knew she could not swim to the side with Travis and, if she released him, he would surely drown. "Come on, little horse, you can make it," she encouraged the frightened animal. "That's it. Don't be afraid. Not much farther. You must help Rana, little horse. Rana will take care of you. That's a good horse," she declared, urging him onward.

Clinging to the pommel with one hand and holding Travis's head above water with the other, she prodded the horse toward the bank. Tears of pain and panic flowed down her cheeks, for she gravely doubted she could succeed. "Please help us, Great Spirit," she prayed urgently, for she knew all would be lost if she let go of Travis. She was overjoyed when her frantic prayer was answered, for the horse suddenly seemed to feel a burst of energy and strength and fought the current valiantly.

Yet it seemed as if they would never reach the other side, though this had been her only alternative when she had been unable to turn the animal around in the midst of the swirling river. She glanced down at the man whose unconscious body was pulling mercilessly on her aching arm. The attacker's bullet had torn through his headband, and she saw blood soaking it and his hair as it streamed down the side of his handsome face and neck to be absorbed by his shirt. She saw his nostrils moving steadily, indicating that he was breathing, and she wanted to pull him into her arms and cover his face with thankful kisses. Her desire went unfulfilled for the moment, for the danger had not yet passed.

Hurriedly Rana focused her gaze on the bank to make sure they were drawing nearer without drifting too far downriver. She clenched her teeth in grim determination as Travis seemed to get heavier and heavier by the second and her arm weaker and weaker. She was nearly in a state of panic by the time the horse struggled to climb out of the water. Exhausted, the animal staggered and slipped in the mud. Once his head cleared the edge of the water, she

301

carefully released her grip on Travis and hopped off the horse, quickly tying his reins to keep him from running off. She returned to Travis and yanked on his arms until she had his upper body out of the river. Breathing erratically, she dropped to her knees beside him and called his name several times. She stroked his face, then leaned forward to kiss him. He did not awaken. She tore a strip from her sopping dress and, after removing the torn headband and stuffing it into her pocket, she bound his wound.

Having disregarded her frantic words and having crossed the river upstream in the same area that Travis had traversed, Nathan rode up, with Travis's horse in tow. He quickly dismounted and joined Rana, who was fretting over the fallen man. He gingerly removed the bandage, checked Travis's injury, then replaced it. He sighed loudly in relief. "It's just a graze, Rana. He'll be fine. Let's get him on the bank. Far as I can tell, there was only one bushwhacker, and Travis's horse took care of him."

As they worked, Nathan remarked proudly, "That was a brave and reckless thing you did, girl, but you moved and thought quickly. You worried me silly taking off like that. I knew I couldn't catch up with you two in the river; she's moving too fast. After seeing you in action before, I figured you could save him, so I hightailed it over here to help you get him out of the water. That was some rescue."

They laid Travis in a grassy area and collapsed on the ground to rest. Nathan commented to break their tension, "Lordy, he's heavy. How in heaven's name did you hold on with the river yanking on him?"

Rana smiled and replied mischievously, "I knew you would beat me if I lost your ranch foreman, and we would have been forced to do his work, Grandfather. He is our scout, so we need him." She reached behind herself to rub her complaining back near her waist, flexed her aching shoulders, then lay flat to appease her fussing body and to slow her respiration to a more normal level. She held up her left hand and gazed at her bleeding, throbbing fingertips where three of her nails had been torn loose at the quick. Tears filled her eyes, but she tried to contain them.

Travis started coughing and stirring. Rana and Nathan moved to either side of him immediately. His eyes opened to find them leaning over him with worried looks. He remembered being shot and falling into the water. He found he was soaked from head to foot, and his head was pounding. He touched the bandage and gingerly examined his left temple, though the pain caused him to wince as he assessed the extent of his injury. He knew he was lucky, for he realized it was merely a flesh wound that had struck him at just the right angle and speed to render him unconscious. He was fortunate that he hadn't drowned and that his two companions were safe. He eyed Nathan, who was wet from the hips down, then Rana, who was nearly as soaked as he was except for her hair. She seemed on the verge of tears and he tried to sit up, but Nathan's hand on his shoulder prevented it.

"You lie still, son. We're trying to stop the bleeding. You scared ten years off my life, and I ain't got none to spare," Nathan teased to ease his tension.

"What about that snake in the bushes? Was he alone?" Travis inquired sullenly, rankled with himself for getting ambushed.

"Apache did him in good, and I didn't see anybody else. Just a no-good horse thief. You rest awhile," Nathan advised.

As Nathan described the incredible rescue, Travis's gaze went to the drenched Rana, whose expression revealed pain. He noticed how tense and pale she was and how she was bravely trying to conceal something. One

303

hand was clasped tightly in the other one, and blood was seeping through her fingers. Not only had he been rescued, but this slip of a girl had done it and at great risk to herself.

Travis insisted on sitting up. He reached for Rana's left hand and pried it free of the other one as she lowered her gaze to avoid meeting his. He had ripped off a single nail before, so he knew how badly she was hurting with three gone. Glancing at the front of his shirt, he realized it was her blood staining it, not his, just as he realized how difficult his rescue had been for her. Considering the rapid action she had taken and the anguish she had endured, she had to be the bravest and most generous woman alive. She had given no thought to her own peril and had not quit when the task had become arduous. She had literally saved his life! She was amazing, unique.

Her hand quivered in his and felt cold. Blood oozed around the ragged edges of her missing nails and raw flesh was visible. He recalled his Indian training for such injuries and that Lone Wolf had given him a *pezuta wopahte* in case it was needed on the trail. "Nate, get that medicine bundle for me. I need to take care of Rana's hand."

Travis's grip was warm and gentle, and it caused her to tremble. She was all too aware of her grandfather's presence as Travis eyed her hand and grimaced, sharing her pain. He asked why she had not told him she was hurt. She tried to pull her hand free as she softly remarked, "I will wash it and tend it. You must rest. The trail is dangerous and we have need of our scout. Do not worry over me," she urged, though what she really wanted was to fling herself into his arms and cover his face with kisses.

A half smile teased at one corner of his mouth and brightened his eyes. "Like you didn't worry over me when I was being swept away by that greedy river?" he hinted roguishly as he caressed her cheek. "From the way it's been looking, you make a better scout than I do."

She debated instantly, "We do not blame you for a tiny mistake. No man is perfect, Travis Kincade, and you must learn to accept this fact. Grandfather wants only your best, and you give it to him. Do not punish yourself for deeds that do not belong to you."

Travis eyed her strangely, for he found many interpretations in her words. Nathan handed him the medicine bundle suddenly and Travis's attention was momentarily diverted from Rana, who was able to recover her poise. "Pass me that canteen, Nate. Rana's hand needs a good washing so I can see what I'm doing." He looked overhead and added, "It's getting late; we might as well camp here for the night. Why don't you start us some supper while I tend to Rana; then we can turn in early. I think we're all tired and jumpy. When I finish, I'll scout around. Maybe I should take your granddaughter with me; she's a fearless warrior and a skilled hunter. If I come across another bushwhacker or get dizzy from this injury, I might need her protection or help."

Rana watched Travis closely and it did not appear to her that he was making a jest. His smoldering gaze inflamed her all over and his voice was as effective as a passionate caress. She was surprised he did not seem irritated at having been rescued by a woman, as she had feared. She watched him tend her fingers so lovingly, so gently. Every so often as he doctored and wrapped each finger separately, he would look up at her to ask if he was hurting her or if a bandage was too tight. His eyes twinkled with merriment as he began to massage her sore arm, then shifted behind her to move onward to her shoulders, neck, and back. She tried to tell him she was

305

fine, but he insisted on continuing his stimulating actions, and she had to admit they felt wonderful and relaxing.

When Nathan walked off to search for wood, Travis leaned forward to murmur, "You should get out of those wet clothes and shoes, Rana. If the night air becomes chilly, you might catch cold. Besides, I'm sure they're uncomfortable. I'll stand guard while you change," he offered politely.

When she turned to respond, her shoulder brushed against his. Their bodies seemed so close and their gazes locked. Travis's right hand slipped behind her head and drew it close to his so he could fuse their lips in a much-needed kiss. When they parted, his eyes helplessly roamed her lovely features. He kissed hers shut to halt their magical, hypnotic pull. "Thanks for saving my miserable life, Rana. Go change clothes before I forget we aren't alone and I have your grandfather wanting to kill me."

Rana opened her eyes to gaze at him. She smiled and replied, "I wish we were alone, *mihigna;* then you could thank me better." She stood up, ignoring how the wet garment clung to her blazing body. She went to her pack of possessions, removed dry clothing, and headed into the trees to find a place to change. She could feel his hungry gaze feasting ravenously on her body, and she thrilled to the sensations he inspired.

Travis glanced in the direction Nathan had taken to search for firewood. He scolded himself for thinking even briefly about following Rana and making her words— "my husband"—a blissful reality. With Nathan around, they lacked the necessary time and privacy for another joining of bodies, a joining that was certain to happen again soon, for the bond between them was getting stronger each day. He went to his horse to retrieve his own dry clothing, then sought one other source of comfort. Withdrawing a bottle of whiskey from his saddlebag, he took a long swig from it. After replacing it, he gazed longingly at the area into which Rana had vanished, then cursed his bad timing as he changed clothes.

After they had eaten, an exhausted Nathan drank freely from the whiskey bottle to release his own tensions and worries, finally draining it under Travis's watchful eye. The older man then reclined on his bedroll and was soon sleeping deeply. When Travis glanced at Rana, her keen gaze was leaving Nathan's slumbering body to look at him. Their eyes met and spoke messages of intense longing.

Travis's gaze roved her enticing features and he warned himself to curb his perilous thoughts, for her expression told him she was thinking along the very same lines. He glanced at Nathan again and was assured the man would not awaken until morning. Even with him lying there, they seemed enveloped in a smoldering solitude. He went to kneel beside Rana to whisper, "I need to scout the area before we turn in. Besides, I need some fresh air and exercise or we're in trouble," he teased in a mellow voice, his green eyes twinkling.

Rana smiled and caressed his cheek. She was delighted when he bent forward and kissed her hastily before leaving the clearing. She looked at the slumbering Nathan again, then toward the forest. Could she brazenly seduce him? She grinned. After a short time, she lifted her blanket and walked to the edge of their camp. She boldly removed her shirt and dangled it invitingly over a bush. A few feet away, she removed one boot and discarded it, then another as she moved along the path. Next, she left her pants and, lastly, her bloomers hanging on bushes to create a provocative trail to her. She spread the blanket and lay down on it, awaiting his arrival and his reaction. The night air wafted over her naked body, but it failed to cool its heat. She closed her eyes in anticipation.

"Do you know how dangerous this is?" Travis murmured as he joined her, having collected her belongings and deposited them nearby with his own. He knew this was the meaning of the message that had passed between them, and he could not resist challenging any evil or peril to have her.

"There is danger in all things, but reward in few," she replied, pulling his head down to fuse their lips.

Travis's mouth explored hers in a long, stimulating kiss. Her arms encircled his neck as his kisses seemingly branded her mouth, face, and throat as skillfully as he might brand a newborn calf or colt. Gradually all restraint left them and they clung together, quivering in each other's embrace. Each could feel the other's naked body pressing closer and closer until no space was left between them. His arms tightened around her possessively as their mouths meshed.

Travis leaned away from her to stare into her compelling eyes. Leisurely his gaze roamed her face and he marveled at her beauty, becoming inflamed at the glaze of passion in her eyes. His hand drifted into her hair, enjoying how it felt surrounding his fingers. He knew their time was limited, but, for now, all he wanted and needed was to look at her, to touch her, to feel her next to him, to absorb her surrender. He knew she was here in his arms willingly and trustingly, and that knowledge caused his spirit to soar and his heart to beat swiftly. His mouth came down on hers again, tasting her sweet desire and eagerly seeking her unbridled response. He claimed her with skill and resolve.

Rana was dazed with love and hunger for Travis. He caused her to flame and quiver all over, and she reveled in these feelings. He took control over her life, her will, her emotions. His hands moved over her flesh, tantalizing her to heightened desire. Her body seemed to urge her talented lover to invade and conquer it. So many wonderful sensations attacked her simultaneously. Her hands began to travel up and down his back and she writhed on the blanket, revealing her rising need for him.

Slowly, dreamily, Rana's fingers drifted over his sleek flesh and increased his yearning for her. Muscles bulged here and there to tempt her hands to explore them, for they revealed such strength and beauty. She felt his respiration quicken and his body shudder. She loved the feel of his flesh against hers. Hunger stormed her body and demanded feeding. Pressing closer to him, she moaned softly.

Her responses caused him to become bolder with his actions. He was sensitive and vulnerable to her every movement. His whole body burned and pleaded to fuse with hers, but he would not rush their joining. He wanted to invade her very soul and claim it as his own. The first night they had relented to passion's calling and it had been wondrous; tonight their lovemaking was sheer bliss. His hand traveled down her flat stomach and teased along her silky thighs, using long, gentle strokes, each one coming closer to her womanhood. Finally he touched that secret place, sending her world spinning with pleasure. It was ecstasy; it was rapturous torment. He wanted her to enjoy this experience to the fullest. His hands and tongue prepared her and tempted her to take him greedily and without reserve.

When he had stimulated her to the point where her body was pleading feverishly for appeasement, he slipped between her thighs and eased within her, where she greeted him with urgency and delight. He moved slowly and seductively within her receptive body, rhythmically creating a wildfire that threatened to consume them. Her breathing became erratic and her head thrashed from side to side as he brought her to the edge of conquest, then lovingly held her there to savor the wild and wonderful pleasure before carrying her over the peak.

Rana took him within her with an intensity and hunger that was exciting and stirring, and soon she had created a turbulent, wild fervor that could not be contained. As his thrusts increased in speed and purpose, she titillated him with caresses and responses that heightened his fiery desires. Their bodies were working as one, taking and giving and sharing sweet bliss.

Travis placed lingering kisses on her face and throat and shoulders, each one more possessive and tender than the last. His shaft was like a flaming torch that cried out for a merciful dousing, mercy he did not truly wish or allow. He drove into her time and time again, each stroke a blend of ecstasy and torment. She was responding to him instinctively, fiercely. When her legs draped over his and she matched his pace and urgency, he feared his control was in danger.

Rana could no longer deny her body what it craved, no matter how much she wanted to continue savoring these sensations, and she lacked the knowledge to control and pace her passions. She clung to him and kissed him savagely as her body seemed to explode into many flames and overwhelming feelings. She stiffened slightly and hugged him tightly to her.

Travis knew her release was devouring her and he unleashed his restraint to join her, allowing them to experience the sheer delight of each other and indescribable pleasure together. They rode the stallion of rapture locked in each other's arms until the wild beast was tamed and exhausted. Moisture covered their bodies and their breathing was labored. Hearts beating as one, they remained entwined until all sensation had been drained.

A tranquil afterglow surrounded and relaxed them. They snuggled together, silent for a time as the reality and meaning of this union washed over them, cooling their sated passions and sealing their bond.

Rana shifted her head to gaze into his placid expression. "I hope you are not angry with me for tempting you again. My hunger for you was so great I could not master it."

Travis responded huskily in the Lakota tongue, "I have chosen you to share my life-circle. I am your protection. I am your provider. You are mine, and I will be all things to you, as you must be all things to me. My word of honor is yours until death."

Rana's eyes misted as he tenderly repeated the stirring words from their joining ceremony, repeated them as if he truly meant them this time. Her heart overflowed with joy and love. "You are all things to me, and I am yours until death. You are the one true man who can tame the wild wind, for I do not wish to battle you or resist you."

"When we reach home, there are many things to be settled between us, Rana. I need you and I want you, but I have important matters to handle first. Trust me and wait for me," he entreated.

"Do what you must until you can come to me with an open heart."

It was very late, but they made love a second time with a tenderness and passion that entwined their hearts and sealed their destinies as one. Afterward, Travis suggested they freshen up and return to camp. They shared a quick bath and slipped back to the dying campfire, sleeping on separate sides of it to resist further temptation. From all appearances, Nathan had not stirred during their absence.

On the Circle *C* Ranch outside of Fort Worth, Clarissa Caldwell stared across the table at Mary Beth Sims, whose father, Clifford, owned a large hotel and fancy restaurant in town. Clifford Sims was one of the many men who owed her father heavily for several favors. Clarissa accurately suspected that her father had been discussing more than legal problems with their male guest, for this was the third time recently that Mary Beth and Clifford had been entertained in their home. It was not like her father to invite wives or children to his special dinners unless he had a lucrative purpose in mind. Clarissa knew that her father had been visiting and eating at Clifford's hotel regularly during the past few weeks, and by now she could tell that Harrison Caldwell was making crafty plans to obtain something he wanted. She recognized that covetous gleam in his eye and his anticipatory tone of voice.

Clarissa smiled deceptively as she scrutinized this woman who had obviously caught her father's attention, for he had been suspiciously secretive about his stealthy pursuit. He had not mentioned his plans for Mary Beth to her and had pretended that these dinners were part business and part social. She was certain they were not, at least not in the sense he had insinuated. She tingled with alarm and raged at his guile. Mary Beth Sims was not the kind of woman to become a man's mistress, not even a rich, powerful man like her father. Something was going on inside her father's head, something she did not like.

The green-eyed brunette was a pretty girl of eighteen who had a very shapely figure, one which her father had been eyeing furtively all evening. Harrison had been laughing and joking while the best foods and drinks were being served. He had slyly mentioned the many times he had saved Clifford's business and how he had been instrumental in getting Clifford elected to the town council. Clearly her father was preparing to call in those debts, and Mary Beth was intimately concerned.

From what she could see and hear as she observed the two men, Clarissa realized that Clifford was eager to

312

please her father. Sims was smiling and joking easily, and cooperating fully with her father's desires. Evidently the manner of repayment was most agreeable to him. Perhaps the man had created a larger debt to Harrison than that of which she was aware, or he soon planned to increase that debt. Considering their positions and how much time and attention her father had given this girl lately, she concluded that his actions could be leading in only one direction: marriage.

Clarissa fumed as she recalled how her father had warned her to be on her best behavior each time the Simses had visited them. He was always complimenting the girl's looks and praising her wit, pretending she was the most fascinating creature alive. She wanted to laugh in her father's face for his ridiculous behavior and plans: a fifty-six-year-old man of his importance marrying a timid eighteen-year-old child! Whatever was the man thinking? she wondered angrily. After all these years of being a widower who came and went as he desired, why marry now and why this little thing? But of course, she decided peevishly, no wife would halt him from doing as he pleased.

Clarissa was aware of other facts that she doubted her father knew: Mary Beth was in love with Cody Slade, who worked for Nathan Crandall on the Rocking *C* Ranch, and the girl did not like Harrison in the slightest and felt ill at ease around him. Naturally Mary Beth was too much a lady and dutiful daughter to expose such feelings to either man, but Clarissa had seen how Mary Beth had glanced at Harrison when she had thought no one was watching. The girl's expression had been one of repulsion and fear. Clarissa wondered if Mary Beth was aware of what was going on before her eyes and behind her back. She also wondered if Clifford Sims would force his daughter to marry Harrison Caldwell even if she could not stand him, for evidently she could not. Yet she realized only too well that women naturally had little to say about their fates.

Clarissa lowered her head to smile spitefully as she envisioned this genteel girl refusing Harrison Caldwell's affection and proposal, as Marissa Crandall had done long ago. She could not help but imagine her father's rage and embarrassment if he were to learn how she had spied on him and Marissa years ago. The old buzzard had always underestimated her cunning and daring, and her hatred! she reflected angrily.

When she had been a child and he locked her in her room during Marissa's secret visits to his ranch, she would climb out her window, edge along the narrow balcony to his, and peek inside. Sometimes she had watched and listened for hours as the two had played in her father's bed. She had been mesmerized by their actions and the intense emotions that had flowed between them. By observing them, she had received vicarious pleasure and happiness and had savored her father's love. Little did her father suspect that he and Marissa had been the ones who had taught her all about sex and had inspired her greedy appetite. She could still remember how eager she had been to come of age and to find the courage to begin her own life of splendid enjoyment. Since her father had refused to give her love and attention, she had found plenty of men willing and eager to do so. Unfortunately, however, only Travis Kincade and Nathan Crandall had been man enough to stand against her father, and neither had become enchanted with her. But other men had loved her and desired her and had filled the void in her life, however briefly. As a child she had learned that her father did not love her or want her. She had done everything, anything, to capture his attention. His only reaction had been anger whenever she embarrassed him publicly. Yet he had not minded asking, or ordering, her to whore for him as

314

Raymond had forced Marissa to do. What kind of father was that? she asked herself with a sneer. Her father was to blame for her behavior, for her misery, for her hatred! One day, she vowed, he would be sorry.

As the two men smoked their cigars and sipped their port and Mary Beth excused herself, Clarissa reflected on her father's past love life. She had to admit he was a handsome man and a superb catch, but she doubted he would be able to ensnare Clifford's daughter. No doubt Mary Beth would do what Marissa had done: reject her father and run off with another man; in Mary Beth's case it would probably be Cody Slade. Of course, Marissa's predicament had been vastly different from this girl's.

Clarissa knew why the blue-eyed enchantress had married Raymond Michaels: to get far away from this area so that her vile secret could be safeguarded. Poor Marissa had never imagined that a cheap saloon harlot would devastate her life with a favor and a betrayal of that favor. Nor had Marissa imagined she could not bewitch the handsome and charming gambler who had pretended to be madly in love with her in order to wed her for her money and status. Harrison had been away for months when Marissa had discovered she was pregnant; otherwise Marissa doubtlessly would have married him. If she had, the flaming-haired bitch would have fared far better than she had under Raymond's insidious hands.

She had despised Marissa for intruding on her life and for gaining a hold on her father's life and affection, a hold she had never possessed. When she had been a teenager and Marissa had returned home for visits, she had faked a friendship with the ill-fated vixen in order to find a way to destroy her. She had thought she had discovered how when she had learned of the hostility between Raymond and Nathan, for Raymond had always stayed in town while Marissa and her child had visited Nathan. She had found a clever way to meet Raymond and had sought her revenge by plotting to steal Marissa's husband, though she had remained ignorant of the couple's shocking relationship until she and the devilish gambler had begun a torrid affair. One night she overheard the sordid truth during a violent argument between Marissa and Raymond, and later confronted her lover; afterward they had shared secrets about Marissa. She had plotted with the handsome rake to get rid of Marissa and Harrison so they could marry and take possession of both ranches, using Marissa's past, present, and bastard child as their weapons. Clarissa tingled as she recalled the secret times she had made passionate love to Marissa's husband. She had hated Marissa even more for obtaining—no matter the reasons—one of the few men who had truly made her body and blood boil, for Raymond's matchless sexual prowess, abundant charms, and superb looks had been his greatest assets. If the Indians had not killed her dreams . . .

It was too late to fret over that annoying defeat. Thinking back on the whole situation, she was glad she had not become partners with Raymond Michaels, for at times he had been cruel and untrustworthy, very much like her father. Raymond had married Marissa before learning the truth about her, then had blackmailed her and made her whore to support him, just as her own father demanded she whore for him so that he might attain his diabolic ends. Marissa had married Raymond to escape her wanton trap, and Raymond had claimed to have married her for her wealth and position. Clarissa admitted she had been enamored for a time by the virile, handsome charmer, for he had had a winning way with women and had been intoxicating in bed, and perhaps his devious character had unconsciously reminded her of her father, whose love and attention she had craved yet had been denied. With her years of experience with men and life, she had learned how to handle and judge men

316

and situations, at least most of them.

With Raymond, Marissa, and a saloon whore dead, she was the only one who knew the truth about her father's ex-mistress, though there appeared no way she could use or profit from that shocking information. She had never told her father, for she believed she might one day be able to twist that staggering truth and use it to her advantage. In time she would find a way to destroy her despicable, selfish father, as Marissa had been destroyed. Poor Marissa, she mused cruelly. She never knew the truth about her child's father, a truth that could have freed her from her nightmarish life with Raymond . . .

Clarissa thought about Marissa's last visit to the ranch shortly before her death. She had known Harrison had been up to something that day, so she had sneaked back to the ranch at night. She had witnessed the depth of his cruelty and the height of his infatuation for Marissa. What she had not known then about them or Marissa, she had learned that night as they had quarreled and battled. After Marissa's departure, she had watched her father gloat over his behavior and power and had overheard him talking to himself about his plan to murder Raymond so he could take possession of the flaming-haired witch, now that she had been properly punished for her past rejection. Determined to keep them apart, she had warned Raymond, a warning that had impelled him to flee to his death. At first she had been sad and sorry and had blamed her father; later she had calmly accepted the situation and had begun searching for another path to her victory. Looking back, she realized it would have been a careless mistake to have become partners with an untrustworthy beast like Raymond, especially since her father was steadily increasing holdings that would soon be hers alone.

After the Simses had departed, Clarissa looked at her grinning father and boldly questioned, "Papa, what do

317

you want with a silly child like Mary Beth? I've seen the way you've been eyeing her. What are you planning?"

"Why, Clarissa Caldwell, you sound jealous," Harrison teased playfully. He realized he would have to tell her something or she might be prompted to interfere. "I've got plans for Miss Mary Beth Sims. When I take over the rest of this area, I'm going to need a proper wife to entertain my friends and clients and take care of me. Surely my daughter isn't going to be around much longer, not if she doesn't want to be called a spinster. You've got to start thinking about marriage and children. Since I'll be in need of a wife, she suits my purposes perfectly."

Clarissa argued, "Even when I marry, Papa, I can stay here to take care of you and the ranch. Who deserves to become the mistress of your new spread more than I do? I've worked just as hard as you to obtain it. Why not find a nice widow closer to your own age? I tell you, Papa, you're wasting your time and energy on her."

Harrison frowned. "Don't go telling me how to handle matters, girl. If you had done your part, Kincade would be on my side, you two would be married, and the Crandall ranch would be ours. They've been gone nearly two months. You didn't even know he was leaving, and you can't find out where they are. I'll make sure you get what's coming to you, so don't you worry none. As for my taking a wife, it isn't any of your concern or business. Surely you don't begrudge your dear father a little happiness and excitement with another woman. Pretty widow or not, I don't want any man's leavings. In case you don't have eyes, girl, I'm still a virile man, and sometimes I get itches stronger than yours. I want Mary Beth Sims to scratch them because she's pretty and young and innocent, and I can train her as I please. Your mother has been dead since '44, and I raised you all alone. Don't you think I get lonesome, and tired of using

318

those cheap women in town?"

Clarissa wanted to shriek at him: *Like you trained that young and innocent Marissa?* but she restrained herself. "You misunderstand me, Papa," she guilefully protested. "Mary Beth has a sweetheart: Cody Slade, who works for Nathan Crandall. Even if you and her father try to convince her to marry you, I doubt she will. She loves Cody and plans to marry him. You don't want to be embarrassed by having her reject your proposal. Besides, she's such a fragile, timid creature. You need a woman with backbone, one who can stand at your side and help you run your holdings, a woman who knows how to take care of a home and a husband. Don't reach for the impossible," she entreated softly and slyly.

Harrison was vexed by his daughter's words and her attitude. "I don't care about Mary Beth's girlish feelings for Slade. She'll do as her father commands. You think Clifford would allow her to marry Slade when I've asked for her? Never. Once she get settled in here, she'll do exactly as I say. It won't take long for her to realize how lucky she is to have married a wealthy and powerful rancher instead of a cowpuncher who can't earn in his lifetime what I spend in a year. She's got manners and breeding, and she's educated and charming. She's perfect for my needs, Clarissa, all of them. Besides, no wife of mine is going to refuse me anything or disobey me."

"Does she know that you and her father are discussing marriage?"

"Not yet. I'm giving her a taste of what I have to offer. Once I get my hands on Nate's ranch, then I'll reveal my plans for her."

"Are you sure her father will go along with you after she cries and begs to marry Cody? He loves his daughter. Surely he wouldn't force her to marry you."

"That's what you think, girl. Sims owes me plenty, and soon I'll have his neck in a financial noose. She'll do as I say, one way or another. You see, girl, her father's done a few things that the law will frown on if I choose to expose them. As his lawyer, I know all about him and his dealings. She'll agree, to keep her father from being hanged. That's something you should learn, Clarissa. Always have an alternate plan, and always know the strengths and weaknesses of your enemies and rivals. That's the only way you can succeed with your plans or defeat a foe. Just make sure you've got the guts and wits to stand firm once you make a decision to go after something or someone."

Clarissa decided she needed to learn what that "financial noose" was so that she could secretly tie it. Too, she would find some clever way to warn Mary Beth or Cody about her father's devious plan. If those two could elope before her father staked his claim on Mary Beth, it would halt his scheme. She did not want another woman in her house, especially one who could give her father a child and give her an unwanted rival for his inheritance. No matter what she had to do, she would prevent him from marrying before she could take all he owned, including his miserable life. If only Travis would return soon, she reflected, and she could find some way to win his heart and help. Women had ways of entrapping resisting men, and she vowed to use any or all of them if necessary.

Help, she mentally echoed, then smiled wickedly. If she were cunning and daring, she could beat her father at his own game with his own hirelings! If she played her cards right, as Raymond had once done, she would undermine the entire situation with the very men her father had hired to help him attain his goals . . .

Chapter Eleven

After they had eaten the next morning and were preparing to break camp, Rana handed Travis the red headband that she had removed the day before when tending his wound. "I will sew it for you later," she offered, pointing to the bullet hole. She tingled at his nearness and longed to embrace him on this new day.

Travis grinned and said, "Thanks for saving it; it's my lucky charm, or used to be. An Apache shaman gave it to me after I saved his hide. He told me to wear it every time I rode into Indian territory and the Great Spirit would protect me from all harm. It worked until yesterday when you had to save my hide," he remarked, then chuckled. His smile and laughter seemed to flow over her and coat her like warm honey, and she gave him her full attention. He observed how she was looking at him and how her cheeks flushed with desire, and his smile broadened. He wondered if she was aware of how potently she affected him. All it required to send his senses soaring was a smile, or a laugh, or a glance, or a casual touch. His blood raced inside his body as his igneous eyes roamed her features and his senses drank in her aura. Visions of her naked body lying beneath his in the moonlight filled his mind. He knew he would have to halt his fantasy, for his body was responding.

She noticed how tiny, golden brown flecks seemed to appear and dance in his green eyes when he was in a tranquil mood, a mood that caused her body to tingle and her heartbeat to increase. Little creases that suggested his sincerity and happiness teased at the corners of those entrancing eyes and deepened the lines near his mouth. He had shaved at first light and his strong jawline was now visible to her wandering gaze. She watched him remove his bandage to secure the red strip around his head, then fluff his sable hair over it, thick hair that seemed to fall into a natural part just off center and cause his wispy locks to settle in careful waves. Evidently he had used his sharp knife to keep his hair from growing too long on the top and sides or past the nape of his neck. She noted how his brows grew at an angle that gave him a devilish or arrogant look when he arched one or narrowed his leafy green eyes. His face was lean and his features well defined, as if carved by a loving and talented creator. She recalled that very little dark hair grew on his chest, not enough to conceal his scars or his muscled torso. With a smile, she debated, "It did not fail to protect you; you are alive. How did you meet this enemy shaman and save his life?" she inquired, snared by curiosity.

He did not hesitate before answering. "Years ago, I scouted for the Army for awhile, until I got tired of their lies and tricks. I was at loose ends; I didn't have any place to go or anything special to do. At the time, it seemed like a good way to learn about the white man and his world; you might say it was one of the safest ways for a half-breed to move around in dangerous territory without being trapped between two sides that hated each other. You see, Rana, whites despise half-breeds more than Indians, but they don't mind using them as trackers and scouts. At first, I didn't try to hide my mixed blood. I was

322

too cocky and bitter to care what anybody said or thought about me. It didn't take long for me to realize how foolish that was. It caused me too much trouble; I was always having to fight or kill some man who couldn't let the matter pass. Not that I was really looking for friends or a home, though the truth would have made that impossible. That's the trouble with people; they judge you by the wrong measure and they're always looking for a way to use you to get what they want. Thing was, the Army needed my skills and Indian contacts, so they kindly overlooked my heritage," he said with a sneer, exposing his lingering resentment and the anguish he had endured since birth.

"On my last assignment, I was guiding four soldiers to a secret meeting with some Cheyenne chiefs. We came upon an Apache shaman who was on a vision quest. He was sitting on this big rock, praying and chanting for a message from the Great Spirit. The soldiers decided to have some fun, as they called it, with the old man. You see, soldiers love taking on defenseless Indians and collecting souvenirs."

She was delighted he was revealing part of his past and his emotions, though she realized how difficult it was for him to speak of these painful memories. She wondered if he was afraid she might think badly of his mixed blood and troubled past. When Travis grew silent for a time, Rana softly probed, "What happened?"

Travis looked her in the eye and calmly divulged, "I killed the bastards." When she did not appear shocked or distressed by his revelation, he continued, "I tried to talk them out of tormenting the old man and killing him, but they laughed and ordered me to stay out of it. I told them that it was bad luck to intrude on a vision quest and that the old man was harmless. The shaman just stood there with his eyes closed, chanting and waiting to die with courage and honor. I had no choice in the matter. When the battle was over, the old man smiled at me and nodded his understanding," he remarked casually, amazing her with how modestly he had revealed what must have been a fierce and dangerous battle against four soldiers and increasing her respect and admiration for him.

"The old shaman removed his headband, said a prayer over it, tied it around my head, and told me it would protect me from evil spirits. He said I could never die as long as I was wearing it. I sure am glad he didn't say I couldn't be defeated or injured, 'cause I would have known it was worthless and thrown it away a year later. He asked my Indian name, then carved those initials on a hunting knife and handed it to me. It had a thunderbird painted on the handle and he said I would receive power from it every time I used the blade. Somewhere a rattlesnake is carrying that knife and, when I find him, he's dead," he murmured coldly, his eyes glittering with hatred and desire for revenge as that infuriating betrayal and defeat flooded his mind.

"When he tried to give me his horse, I told him he was being too generous. He smiled again and said a man's life and honor were worth far more than a headband, knife, and horse. That's how I got Apache here," he told her, stroking the animal's forehead. "I don't know what the shaman whispered in his ear, but he won't allow anyone on his back but me, and I know he would give up his life for mine. He's gotten me out of many a scrape, like yesterday. He's mine until one of us dies." As if knowing his master was speaking highly of him, Apache nuzzled the side of Travis's head and brought a smile to his lips.

"How did you lose the knife?" she inquired, aware of how important those belongings and that episode were to him.

For an instant, he tensed, then forcibly relaxed his hard body. "I didn't. I was ambushed by two cutthroats when I was twenty. After they tortured me, they stole everything I had but Apache. He wouldn't let them near him. For months he had rope burns on his neck from trying to get free to save my life." Travis remembered the pistol he had been wearing that fateful day, one he had taken off a gunslinger who had challenged him to the death, a pistol that had revealed the man's prior victories in gun battles in the tiny stars notched on its butt.

Rana glanced at the animal to discover that the scars Travis had described were still visible if she looked closely. "Why did they not steal your *wanapin?*" she asked, wishing he would explain its significance, for a warrior's markings on his possessions and body told much about him. Delving into his dark past made him tense, she realized, so she probed lightly and gingerly and was ready to end the conversation the moment he desired it.

Travis absently touched the sacred token that had been carved and given to him by the legendary Sitting Bull. Only twice had it been removed from his neck—the day he had handed it to Buffalo Slayer to give to her if he did not survive his pursuit of Claude Chambers, and the day Lowry's hirelings had tried to steal it. Both times he had recovered it. "One of them cut it off, but he dropped it. Nate found it when he found me, half-dead. He took me to his ranch and brought me back to life, in several ways. That's how we met seven years ago."

"You searched for these men to slay them?" she pressed, acting as if she knew nothing of the circumstances.

"Yep, but their trail was too cold by the time I healed. The man who hired them had been murdered, so I couldn't beat any clues out of him or his . . . Nate was the first person who had accepted me and needed me since I had left the Hunkpapa camp, so I returned to the ranch to help him and stayed there. It took him years, but he settled me down. I owe him my life and loyalty, Rana," he explained pointedly. "I wouldn't want to do anything to disappoint or hurt him."

Rana watched him intently as he spoke so openly and sincerely. Every day, nearly every hour, he touched her heart more deeply. It was clear to her that he had endured a hard, painful life. She was glad he had been thrown together with her grandfather and cast into her life. "I am happy Grandfather found you and saved your life."

"Are you, Rana?" he asked, gazing into her liquid blue eyes.

She looked deeply into his before replying, "If not, he would not have found me and I would not be going home. The Great Spirit works in mysterious ways. He sent Grandfather to your side and sent you to find me to bring me home. All is as it should be."

"I'm glad you see things that way. I must admit you had me worried for awhile," he confessed, grinning at her.

"As you had me worried," she playfully retorted. "Have I not proven the bad tales about Wild Wind are false, or too great? The Oglalas did not understand how important it was for me to be as I am, to be all I am. You and Grandfather understand and accept me as Wild Wind or Rana. This makes me happy and thankful. You are good for me."

"Does this mean we can become friends now?" he hinted, allowing his appreciative gaze to wander over her from head to foot.

"We are friends, Travis Kincade, and more," she added. "I am sorry you suffered so much before meeting Grandfather, but it has made you as you are, a very special man who warms my heart. You carry the best of two bloods; be proud of both, for they are you. Promise you will never leave Grandfather and the ranch. They need you, as I need you. I will never reject you or scorn you. I am yours by choice. Lone Wolf was wise to make us join before releasing me to you."

Their gazes met and they exchanged smiles. Nathan joined them then and asked, "We ready to ride? I'm anxious to get home."

"So am I," Travis cheerfully concurred.

Rana smiled at her grandfather and nodded her agreement.

When they approached the ranch two days later, it was dusk, but they were filled with energy and anticipation. Travis and Nathan had been away for fifty-seven days; Travis and Rana had been joined for thirty-three, a fact that neither could ignore or wanted to forget.

Rana's eyes darted back and forth as the two men filled her ears with information about the ranch. As they rode under the arch, from which a large C resting on a rocker was suspended from a crossbar, her eyes grew wide with disbelief. Nathan claimed ownership for land as far as she could see and more. Fences snaked along the dirt road for miles, restraining many animals. She wondered how anyone could go hungry or be cold with so many animals, or fear any foe with so much power. It was difficult for her to comprehend the extent of Nathan's wealth and ranch. As they neared a large wooden dwelling, Nathan told her it was her new home and that he was eager to show it to her.

Not far away, she could see more wooden dwellings, which Travis told her were barns, work sheds, and bunkhouses, and he explained how each structure was used. The closer they rode to the neat settlement, the more noises she heard: men's laughter and singing, strange music, the lowing of cattle, and the neighing of horses. Travis related how Saturday and Sunday were the days the hands could relax from the week's work, with half of the men taking off Saturday and half taking off

Sunday; this schedule was switched the next week, for there were chores to be done every day and the ranch could not be left unprotected. If a man had special plans, he could usually find another hand with whom he could swap days off or he could pay someone to work in his place. Usually the men would use the time to play cards or games or make music, and some would sing or dance. On Saturday, many would ride into town to visit and drink with friends who worked on this or another ranch. He did not tell her that many of them would go there to spend time with the women who worked at the Silver Shadow Saloon, as he had done on occasion. On Sunday, some would go to church or simply rest. Because it was now supper time, most of the hands had returned and were enjoying their last few free hours before preparing for the new week.

They dismounted near the house and Travis collected the reins to take the horses to the stable. Nathan instructed genially, "See if you can locate Cody while I show Rana inside. I need to know what's been going on during our absence, but I don't want the men crowding my granddaughter tonight. I'll introduce her around later."

Travis nodded, then smiled encouragingly at Rana before he walked toward the two men who were heading their way at a rapid pace. Out of her hearing range, they met and halted briefly as Travis spoke with them. The two men gazed past the handsome foreman to stare openly at the flaming-haired beauty who seemed a ghost to them. Travis chuckled as he led the men away and answered some of their questions. All he could think about was being alone with Rana, but he knew privacy would be difficult, for they would have to keep their love affair a secret for awhile. He knew he would have to settle this matter with the Caldwells before he could claim her. Travis asked the whereabouts of Cody Slade, the man they had left in charge of the ranch during their long journey; he and Nathan needed his report as soon as possible.

Rana observed their expressions before taking Nathan's arm to be escorted into her new home, a dwelling that now seemed vaguely familiar, though whether that familiarity came from her memory or from Nathan's talks she could not determine. Turning her full attention to the house, she noted that it was white with a long porch spanning the front on which had been placed six rocking chairs. Inside, Nathan intentionally began his tour to their left. She was shown an eating area that Nathan called a dining room, and a kitchen with a large pantry and side entrance. As they walked down connecting hallways that formed a T, Nathan pointed out three bedrooms—his, Travis's, and Marissa's old room, which would be given to her. At the door to this room Nathan remarked about the need to get her proper clothing as soon as possible. Next to her room at one end of the second hall was a bathing closet, which had been built for his beloved Ruth; at the other end of the hallway and next to Nathan's room was an office, where he did his bookkeeping. Lastly, they returned to the long front hall and entered a large but cozy sitting room with an enormous fireplace and decidedly masculine decor.

Intrigued, Rana glanced around and her gaze halted on the stunning portrait over the mantel. Nathan needlessly told her that the woman was Marissa Crandall Michaels, her mother. As Nathan placed the two paintings of Rana on either side of her mother's portrait, he murmured, "See how much you look like your mother? That's how I knew Wild Wind was my little Rana from the moment I laid eyes on these pictures."

Rana went to stand before the fireplace to study the image that had filled her dreams many times. There was no denying the obvious resemblance. She could hardly believe that the large portrait was not a likeness of her. As portions of her nightmares flashed before her mind's eye, she realized she had been dreaming about her mother; that the dark-haired villain had been attacking Marissa, not her. And if the woman in her nightmares truly was her mother, then the man must be . . . She forced such intimidating memories aside, for this was not the time or place to deal with them, and she hated to think that the cruel man in her nightmares had actually been her father.

Nathan was saying, "Rachel Raines does the cleaning, washing, and cooking for me and Travis. She's married to one of my best hands, Todd Raines. She comes in a few hours every day but Sunday to take care of us. It's a shame those two don't have any children; they're good folk." He shook his head and shrugged as he realized that Todd Raines could have been Rana's father if Raymond Michaels hadn't come along, or that he could have been his adopted son if Travis had not come upon the scene.

"You don't need a housekeeper asking you hundreds of questions and making you nervous, so I'll give Rachel a week or so off while you get settled here in privacy. I'm sure she's got plenty of canning and quilting to do; that's how she's helping Todd earn enough money to buy a little place of their own."

Nathan could tell Rana was nervous and that his chatter was distracting her, so he talked on. "Todd's away on the spring cattle drive with Mace Hunter. I think I told you Cody Slade has been looking after things while Travis and me went after you. Travis is my foreman and boss, but Mace and Cody usually take care of things for him. I've got me some good hands, Rana; you'll like my men. Only two of them are married; Todd and one of the Davis brothers. 'Course I suspect Cody will be getting hitched before winter. He's been seeing Clifford Sims's girl since summer last. Not many cowpunchers marry

330

young. I guess because it's a hard, busy life. About five miles away I have four small houses that I rent to married hands for a small amount. That's where Todd and Rachel live, and the Davises, Darby and Lettie, with their passel of little ones. Darby's brother, Bart, works for me too, but he lives in the bunkhouse with the boys."

Rana smiled and commented, "You love your land and people very much, Grandfather. It will be good living here."

"Why don't you go to your room and get washed up and rested while Travis and me speak with Cody? We've been gone a long time and there's no telling what's been going on here. When we finish, we'll join forces in the kitchen and rustle up some chow."

Nathan filled a pitcher of water from the pump in the kitchen and carried it to her room, then showed her where the washclothes were kept. "If you need anything, Travis and me will be outside. Rest, or look around all you want. I love you, girl, and I sure am glad to have you home," he stated hoarsely, then embraced her tightly before rushing out the door.

Soon after, Travis entered Rana's room to find her standing before a closed window. When he called her name, she immediately whirled and looked at him as if she had been doing something wrong. "I brought your saddlebags and *parfleches* so you could unpack and get settled while we talk with Cody. He escorted Rachel Raines to church and stayed over for Sunday dinner. I sent Bart Davis to fetch him." He glanced at her pitcher and noticed it was full of fresh water. "We'll have supper as soon as we finish our meeting with Cody. You need anything else before I leave?" he inquired, wanting nothing more than to remain at her side during this trying period. He wondered if memories, good or bad, were surfacing to haunt her. He knew about her past visits to the ranch, though she had been only a small

331

child then.

While he was speaking, Rana picked up her *parfleches* and placed them in the corner of the room, as she had done in the tepee. To him, she appeared timid and apprehensive, and perhaps a little lost in the big room that he suspected she could not quite remember or did not wish to recall. As a baby or a small child, she had visited here only a few times, and many things had changed over the years. Progress had transformed much on the ranch and in the white man's world.

Travis wanted to pull her into his arms and cover her face with kisses. This privacy was too stimulating and tempting, and he was too cognizant of her allure and the big bed nearby. He dared not touch her in fear of losing his control, when someone could arrive at any moment and catch them. Here, no one knew of their Indian marriage, a union not recognized under white law. He could not tell anyone she was his wife, or be discovered treating her as such. Yet he no longer felt guilty about their involvement, even if he knew it was best to keep their relationship secret for awhile. He could not bear the thought of anyone thinking badly of her, or of Nathan believing he had taken advantage of his young grand-daughter. Twice he had made love to Rana behind Nathan's back, and he was not sure his friend and adopted father would understand his weakness. If it were another woman, perhaps; but Nathan's grandchild . . . Nathan would have expected him to have had the respect, loyalty, and strength to have waited. "Why don't you put your things in the chest?" he inquired, trying to stall his departure and help her relax.

"Chest?" She repeated the confusing word, then looked down at her own body, for she had forgotten the use of such furniture over the years. "I do not understand. Is it wrong to place them there?"

Since she seemed so nervous and sincere, Travis

332

suppressed his amusement and retrieved her leather pouches. The room was almost as large as the entire tepee in which she had lived for ten years, and without furniture. No wonder she was baffled, he decided, certain that she would learn or recall such things. He placed the *parfleches* and saddlebags on the bed and opened them. Removing several items, he walked to the chest, opened the drawer, put the items aside, and closed it. Rana watched him quizzically, then her eyes grew wide as if she believed the wooden chest had devoured her belongings.

He patiently showed her how to use the chest and closet, promising to get her enough clothes to fill them, then explained about the bed and its covers. He refreshed her memory on the use of chairs, how to open and close windows for fresh air, the use of doors and curtains for privacy, the use of safety matches and lanterns for light, and the purpose of the chamber pot beneath her bed. Since these last instructions appeared to embarrass her, he quickly returned to the lantern to caution her about its safe use and to warn her about hot chimneys and broken glass, which reminded him to explain about the fireplace in her room, although it would not be needed until winter.

Rana followed Travis around the large room, watching and listening as he instructed her about her new surroundings. "It is easier to live in a tepee or outside," she remarked mirthfully.

Travis chuckled. "I'll show you how to use the bathing closet and kitchen later. We don't cook over open fires or fetch water from a stream, or wash our clothes and bathe in rivers. You've got lots of things to learn or remember, Rana, but Nathan and I will help you, so don't be intimidated by all these differences. Be patient with yourself; it'll take time and work, but you can do it," he encouraged confidently.

Her gaze softened. "You judge me very highly, and I

am pleased. Your friends will wonder why Rana does not know such things. Will they laugh at me and tease you?" she asked worriedly.

"If anyone makes fun of you, I'll beat him senseless, or her. Just relax, 'cause Nate and I won't let anyone come near you until you've had time to learn your way around. We'll decide at supper what we're going to tell anyone who asks questions about you."

Rana's thoughts now matched Travis's earlier ones. She wanted to feel his arms around her and his lips on hers. She wanted to make passionate love and fuse their bodies into one. But this world seemed so strange and intimidating, and she needed to learn her way around it. She did not want to shame them with her ignorance or errors. She knew what whites thought about Indians, or people reared by them, or women enslaved by them. She was also aware that at any moment her grandfather or another could enter this wooden tepee and find them together, so she dared not reach out to him. She did not feel their relationship was wrong, but her grandfather might. She did not want him to become angry with Travis, or blame him. "Your sky is different," she said aloud. "I cannot read the time and season in it."

Travis smiled and stroked her hair, aware of her trembling and loosely leashed emotions. "I will teach you to read the sky over Texas, and I will teach you to read the white man's clock."

"Clock," she echoed, recalling pictures of them in the books that the teacher had guarded with her life. There was too much to learn and her family had been too kind to be fooled any longer, so Rana told Travis about the captive schoolteacher and her past lessons. "If you help me, all the words and numbers will return. I will try to remember and speak as she taught me. It will be easier here where I do not have to go back and forth between English and Lakota. I wish you and Grandfather to be

334

proud of me. I must stay in this . . . room until it is so."

Travis could not keep himself from embracing her. "You are a wonder, Rana Michaels. It's nice just being around you. Be yourself and everyone will love you, no matter how much or how little you know about the white ways. But don't rush things or they'll overwhelm you. This is all new to you; take it slow and easy. I won't let you suffer as I did."

Rana hugged him tightly. "Please help me not to shame my grandfather and my . . . you. Is it so that no one is to learn of our joining?" she queried, keeping her face nestled against his firm chest. His arms and words were so comforting, and his nearness tempting.

He tensed slightly and took a deep breath. "It must be our secret, Rana," he finally responded in a strained voice. "The whites do not accept Indian laws and customs; neither does Nathan. To him, we aren't married." He leaned back and looked into her upturned face. "Perhaps I have too much Indian blood and spirit, for it is not true with me."

When Travis heard Nathan calling him from the front porch, he gently set her aside and told her he would return later.

Rana cast a longing glance at his retreating back. She felt she could trust this man, and she hoped she could win his heart. She continued with her unpacking as he had instructed. In the bottom drawer of the tall chest she found her old doll, the one Marissa had hidden there before their fateful journey. She stared at it for a long time before lifting it and clutching it against her heart, as she had done that day long ago when Nathan had given it to her. Closing her eyes, she hugged the cherished treasure and rocked back and forth as several memories swirled around inside her head, and this time she did not try to halt them. Flashes of her last visit to the ranch, her terrifying travels with her parents, happy times with

Nathan, and the receiving of this doll passed through her mind.

As if it had been a real baby, Rana lovingly snuggled the doll in her protective arms as tears rolled down her cheeks, for she remembered her mother now, just as she remembered how intimidating her father had been. She grasped Marissa's heart-shaped necklace and rubbed it between her shaky fingers. Because of Raymond Michaels's wickedness, the two precious possessions had been left behind. She recalled crying for the doll and her mother saying, "Do not fret, little one. We will return for your baby very soon. Then we will be free and happy." In light of the Kiowa attack, she was glad these treasures had survived.

As with Travis's parents, her father had been evil and her mother had married the wrong man. How she wished someone had rescued Marissa from her evil husband and had given her mother the happiness that she was experiencing with Travis. Marissa's life had been so brief and painful, and she had caused her father so much grief. For some unknown reason, Rana was convinced that Marissa had not meant to do so. If only she could discover the truth . . .

Perhaps her mother's tragedy had proven that defiance and obstinancy were bad traits, dangerous ones, and that she must cease them or she and others might suffer as Marissa had. At last the Great Spirit had sent her home to help and comfort Nathan. "I am home, Mother, and I will take care of Grandfather for you," she promised.

On his return, Cody Slade gave Nathan and Travis a shocking report on what had happened during their two-month absence. The hazel-eyed, sandy-haired man of twenty-six related infuriating news of cattle and horse

336

rustling, the tearing down of fences, the burning of two hay fields, the surprising departure of James McFarland and subsequent purchase of his ranch by Harrison Caldwell, and the Caldwells' intense curiosity regarding their whereabouts. Anger laced his voice when he revealed how Harrison had been seeing too much of his sweetheart, Mary Beth Sims, and told how the Caldwells had sat with the Simses in church earlier that day. He explained that the reason he had been escorting Rachel around had to do with the strange accidents that had befallen some of the women on McFarland's ranch, which had driven off many of the Flying *M* hands.

"What did the sheriff do to help Jim?" Nathan questioned.

"Wasn't much he could do, sir. Nobody would speak out; they were too scared. After McFarland lost so many hands and things got so dangerous over there, he sold out. Caldwell bought his place fair and square, or made it look that way. 'Course nobody bid against him.''

"Everybody knows Harry is behind all this trouble," Nathan accused. "He's sitting around us like a tight horseshoe! I never thought Jim would weaken, but I don't blame him under those circumstances. But Harry's crazy if he thinks he's going to run us out and get my ranch. As soon as the rest of the boys get back from the cattle drive, we'll take care of those rustlers and fence cutters. We'll set out guards and handle this trouble ourselves. We'll teach that Yankee lawyer what it is to tangle with real Texans. When the election comes around, that sheriff's gonna be real sorry he's in Harry's hire. Cody, you make sure Harry doesn't get his bloody hands on Mary Beth."

"I'm doing my best, sir, but she's mighty scared. Ain't no secret Sims is beholden to Caldwell. She'll have it rough if her pa insists she marry him. I'll kill him first!" Cody vowed, imagining his love caught helplessly in that

337

vulture's clutches.

"Maybe we should send for a U.S. Marshal to do some nosing around," Nathan suggested with mild sarcasm. "The government owes us something for holding us captive in the Union."

"Won't do any good, sir. Caldwell's covering his tracks better'n an Apache. He's been reporting the same kind of trouble we're having. It ain't nothing but a trick to look innocent. While you were gone, he hired two gunslingers; claimed they were for protection of his property and people. If you ask me, I'd bet they're the ones doing the killing and raiding. Mean-looking cusses, sir. From what I hear, they rode with that cold-blooded Quantrill, so folks around here won't rile 'em."

Hearing of Caldwell's latest deceptions caused Travis to recall how the unscrupulous lawyer had achieved his power. The Civil War had ended two years earlier and very little fighting had taken place in the Lone Star State, but many Texans were bitter over the Rebels' defeat and the terms of peace. Although most of the ex-slave owners lived in the eastern and southern parts of Texas, the aftereffects of the war were still being felt in more widespread areas. Texas had once been a republic with its own president, and she continued to feel and flaunt her streak of independence with such acts as flying the Texas flag on the same level with the American flag. Texans were proud and resilient folk, and now that the ex-soldiers had returned home and Reconstruction was underway, huge, prosperous cattle spreads were being created across this vast and rugged state.

Travis and Nathan were very much aware that during the war and shortly afterward, lawyer and rancher Harrison Caldwell had begun taking control of local politics and absorbing neighboring ranches. Well acquainted with the law, on the books and in the political offices, Caldwell had carried out his grasping process legally in the public eye and deceitfully in private. It seemed no one could stop him from achieving his dream of creating one of the largest and most lucrative cattle empires in the west.

America needed what Texas and Nathan had to offer, and Nathan had been doing extremely well until nature had begun dealing him some harsh blows. By borrowing money for survival, he had opened a door that a clever and daring thief like Caldwell could enter if Nathan could not find a way to close it soon. Years ago the Rocking C had been bordered by four separate ranches and a river; today it was bordered by the river and a horseshoe-shaped Circle C Ranch.

Travis had been silently taking in Cody's new information, reflecting that it would affect him personally by making Rana a target. "You said Clarissa has been checking around on us. What did you tell her?"

"Like you ordered, boss, I told her you two had private business and didn't tell us where you were heading or why. She's been real busy trying to uncover something. She even had that painter do her picture, but he didn't tell her nothing either. Before he left town, he came out to tell me she had been pumping him for information and that he wanted you to know he had kept his mouth shut about your granddaughter. I'm glad you two got her home safely. Bart said she looks just like . . ." Cody halted, wondering if he should mention Nathan's deceased child.

Nathan smiled knowingly and nodded. "Yep, she's almost the spittin' image of her mother. Got Marissa's spunk, too. Tell the boys to keep quiet about her; Rana needs time to get settled before people start trying to get a peek at her, especially those Caldwells. They might consider her a tangle in their plans."

Cody knew Bart had announced Rana's arrival and supplied details of her appearance to his brother, Darby, and to Rachel Raines. No matter their orders and good intentions, the hands would not be able to keep news like this quiet very long. He also knew this would be a frightening, difficult change for a young girl, particularly one to whom men would be attracted. Cody could understand Nathan's concern, and he promised to help protect Rana.

Travis ventured, "Maybe we should send a few of the boys to join up with Mace and warn him about this new trouble. We'll be in deep mud if anything happens to the cattle money. We've got that loan due at Mason's bank on August first. If we can't repay it, Caldwell will have an open door to buying us out real legal. We need to be careful and alert. I think it would be a good idea to hire a few extra men, Nate; we could round up the herds and set guards on them for awhile, at least until we can find a way to unmask Caldwell."

"Won't be easy, Travis; he's real clever. You'd best watch out for those two varmints he hired. If anything happened to you, Caldwell would find it easier to push Mister Crandall around," Cody warned, aware of the potency and importance of Travis's reputation.

"Do you know who they are?" Travis asked.

"Wes Monroe and Jackson Hayes, real bad types," Cody Slade replied. "You want me to join up with Mace and Todd?"

Travis did not respond. He was stunned by the possible identities of the two gunmen, for their first names were familiar. If he had not been badly injured and in Texas when the Lowrys had been killed, he might have been charged with their murders, for he had had a strong motive. The Lowrys had hired men called "Wes" and "Jack" to ambush him! His gut instinct told him these were the same two men who had beaten him senseless near St. Louis. If so, they were cruel and unfeeling bastards who would stop at nothing. At last he might be given a shot at revenge, or rather justice. Yet he had to be careful, for more was at stake than his own personal war with them. No doubt they had robbed and slain their boss long ago, implying that even the code of honesty and loyalty among criminals meant nothing to them. If the Caldwells felt threatened by Rana's arrival, they might sic . . .

He saw that Nathan and Cody were staring at him inquisitively. He promised himself he would handle the problem of Wes and Jack later. "I think you should stay here, Cody, and take care of some other matters for me. Pick out our three best shooters and send them. We'll talk again tomorrow."

After Cody left them, Nathan turned to Travis and asked, "Something caught your head, son; what was it?"

When Travis exposed his suspicions, Nathan looked worried. "If they remember you, son, you'll be in grave danger. You know they don't want anybody exposing them to the authorities."

"They've killed so many people I doubt they'd remember me. After supper, I'll sneak over to the Circle C. Just in case it is them and their memories are good, I'd like to sight them first."

"You're going to kill 'em, aren't you?" Nathan probed.

"Yep," he stated casually. He couldn't forget the almost lethal beating they had given him, or witnessing the Indian girl's rape and murder. Except for the Hunkpapa betrayal, once he resolved the Caldwell and Lowry matters, his past and present would be settled; and afterward he could work on his future, which looked brighter and happier since he had met Rana "Wild Wind" Michaels. He couldn't allow anyone or anything to harm her or endanger their future.

"I won't ask you to turn this matter over to the sheriff, because there isn't any proof against them, here or back in Missouri. I know you've got to take care of this, son,

341

but do me one favor; don't get caught. I don't want you hanged for getting rid of dung like that, and you can bet Caldwell will sic the sheriff on you if you're seen."

"Don't worry, Nate. For now, I'm only going to make sure it's them. Hopefully they won't recognize me. But like the Apaches say, it's easier to kill a man than capture him. This time, they won't get away." Travis looked at Nathan and reasoned, "It isn't just for me, Nate. Those bastards have tortured and killed lots of innocent people. I have to stop them. I'm willing to swear they killed Lowry and his daughter and took more than their payment for taking care of me, and I watched them torment that Indian girl before slicing her throat. A man doesn't forget a sight like that. As I recall, the one called Jack didn't have much sense. Wes was the one who gave the orders. If he's still got my knife, I'm going to kill him with it. Trust me, Nate; I'm going to defeat them and Caldwell."

Nathan changed the grim subject. "I plan to go into town in the morning. I need to speak with Wilber Mason about my loan and see if I can learn anything about McFarland's sale. While I'm there, I'll hire a seamstress to come out and get started on some clothes for Rana, and I'll see if I can hire that schoolteacher to help her with her lessons. I think you should hang around the house until I get home. I would feel better knowing you're here to protect my granddaughter."

"You're right, Nate. We shouldn't leave Rana alone with all this trouble scattered about. When you get back, I'll check on things." Travis recalled what the two bushwhackers had done to the Indian girl who had warned him about Elizabeth's treachery and what Cody had told them about incidents involving women on the McFarland ranch. He would make certain Rana was not left unprotected for a single minute! He would also teach her how to fire a pistol and rifle tomorrow. He was glad

Rana was smart and brave and knew how to fight. But even so, men like Wes, Jack, and Harrison were deadly.

Because of her injured hand, Rana was not allowed to assist Nathan and Travis in the preparation of their evening meal. As they worked, the two men taught her how to use the water pump and wood-burning stove. They showed her the pantry and explained about their foods and the use of their dishes. While the meal was cooking, Travis guided her to the bath closet in the hall and related its function. He told her that Rachel would teach her about doing the laundry when the housekeeper returned in a week. "You'll like her, Rana, and she'll be glad to help you with anything. Don't be embarrassed to ask questions."

"There is so much to learn," she murmured, feeling ignorant and insecure in this strange place.

He tenderly cuffed her chin. "I know, but you can do it. Nate's going to town in the morning, so I'll work with you most of tomorrow. I plan to teach you how to shoot a pistol and rifle, so I won't worry about you when I'm gone."

"Gone? Where are you going?" she asked as if panic-stricken.

"Just around the ranch, *micante*." He saw her smile as he called her "my heart." "I have to check a few things. We had a little trouble while we were away fetching you. Somebody's been stealing cattle and horses and cutting holes in our fences. The man who owned a neighboring ranch got scared, sold out, and left. It's best not to let this kind of trouble get out of hand."

"Another tribe raids on our lands?" she inquired in surprise. "Who would dare challenge you and Grandfather?"

Travis chuckled. "Renegade whites are trying to raid

343

our lands, but we'll stop them now that we're home again. Don't worry."

"Rana will help you defeat them," she bravely announced.

"No, Rana will not. Rana will stay at home and study her lessons. When you've learned them, I'll teach you all about ranching, and rustling, and shooting. Then, if there's any more trouble, you can ride against the varmints with me. We both know how well you can fight; right now, your lessons are more important than helping me defeat a few raiders. Agreed?" he softly demanded, not wanting her to confront the Caldwells or Wes and Jack.

She smiled at him and nodded her head. She sensed his worry over her and it warmed her heart. He did not doubt her capabilities, she realized; he only wanted to protect her. "I will obey."

"Good." He caught her hand and, after stealing a blissful and heady kiss, led her back to the kitchen.

As they ate and Rana practiced with the utensils, Nathan told her what he and Travis had decided to reveal about her past and the reasons for her return. "We'll tell anyone who's bold enough to ask—and you can bet there'll be a few people who'll do so—the simple truth. We haven't done anything wrong and we've got nothing to be ashamed of, so why get tangled up in fancy lies? It won't take our friends long to love you and accept you. If we stick to the truth, we won't have to worry about getting our stories crossed and having people think we've got something terrible to hide. The only thing we'll keep quiet about is that false marriage between you two. Is that all right with you, Rana?"

Travis added before she could respond, "I doubt anyone will be fool enough to say anything ugly to you, or about you, Rana. If someone does, he'll answer to me. Anyone with eyes and ears can see you haven't lived as a

344

wild savage or an abused white captive. Just remember, you don't have to explain anything to anybody. Some people will be genuinely interested and some will be downright nosy or rude. You decide how you want to handle each one, and we'll back you."

Rana smiled at both men. "Do not worry about me. Remember, for many years as Wild Wind I accepted good and bad teasing. I will not allow their words to harm me or to make me forget my honor. I will let my actions and face speak for me and prove my worth. It is good to speak the truth, for lies and tricks can do much harm."

Later that night, as Rana snuggled into her bed, she savored its comfort and softness. In spite of the awesome learning task before her, she felt happy and relaxed. The word "home" kept drifting across her sleepy mind like a peaceful cloud in a tranquil blue sky. She cuddled the doll in her arms as if it were a tangible link to her deceased mother, for it brought back good memories of nights when she and Marissa had shared this bed, had laughed and whispered and made up beautiful fantasies that had not been allowed to become realities. Yes, she decided, her destiny was here with her grandfather and her husband. *Husband,* her mind echoed, then she smiled.

With Nathan and Rana in bed, Travis stood before the fireplace in the sitting room and admired the three portraits above the mantel. His gaze finally settled on his favorite of Rana. She was so beautiful and radiant and she was so close, but so was Nathan. Lordy, how he wanted her, he reflected. It had been days since that night in the forest when she had declared that she had chosen him to share her life. She was like sunshine, and

345

flowers, and a fresh breeze; she was a rainbow, a child, a rare treasure; she was all things good and pure and priceless. Her eyes, so large and mellow, held such magic and allure. It was as if every inch of her called out irresistibly to be touched ever so gently. Her tumbling tresses presented an enticing aura of sensuality. This angel displayed overwhelming charms and she was . . . almost his.

Travis stared at her painted image and yearned for her. He imagined her lying in bed a short distance away, waiting for him. These next weeks pretending she was his "sister" would be unmerciful, yet he needed to protect her life and reputation as much as he needed to be with her. Could he betray Nathan's trust in his own home? What if Nathan caught them together? It could damage their relationship. Even if they declared their love, would it excuse or justify their intimacy? There was no safe way they could marry until this danger with the Caldwells was past and, until they were legally wed, would Nathan understand and accept their wanton affair? It was indeed a predicament.

Travis paced the sitting room, wondering if he should go to Rana. He needed her and wanted her, but could he risk discovery? Twice he had challenged it on the trail; how long could his luck hold out? He doused the lanterns and headed toward his room.

In the hallway, Travis glanced to his left to find Rana poised in her open doorway, smiling at him and mutely beckoning him to her side. He looked toward Nathan's closed door and sighed heavily. If he learned the truth, Nathan would have to understand that he could not resist Rana or deny these passions burning within them. He quietly headed toward her. She opened the door and allowed his entrance.

Travis closed and locked the door behind him. His hands captured her body and pulled it into his embrace, creating a blissful contact. The dam that had checked their passions for many days suddenly shattered and a surge of powerful passion spilled forth. Her nearness caused his heart to race with desire. With the slowness of a snail, his hands moved over her face, down her throat, over her shoulders. His fingers deftly drifted over her bare flesh, causing her to tremble. Bending forward, he fastened his eager lips to hers. His tongue tentatively mated with hers, then darted between her lips to play joyously within her mouth. He kissed her nose, then her eyes, then sensuously attacked her ears, where his respiration caused her trembling to increase. Slowly, seductively, his mouth traveled down her neck and wandered over her shoulders. At the same time, his hands slipped up her body to capture two passion-swollen breasts and tantalize her taut peaks.

Rana shivered with longing. Her body quivered in delight. She had been waiting for him to come to her, fearing he would not. It had been too long and she craved him. Her breath came in shallow, sharp gasps as his tongue and hands brought titillating sensations to her. Suddenly her breath was stolen by feverish kisses and a fierce embrace. Her entire body experienced a rush of heat and tingling. His hands tenderly squeezed her thrusting peaks as his tongue probed her mouth. Then they slipped around her body to grasp her buttocks and fondle them, pressing her snugly against his rapidly enlarging manhood. Slowly his hands began to move up and down her body, stroking here and there.

Her fingers pushed aside his shirt and allowed it to float to the floor so she could press kisses to his throat and chest. Her arms encircled his taut body as her mouth worked its wonders. Her actions revealed her inexperience, yet she stimulated him to the edge of mindless surrender. She had craved him for days and she could not wait any longer. Her body was like an ember lying near a fire, waiting to be ignited and consumed by its heat and sparked to blazing life.

Travis's hands captured firm mounds and gently kneaded them. His mouth wandered over her face and his nose inhaled her heady fragrance. His manhood throbbed with painful cravings, flaming with a need only she could extinguish. Their tongues touched and explored the taste of the other. Her breasts burned like two coals against his chest. He groaned in achingly sweet need of her as his lips worked between her mouth, ears, and neck, and his talented hands stimulated her body to quivering desire. Down his hand drifted, over supple breasts, past a slim waist, over rounded hips, and into a beckoning fuzzy mound that radiated a heat to rival the July sun. Slowly and provocatively his hand stroked the hardened peak it located there until their starving senses were ravenous and pleading.

"Love me," she entreated, enslaved by rapidly rising desire.

Travis could wait no longer to feel her body clinging to his. He lifted her and carried her to the bed. After placing her there, he quickly removed his clothes and joined her. He wanted to feel each sensation and to savor each emotion. She was so close, so intoxicating, so eager. He could think of nothing except her desire for him and his for her. Her flesh was as soft as Texas cotton and he longed to caress it. Her body was lithe and enticing, calling out to him to give it pleasure. Needing to feel her flesh against his, he assailed that body eagerly.

Rana's hands moved over his compelling frame. He was so strong, so firm, so sleek. It felt wonderful for her hands to glide over his body, and she relished its feel and the power she possessed to stir him to life. Her fingers roved broad shoulders and a nearly hairless chest on which muscles stood out prominently before flattening to a taut stomach and lean hips. Her respiration quickened and her insides quivered with anticipation of what lay ahead tonight. His embrace was enticing, stimulating, irresistible. It was too dark to see his handsome face, but she could envision it. Her senses were alive and alert, yet mindless and dazed. He demanded and controlled all she was, and she did not care. Her body was susceptible to his every move and touch. She wanted him to take her fully, for every area of her body and mind ached for his conquest.

Travis suppressed his groans of desire and pleasure as his hands and mouth wandered over her receptive body. Staggering sensations flooded his mind and inflamed his flesh. His lips found hers and urgently possessed them. He claimed her senses with skill and determination, wanting to be her only reality. His hunger could not be denied.

A flood of sensation washed over Rana. Her body relaxed and tensed simultaneously as he created ecstasy and torment at the same time. Some kisses and caresses sated her, while others tantalized her. Her hands grasped his shoulders and pulled him tightly against her smoldering body. She wanted . . . She needed . . .

Their contact and her eagerness were playing havoc with Travis's control. Their naked bodies clung together and their mouths fused feverishly. His shaft demanded entrance to that moist haven, which could both cool and inflame it. His hand provocatively traveled down her stomach and teased along her silky thighs, encouraging her desires to burn brighter and more fiercely. He called on all he knew about women to give her the ultimate pleasure while trying to contain his rampant need.

Rana writhed on the bed as Travis toyed with the sensitive peak, which delighted and encouraged him to continue his actions. His lips found hers and sent reality spinning. His talented lips shifted from her mouth to her breast, then back and forth, causing her to squirm beneath his artful seduction. Soon her body was pleading for appeasement. Her appetite was whetted beyond resistance or denial.

By then, nothing mattered to either except the dousing of the fires of passion that enflamed and consumed them. Yet Travis continued to use his deft hands and lips upon her pliant body. Her hands roamed his body, their pressure on it revealing the intensity of her desire. Aquiver with fierce longing, his mouth encased a taut peak and drove her wild with blissful torment. His mouth moved upward then to willfully invade hers, his hunger intense and his skill enormous. Her body was responding wildly and eagerly to his and his heart surged with joy. He soon became lost in the wonder of her love and response.

Her fingers lovingly traced the lines on his face and body. They drifted into his hair and played amongst its waves. They moved seductively over his lips, then drew his mouth to hers. Greedily she feasted at his love's well, partaking of its heady nectar. She moaned against his mouth and covered his face with kisses. As his fingers worked on her body, sliding over her throbbing peak and thrusting into her aching womanhood, she yielded her all to him, entreating more stimulation, which he eagerly and happily granted her.

At last, she murmured hoarsely and weakly, "I must have you now, my husband. Enter me and feed this hunger."

He responded huskily, "If I took you twice a day for the rest of our lives, my hunger for you could never be sated. Each time I take you causes me to want you even more." He shifted between her inviting thighs and drove gently within her encompassing womanhood. She arched upward, craving and accepting his entire length. She sighed with temporary relief, then felt the burning flames attack her once more as he moved with caution and experience. She needed him so desperately that she feverishly matched his rhythm, even as he warned her to move slowly and carefully. Wildly, skillfully, he guided and instructed her along this fiery path.

His mouth claimed hers and worked ardently before shifting its attention to her pleading breasts. As his warm, moist lips closed over one nipple, she writhed beneath him. He lifted her hips to drive more deeply into her body. His worked deftly, thrusting and thrusting until he feared she would cry out in sweet yearning. Lordy, how he wished they didn't have to be careful with their voices and actions. It was sheer agony to have to control anything tonight.

Travis could barely restrain his desire to plunge into her body over and over again until his release came. Each time he advanced and retreated, he feared it would be his final movement. She was enjoying this night too much to end it swiftly and he wanted her to claim all the pleasure she could extract or he could give. He labored to master his heated flesh, as he wanted to prod her more slowly up that mountain she was climbing so rapidly. Each time he ceased his probing to cool his blazing desire, she would wiggle and entreat him to continue. He knew she was too dazed by passion to hear or comply with his warnings, so he ceased murmuring them in her ear and labored silently to send her over love's precipice.

Rana thrilled to the way his manhood teased along the sensitive sides of the dark, damp canyon between her parted thighs. Her heart was pounding rapidly and her body was ablaze. Each time his tongue flicked over her nipples, she had to force herself not to cry out in pleasure. Her legs overlapped his and she matched his thrusting pattern. As her mouth clung to his and her hands pressed him tightly against her, she strove for the rapturous climax that had begun to melt her very core.

Their hearts and bodies were fused and their desires matched perfectly as they cast off all restraint and caution. Their bodies blended time and time again, and they unselfishly urged each other up the spiral road of passion. Higher and higher they soared, until a staggering release struck them forcefully and sent them spinning wildly back toward earth. Blissful spasms racked their bodies and tossed them on a sea of sated contentment. They lay in an embrace of love and tranquillity, exhausted and enchanted.

Travis rolled to his back, refusing to release her. His heart was pounding and his body was soaked. Never had he experienced anything like this union of bodies, hearts, and spirits. It was wonderful, exciting, all-consuming, and powerful. They shared passion, tenderness, urgency, and ecstasy; they shared a beautiful love. This thing between them was good, and pure, and right; and no one would destroy it.

Rana curled against him, feeling and thinking as he did. She listened as his heartbeat and breathing returned to normal. She did not mind the wetness of his body, nor that on hers. The musky fragrance that filled the room brought a smile of happiness to her lips. His fingers were slowly, absently trailing up and down her back and she sighed happily and nestled closer to him, delighting when his embrace tightened and he rested his jawline against her forehead. A special peace filled and enveloped them. Their legs were entwined and their flesh joined as one. She closed her eyes and gradually drifted off to sleep.

Travis reluctantly drew away from her, arose, and, after kissing her damp forehead and covering her slender body, returned to his room, yearning for the time when he could remain with her night and day.

Nathan left for town the next morning after breakfast. Travis was cheerfully clearing the table and washing the dishes as Rana argued about helping with the chores, but

Travis won their genial debate by kissing each bandaged fingertip and telling her, "Just keep me company while I work. Since you hurt these lovely fingers saving my hide, the least I can do is wait on you while they heal properly."

"They were injured many days ago, Travis. A little water and work will not harm them. It is wrong to be lazy and selfish."

"You can't fool me, woman. I know they're still sore and sensitive. The only water I want them in is your bath, understand?"

"You treat me like a child or a captive," she teased.

"Sometimes I think it would be easier on me if you were a child. You know good and well that if my hand were hurt, you'd be treating me this same way. Am I right?" he challenged, and her expression answered him.

When Travis went to give orders to Cody and the hands, Rana entered the water closet to take a bath. She plugged the hole with the wooden stopper and pulled on the cord to allow the wooden tub to fill itself. She grinned as she stepped into it, for she liked the ease and privacy the closet afforded. For a brief moment she could almost hear and see herself splashing in this tub long ago. When she finished, she wrapped a drying sheet around her silky frame and prepared to return to her room to dress.

Since Rana's door was ajar, Travis thought nothing about pushing it aside and walking into her room. There was a noise behind him as she reopened the closet door, which his entrance had shut on her. As he turned to locate her, he was saying, "Why don't we go for a walk and I can show—" He ceased talking and his mouth remained open, for she was nude, a vision of magic and temptation that set his passions boiling. He could not

353

stop his gaze from instantly roaming every inch of her arresting face and figure. He had seen her naked several times in moonlit shadows, but this magnificent view in brilliant light staggered his senses and increased her enormous allure. Her shapely figure was perfect and intoxicatingly appealing. His hands itched to wander over her silky flesh, to leisurely explore curves and peaks and valleys and entreating crevices. He moistened his lips as his mouth craved to do the same. His eyes seemed to scorch her skin, to singe the flaming forest between her sleek thighs, to cause her nipples to grow hard and prominent. He smiled as he observed his effect on her, for she was glowing with desire.

Coming alert, Travis shifted nervously. "I . . . I'm sorry, Rana. I didn't know you were . . . dressing. Call me when you finish," he said, feeling he was infringing on her privacy. At other times, he had been too consumed by mindless hunger to think about his behavior and its consequences; today he was fully aware of his responsibilities and obligations to Nathan and to Rana. Could he brazenly take her every time and any place the mood struck him? Just hop into bed and make wanton love to her every time Nathan's back was turned? Damn, he cursed silently. Sometimes he hated this conscience that Nathan had inspired and despised the white man's idea of morals! As much as he wanted to be honest with Nathan about this situation, he knew he could not, for Nathan was her grandfather and he was very old-fashioned. Without a doubt, Nathan would feel betrayed and duped; he would feel Travis had dishonored his innocent grandchild and used her selfishly. Like him, Nathan would be unable to think clearly and without bias about Rana.

Retrieving the drying sheet that had slipped accidentally from her body, Rana covered herself. Had his cheeks actually flushed and his tongue twisted? she

354

mused, warmed and amused by his behavior. Since he looked unnerved by their privacy, she asked, "This is not the first time we have been alone or touched. Why do you behave this way?"

Travis inhaled raggedly as his yearning gaze wandered over her bare shoulders and exquisite face. He revealed what he had been thinking. "No woman has ever tempted me or affected me like you do, Rana Michaels. I can't seem to keep my hands and mind off you. I'd best git out of here while I can. Somebody could come searching for me, and it would appear mighty strange for me to be locked in your bedroom with Nate gone. Much as I crave you, it's too risky for us to be together this morning," he explained, though his eyes told another story.

A fetching smile teased over her lips. "We must not feel guilt or shame over this special bond between us. It is sad we cannot tell Grandfather about it, but must we reject each other to obey laws and ways that we know are not right for us? Must we stay apart because the white-eyes say it is evil for us to be together on a sleeping mat? Must we suffer loneliness and separation because Grandfather was taught these foolish and tormenting customs? You have never dishonored me or used me selfishly; I have come to you willingly and eagerly each time. I choose to belong to you, and I care not who says my feelings are wrong or my actions are wicked. Have you forgotten how short life can be? Must we suffer painful denials by living as others demand? We hurt no one by holding our feelings and actions a secret; they are for us alone to share and know. Grandfather is gone and no one should enter your tepee uninvited. We have little time alone. Is it not best to seize each moment and joy?" She hesitated. "Do I speak and act too boldly?"

Travis realized they would be alone for hours and they had total privacy. He could read the matching hunger in her eyes, as she had in his. "Again, your words are true and wise, and spoken with great courage and daring. I must have lost my mind over you, Rana Michaels. Every time I'm near you, I want you like crazy. This pull between us is too powerful to resist, so thank heavens I don't want to fight it or have to fight it. I don't know what I would do if you didn't feel this way about me. I never thought I would hear myself saying this to any woman, but I love you, Rana Michaels, and this isn't White Eagle speaking. With everything I am and with both my bloods, I need you and I want you—today, tomorrow, and forever. I don't like sneaking around behind Nate's back and I don't like feeling guilty over taking you, but you're right about this matter remaining between us. As soon as I settle our problems on the ranch, I'm claiming you totally."

Travis stepped closer to her and gazed into her compelling face. "White Eagle desired and claimed Wild Wind's heart, body, and life; now Travis Kincade hungers to do the same with Rana Michaels."

Rana's hands slipped up his chest to capture his face between them. She went up on tiptoe to seal their lips after telling him, "Your thoughts and feelings match mine. I love you, Travis Kincade."

Travis released the drying sheet and allowed it to settle around their feet. He reached past her to lock the door, then scooped her up and carried her to the bed. After removing his boots and clothes, he lay down beside her. Had it only been a few hours since they had made passionate love in this bed? he mused. They had spoken little the night before, for it had not been a time for talking, and silence had seemed to enhance the romantic solitude of her dark room.

Her breath was stolen by the pervasive kisses he could not hold back and by his powerful embrace. He could see and feel her eager responses, her heightened desires, her love and commitment to him. His green eyes darkened with desire as his lips and hands went to work lovingly on her body.

When their bodies could tolerate no more teasing and tempting, he tenderly eased his flaming shaft inside a haven that received him ardently and gratefully. Mastering the urge to ride her swiftly and hard in order to end his bittersweet hunger, he remained motionless for a brief time, his throbbing manhood behaving as if this were the first time they had joined. He shuddered as it quivered threateningly and he concentrated fiercely on maintaining control. As he set his pattern, her legs closed over his and locked around his lower body. She worked in unison with his movements, arching to meet his rapturous entries and relaxing to endure his mandatory withdrawals. She was driving him wild with her uninhibited behavior. When her mouth nibbled on his ear and she pounded her body forcefully against his, she tempted him to race blindly and rashly for victory. He was ecstatic when she claimed her blissful prize, for he would have been unable to restrain himself any longer.

Together they rode passion's waves and were rewarded with soul-stirring pleasure. They drank from love's cup until every drop of its intoxicating liquid was drained and savored. They lay exhausted, but enlivened, in a serene setting of total contentment.

As they snuggled together in the afterglow of love, she entreated dreamily, "Tell me more about White Eagle becoming Travis Kincade."

Travis patiently repeated the story of his past to her and gave her some new information. Still he left out details of his necessary relationship with Clarissa Caldwell, the threat of destruction from Harrison, and the reappearance of Wes and Jackson in his life. He did not want this beautiful moment spoiled by such ugly and intrusive realities. This thing between them was too special to damage even with defensive lies, so he vowed to be careful about what he said and did. Besides, Rana had just arrived home; she had enough to learn and to handle without him burdening her with those distasteful and dangerous problems. Too, he was afraid she would insist on becoming a "warrior" to help him battle his foes, and he could not bear the thought of seeing her injured or slain. In a few days, he would explain about the Caldwells and their gunslingers, and why she had to stay out of that situation, and why she must allow him to dally with Clarissa. He would protect her, even from her own skill and confidence, which would cause her to insist on riding at his side.

At present, he knew she was simply very curious about him. He believed that if he was open and honest with her about himself, then eventually she would be able to look upon her own past in the same way. Therefore he was able to explain, "Right after I escaped the Hunkpapa camp, I worked several jobs to spite them, until I realized I couldn't hurt any or all Indians because of what the Hunkpapas had done to me. Besides, the only one getting hurt was me. When you aim for revenge, you always fire two arrows, and one is pointing at your own heart. That was one of my first and most painful lessons. When I became a U.S. Marshal, I think it was to give me an excuse to hunt down and kill evil men like my father and his partners so they couldn't hurt innocent people like my mother and me. I finally stopped fooling myself and endangering my life when I discovered why I had been hired. If I recall the words correctly, they went something like, 'That half-breed can get rid of lots of bastards for us and if he gets killed doing it, what does it matter?' You see, *micante*, selfish people use gullible people all the time; and people are more gullible when they're hurt or seeking revenge."

Rana nestled against his firm body and sighed peacefully. Her gaze roved each marking on his *wanapin* and each scar on his chest and arms. As if trying to determine the agony he had endured with each wound and to comfort them belatedly, her fingers lovingly traced each one. He still retained the honed body, keen instincts, and noble spirit of a highly trained warrior. She had seen him get angry but not lose his temper and control or become violent. She had seen him accept pain without even a soft whimper, and she had seen him use his courage and wits in the Oglala camp. She doubted he had ever cried out during the Sun Dance or his torture. He was so strong and proud, yet so sensitive and vulnerable beneath that seemingly impenetrable surface.

She listened to him talk about his days with the Apaches and how much he had learned from them, even things the Lakota warriors did not know. He talked about riding with outlaws for a time, claiming it was to show the white law that he was invincible and could do whatever he wanted and no one could touch him. She heard him admit he had been trapped between two sides and could not choose which one to help or hurt, until he finally learned he was the one being harmed the most. Under Nathan's hands, he had come to accept the fact that he could not change the world, only himself. Again, her fingers traced his scarred flesh—which in no way detracted from its beauty and appeal—and caressed his virile body as she absorbed his soulful confessions. She toyed with the Lakota *wanapin* as he told her about it. He had faced so many perils and hardships and had known such anguish. Yet she realized how each incident or job had molded him and honed him into the man he was today, a man who stood above others in so many ways.

Travis kissed her, then left the room to wash up and redress. He returned shortly to find her still reclining on the bed and smiling provocatively at him. He chuckled and teased, "Don't you go looking at me like that, woman. I have no willpower where you're concerned, and Nate could return home in an hour or two. Get up and get dressed so I can show you around your new home."

Rana did as Travis suggested, rising and leaving the room to refresh herself before dressing. Travis straightened the bed and placed the doll where it had been before their heady bout of lovemaking. He gazed at it and smiled, for he knew that someday they would have a baby, and he vowed their child would never experience the pain its parents had. Strange, he hadn't given love, marriage, or children any serious thought until he had met that entrancing vixen who had practically turned his gut inside out until he had finally won her heart and acceptance. A child . . . Nothing would make him happier than making and sharing a child with Rana Michaels. After all, they were married and . . . Damn, he cursed silently. There were some problems he would have to correct as soon as possible. There was a legal entanglement that now prevented a marriage between them; there was his concern over not getting Rana with child before they were joined under the white man's law; and there was the matter of getting rid of several dangerous enemies who could be lethal threats to her and Nathan . . .

Chapter Twelve

Travis saddled two horses and took Rana riding. Without going too far and getting out of sight in case of danger, he spent three hours telling her about ranch life and escorting her around the areas of their spread that were visible to those laboring near the wooden structures or the hands working on horseback. She was fascinated by the branding process, which he allowed her to view through his field glasses. She was concerned that the animals were being hurt, so Travis explained the procedure in detail without allowing her to approach the hectic scene. She observed the hands who were herding wild mustangs into a large corral so they could be broken and sold in two months. In the Oglala camp she had witnessed the mastering of wild horses and knew it was a dangerous task. Yet she eagerly asked Travis if she could watch what he had called "bronco-busting."

He chuckled and nodded, wondering how she would feel when she watched him nearly busting his butt and ribs on one of those wild beasts that could suddenly seem like a bundle of energy, sharp bones, and flaying hooves. Bronco-busting always gave him a sense of power and victory, and a thrill that was hard to describe to anyone who had not experienced it. There was something about challenging danger, even death, that made him come alive and sharpened his wits. He began thinking that since he was planning on a family soon—a wife and children—perhaps he should cut out some of the dangerous things he had been doing. Certainly Nathan would agree as soon as he was told of the love he and Rana shared. Soon he would become more than Nathan's adopted son and legal heir, and hopefully that would please the older man. Yet he understood that he could not legally wed Rana as long as he remained her uncle by law, a fact that would have to be altered after any threat to her was removed.

To avoid the tension of her having to meet so many strangers while she was getting settled, he stayed clear of the wranglers and the families in the married settlement. In about a week, he and Nathan would introduce her to a few people at a time, beginning with those important to the ranch, such as Cody Slade, Mace Hunter, Todd Raines and his wife, Rachel, Darby Davis and his wife, Lettie, and Bart Davis.

This first day of July was lovely and mild, and the landscape seemed to be showing its gratitude to nature by having donned its prettiest face. Travis could tell that Rana was amazed by the size of their spread and impressed by its beauty. The smiling foreman observed Rana as she twisted this way and that in her saddle to take in everything around them. Each time she looked at him to ask a question or to make a comment, their gazes met and they smiled before speaking.

He told Rana he would show her the rest of their land another day, as there was too much territory to cover so quickly and it was past lunch time. After they had returned to the stable and were heading for the house, he asked her if she would be ready and willing to learn how to handle a pistol and rifle that afternoon.

Excitedly she replied, "Yes, teach me now."

"After we eat," he informed her, then grinned. She was so full of energy, vitality, and curiosity. He enjoyed watching her and sharing time with her. She was such a rare and special woman, and he was delighted she belonged to him. He admitted to himself he was not sorry for staking his claim on her and was eager to increase it. Remembering what they had shared warmed his heart and his body. His gaze engulfed her possessively, proudly. His woman, his wife . . .

Rana smiled and her cheeks glowed as she read heart-stirring emotions in his eyes. "You do not think of eating food, *mihigna*," she teased cheerfully as her eyes lovingly adored him.

Travis arched one brow devilishly and replied, "You're right, *micante*. Today it is not the rumbling in my belly that calls to me."

Rana laughed merrily, for she recalled that first night in Lone Wolf's tepee when he had scolded her with similar words. "It is good, *mihigna*, for Myeerah's tepee is too far away for me to fetch food to quiet it. We have both changed much since that first night."

Rich masculine laughter filled the air as Travis realized to what she was alluding with her jest. "Yes, we have both changed, Rana," he concurred, reaching over to caress her flushed cheek. At that moment, he did not care who was watching or what anyone thought.

"My grandfather has tamed you, and you have tamed me. I will no longer behave like a rebellious child or a wild spirit."

Travis's brows lifted and his eyes widened in surprise. Slowly the reaction faded and his gaze revealed sparkling eyes that narrowed slightly to form tiny lines at their corners. White teeth gleamed as his smile broadened and those creases deepened. Astonishingly he vowed, "I don't want to tame you, Rana; I like you and want you just as you are. You possess just the right blend of

363

strength and softness. You're kind and generous, and you're the smartest and bravest woman I've ever met. Stay as you are, my fiery-haired temptress. You have so much spirit and life, Rana, and you make me feel good just being around you. I wish you to grow by learning, *micante,* but do not change."

She was deeply touched by his words and her eyes grew misty. "But I am stubborn and defiant," she softly refuted.

"Only because you wanted to do all the things you loved and needed to do, and the Oglalas wouldn't allow it. Here, Rana, you can do *almost* anything," he informed her, stressing the one vital word. "You have plenty of skills and talents, but you have to learn where and when to use them, especially on me," he teased.

To control his desire for her at this inconvenient time, he changed the subject. "The white man's laws and ways are different. I'll teach them to you, and you must obey them. Here, only bad men raid, and when they're captured they're punished. If we want something, we work for money, then we buy it; we never take it. If a man does wrong, we don't kill him; he's captured and punished, by jailing him or hanging him. Don't worry, I'll teach you all you need to know," he encouraged when she frowned in dismay and confusion. He tried to explain the American government, Texas laws, trials, justice, and more, but he could tell this information was overwhelming, befuddling.

She thought a minute, then asked, "What if the bad man flees before this . . . sheriff comes to . . . arrest him? This man called a lawyer—what if he tricks others with clever lies? What if the jury does not believe your charges? Will he go free?" she inquired, disliking this seemingly irrational form of justice. She insisted, "It is a man's responsibility to defend his own life and lands, and those of his family. If another does evil deeds, his guilt is known and he should die. It is right for the one who suffers from his evil to punish him."

"A white man cannot take the law into his own hands, Rana. If he does, he's guilty of breaking the law and can be punished. In America, the white lands, justice must be carried out legally. It protects an innocent person who's been falsely or mistakenly accused of a black deed, which we call a crime. Years ago I could have used a lawyer and a jury trial in the Hunkpapa camp and maybe I would have gotten a fair shake," he remarked to make his point.

She considered those words, then shook her head. "This makes no sense, Travis Kincade," she argued softly. "If a man does evil to you and the white law does not punish him, will you let him go free to harm another? Does this white justice always work?"

Travis grimaced at her painful point, for that was exactly what he would not do. Embittered or mistreated men often took the law into their own hands, just as, if necessary, he was planning to do very soon. How could he honestly tell her, "Do as I say, not as I do"? Trapped, he wondered how to answer her sincere question without lying or causing confusion in her new education.

Suddenly Rana smiled mischievously. "I understand. You must obey white laws when possible; but if justice fails you, you must appear to accept such laws while you carry out your own justice in secret, and you must not be captured while breaking these laws. Is this not so?"

"Lordy, women, you're too clever to fool or argue with. The trouble with taking the law into your own hands is you risk hurting those you love. Your family and friends can be accused of helping you and they can be punished. Besides, the white law is powerful and persistent. If you challenge it, you had better be ready to die, 'cause some of those lawmen will chase you to hell and back. I know; I did it several times when I was an Army scout and U.S. Marshal."

"What of these men who raid our lands? Why does the white law not capture and punish them?"

"The sheriff says he doesn't know who's responsible. The rustlers strike at night and nobody sees them. If people do witness their crimes, they're too afraid to give out their identities. They're like shadows, Rana, and you can't capture a shadow. Once they become real men, the law will punish them. I'm going to try to unmask them. All I need is evidence on who's behind all this trouble."

"To capture a dark shadow, you must become a darker shadow. Remember how we set traps for the sly fox and crafty raccoon? One who does mischief or evil must be snared. When you capture them, must you give them to the sheriff? Or will you punish them?"

"I'm supposed to hand them over to the law," he replied vaguely.

Rana eyed him for a few moments, then stated confidently, "You know who leads this band of night raiders. You are planning how to defeat them. Let Rana help you," she entreated earnestly.

Travis stared her in the eye as he warned, "Listen to me, Rana Michaels. These men are dangerous, and I don't want you getting hurt. Don't talk about this to anyone except me and Nate. We want you to stay close to home until this matter is settled. Understand?"

"But I can help you defeat them. Did I not prove my fighting skills on the trail? You will be in danger, and I wish to protect you."

Travis sighed heavily. "Darn you, woman, I can't be careful if I have to worry about you. In case you haven't noticed before, you are most distracting. If those men got one look at you . . ." He halted and shook his head vigorously. "No, *micante*. Please don't fight me on this. If anything happened to you, I couldn't stand it."

Rana could not suppress a happy smile. "I wish to help you and Grandfather, but I will obey."

Travis sighed in relief and cuffed her chin playfully. "Good. You don't know these people and, if you said or did the wrong thing, you could endanger all of us and the ranch. We have to be very careful and alert. You see, *micante*, until we know who's involved, we can't trust anyone. Right now, all I can do is watch and listen for clues. When I get evidence against the guilty ones, I'll let the sheriff handle them, or I will," he added with a sly grin.

As he prepared their meal, Rana observed the man who ruled her emotions. Earlier this morning he had tended her injured fingers and rebandaged them, and now he had refused to allow her to help him prepare their food or wash up afterward. Nathan arrived just as they were leaving the house to begin her pistol and rifle lessons. The session was delayed when Nathan asked Travis to join him in his office for a talk.

Nathan smiled at Rana and said, "You sit here on the porch and I'll be finished with Travis soon; then he can teach you to shoot. I talked with a woman in town this morning. She'll be coming out tomorrow to take your measurements so she can make you some clothes. And I spoke with the schoolteacher; he's agreed to come out here a few days a week to help with your lessons."

Rana hugged Nathan and said, "You are very kind and generous, Grandfather. I will wait here for Travis." She realized Nathan was worried about something and wanted to discuss it privately with Travis, and she quickly surmised it was the trouble with the evil men. She watched them go inside, then she sat down on the top step to relax and think.

Time passed as Rana awaited their return, and she was so caught up in her thoughts that she did not notice the young man who approached the house. As he sighted the beautiful, flaming-haired girl, he stared, then smiled genially. Halting at the bottom porch step, he declared,

"You must be Mister Crandall's granddaughter. I'm Cody Slade. Are Mister Crandall and the boss inside?" he asked pleasantly.

Rana recognized the man's name and noted that he seemed very friendly and polite. "I am Rana Michaels. Grandfather and Travis entered the house to speak privately. We must wait here for their return," she informed him, trying to speak properly and cordially.

Cody propped his boot on the lower step to follow her advice. "I know Mister Crandall sure is happy to have you home again, Miss Rana. You're going to love it here. This is one of the finest ranches anywhere, and there's nobody better to work for than Travis and your grandfather. I've been with them since I was knee-high to a weaning calf."

Rana tried to keep the confusion that filled her at his unknown phrases from showing on her face, but she could only guess the gist of his words. She did not know how to converse with this sandy-haired, hazel-eyed male whose looks and manner were pleasing to the senses, so she remained silent and alert after she had smiled and thanked him.

Cody could not get over how exquisite she was, even though he had seen the portrait of Marissa and had been told she looked like her mother. To confront such radiance and beauty in person was stunning and gratifying. Unconsciously he indulged his stimulated senses. He had seen a few women who had been called ravishing, but all of them put together could not compete with this glorious angel before him. She looked so sweet and innocent to possess so much earthy sensuality. Everything about her seemed perfect, but it was her expressive gray-blue eyes and the fiery curls reaching to her waist that snared his attention time and time again. He wondered how Travis Kincade, who had traveled with her for weeks and was now living in the same house with her, could think about anything besides this bewitching creature. If he was not in love with Mary Beth Sims, he would feel compelled to pursue Nathan Crandall's granddaughter.

Wanting to hear that voice again, which seemed simultaneously to be able to soothe and stimulate a helpless man, Cody inquired, "Has Travis shown you around the ranch yet?"

"We rode nearby this morning," she answered slowly as she selected her words and tried to speak in the white man's style. "Travis told . . . me the ranch is too large to cover in one day. I have been away for many years and there is much to learn before I meet others."

"I guess it is a scary thing for a woman to come to a new place with so many strangers. Don't worry, Miss Rana; everyone here will help you in any way they can. You'll make friends easily and quickly."

Because of his tone and sincere smile, she did not take offense at the suggestion in his first sentence that women were prone to fear, nor did she correct him. "You are very kind, Cody Slade. Ra . . . I will need friends and help here. You are the first to speak with me; it is good to call you friend."

Cody wanted to ask all about her and her absence of eleven years, but he knew that would be too intrusive and bold. "There aren't too many girls your age around these parts. As soon as you get settled in, I'll introduce you to a close friend of mine, Mary Beth Sims. She's eighteen, and real nice. You two will like each other. She's about this tall," he related, indicating a height of about five feet, five inches. "She has green eyes and brown hair, and she's real pretty. Her father owns a fancy hotel in town. She doesn't have many friends her age, so I know she'll enjoy meeting you."

Rana observed the telltale glow that filled Cody's eyes and comprehended how much this girl meant to him. She warmed to a man who could show such deep emotion without being embarrassed. "Soon, I will ask you to bring her to visit me. It is good to have a special friend." Rana thought about Myeerah for a time and thrilled at the idea of making a good friend in her new home. If Mary Beth Sims was close to this pleasing man, she would be a very special person.

"Do you wish to sit with me until Grandfather returns?" she invited amiably, knowing he must feel awkward towering over her. Cody grinned and sat down on the middle step, within a few feet of her. "Tell me about . . . bronco-busting," she coaxed to relax him. "I saw the wild horses this morning. Travis said I could watch."

Cody eagerly slipped into an explanation of the taming procedure. As he spoke with knowledge and enthusiasm, he leaned against the next step and rested his elbow on it. Intrigued and attentive, Rana placed her chin on her hands, which were lying flat on her raised knees. Her head and Cody's were very close as he shared tales of past events.

From the hallway, Travis eyed the rankling scene on the front steps. Consumed by a novel burst of jealousy and possessiveness, he joined them, halting to hunker down behind Rana so he could boldly display his claim on her by the way he stroked her hair, then rested his hand on her shoulder. "Just what is this cowpoke filling your ears with?" he inquired jovially, concealing his irrational feelings from them.

Rana half-turned to meet his gaze and to respond, "Cody is telling me about taming wild horses. Can I choose one to replace *Mahpiya* as you promised?"

Cody observed the way Travis looked at Rana and trailed his finger across her flushed cheek as he nodded. His foreman and friend appeared to be mesmerized by those remarkably alluring eyes. Smiling, he decided that the two were deeply attracted to each other. He was pleased for Travis, for he felt this man deserved the best in a woman.

"As soon as we get them broken in, you can take your pick. Were you looking for me, Cody?" Travis queried, glancing his way.

Cody stood up and nodded. "I hired those men we talked about last night. You want to meet them and give 'em orders while they're getting settled in at the bunkhouse?"

"I'll be right along," Travis replied in a dismissing tone.

Cody smiled at Rana and told her, "It was a real pleasure meeting you, Miss Rana. If you need anything, just give me a holler." Cody noticed the way Travis tensed and frowned. Chuckling, he said to the half-blooded foreman, "See you at the bunkhouse, boss." Grinning broadly, he turned and strolled off at a jaunty pace, whistling.

Rana pondered why Travis was looking and acting so strangely. Wondering if he thought she might have said something wrong to Cody Slade, she related the entirety of their conversation. "Are you angry with me? Was it wrong to speak with your friend?"

Travis calmed himself, for he knew he had over-reacted. "No, I'm not mad at you. It was all right to talk with Cody, but you have to be careful when you meet strangers. Cody might not have been a friend."

"But you and Grandfather spoke of him many times."

"I know, *micante*, but what if that man hadn't been Cody Slade?"

"Eyes do not lie, Travis Kincade. I read friendship and kindness in his. I like your friend. He is a good man, one who loves a woman named Mary Beth Sims," she reminded meaningfully.

Travis shrugged and mischievously asserted, "Must be

that Indian blood acting crazy inside me. Can White Eagle help it if he's jealous and possessive of his wife, Wild Wind, when he can't claim her publicly?"

Rana laughed. "You do not trust your friend or your wife?"

"Trust any man around you? No, ma'am. You stay right here until I see my new hands." Travis chuckled heartily when her eyes filled with that now recognizable bewilderment. "Not these hands, *micante;* the men who work for us. They're called hands, cowpokes, wranglers, cowpunchers, cowboys, and a few other names."

"This white man's tongue will be hard to master. So many names, for one thing. Explain Cody's words, 'knee-high to a weaning calf'?"

Travis explained what calves and weaning were, then tried to explain slang. "He was saying he's been working here since he was a young boy, fourteen to be exact. Nate used to take in lots of young boys after their parents were killed, usually by Indians. You were right about Cody being a good man. I'm surprised he wasn't occupying the place Nate gave me. The same can be said of Mace Hunter. Those two are my best friends. I don't know how to explain the bond between me and Nate. As soon as we met, it was like father and son, and Nate insisted on making it legal so I wouldn't have any trouble getting the ranch after he died. 'Course the ranch is yours by right of blood. I was damn lucky Nate hadn't taken Cody or Mace as his son, or they might have doctored me and left me in Missouri and we wouldn't have met. Lordy, woman, listen to me rambling on and on. I never used to talk this much. Something about you just opens me up, makes me feel real comfortable, like a good pair of leather boots."

"It is the same with me, Travis. I feel I can say anything to you, and you would understand. It is good to be so close with you."

Travis gazed into her entreating eyes and stated mysteriously, "Soon, there'll be something I have to get straightened out before we can have a serious talk about our life together." He knew Rana did not realize the importance of the fact that he was legally Nathan Crandall's son and she was Nathan's granddaughter, making her his niece by law and making marriage between them impossible. Somehow he would have to find a way to void those adoption papers so he could marry Rana. Trouble was, he dared not start any obvious legal proceedings until lawyer Harrison Caldwell was out of their way. So many things appeared to be complicating his life these days, especially the matters concerning her.

Rana stood on the porch until Travis had vanished into the bunkhouse. She wanted to be near him all the time. She received so much pleasure just by looking at him or being near him. The sound of his voice seemed to tease over her entire body when he spoke. His caress and his scent enticed her, and his consuming gaze inflamed her from head to foot. She wanted to touch him, to taste him, to see him, to hear him, to enjoy him, and to share all things with him. She could not seem to get enough of him. He made her feel so calm, yet so stimulated. He made her feel as if he were everything, yet with so much more to explore or obtain. He was open, yet a mystery. He could satisfy her completely, yet leave her hungering for more. So many complex emotions filled her body, and they all centered around Travis Kincade.

Travis returned sometime later to tell Rana not to wait for him, for he was needed to instruct the new men and to make plans to overcome these new problems that had arisen. He suggested that she join her grandfather. Disappointed, Rana entered the house and headed for Nathan's office.

* * *

373

Nathan Crandall was leaning back in his chair and staring at the map over his desk, the one that had been altered today to indicate the unexpected enclosure of his lands by Harrison Caldwell. Over the years, Caldwell had added Sam Kelly's Box *K* Ranch and Harvey Jenkins's Lazy *J* Ranch to his Circle *C* holdings. Nathan had not truly been worried about Caldwell succeeding with his dream to forge a new cattle empire until James McFarland had sold out while he and Travis had been gone. If he had been here, he could have helped and advised his old friend. After his talk with Wilber Mason at the Mid-Texas Bank in Fort Worth, it had become clear from the terms of the sale and the price that Harrison Caldwell had practically stolen the Flying *M* Ranch, though legally, as he had supposedly acquired the other two spreads. Except for the river boundary, which was one reason why the Rocking *C* Ranch was so prosperous and coveted, Nathan's land was now encircled by that devious, determined rival who wanted his land and whose daughter wanted his son. They would never get either, Nathan resolved confidently.

It was hard for Nathan to imagine that he and Harrison had been genial acquaintances many, many years before. Not that they had ever been good friends, but they had been neighbors and their wives had been close. In fact, Harrison's wife, Sarah Jane, had been with his beloved Ruth when she had suffered her worst bouts of fever shortly before her death in '39. The poor creature had never recovered from that trying period, and she had been unable to face him again before her own demise in '44. One would have thought two neighboring widowers with small girls would have become good friends, but it was never to be, for Harrison Caldwell was nothing like Nathan Crandall.

Nathan admitted that perhaps he had kept to himself too much after his cherished wife's death, for he had not realized what Harrison Caldwell was plotting until the man's plans were well underway. Before he knew or suspected a thing, Caldwell was the owner of three of the four ranches that bordered Crandall holdings. While he and Travis had gone to recover his granddaughter, the last spread had been gobbled up. Ever since Caldwell's return from back east around the time Marissa had married and left home, the man had seemed bent on obtaining his ranch. It was almost as if something terrible had happened to Harry around that time to rile and embitter him, for he had become worse than ever after his return home. In the past few years, the guileful lawyer had made three offers for the Rocking C Ranch.

Nathan's mind drifted back to the day of his last overture. Caldwell had offered him any price for his ranch, saying Nathan could buy another ranch anywhere and still have plenty of money to spend. Harrison had told him how important it was for a big rancher to own lots of connecting property with plenty of water and grazing land. They had talked, then argued, with Nathan vowing never to sell and Harrison claiming he would own this entire area one day.

Nathan slammed his fist down on his desk. If only he and Travis could find evidence to prove that Harrison Caldwell had driven the other ranchers away illegally. Somewhere papers and altered branding irons had to exist, as Travis had suggested on several occasions, and somewhere there was a witness who could be compelled to tell the truth. The trouble was, Harrison Caldwell was getting desperate and was playing dirty by hiring gunslingers. Nathan hated to imagine the things happening on his ranch that had taken place on McFarland's. He could easily understand why the older man had given in to such malevolent forces.

What made things worse, if anything could be worse, was the fact that the two hirelings were the same two men from Travis's past. This posed the danger that Travis's personal feelings would get in the way of his thinking clearly. They could not expect any help from the sheriff—that had become obvious at their meeting this morning—unless the incompetent lawman was forced to take sides because of undeniable proof against Caldwell and his cohorts. If anything, the sheriff would turn on him and Travis for taking over his job and doing it efficiently and correctly. It had become a touchy situation that had to be handled gingerly as well as secretly.

Nor could he expect any help or leniency from Wilber Mason. The man had come right out and admitted that his bank would foreclose on Nathan's loan after six o'clock on August first, if the debt was not paid in full. Of course, the lawyer for the bank was none other than Harrison Caldwell. Wilber Mason had even refused to discuss extending or renegotiating the loan. Clearly Caldwell was pressuring the banker. The only way he could repay the loan and pay his hands was with the money from the cattle sale in Sedalia. He shuddered in horror when he thought of the possibility of that money being stolen. His men, under Mace Hunter and Todd Raines, had always been careful and loyal, but he was glad Travis had ordered Cody Slade to send more men and a warning to guard the cashbox.

He could still envision Caldwell's gloating face as it had been when they had met in town earlier today. He had vexed the Circle *C* owner by refusing to comment on his lengthy absence or to show concern over McFarland's bad luck during that absence. Neither had he told Harrison about the return or existence of his grand-daughter. The insidious man would make that discovery soon enough, as would his daughter, Clarissa. Maybe news of Rana would shock the malicious vixen into . . .

"Grandfather?" Rana called to him. "Do you wish me

to do some work for you? I do not understand the chores of your lands and home, so I laze here with nothing to do."

Nathan cast aside his troubling thoughts to spend time with her. "There's nothing that needs doing today, Rana. We'll let everything go until Rachel returns next week; then she can teach you about the house." In an attempt to keep her from being disquieted or embarrassed during the seamstress's and teacher's visits on Tuesday, Nathan went over what would be expected of her and the important purpose each would serve. He then gave Rana another tour of their home and explained its features in greater detail.

By the time Travis returned, she and Nathan had supper ready and waiting. It was after the evening meal was eaten and the dishes had been washed and they were drinking coffee in the sitting room that an unexpected, though anticipated, incident took place. Clarissa Caldwell arrived to see Travis, having learned of his return from her father. Even though it was nearing bedtime, the audacious woman had ridden over, after realizing with some annoyance that the handsome foreman was not coming to visit her on his second day home. To ensure their privacy, Clarissa had sent one of the hands to the house to fetch Travis to the yard.

After answering the summons at the door, Travis returned to the sitting room. He sent Rana a wry grin before he explained the rankling situation to Nathan. "Harrison Caldwell's daughter is outside and she wants to see me privately. What do you think, Nate?" he inquired casually, wondering how they should deal with Clarissa's immodest visit. Knowing that James McFarland had been squeezed out during their absence, both hoped that, in her eagerness to snare Travis, Clarissa might carelessly drop a clue about her father's activities. Yet, Travis dreaded conversing with the conniving vixen and being forced to enlighten Rana about her. He wished he had already told Rana about Clarissa and had explained their predicament with the Caldwells, especially the reasons for his past and present pretenses. He hated to imagine what Rana would think and feel about this oversight and his behavior toward Clarissa. In a way, he had promised not to deceive her or withhold vital information again, and nothing could be more vital to their relationship than a woman who was trying to captivate him while he pretended she might succeed. There was no way they could keep her from learning of the problems they were facing, and it would be in her best interest that she be well informed about them and about the people involved. He would have to see Clarissa, he decided, and get this distasteful matter over with tonight.

Neither of them wanted to subject Rana to Clarissa Caldwell this soon. That was an introduction both men wanted to put off as long as possible. Nathan saw Travis's reluctance and vexation, and he was slightly curious, for his adopted son usually enjoyed matching wits with both Caldwells, even if he could not stand either one. Maybe Travis wasn't in the mood for clever games tonight, Nathan mused. These past two months had been hard on his adopted son, and now he was facing more ghosts from his past and more danger from Harrison. Still, this task had to be done, and the sooner the better. "Considering what's been happening while we were gone, I think you should see her. Maybe you can learn something. Tell her whatever you think is best; just don't bring her inside."

Rana sensed a disturbing undercurrent in the room. From what the men had told her, Harrison Caldwell was their neighbor; yet they did not seem pleased with his daughter's visit. An aura of mystery and hesitation filled the room, making her suspicious and apprehensive. She could not understand why a woman would come to visit Travis so near to their sleeping time and why the men

378

would need to discuss whether or not to see her. "Do you not wish me to meet this neighbor's daughter, grandfather? It is late and dangerous for a woman to be riding alone. Does she bring bad news?"

Neither man spoke for a time, which increased Rana's anxiety. Finally Travis replied, "I should have told you about Clarissa and her father before this. You'll have to meet her one day, Rana, but not tonight. She isn't the kind of woman you'll like or want to be around. I'd rather not see her tonight, but we need to know a few things—if she'll reveal them, which I doubt. Don't worry; I'll explain it all in the morning. You two go on to bed; it's late, and both of you have a busy day tomorrow. Hopefully I won't be long."

"If you and grandfather do not like her, why does she come to visit and why must you see her? Why do you refuse to allow her to enter our home?" she inquired, observing both men with rising suspicion. She knew that Travis and Nathan were not men to allow anyone to force them to do anything, so something was terribly amiss. Worst of all, her beloved looked nervous, and guilty of some wrong.

"I'll explain in the morning; just trust me," he coaxed.

Aware of how she would soon handle this distressing matter, Rana did not want to lie, so she chose her words carefully when she answered, "I will try to do as you say, but this matter is confusing."

Rana and Nathan said their good nights and went to their rooms. Travis dismissed the man who had been waiting on the front porch for further orders after delivering Clarissa's message.

The formidable man left the house to meet with Clarissa, who was pacing near the corral. The dark-haired, dusky-skinned woman halted to watch Travis Kincade's approach. Her deep brown eyes sparkled with desire and eagerness. She licked her lips in anticipation of fusing them to his. Her entire body began to warm and itch with barely suppressible lust. She could hardly wait to get this virile male in her arms, in bed or anywhere he chose. Someday and somehow she would break down his resistance; then he would be hers.

With a leisurely stride that exposed his confidence, agility, and a hint of arrogance, Travis reached her. He flashed her a devilish grin as he lazed negligently against a large post, then asked, "Isn't it a bit late for such a lovely lady to be out calling on neighbors? Cody tells me there's been some trouble in these parts while we were gone. I know you're a fearless and stubborn girl, but I'm surprised your papa let you leave home with so much danger lurking."

As her appreciative gaze roamed his face and body, Clarissa offered him a seductive pout and throaty laugh. "No man, good or bad, would dare attack Harrison Caldwell's daughter. Since you haven't come over to see me since your return, I've cast all shame aside to visit you."

Travis chuckled heartily. "I've only been back since last night."

She added petulantly, "And you were busy all day. You've been gone for months, love, and I've missed you terribly. Is this any way to greet me?" she asked provocatively, stepping forward to press her body against his intimately. "You're a cruel and selfish beast, Travis Kincade. Why do I allow you to treat me so badly?" she teased, running her fingers through his sable hair before using them to pull his head down to hers to seal their lips.

Travis was tempted to spurn her and her kiss, but he knew the only way to extract information about her father's insidious dealings was by faking a response. His arms went around her and tightened to expose his strength and control, and his mouth seared over hers, causing her to tremble with hunger. Lordy, he hated touching this woman and being nice to her! If there hadn't been so much at stake, he would have sent her on her way, after telling her how he really felt about her. Yet there were limits to his game with her; he would never bed her for any reason. It was not that Clarissa wasn't a very attractive and sensual woman, and no doubt skilled in lovemaking, but her character made her ugly and repulsive to him. During the time he had known her, he had never been tempted to accept sex from her, and she had offered it countless times. Over the years since his coming of age as a man, he had been able to separate his emotions from his sexual urges. After that perilous incident with Elizabeth Lowry, he had become very selective about whom he bedded, even on the occasions he had visited the Silver Shadow Saloon. But having taken Rana and having blended emotion with love-making, his feelings would never be the same. Now the only woman with whom he wanted to unite his body and share his passion was Rana Michaels. She had taught him that the act of mating was something special and that it should not be performed with just anyone, even if one's body was screaming for release.

When Clarissa's hands began to wander boldly over his body, Travis grasped them to halt the wanton display. He leaned back and taunted, "Behave yourself, woman. My cowpunchers are still up and around. We don't want them teasing their boss or thinking naughty thoughts about you. Seems a lot happened while I was gone. From what the boys have told me, it's dangerous around here for women. You'd best get home, and I'll see you in a few days."

"It's been months, Travis. I want to spend some time with you. Besides, if it's so dangerous out there, you should escort me home safely," she cajoled, yearning to get him alone.

"What about those two gunslingers your papa hired? Aren't they supposed to guard you as well as Harry's property?" he jested, lifting a curl with which he began teasing her nose. "Tell me, you clever vixen, how did you sneak off with your place being watched? If you can slip past them, they must not be very good at their new job."

Clarissa chuckled at the tickling sensation. She captured Travis's hand and placed kisses over it, then erotically trailed her tongue over each finger and across his palm before suggestively and lasciviously sucking on several of his fingertips as her gaze seduced him. "When I want something badly enough, I find a way to get it," she replied breathlessly, for her actions were stimulating her to feverish desire. "If I tell you or show you how to sneak through Papa's guard line, will you use the information to visit my room tonight?" she inquired sultrily.

Travis playfully traced his forefinger from her nose, across her lips and chin, over her throat, and down her chest, to halt at the swell of her breasts where the first button on her shirt was fastened. His roguish gaze never left hers as the finger began to slip very slowly up and down her deep cleft, visibly increasing her respiration and pulse rate. He mischievously chided, "I've told you before, hot-blooded lady, I don't get involved with daughters of important or dangerous men. If Harry caught us together like that, he would skin my hide, or force me to take a wife if you were to get with child. Sorry, Clarissa, but I'm not ready to settle down or to risk getting run out of this area. I've put in my best years on this ranch and Nate has claimed me as his son and heir; I don't aim to waste or spoil that by upsetting him, 'cause you know how he feels about your papa. One of these days I'm gonna find out why those two hate each other so much. I'd bet my year's ages you know the truth, but you ain't talking."

Travis watched a telltale grin form on Clarissa's mouth, but she held her silence. "When I do get ready to settle down with a wife and home, there's one thing for sure, Clarissa. There's only one tempting female around here. I still got me a few wild years and urges left. You just be patient and obliging while I tame 'em. Now, get along. I have to get up early. Work piled up while Nate and me were on the trail. Then there's this trouble that started brewing during our absence. Harry got any idea who's behind all the rustling and fence cutting?"

Deceitfully she vowed, "If I knew anything, love, I would have told you by now. Poor Mister McFarland, he got so scared he sold out and left. I suppose he was too old and weak to put up a fight. Did you know one of his sons asked me to marry him?"

Travis frowned as he arched one brow and narrowed his green eyes, acting as if he were jealous. He winced inwardly as he lied to Clarissa to entrap her. "You'd best be glad you said no, woman. McFarland ain't got no son with guts, or they would still be over at the Flying *M* Ranch. Even if a gang of devils and demons rode in here, I would never be pushed off my land. All of my blood would soak into this dirt before I deserted it. Besides, like me, you aren't ready to settle down to marriage and children yet." They both laughed. "Nate talked with the sheriff, but that fool doesn't know anything. If you ask me, we ranchers will have to handle this matter ourselves. Maybe we should hire us some fancy gunslingers like your papa did. Except every hired gun I've ever met eventually turned on his boss and killed him. One person you can't trust is a man who hires on for money, 'cause somebody always has more money and can lure him away, or he kills you and takes more than his share of blood money. You be careful around them."

"I warned Papa those crude men might be trouble. If anything happens, Papa has only himself to blame for

383

hiring such lowbred ruffians. I wouldn't be surprised if they've ridden as outlaws or if they try to rob Papa. You don't have to worry about me; I try to stay as far away from them as possible. But you know Papa, Travis; he thinks he can handle anyone and anything. Sometimes he's so mean to me. He became furious when I begged him to fire those beasts. Sometimes I can't wait until Papa is gone and our ranch is mine, and Nathan is gone and this ranch is yours. What an empire we could build together!" she exclaimed, wondering how he would react to her statements.

"Those dreams are a long way off, Miss Caldwell. Right now, I need sleep so I can catch up with my chores."

"You wouldn't need to catch up if you hadn't been gone so long," she scolded peevishly, finally reaching the topic that intrigued her the most. She felt she had avoided it long enough to begin questioning him without overly arousing his suspicion or annoyance. "Wherever did you go, love, and why were you away so long? Cody wouldn't tell me anything, and I was so worried about you. I think he's mad because Papa's been seeing his little sweetheart. Isn't that a laugh, Travis? A man of Papa's age pursuing a child bride? He's making a fool of himself."

"Is he really interested in Mary Beth?" Travis probed.

Clarissa wanted Travis to warn Cody to snap up the little creature before her father did, and so she confided, "It's a big secret between Papa and Mister Sims, but they've discussed marriage. That's all I need—a stepmother younger than I am! I told Papa that Mary Beth and Cody were sweethearts, but he doesn't care. Papa says he needs a wife, and she's the best choice."

"And Sims is going along with this ridiculous demand?"

"He's most agreeable. Don't you tell a soul about this, or Papa will skin me alive. He says I've been bossing him too much lately. I don't know what's gotten into him, Travis; he's behaving like a crazy man."

"I take it you won't be upset if me and Cody save Mary Beth from your father?" he teased, tugging gently on a lock of ebony hair.

"Please do, and spare me the humiliation of this absurd marriage. Let's talk about you. Where did you go, and why?"

"You'll never believe what happened in early May. Nate got news about his missing granddaughter, Rana Michaels, the one who was taken captive by Indians eleven years ago. We rode to the Dakota Territory to find this girl who favored Marissa."

The dusky-complexioned woman stared at Travis. "Well?" she probed anxiously when he did not continue. "Was it Marissa's child?"

"I'm afraid it was. She's in the house asleep right now. It cost us five thousand dollars to buy her from the Indians, and nearly cost us our lives. Seems a chief took a liking to her and adopted her as his daughter. She's been living as an Indian princess for ten years. Lordy, she's a willful, spoiled little creature. The chief named her Wild Wind, if that tells you anything about her. I practically had to hog-tie her and drag her all the way home. I've never been more tempted to turn a girl over my knee and whack her good than I was with that little brat. She fought me tooth and nail, and I probably still have scars to prove it. But it didn't take the little minx long to see that this ranch was a good thing. Knowing her, she'll probably try to weasel the entire spread out of Nate. She's a crafty little savage."

"I take it you aren't too pleased with her or her return?"

"Are you *loco*, woman? I've heard plenty of stories about her mother, and believe me, she's just like Marissa Crandall, or worse."

Clarissa scoffed rashly, "You don't know the half of it, love; Marissa was far worse than most people realized. If Nathan knew the truth, he would deny Marissa and this Rana Michaels."

Travis stared at her, sensing something mysterious in her tone and look. Clearly this woman knew some secret that few, if any, others knew. "What about Marissa?" he probed nonchalantly. "I thought you two became close friends before she was killed."

She laughed coldly, then murmured, "One day I might tell you all about Nathan's wicked daughter. What does this Rana look like?"

"You've seen the picture of Marissa over the fireplace. Let's just say that at first glance you'll think you're seeing a ghost."

Clarissa swallowed and digested this bitter information. Hatred and alarm coursed through her body. She wondered what her father would think and do when he discovered this shocking news. And, she fretted angrily, what about Rana's effect on Travis? Another Marissa to battle for the men she craved . . . "Marissa Crandall Michaels was a very beautiful woman. If Rana favors her, then why aren't you inside with her instead of out here with me? You could have her and the ranch with one bite. No doubt her mother's whoring blood runs through her," she commented scornfully, watching how he took this insult.

"No doubt it does, but not where I'm concerned," Travis replied, having successfully concealed his fury. "She's a little brat, Clarissa, and she nearly drove me crazy. She still expects to be treated like a princess, and I won't bend to her wishes. I can't count the number of fights and quarrels we had on the trail. Damn, it's good to be home again. Facing rustlers will be a pleasant change from battling her."

"Why didn't Nathan tell Papa about her this morning?"

He scowled. "Like I said, she's little more than a savage. Nate plans to keep her hidden in the house until that schoolteacher and the seamstress can have her looking and acting half civilized."

"Is she very crude? Can she speak English?"

"Yep, the chief took a schoolmarm captive and forced her to teach the little brat English so she could question prisoners. Oh, she can look and talk white, but underneath she's wild and vicious. She's always trying to bite me or scratch me when she gets mad, and those little teeth and claws are mighty sharp. One hand's bandaged now where she broke several nails attacking me a few days ago. Her Indian father died a few months back, and she was giving her Indian brother fits. He was glad to get rid of her. Now I see why. I can tell you one thing, Miss Caldwell. I'm gonna tame that wild wind for Nate."

"What if she tames you first, my proud and carefree wrangler?"

"What if the sun doesn't rise tomorrow?" he said with a sneer.

"Tell me, love, are you really angry because she's so beautiful and she spurns you?" Clarissa held his gaze as she sought signs of deception.

Travis chuckled. "Would you like to know how many times I've kicked her off my sleeping roll? If I wanted Rana Michaels, my jealous vixen, I could have taken her plenty of times by now. Her hot blood even outblazes yours, and she has no morals or manners. She's been raised wild and free, to take whatever she wants. She rides bareback and goes barefoot, and thinks nothing of shucking her clothes and going for a swim when the mood strikes her. Her temper is as fiery as her hair. Maybe my stinging rejections riled her, 'cause I ain't sharing no

387

bedroll with a wildcat." A playful grin crossed his face as he added, "Maybe I should relent just to have peace in the house. 'Course, like your papa, Nate would tie me to that little vixen if I shared her bed like she keeps inviting. Lordy, Clarissa, I can't think of anything worse than marrying a real bitch, can you?"

"Are you afraid Nathan might turn the ranch over to her? He did make you his son and heir. He would have to disown you."

"I won't let him, and I won't let her take it," he replied smugly.

"If you lose this ranch, love, you can marry me and take over the Caldwell holdings, which are increasing every year," she offered.

"The Caldwell empire doesn't have my blood and sweat all over it. This ranch is mine, one way or another, after Nate's gone."

"If you come home with me tonight, I'll tell you how and why you're Nathan's only legal heir. If you get the right information and help, Rana Michaels can't claim an inch of this ranch."

"Just what are you trying to tell me without coming right out and saying it?" Travis pulled her close against him and kissed her soundly. "If you know something that can help me, spit it out," he entreated huskily, then nibbled at her ear.

"You're teasing me and tempting me unmercifully, Travis. I'm sure my lips and wits will loosen while you're making love to me."

"So, that's it, a trick to seduce me," Travis accused wickedly.

She nibbled on his lower lip and rubbed her body against his as she stated, "I swear to you I know something about Marissa that can end your worries, but you'll have to prove I can trust you."

Travis eyed her speculatively. "By sleeping with you

tonight?" When she nodded, he argued, "Come now, Clarissa; I could sleep with you a hundred times and that wouldn't prove you could trust me. Don't you realize by now, if I considered you just another woman, I would bed you without a care. You mean something very special to me, so I can't use you or treat you lightly. If you can't understand or accept that, we don't need to see each other again. I have enough problems right now with the ranch and that little brat without your adding to them. Lordy, woman, you know I don't see anybody but you."

"But you don't see me enough, Travis," she wailed greedily.

"I'll tell you what. Let me get things straightened out over here and then we'll start seeing each other more, and talking seriously. I told you I ain't ready to get married yet, but we might get promised soon if things work out. Like I said, be patient and trust me."

"You aren't teasing me, are you?" she challenged.

"I don't see anybody but you, and getting promised would stop you from seeing anybody but me. I'm the one who has to worry, not you. Who could Travis Kincade Crandall choose besides the most beautiful and passionate woman around?"

Clarissa was mostly taken in by Travis's silky words, though he had actually been referring to Rana each time. Blinded by vanity and overconfidence, she naturally assumed Travis was smitten with her and would eventually marry her. If he wanted her to behave like a lady, then she would do so, at least around him. She felt he must be anxious to get his hands all over her, and would soon tire of denying himself that pleasure. Now that he was worried over his inheritance, perhaps he would come around to her way of thinking, and perhaps together they could get rid of Nathan and her father and take over both ranches. But she would have to be careful.

Rana Michaels, Marissa's little bastard, would never

interfere with her plans! If necessary, she would expose the truth about Marissa's vile birth. Perhaps one day soon she would tell Travis that Marissa was not Nathan Crandall's daughter and legal heir, and that Rana Michaels was not Nathan's granddaughter. Perhaps she would tell Travis what Ruth Crandall, Nathan's beloved wife, had revealed to Sarah Jane Caldwell while in a delirium before she died. Once she had heard Ruth's secret, Clarissa's mother had never been able to look Nathan in the eye again. Travis might be relieved, and deliciously grateful, to discover that Ruth had been raped by three outlaws during Nathan's three-month absence thirty-eight years ago. Ruth had never told Nathan, even though she had borne a child of that brutal assault. Ruth's fever-dulled mind and loosened lips had even caused her to divulge which of the three villains had been responsible: a flaming-haired, blue-eyed Scotsman who had been called "Red." The old fool, Nathan, had actually believed that the baby girl named Marissa had arrived over two months early. For a fact, neither Nathan nor Marissa had ever learned about Ruth's ravishment. If Marissa had known the truth about her birth . . . But no matter now.

Perhaps she would tell Travis how Marissa had whored with her father for two years and for her husband for many years. Perhaps she would tell him that Rana was not Raymond Michaels's daughter, just as Marissa was not Nathan's child. Perhaps she would tell him who Rana's real father was. No, that would spoil her plans . . .

Travis was gazing inquisitively at the brown-eyed beauty. She had been silent for a long time. Something was running wildly through her head, and he wanted to know all about it. What, he wondered, did she know about Marissa that could affect his life, and Rana's too? "Like the Indians say, you've got a fox running around inside that pretty head. Marissa told you a big secret. What was it?"

"I'll tell you another day, my love. I should get home before Papa misses me and your hands think I'm unworthy to become your wife. As you told me, be patient and trusting a while longer."

Travis knew it would be a mistake to press her tonight, so he allowed the intriguing matter to drop. "Wait until I saddle Apache; it's too dangerous for you to be out alone, even if you were anxious to see me. Next time, woman, you control such reckless urges. In spite of what you think, some men aren't afraid of your papa. Promise me you won't go riding after dark again."

"I'm sorry for behaving so foolishly. I promise," she whispered, then kissed him ardently. She couldn't tell him she was safe because the villains worked for her father and would soon be working for her . . .

Travis left her then, but he was soon back at her side with Apache and her sorrel. He helped her mount and they rode off together.

Rana leaned against the house and closed her eyes, which forced her pent-up tears to overflow and stream down her cheeks. How she wished she could have gotten close enough to hear their words, for their behavior had seared her heart. She slipped around the house and climbed inside her room, wishing she had not crawled out her window to spy on Travis and that infuriating female called Clarissa Caldwell. She flung herself across the bed and wept as she recalled how Wild Wind and White Eagle had spent this morning in each other's arms. Was this woman the "something I have to get straightened out before we can have a serious talk about our life together"?

Suddenly Rana sat up and scolded herself. No matter how that scene had looked to her, there was probably a logical explanation for it. It was wrong to start doubting her husband, or to renounce him. She must trust him, as he had entreated earlier, and fight for him! If she let this matter pass, it would eat her alive inside. The best thing to do was confront Travis and give him the chance to tell her the truth. Their relationship was too new and special to allow misunderstandings to damage it. She loved Travis, and she believed he loved her; so why should she suffer unnecessarily? Yes, she must give him a chance to defend himself, she decided, just as soon as he returned home.

Travis and Clarissa headed for the edge of the Circle *C* Ranch that was nearest the Caldwell house. At a safe distance, the clever Travis told her, "Now you get in that house and stay there. I don't want anything happening to you. I'll come by Wednesday or I'll see you in town Thursday." He leaned over and kissed her as if feasting on the sweetest mouth of any woman alive. He smiled and waved, then rode away.

It was late, but Travis was restless tonight, and he decided to ride along the northeast fence line, which had once bordered Sam Kelly's Box *K* Ranch. Their largest herd was grazing in that area, and he wanted to nose around before returning to the ranch. Besides, he had some serious thinking and planning to do. He would need to explain to Rana about the Caldwells and obtain her help with duping Clarissa. That wasn't going to be easy, for what woman in her right mind would want to aid her lover's pursuit of another woman, even if it was only a false chase? He had to convince Rana that Harrison and Clarissa were dangerous, that they wouldn't hesitate to destroy anything or anyone who got in their way. Rana was smart and brave; she would understand this predicament and help him, he decided. Squaring his shoulders, he rode off in search of answers, for himself and for the ranch.

Clarissa made certain that Travis had not hung back after delivering her to her ranch, then she rode off toward the cabin where Wes Monroe and Jackson Hayes were staying. There was only one horse standing near the cabin. She sneaked to a window and peeked inside to find Wes lying naked on a bunk in one corner and, surprisingly, reading a book. She smiled wickedly as she noticed he was alone, which suited her perfectly. When she knocked on the door, Wes answered, wearing nothing but a cotton sheet he had grabbed and wrapped around his hips. She watched him lower his pistol, eye her up and down, then grin pruriently.

Lacking all modesty, he leaned against the door jamb and asked, "What can I do for you, Miss Caldwell? You can see I wasn't expecting company, especially the boss's daughter. Did you need something?"

Clarissa glanced over his bare shoulder, as if checking to see if he was alone. "I need to talk about something personal," she replied, allowing her gaze to roam his face and torso. "Is your partner around?"

"Nope, and he won't be back until morning. Why don't you come inside and take a chair, if you ain't afraid of me."

"I'm not afraid of anyone, Mister Monroe," she vowed smugly. "But I want this matter to remain between you and me."

He motioned her inside and closed the door behind her. "The name's Wes to such a beautiful woman. Care for a drink?"

She nodded, then slithered seductively around the

393

room while he fetched a bottle of whiskey and two cups. Clarissa downed the golden liquid easily and quickly, then held out her cup for another drink. She noticed how Wes was watching her as she leisurely sipped the second one. Her gaze drifted over his bare chest and legs and returned to his eyes, eyes that did not conceal his lust for her. Yes, she concluded, this man was deceitful and dangerous, and those evil qualities excited and aroused her. She would ensnare Wes with money and her charms, use him, and be done with him before he realized what was happening. When she was finished with him, she would kill him herself while he was dozing in the afterglow of sated passion, or perhaps kill him at the instant of his final release. That would be one of the most stimulating and erotic moments of her life, to watch a man's expression shift from the ecstasy of passion as he comprehends the horror of his own death. She licked her lips and smiled. "You mustn't tell my father or your partner or anyone I came here tonight. This is strictly between us. I want to hire you to do a job for me. How much will your complete loyalty cost me?"

"What kind of job would a pretty lady like you need doing?" Wes asked, pouring more whiskey into Clarissa's cup.

"I need an important man killed," she stated simply.

Wes's face revealed surprise. He eyed her keenly, then grinned. After downing the contents of his cup, he asked, "Who, and why?"

Clarissa laughed sultrily. She set down her cup, strolled to the door, and opened it. She pressed the center of her back against the frame and, on either side of her hips, clasped the edges of it with her fingers, striking a pose that caused her bosom to jut out noticeably. She rubbed her fingers over the hewn logs behind her, relishing the feel of the biting splinters and rough surface. She looked outside and inhaled the breeze that carried with it the blended odors of wildflowers and grasses. It was dark, for only a quarter moon was shining and clouds concealed most of the stars. Hints of a possible thunderstorm filled the air and she hoped it would strike, for she loved the awesome power of raw nature. The cabin smelled of cheroot smoke, whiskey, gun oil, leather, and masculine sweat: sensual and stimulating fragrances to her. When Wes joined her at the door and leaned against the other side, she murmured, "Do you ever do jobs only for the money and without questions? You didn't ask how much I'm willing to pay."

Wes straightened and stepped toward her. He trailed his fingers up her left arm and down the opening of her shirt until a button halted him. His right hand slipped over one breast and cupped it, then his forefinger and thumb kneaded the taut point between them. He was stirred by her lack of a chemise and the way her peak responded to his touch. He kept staring into Clarissa's eyes as he made move after move on her body. She returned his gaze, and not once did she attempt to stay his hands or scold him. As Wes's left hand drifted down the outside of her leg, then made its way up the inside of her thigh, he asked in a hoarse voice, "I always have to know who I'm killing and why, 'cause some jobs ain't worth the risks. Money is useless if you're put in jail or six feet under." Wes's hand made contact with a fuzzy patch between Clarissa's thighs. He realized she wasn't wearing anything but a shirt and skirt and a pair of boots. Pressing his hardened manhood against her thigh, he began to massage the greedy bud beneath her skirt. "Tell me, Miss Caldwell, what is a beautiful and desirable woman willing to pay for this important man's life?"

Clarissa undulated her hips against his hand and responded breathlessly, "Tonight, I only want to know if you're for hire. In a few weeks, I'll tell you who and why, and how to do it. First of all, I have to make sure I can trust you to do the job perfectly and secretly."

"Unbutton your shirt," he commanded in a ragged voice. After she obeyed, he replied, "You've got a deal, Miss Caldwell, if I like your first payment tonight." His mouth closed over one breast and his finger slipped inside her moist body.

Clarissa loosened the sheet and let it fall to the floor. She grasped his manhood and murmured, "I'll make certain you don't change your mind, Wes. You do this job for me, and you can name your price."

He looked her in the eye and said, "The price is you, woman."

Clarissa smiled and drew his mouth to hers . . .

Chapter Thirteen

It was nearing two o'clock when Travis reached the house. He removed his boots at the front door and entered stealthily. Taking the low-burning lantern from the front hallway, he slipped quietly to Rana's door. Deciding it was too late to disturb her, he went to his room and undressed. Before he could toss the cover aside and lie down, his door opened and Rana came inside, closing it after her entrance, and seeming not to notice that he was standing nude near his bed. Even if she had noticed his condition, it did not seem to trouble or embarrass her or deter her from her purpose.

The lantern on the bedside table gave off a soft glow, which lovingly bathed her in its adoring light and enhanced the colors of her flaming hair and gray-blue eyes. Without a word or hesitation, she came forward and halted before him, leaving only a few inches separating their bodies as she looked up into his striking face. Her yearning gaze locked with his and each absorbed the bond that stretched between them and encircled them. Only their soft breathing could be heard in the quietness. As if magically transfixed, neither spoke or moved; they just looked at each other, each sensing the other's matching need.

A light breeze played with the thin covering over the open window and sent stirring fragrances into the shadowy room. Beyond it, if they had not been so enraptured by each other, they would have heard cattle lowing, night birds and insects singing soulfully, and the distant rumble of thunder. The lantern light danced across their entranced features and susceptible bodies, highlighting certain areas as each admired the appeal of the other. It was as if all else was moving very slowly in an attempt to postpone the intrusions of a new day.

Travis lifted one hand and tenderly caressed her face, touching and enjoying each arresting feature. Rana did the same to him. They looked, and touched, and savored each other as if mesmerized. Travis's hands cupped her face and he brushed his lips so lightly over hers that it seemed their mouths were barely touching. His lips drifted lazily over her face, making contact with each rise and fall of its beloved features. His warm respiration was tantalizing at her ear as he buried his nose and hands in her thick hair. His mouth moved across her forehead and kissed each closed eye and then her nose before gently claiming her mouth. The kiss was leisurely and romantic, and ever so gradually he deepened its pressure and intensity, revealing his immense pleasure and yearning. His hands slipped down her neck and across her shoulders and he released the quilt that was wrapped around her, bringing their naked bodies together. His kisses softened once more, for he wanted this stimulating period to stir her thoroughly.

Rana's fingers trailed over Travis's firm yet pliant frame, stopping her and there to caress a bulging muscle or to admire the supple sleekness of his physique. His golden flesh felt so warm and vital, as if she were caressing the soft underbelly of a mighty buck. Her fingers traced over tiny scars that told of his battle-riddled life and enormous prowess, and she lovingly touched those that had gone much deeper than his skin. As he nibbled on her neck and shoulder, she nuzzled his ear and the side of his head. It was sheer bliss just to touch him and to be touched by him. Her hands grew bolder in their wanderings, as did his.

Travis lifted her and placed her on his bed. After dousing the lantern, he joined her. Time passed as they kissed and caressed and explored sensations that heightened their passions. There were no inhibitions or hesitations, no shame or guilt, but only the richness and beauty of their unique love. Both seemed to want to know every inch on the other's body, and how it affected the other when that area was touched and kissed in different ways. It was as if they had forever to enjoy this rapturous enlightenment, and as if they had been a part of each other longer than time itself. But fiery desires, which had been kindled so skillfully and rigidly held at a smoldering peak while they savored these stimulating pleasures, gradually seared through their control and ignited their flaming passions into one roaring blaze.

Their kisses and caresses expressed the depth and urgency of their mutual desire. As their bodies fused into one, Travis murmured against her ear, "I love you, Rana, more than anyone in my life. I waited a long time for someone special to enter my heart. Be mine forever, *micante.*" He kissed her possessively, hungrily.

She felt weak and breathless from the intensity of her emotions. "I am yours forever, *mihigna.* My heart is filled with love for you. Let no one and nothing come between us, or part us."

Together they scaled and conquered the heights of blissful ecstasy and, afterward, settled peacefully in each other's arms. Travis lay on his back and cuddled her snugly against him. He continued to caress her tenderly until his breathing rate was restored to normal. "We have to talk, *micante,*" he finally murmured, hating to allow anything to intrude on their meager time together, particularly the Caldwells, but knowing he should speak promptly to avoid misunderstanding.

"About Clarissa Caldwell and her father?" she asked knowingly.

Travis tensed uncontrollably, and wished he had not. "Lordy, Rana, how do I explain a dirty mess like this? I should have told you about them earlier, but it's such a bitter matter. It makes me mad every time I see them or think about them, and it riled me good when Clarissa raced her fanny over here tonight. I hope you didn't get too upset with me for meeting with her outside. By the time I escorted her home, I was so agitated I had to go riding to settle down." His tone changed noticeably as he continued. "They scare me, Rana, and I don't scare easily. They're evil, and cunning, and greedy. I don't want you getting involved with either one of them, but I doubt that's possible. Promise me you'll hear me out before you get mad, 'cause I've done some things and plan to do others that you won't like."

When he seemed to have difficulty finding the right words to begin, she coaxed, "Do not be afraid to speak what is in your heart. I love you. I will understand . . . and obey, for you would not ask me to do anything that does not matter greatly to us. We are as one now, and what harms you harms me. Reveal your fears and pain."

He hugged her fiercely. "Lordy, woman, do I even deserve you? I love you and trust you, Rana, but what I have to tell you and ask you will prove hard and painful, for both of us. And it's very dangerous."

"My father . . . I mean Soaring Hawk, told me that waiting makes it no easier, and sharing pain makes it less. Love and trust are powerful weapons, my beloved husband, and they can defeat evil if you believe in them strongly and use them against your enemies."

"I don't want to do or say anything that might cause

trouble between us. I love you and need you, Rana. If you don't agree with what I suggest, I swear I won't do it, no matter what the consequences might be."

"Consequences?" she echoed in confusion.

"Things that happen because of something we say or do. Usually consequences are bad things that happen after we make a mistake," he explained. "Let me tell you about Clarissa and her evil father; then you'll see what we're up against." Travis revealed what he knew Harrison had done and what he believed the man was going to attempt. He discussed his past deceit with Clarissa and his current scheme to extract information from her by pretending she was special to him. He told her what had taken place at the corral and what had happened afterward. "I promise you it won't ever go any further than that. It makes me sick just to fake responses and touch her. It's even harder now that I have you. You'll have to play along with this game, Rana, or I'll have to stop it right now. Do you understand how dangerous it can be for all of us, especially you, if Clarissa and her father see you as a problem?"

Rana sat up and lapsed into deep thought. Several things became very clear to her: if Clarissa doubted she could win Travis, the selfish creature would consider him of little use, and his life would be in danger; also, her grandfather would be safe only as long as the Caldwells retained hope of getting the ranch peacefully through Travis and Clarissa. Until her unexpected return, Travis had been Nathan's only heir, but now that she stood to inherit the property, the Caldwells might view her as an obstacle to their evil plans. She was worried about the proximity of the two gunslingers who had once tried to murder her beloved, and deeply concerned over the evil those men could do in league with the Caldwells. Travis was right; they must join forces to unmask and overcome them.

401

"Rana?" Travis whispered apprehensively. He had not told Rana about Clarissa's insults and insinuations about her mother, and he feared that perhaps she sensed he was withholding something. But he refused to tell her things that could be lies and would pain her deeply. "Tell me what you think," he encouraged, sitting up beside her. He wished the room hadn't been so dark, for he yearned to see her expression; yet he could not blame her if she chose to be angry about what he had said and done with Clarissa.

She snuggled against him. "You love me, and you need my help and understanding. You will have all of them, and all of me. We must make plans and decide how much we will tell Grandfather. He will be sad if he does not know why we behave so coldly to each other."

Travis seized her and hugged her with overpowering love and gratitude. "We'll tell him how much I love you and want to marry you just as soon as this mess is over, if you'll say yes a second time."

"Are you sure you wish to make this choice so soon?"

He kissed her forehead. "As far as I'm concerned, we're already married, by our choice. All we need to do is make it legal under the white man's law. Well, what do you think about marrying me again?"

"I love you and would marry you again and again," she responded happily. "We must tell Grandfather about our love and plans for a new marriage; he will help us keep our secrets and fool our enemies. It will be good to work as a family to defeat such evil foes. But we should not tell Grandfather about this," she murmured playfully, pressing him to the bed and running her hands over his body. She kissed and caressed him feverishly, stirring new passions to life. When he was completely ensnared by heady desire, she confessed her earlier spying. They both laughed.

There were only a few hours remaining before dawn.

Travis kissed Rana gently and told her she must return to her room and bed. She did as he requested, anticipating the day when such secrecy would no longer be necessary. Never had she been so happy, or so nervous about their impending actions. She snuggled into her comfortable bed and closed her eyes, pleased that she had gone to him, thereby preventing any problems.

Hours later, Rana smelled breakfast cooking. She slipped into the bathing closet to refresh herself and to dress for this busy day. As she entered the kitchen, she found Nathan sitting at the table and drinking coffee. They exchanged smiles. Nathan told her that Travis had left earlier to handle the morning chores. She ate while Nathan sat smiling at her.

"Grandfather, did Travis tell you a secret this morning?" she asked, unable to contain her joy any longer.

Nathan beamed. "Seems my family will be getting closer but not bigger real soon. I'm happy and pleased, Rana. You and Travis are perfect for each other. And I'm glad you understand about this mess with Harry's daughter. Think you two can fool her? Hiding love isn't easy," he teased, adding milk to another cup of coffee.

"We must do this until our enemies are defeated. Again we will fight side by side, Grandfather. We will be brave and cunning, and we will defeat them as we did the bluecoat foes on the trail."

"I'm proud of you, Rana, and of Travis. But I want you two to be real careful. Those Caldwells are dangerous and wicked."

"I understand, Grandfather. I will follow orders."

When the pudgy seamstress arrived mid-morning, the

cheery woman was delighted with the lucrative task and the lovely girl she would outfit. She quickly took measurements and discussed clothing with Rana and Nathan, who ordered everything Rana might need or want. Mrs. Clara Dobbs told them she would begin the new wardrobe that very day and would send out a few ready-to-wear garments for Rana's immediate use. When Nathan asked the woman if she would help Rana learn how to dress properly, Clara Dobbs replied that she would be delighted to instruct Rana in any way she could. Moreover, the harrowing tale of the girl's past misfortune did not trouble Clara in the least. Mrs. Dobbs was charmed by the gentle, beautiful girl, and she was certain others would be also. With a genuine smile, the pug-nosed woman bid them good day and departed with one of the hands, who would accompany her to her shop and retrieve the promised ready-made items.

After the noon meal, the local schoolteacher arrived. Nathan introduced Rana to Aaron Moore, then left the two alone in the sitting room. Aaron used his first session with Rana to question and test the extent of her knowledge. He was pleased by how much she knew and by her quick and keen intelligence. He could tell he was going to enjoy tutoring this radiant, eager pupil. Finally, he told her he would return the following day to begin their lessons. Rana was delighted when he promised he would also teach her customs, etiquette, and dancing.

After bidding the teacher farewell, Rana relaxed in the sitting room and glanced through the books Aaron Moore had left with her. She realized her journey back to the white world would be hard, but she was proud of the fact that she was learning things every hour. So far, everyone seemed so friendly and helpful. Yet she knew there were some nearby who would despise her and try to hurt her. But she had Travis and her grandfather, and together they made a happy family. Her life had changed so much since the winter snows had left the Oglala lands, and those changes had been good ones.

Rana rested an open book against her chest as her gaze traveled to her mother's portrait. Laying aside the volume, she walked to the fireplace. She looked closely at Marissa's image, then at the two portraits of herself. Comparing them, she noticed how closely she favored her mother and that pleased her, for the resemblance seemed to provide a bond between them, one that overcame even the dark barricade of death. Yet there was also an eeriness in being the reflection of another person, one who had suffered greatly in life and who had died so young and tragically. Rana wanted to know everything about her mother, but she suspected that few, if any, knew the truth or had known the woman. Intelligence and courage were reflected in Marissa's eyes, traits that should have prevented such a woman from marrying a brutal, evil man like Raymond Michaels. Even now, Rana could not imagine that man being her father, though she knew she could not alter the circumstances of her birth.

Rana wondered what her life would have been like if Marissa had married another man or had remained on the ranch after her last visit, or if Travis had arrived to find both of them living here, one older and one younger than himself. Would the sensuous Marissa have won his heart? she asked herself. A strange, unwanted jealousy consumed her as she pondered which of them might have caught Travis's eye first. Quickly Rana forced such foolish thoughts from her mind.

She was eager to meet Todd Raines, who had loved Marissa, and whom she hoped could tell her more about her mother. Her mother's past now seemed very much like the Oglala game in which a group of colored sticks were tossed into a pile to form a pattern about which one player asked a question and another player guessed the answer from the sticks' arrangement; but too many

405

pieces were missing in Marissa's game of life to make guessing any answers possible. But perhaps Todd Raines could add a few sticks to the pile. Raines . . . Rana . . . she mused silently. How strange it was that their names were similar. Then again, she realized, Rana and Raymond were similar. If Raymond Michaels was the villain in her nightmares, the man with night hair and deer eyes, it meant she did not favor him. Perhaps it was not proper to be so happy about such a little thing, but she was.

"What drove you from your family, Mother?" she unconsciously asked aloud, empathizing with the woman who had borne her, a woman who was alive only in her dreams and almost a stranger. "Why did you stay joined to such a cruel man? I remember how he beat you and cursed you many times. All those nights I dreamed some evil man was chasing me and hurting me, it was you I saw in my sleep. Why did you not leave him or slay him? Why did you not ask Grandfather for help? I hated him, and I'm glad he's dead. How could you have endured such evil? Even love would not explain such a bond of loyalty."

Rana closed her eyes and leaned her forehead against the mantel as flashes of her past flooded her mind, remembrances that had plagued her so many times over the years that she could never forget them. Maybe there was a purpose behind her memories, and she fervently wished the Great Spirit would reveal it or push them aside forever. One dream in particular returned to haunt her, the one that had attacked her the first night she had met Travis. She knew what the white words "bitch" and "whore" meant, and she could not understand why Raymond—she could not call him father or think of him in that light—had called her mother such vile names. Had her mother actually been afraid Raymond would kill Nathan, or all of them, if she ran away? Now that she had

fused her body with a man's, she recalled and comprehended other things she had witnessed; the name
"Fargo" and Raymond's wicked commands caused her
mind to burn with anger, contempt, and hatred for
Raymond and the men who had taken advantage of her
vulnerable mother. How she wished she had been old
enough to protect Marissa from such torment and
suffering. If only she had understood the situation and
had told Nathan.

Raymond's voice shouting ". . . the truth about you
and that brat . . ." thundered across her mind. "What
truth, Mother? What did he mean by 'silence for
money'? Why were you so afraid of him? What secret
kept you bound in such evil as his slave?" she murmured
sadly.

Rana began to cry softly, for she knew some terrible
evil had befallen her mother, an evil that perhaps still
existed in this land and lurked nearby in secret, waiting
to destroy her too. "Help me, Great Spirit; do not let this
evil destroy me as it did my mother. Reveal it to me, and
show me how to defeat it."

Suddenly Travis was there, pulling her around and
embracing her in his strong arms. "What's wrong,
micante? Were Mister Moore and Mrs. Dobbs so rough on
you today? Don't worry, you'll learn everything soon.
You're quick and smart," he murmured comfortingly as
he held her snugly against him. He had watched her walk
to the portrait and stare at it, and had heard her speak
those baffling words. He tucked them away in his mind
together with those he had overheard in Lone Wolf's
tepee and those she had spoken in her sleep that night on
the trail.

She admitted anxiously, "My heart races in fear,
mihigna. Terrible dreams keep filling my head. Memories
flood it like muddy waters and I cannot see through them
to the bottom of my past. There is evil here and I cannot

remember where or in what form."

Travis knew who held a secret about Marissa in her insidious grasp. Somehow he had to force the truth from Clarissa, for he saw that the past was tormenting his beloved and he feared that the malicious creature might find some way to use her knowledge against Rana. Somehow he had to solve the ever-increasing mystery that surrounded Marissa Crandall Michaels. Aloud, he ordered, "Forget it, love. You're safe here with me." He guided her to the settee and pulled her down beside him. "Just relax, my love, and calm down." For a long time, they sat quietly as he held her close. Finally, he teased lightly, "Do you want your grandfather to find you in tears and fire those two for upsetting you like this?"

"But it was not Mister Moore or Mrs. Dobbs."

"I know, love, but you don't want Nate to see how frightened you are. If he does, he won't let you fight these enemies with us."

Rana looked up into his eyes and inquired, "What does 'brat' mean?" She noticed that a curious expression filled his eyes.

"Where did you hear that word?" he asked in a strange tone. "It's what the whites call a really bad child, a child who's spoiled and mean as a snake, one who gives its parents great difficulty when they attempt to control it. It's a hateful and rude child you have trouble liking, one you don't want to be around if you can prevent it. Why?"

Without hesitation, she told him, "I keep hearing Raymond Michaels calling me that in my dreams. I do not understand why. I know it sounds bad, Travis, but I hate to think of him as my father."

He pulled her close to him. "No, love, it doesn't sound bad. I know how you feel. I feel the same way about Jeremy Kincade. Some men are just plain evil, Rana, and they don't deserve our love and respect, even if they're family. From what I've heard about Raymond Michaels, he didn't sound like a fatherly kind of man. Maybe he just didn't like being tied down with a small child. He liked to travel and gamble, and the kinds of places he went were not places for a little one. You probably got in his way, but not because you were a brat. When I was talking with Clarissa, I called you a brat several times to make her think you and I didn't like each other or get along," he confessed ruefully. "I'm sorry, but you know I didn't mean it."

Rana laughed. "Were you afraid I had heard it from you when I spied on you, like a brat?" she teased. "I told you, I could not hear your words from the house. But I wanted to claw out that woman's eyes for touching you as only I should touch you."

"A possessive and jealous wife—good," he remarked roguishly.

Rana kissed him, then hugged him. "I fear I am both, *mihigna.*"

"When somebody asks you what that word means, what are you going to tell them?"

"The same thing you will tell anyone who asks what *micante* means," she laughingly retorted.

"Listen to me, you little brat, we have to be careful what we say and how we act around other people, even our friends, because they let secrets slip without meaning to do so," he warned.

"My son is right, Granddaughter," Nathan stated genially from the doorway. "We all have to be careful. It won't be easy to fool Harry and Miss Clarissa. I think you two should keep your kisses and hugs inside this house," he advised pointedly.

"We will, Grandfather," Rana promised happily. "When we are around your enemies, I will behave as a . . . little brat." She glanced at Travis and they both laughed.

Nathan watched Travis tickle Rana, then observed

how they looked at each other. There was no doubt in his mind; they loved each other deeply and they deserved each other. His heart overflowed with joy. "I can't wait until you two are married and fill this house with my great-grandchildren. I thank the Lord every night for sending you home, Rana, and for sending Travis to me."

"So do I, Grandfather," she agreed, her loving gaze on Travis.

"Would you like to hear a secret, Papa dear?" Clarissa inquired provocatively after Harrison Caldwell had returned from town the following day. She had risen late after her wanton encounter with Wes Monroe and had discovered that her father had already left for business in Fort Worth. All day she had hoped no one would reveal to her father the news about Marissa's daughter's return.

Harrison glanced at his wayward child and asked, "If you've got something to say, Clarissa, don't be silly about it."

"Then I suppose no one's told you where Nathan Crandall went during his long absence or why?" She toyed with him, even though she knew it irritated him when she did so. Tonight she held the winning hand and she was going to savor laying it out before him, one card at a time.

"I don't give a hoot," Harrison stated, scowling at her.

"You don't give a hoot if Nathan found Marissa's missing daughter alive and well?" she inquired evocatively, grinning at him.

Harrison set aside his paper and stared at his obnoxious child. "What in blazes are you blabbering about?" he demanded.

"I thought you might be interested in knowing that Nathan located the girl and brought her home . . . a girl, I was told, who looks like her mother, or better," she casually revealed. "Evidently your hired men aren't as well informed or as talented as I am, Papa. They arrived Sunday evening, so I went to work obtaining information for my dear father. Rana Michaels could ruin your plans, so you might have to take care of her quite soon. From what Travis told me, she's quite a handful."

"Get on with it, girl," he commanded sternly when Clarissa returned her attention to the book in her hands.

The clever Clarissa had added up the clues and had realized how Nathan had learned about Rana: Thomas Mallory. "As I said, Papa, Nathan found Marissa's daughter, Rana Michaels, living with Indians as a chief's daughter. You remember how the Kiowas butchered Marissa and Raymond and abducted her little girl," she reminded him spitefully. "Nathan never gave up hoping and searching for his little Rana. When he heard about this girl who looked like Marissa, he and Travis took off to find her and look her over themselves. It was Rana, so he paid five thousand dollars for her release. Such an expenditure should have left him penniless and right where you want him with his loan at the bank coming due soon. From what I was told, Rana's beauty puts her mother's to shame. Fiery red hair and big blue eyes . . . I believe Travis said it was like looking at Marissa's old portrait, or seeing her ghost."

Harrison's mind began to race. His respiration increased and he paced unnaturally. "You don't seem distressed by having her in the house with your Travis," he taunted as he tried in vain to conceal his turbulent feelings.

"Why should I? She's a little savage and she doesn't have a claim on the ranch. Thanks to Ruth Crandall's friendship with Mother, we both know Marissa isn't Nathan's daughter, so how could Rana be Nathan's heir? After all, Travis is Nathan's legal son and heir. If Nathan tries to hand the ranch over to Rana instead of Travis,

411

we'll just have to tell the old buzzard the truth about Marissa—all of it."

Harrison continued to pace the room, and his excitement was as obvious to Clarissa as the flush on his cheeks. She suppressed an evil grin to speculate, "I wonder if we should get rid of her, just to make certain she doesn't cause us any problems. I'm sure Mister Monroe and Mister Hayes would love to handle her for us. They seemed to enjoy their work on the McFarland ranch. Are you sure those men can be trusted, Papa? They seem awfully evil and dangerous to me."

Harrison grinned smugly and chuckled. "Don't worry, Clarissa dear, I'm holding Monroe and Hayes tightly in hand. Besides, I plan to get rid of them after they handle a few more problems for me. We'll lure them out to that old mining site on the Lazy *J* and drop 'em into that abandoned shaft. Hell, girl, I know their kind can't be trusted, but I'll get them before they catch on and strike at me."

"Let me lure them out there, Papa. You can depend on me to fool them and to handle this secretly." She watched her father pour himself a sherry without offering her one. Yes, she would lure them out there, and push all three down that shaft after she had what she wanted! But she would need someone to blame for Harrison Caldwell's death, a dangerous, despicable villain whose wicked reputation was well known and feared. Everyone knew Wes Monroe was working for her father, and it would not seem suspicious if that evil beast robbed and murdered him. Afterwards, she could shoot Wes in self-defense for trying to rape her. Yes, that plan was perfect! She knew what her father was feeling now— hunger for another Marissa. She would let him discard Mary Beth and make his move on Rana Michaels. It would keep him single and occupied until their final success. But if he were to get too cocky or too close, she

412

would reveal an astounding weapon and use it to stop him from marrying Rana Michaels . . .

"You're a wicked little bitch, Clarissa. Are you sure I can trust you? I've seen your malicious side."

Clarissa laughed as if her father had told a joke. "If you can't trust your own family, Papa, who can you trust?" she teased. "We'll be neighbors too one day. I'll be married to Travis and we'll run the Rocking *C* Ranch, and you'll have Mary Beth and run this beautiful horseshoe empire around us," she remarked, pointing to Harrison's holdings, which were shaded brightly on the map on one wall.

"Are you sure you can snare Kincade?"

"As certain as you are you can snare Mary Beth. As you tell me all the time, Papa, success is the result of clever planning. You taught me to look for a person's strengths and weaknesses, then use them against him. That's exactly what I'm doing, and I'll succeed."

"Then let's both get busy on our conquests tomorrow. This final battle is lasting too long. I'll give Nathan until August first to get out peacefully; then I'll let Monroe and Hayes handle him."

"Why a reprieve, Papa? He might get suspicious."

"Oh, I don't plan to ease up on him, girl, but I don't want to damage property too severely that will soon be mine."

"Mine, Papa," she corrected him boldly, "for all of my help. Maybe if Travis gets nervous about this Rana taking everything away from him, he might be convinced to side with us."

"Don't count on it, not if she looks like her mother. If I were you, girl, I would be plenty worried about losing him completely."

"Come now, Papa. Marissa was a cheap whore. Like mother, like daughter. Travis Kincade doesn't want a woman like that." Harrison eyed Clarissa up and down and laughed wickedly, to which Clarissa angrily replied, "I keep my affairs secret, Papa, so he doesn't know what I've done for you. You should be grateful that I obey your orders—all of them—and not be mean and insulting."

"I was only teasing you, girl. If your mother's blood had been as hot as yours, I would still be missing her today. A real man likes his woman to be a whore in bed and a lady in public. Just make sure you don't ever confuse those two roles and use them unwisely."

"I take after you, Papa. I'm insatiable, and selective."

"Well, how about using some of those insatiable and selective skills on Kincade? Don't tell me they don't have any effect on him."

"You're being mean tonight, Papa. I'm going to bed before I start doing the same," she playfully warned, leaving the room before she was tempted to do just that. How she longed for the day when she could fling his evil crimes in his face before having him killed. She decided angrily that if he did not curtail his hateful treatment of her, she would watch Wes beat him brutally before allowing the crude bastard to slay her father. Or, she mused with a grin, she might demand that privilege herself! The thought of such evil aroused her.

In her room, Clarissa pulled out the small painting of Raymond Michaels that she had kept hidden all these years. She eyed the image of the man who had once enchanted her briefly, then smiled sardonically. Perhaps she would give it to Rana, and tell that little bitch all about what her mother had done for Raymond. Perhaps she could drive Rana away, and prevent her from enticing Travis, for such a day might come if she lollygagged too long. She was all too aware of Travis's potent appeal and Marissa's magical allure, which Rana easily could have inherited. Oh, the destructive tales she could relate to Rana about her mother and Raymond! She remembered Raymond telling her how he had discovered the truth about Rana's conception, and how he had strangled the only person who had known about it besides Marissa. Now, only she possessed that valuable weapon . . .

Clarissa stood by her window, trying to catch the mild breeze. The storm had not struck last night or today and it was still humid, making her restless, but tonight she would be satisfied with the stimulation provided by her evil thoughts.

The next day, Travis spent the morning teaching Rana how to load, fire, and clean a rifle and a pistol. She learned quickly, for she possessed good instincts and had no fear of the weapons. They practiced for hours, with the sounds and smells of gunfire filling their senses. They halted finally in order to partake of the noon meal before Aaron Moore's scheduled arrival to begin Rana's afternoon lessons.

Rana spent four hours with the patient and somewhat timid teacher, who seemed smitten with her. When Aaron Moore left for the day, Travis teased, "Don't tempt him too much, *micante,* or he'll be staring at you rather than keeping his mind on your lessons."

"He is very nice, Travis, and very smart. Do not be jealous. My eyes and heart belong to you. He will not come tomorrow. He explained about the white holiday on July the fourth. It is sad that my people, the Oglalas, cannot win independence from the whites."

"I know, love, but there's nothing we can do to help them. One day, this period will be a bitter memory in history."

"Mister Moore told me about history, so I understand that word."

"Pretty soon, you'll know more words than I do, and

415

you'll be teaching me. What do you say about us starting supper?"

Without knocking, Cody Slade rushed into the house and shouted, "Boss, you'd best get out here *pronto!* Mace and the boys are back, and it ain't good news. We sent those extra guards too late."

Travis grimaced knowingly at his words. "Please stay here, Rana, and I'll be back soon." He left instantly with Cody.

Rana hurried to the front window and observed the action taking place near the stable. She wished she could hear what was happening, or understood what had happened. She knew it was something terrible, but she also knew she should stay in the house as Travis had requested.

It seemed a very long time before Travis and Nathan returned to the house, both looking worried and angered. She went to them and asked, "What is wrong, Grandfather?"

"Bad news, Rana. The worst," he admitted sadly. "Mace was robbed on the way home. Without that money, I can't pay the bank what I owe it, and they'll take my ranch as payment."

"I do not understand, Grandfather. Who will steal your ranch? Can you not fight them? You have many war . . . men to help you."

As Nathan dropped wearily into a chair, Travis patiently explained about money, banks, loans, fore-closures, and the laws governing such things. Their predicament became clearer to her when Travis described how Harrison Caldwell could buy their ranch at a debtor's auction. "By losing that money, we've fallen right into his greedy hands, and there isn't a damn thing we can do to stop him; the laws' on his side this time, and he'll use it to get this ranch."

"What about the enemies who stole Grandfather's

416

money? Can we not go after them and recover it?" she inquired gravely.

"We could, if we knew who stole it and where they were hiding it." Travis laughed coldly. "Oh, we know Caldwell is behind the robbery, but we can't prove it. I wouldn't be surprised if those saddlebags are locked in his safe right this minute." When Rana questioned the meaning of "safe," Travis guided her into Nathan's office, showed her theirs, and explained how it worked.

"Why do we not ride to his lands and force him to open his safe and return Grandfather's money? Will the white law not help us?"

He caressed her cheek and smiled. "It isn't that simple, love. Caldwell would only deny our charges, and then he'd know we were on to him. He would hide those saddlebags where we'd never locate them. If I could sneak into his office in town and the one in his house, I could search them, for more than our stolen money. If I found something to incriminate him and his men, the sheriff would have to force him to open his safe to prove he doesn't have our money. Those saddlebags have rattlesnakes carved on them, so they're easy to recognize."

"Why do your men not tell this sheriff who did this black deed? How could they not see their faces and know them?" she reasoned.

"Harrison Caldwell is very cunning and dangerous. He's hired some deadly and clever gunslingers to do his dirty work. They sneaked up on Mace and the boys where they were camped for the night. The two cowhands Mace set out as guards were killed without a sound, their throats sliced Indian style; then one of Caldwell's men slipped into camp and took the money from Mace's side while he was sleeping. None of our cowpunchers heard or saw a thing. I should have joined them on the trail as soon as I got you and Nate home, but I had other things on my mind," he informed her with a wry grin.

"Mace said they searched the entire area the next morning and tried to track them. They finally had to give up their search because those varmints had covered their trail completely. Mace and the boys feel as bad as we do. They know we trusted them and depended on them. They don't want us to lose this ranch either. Dad-blame-it! We're out the cattle and the money, and pretty soon we'll be out of time. We know Caldwell's guilty, and we can't do a thing about it."

"These white laws and customs are bad, Travis. They do not allow the capturing of enemies and their punishment. It is wrong for the innocent to suffer."

Travis sighed heavily. "I know, *micante*, but we're trapped. We don't have any witnesses against Caldwell; we can't make accusations against him without proof and he knows it, so he'll be real careful to hide his guilt and evidence of the dirty deeds. Remember how you had no choice but to obey and yield when Lone Wolf and the Oglala Council spoke their commands, even when you disagreed with them?" She nodded her comprehension. "Until we can get evidence against Caldwell, our hands are tied. Right now, we need money, plenty of it. We have to figure out a way to get enough to exist and to repay that loan in four weeks."

"Why do you not sneak over to the Caldwell ranch and steal your money from his safe? If he does not hide it there, take his money to replace what he has stolen from us."

"That's too dangerous, love. He knows we're desperate, and he'll have plenty of guards around his place. Even if we could get into his house and safe, if we were caught we'd be in worse trouble than we are now. Much as I hate him and want to defeat him, this isn't the time to do anything reckless. It doesn't show courage, intelligence, or honor to ride into battle blind or without

418

weapons. We have to be patient and cunning until we can trap him. I wouldn't be any use to you or Nate if I were dead or in jail. Caldwell would pounce on you two like a starving wolf on a slow rabbit. I know from experience that being innocent doesn't help much in some situations."

"This safe only opens with certain secret numbers?"

"That's right, and we don't know them. It's too heavy to steal and we can't blast it open. Too much noise. And if I know Caldwell, he'd let me beat him and shoot him before giving me those numbers."

"It's useless, son," Nathan stated dejectedly, entering the room. "We'll never see that money again, 'til Harry uses it to buy this ranch. The bastard!" Nathan exploded angrily. "I can't let him get away with this, Travis."

"Don't worry, Nate. Somehow I'll stop him. Somehow I'll find enough money to . . ." Travis grew silent and his gaze narrowed as he fell into deep thought. "That's it," he suddenly announced. "Why not? It's already been paid for with plenty of lives and suffering!" he murmured aloud, confusing Rana and Nathan.

"What are you talking about, son?"

The Rocking C foreman replied shockingly, "The gold, Nate—the gold my father took from the sacred burial grounds. I know where it's hidden, and I doubt anyone's found it yet. If I ride like the wind, I can get it and return here before Mason's bank can take our ranch and sell it to Caldwell with our cattle money. I'll be careful. It's our only hope, Nate," he reasoned when he saw Nathan begin to shake his head as worry filled his faded blue eyes.

"That gold nearly got you killed once, Travis, so don't go tempting those Hunkpapas by trying it again. Let it go, son," he pleaded. "I'd rather lose this ranch than lose you, boy, and that's God's truth."

"I can't, Nate. That part of my life is still an open wound. It's time I healed it once and for all, and this is the perfect time and way. I deserve that gold, Nate, and I've already paid for it. I'll leave in the morning, and I'll be back before this month's gone."

"I will go with you," Rana told him.

He declared gently, "No, Rana, you won't. I can travel faster and more safely alone. There isn't much time, and I need you to stay here to help Nate take care of things. Just tell everybody I went looking for the bandits' trail. Once this loan's repaid and the ranch is safe, we'll find a way to defeat Caldwell. You keep studying your books and white ways and practicing your shooting while I'm gone; then we'll take on this enemy together when I return. I need your understanding, trust, and help until this matter is settled. Nothing will happen to me, love; I promise. I'll go see Lone Wolf and get him to help me."

"Maybe Harry will settle down now that he's got our money. Ain't no need for him to do more than wait us out," Nathan speculated.

"I hope you're right, Nate, but I doubt it. It might be wise to keep guards posted. You know what kind of men he's hired, so both of you be careful. Before I leave, I'll write Clarissa a sweet little note to keep her panting after me; maybe she can keep her father in line while I'm gone. It's worth a try. Cody can deliver it for me after I'm gone. Speaking of Cody, why don't you help him and Mary Beth get married soon to get her out of Caldwell's reach? There isn't anything her father or Caldwell could do after the fact. You might want to tell Rachel to come back to work Friday, so Rana will have some company and help. Rachel can keep her too busy to worry about me."

"No, she cannot, Travis Kincade. And if you do not return in one full moon, I will come searching for you," she threatened mildly. She was so afraid for him to return to the Dakota lands, but she knew he had to go, and alone. By being stubborn or defiant, she could endanger both of their lives and his victory, so she would stay behind and do her part here at the ranch. "Perhaps you only seek to run away and not marry me again," she teased to lighten his burden.

A playful smile teased over his lips and his green eyes sparkled with mischief. In a warm tone, he warned roguishly, "No chance, my love, so make sure you don't use that false excuse to flirt with my hired hands while I'm gone. You had better be waiting for me when I return, because I've staked my claim on you. Nate, you keep a sharp eye on this restless filly for me. I wouldn't want to turn her over my knee for a good spanking the minute I get home. And another thing, Rana Michaels. Don't you dare do anything foolish or reckless. These men are dangerous and evil. Now that I've snared you and tamed you, I don't want to lose you or have you running wild again. I promise that you can be a female warrior at my side when I come home. Agreed?"

"Have I not proven I am smart and obedient?" she responded, slyly avoiding a direct answer and smiling at him innocently. She did not want to lie to him, and if anything happened while he was away . . .

Travis went into Nathan's office to write the note to Clarissa. When it was finished, he read it aloud to Rana and Nathan:

There's been some trouble over here, so I'll be gone three or four weeks. Mace was robbed of our cattle money on the way back from Sedalia. I'm heading up the trail to see if I can pick up any clues as to who took it and which way they rode off. I been doing some serious thinking about you and I don't want you fretting over me leaving again this soon. Don't tell your father how badly we need that money, 'cause I don't want him hanging over Nate's head like a vulture while I'm gone. If I can't pick up those bandits' trail, I'll be heading on up to St.

Louis to see if I can locate some banker willing to settle our loan with Mason's bank. Since Nate and me stand to lose everything if I don't recover that money or I don't get a new loan, I can't ask you to wait around for me. A man's got his pride or he ain't got nothing, and no real man would take a woman for what she has. If I lose this ranch, I'll be moving on alone. So if you hear anything that can help me and Nate find these varmints who are trying to ruin us, I'm begging you, love, tell Nate while I'm gone and he can put the sheriff on them. Fact is, it's gonna be nice to get away from that little brat living with us! She's about to run me ragged around a tree. You ain't nothing like Rana Michaels.

He halted to laugh and remark, "Lordy, how true that is. If you were like Clarissa, love, Nate and I would have left you with Lone Wolf." He grinned, then continued with his note:

Don't go taking any foolish risks by trying to learn who's behind this trouble just to help me. You stay home where it's safe. I'll send you word as soon as I can. One last thing. Don't tell anybody where I'm going or what I'm doing. See you around the end of the month. Travis.

He looked at Nathan and Rana and asked, "Well, how about it?"

Nathan shrugged, but Rana responded, "If you wish to snare her heart, Travis, you must write words to give her real hope of winning you. Where you say you have been thinking seriously about her, say you will miss her or you will think of her each day you are gone. Where you say you cannot ask her to wait for you if you have no land and home to share with her, you must say you cannot ask but you hope she will wait for you and accept you even if you lose all you own. Where you say you will be moving on alone, you must add, 'Until I can find another home and work and then I will come for you.' When you speak of when you will see her again, say, 'You'd better be waiting for me when I return, because I've staked my claim on you'. I love those words, and she will love them. If she is helping her father with his evil deeds as you believe, she might try to stop him or control him if she knows she might win or lose you over what happens while you are gone."

Travis frowned in aversion. "If I say those things, *micante*, she'll be all over me when I return home. You sure you want me to say them to another woman, even if we both know they're lies?"

She smiled lovingly. "It does not matter, for I know you do this only to save us and our home from wicked foes. She is like an evil spirit that must be fooled, then defeated. When you return and pay the bank this money, you can free yourself of all evils. When she learns you have fooled her, she will become angry and perhaps reveal her evil. Say what is needed to defend our lives and home."

Travis sighed loudly. "I've been rejecting her so long, I'm not sure she'll believe this romantic letter."

Rana recalled what she had witnessed near the corral that night. "She is greedy for you; she will believe what she wishes to believe. She will think you have weakened, as she has expected."

Nathan chuckled and concurred.

"I surely hope you two are right, and that you'll beat her off me when I return home. I can always claim I didn't write this mushy message." Travis returned to Nathan's desk and wrote another letter, including Rana's bold suggestions. When he finished it, he read it to them:

423

I ain't one for writing letters or putting my feelings on paper where the wrong person can see them and read them. But I got some things need saying to you before I leave. There's been some trouble over here, so I'll be gone three or four weeks. Mace was robbed of our cattle money on the way back from Sedalia. I'm heading up the trail to see if I can pick up any clues as to who took it and which way they rode off. I been doing some serious thinking about you and I don't want you fretting over me leaving again this soon 'cause I'll think about you every day and I hope you do the same with me. Don't tell your father how badly we need that money I'm going after, 'cause I don't want him hanging over Nate's head like a vulture while I'm gone. If I can't pick up those bandits' trail, I'll be heading on up to St. Louis to see if I can locate some banker willing to settle our loan with Mason's bank. Since Nate and me stand to lose everything if I don't recover that money or I don't get a new loan, I can't ask you to wait around for me, but I sure do hope you will and I hope you'll still want me even if I lose this ranch. A man's got his pride or he ain't got nothing, and no real man would take a woman for what she has. If I lose this ranch, I'll be moving on alone, until I can find another job and place to live. If you're willing to marry a man with nothing and you'll wait for me while I get settled elsewhere, I'll come back for you. But I'd rather stay on the ranch if I can find a way to keep her. So if you hear anything that can help me and Nate find these varmints who are trying to ruin us, I'm begging you, love, tell Nate while I'm gone and he can put the sheriff on them. Fact is, it's gonna be nice to get away from that little brat living with us! She's about to run me ragged around a tree. You ain't nothing like Rana Michaels and you won't ever be. Don't go taking any foolish risks by trying to learn who's behind this trouble just to help me. You stay home where it's safe until I can get back. I'll send you word as soon as I can to let you know where I am and how things are going. One last thing. Don't tell anybody where I'm going or what I'm doing. See you around the end of the month, and you had better be waiting for me when I return, woman, 'cause I've staked my claim on you and told you things from my heart. Travis."

It was close to midnight when Travis sneaked into Rana's room, where she was waiting eagerly to spend this last night with him. Each longed to embrace and kiss the other urgently, for they knew that death might confront either of them shortly. They would love as if that black spirit was truly about to claim them and there would be no more happy days or blissful nights for them to share.

"I love you, Rana Michaels, and I want to marry you and let everyone know you're the woman of my heart and life."

She responded ardently, "I love you, Travis Kincade, and the Great Spirit will hear our prayers and answer them. You will return to me soon, and we will claim each other under white law. You must think of nothing and no one while you ride this dangerous trail to the Hunkpapa lands. You must think only of your safety and victory."

"Come, my beautiful wife, and soar on the wild wind with me; then later we will talk." Travis's lips and hands claimed her full attention then as they began their rapturous journey on the wings of love.

Travis lay beside her, holding her, caressing her. The door was locked and one candle glowed softly in the quiet room. For a time, he made love to her with his eyes, storing up exquisite images to carry him through the rough days ahead. Slowly he came forward until his chest grazed hers and his lips brushed over her mouth. His fingers seemingly danced over her face and through her silky hair. He rained kisses over her throat and gently devoured her breasts, bringing the brown peaks to instant life.

She groaned softly as he ignited and fanned her smoldering desires into a raging fire of blazing passion. She savored the way his experienced, talented hands roamed her body, his one hand drifting over her stomach and causing it to tighten with anticipation of the path it would forge toward her womanhood. She was stirred and tempted and could not keep from drawing his mouth back to hers and ravenously meshing her lips to his. Her hands roved his body then, stroking its tanned flesh, admiring its beauty. She closed her eyes and absorbed the stimulation of her unbridled senses. She relished the tautness of his chest as her fingers lovingly mapped his torso. One hand rose to travel through his sable hair. The other played over his body and boldly captured his rigid manhood. Lovingly she caressed its warm, smooth surface. His loins instantly responded to her touch and he writhed in pleasure. She felt him tense and relax at her tantalizing touch and she smiled happily.

Travis's lips returned to the brown nubs on her breasts and blissfully tormented them, increasing her hunger for him and what lay ahead for them this night. He saw the dreamy smile on her lips and silently vowed that this night would be unforgettable. His hands tenderly kneaded her breasts and he deftly squeezed their hard tips as his mouth drifted between them and her lips, bathing her in intense sensation. He grasped her buttocks and fondled them before pressing her core snugly against his enlarged staff, which pleaded for encompassing contact. Again his hands returned to her eager mounds to

426

sweetly torment the thrusting peaks. Slowly and deliberately his fingers began to trail up and down her sides until one continued down her flesh into her fiery triangle and carefully, sensuously stroked the straining peak there. He could feel the tension and anticipation throbbing within her body, especially at that sensitive spot. As his mouth lavished attention on her taut nipples, a deft finger entered her entreating womanhood and moved expertly until her head was thrashing upon the bed, signaling her uncontrollable desire.

Rana's hands roamed Travis's hard, smooth frame. They teased over sinewy muscles that rippled with his movements. They wandered down his back to examine his firm buttocks that could forcefully drive his manhood into her body with such skill and delight. He was making her wild and stealing her wits. Again her fingers moved provocatively over his groin, playing in the crisp hair that surrounded his rearing stallion, so full of heat and need. She felt him trailing kisses down her stomach, and he shifted his body to continue along her thighs, taking him out of her reach. His fingers teased over her hips, ending their stimulating journey in her auburn forest, and he smiled triumphantly when she shifted her legs apart to welcome his invasion.

Travis's hand stimulated the tiny mound before he pressed kisses to it, causing her to stiffen in surprise and intense delight. He grinned as she glanced down at him, her expression questioning his action. He smiled, encouraging and relaxing her completely. His strong hands drifted up and down the insides of her silky thighs, each time barely making titillating contact with the sensitive area. He pushed aside her soft hair and his finger lovingly massaged the delicate peak. Another finger slipped within her secret haven to create a pattern that matched that of his manhood when he was thrusting deeply within her. Her moist, snug paradise told him she

427

was eager to accept and enjoy any pleasure he wished to give her. Gently he tantalized the tiny bud, which had grown hard and hot beneath his touch. Slowly and purposefully his head bent forward and his tongue replaced the finger on the peak. He teased it with his teeth, providing a thrill she had never experienced before. His tongue flicked and circled, sometimes swiftly and sometimes leisurely. At times he would grasp it hungrily and suck upon it as he had her nipples, the action causing her to thrash wildly. Together his mouth and fingers worked to bring her to the point of torturously sweet abandon and unspeakable rapture.

Rana squirmed as the tension built within her. She wanted to relax, but found it impossible. Her body seemed taut with anticipation of something she knew would be wild and wonderful. Passion's flames licked over her body and seared it. The peak and canyon located in the core of her womanhood throbbed and pulsed as he delivered an erotic attack on them. She cautioned herself to remain alert and silent, but she feared she was losing her wits and would cry out in sheer bliss. Her hips began to arch madly as overpowering spasms assailed her, inspiring him to increase his endeavors to give her supreme satisfaction. While her womanhood was still quivering from the thrill of his success, he moved atop her and thrust his aching manhood deep within that tingling crevice. To his surprise, her passion and hunger returned instantly, indicating to both of them that her womanhood was extremely sensitive to whatever he chose to do there. As if insatiable, she responded feverishly to his thrusting.

His lips greedily drank from her hardened nipples as his hips repeatedly and seductively pounded his manhood into her receptive body. Her total surrender, her fiery responses, and her coaxing actions sorely strained his control. She was moaning against his lips and clinging to him, revealing the height of her arousal. His mouth was insistent upon hers, his tongue teasing over her lips before his own hungrily fastened on hers. She matched his pace and they worked in unison toward the mutual goal looming before them. Ecstasy exploded within her again and her teeth sank almost savagely into his shoulder as she attempted to halt her outcry of rapture and victory. He felt her clinging to him as if in fear for her life. He was charged with energy and fierce cravings, and he rode her as skillfully and wildly as a wild mustang. Together they scaled the summit and experienced the power of passion's fusion. Then slowly and dreamily they drifted back to reality.

Rana felt exhausted but totally content. This bout of lovemaking had been a journey into ecstasy beyond description or comparison. Her body felt limp and aglow; her heart was surging with love and peace. He was a skilled lover, and his sexual prowess had rewarded her greatly. He was so gentle, yet so demanding and giving. She wiped away the glistening beads of moisture from his face and smiled into his twinkling eyes. "You know many mating secrets that you must teach me," she whispered into his ear.

The candlelight flickered over her serene face as he suppressed happy chuckles, for he knew what she was feeling at that very moment and what rapture he had given her. He tingled at the memory. Drawing her ear close to his, he murmured, "I will teach you all I know, *micante,* and we will enjoy and improve our skills together when I return. There is no spot on you that I do not love and desire. There are many exciting nights ahead for us."

She shifted her head to stare into his eyes, beaming with love and anticipation. "Many nights, and many days, my love. Promise you will return safely to my life-circle. It cannot be complete without you."

He hugged her fiercely and vowed, "With the guidance and love of *Wakan Tanka,* I will return to you, my love. But if I died this very night, I would meet the Great Spirit knowing you have given my life its true meaning and have brought me happiness beyond measure."

Their lips fused and they nestled into each other's arms, knowing and dreading what the new day would bring.

Chapter Fourteen

Shortly after dawn, Travis quietly dressed and headed for the cookhouse to meet with Mace Hunter and Cody Slade, who were awaiting his arrival and final orders. Darby and Bart Davis were standing with Mace and Cody outside the wooden structure, and all four men were drinking coffee and discussing the current situation. Before Travis reached them, Todd Raines rode up and, after securing his mount's reins to a corral post, joined the small group. Travis eyed the five men as he walked toward them and realized how lucky the Rocking *C* Ranch was to have these loyal and skilled hands working on it.

After they exchanged congenial greetings, Travis told them the same false tale he had written in Clarissa's letter. He hated to deceive these good men who were his friends, but he could not allow even the slightest chance of anyone carelessly dropping a hint about him in the wrong ear or being coerced by brutal force into revealing his daring plan. Few men could hold silent while being tortured or while watching a loved one undergo such pain, and Travis knew that Caldwell was not above obtaining information by any means necessary. If he was lucky enough to retrieve the gold—their last chance to retain the ranch—he certainly couldn't risk having any of Caldwell's men ambush him and steal it.

After the Davis brothers and Todd Raines had headed off to begin their chores, Travis advised Cody Slade, "If I were you, Cody, I would settle my claim on Mary Beth Sims *pronto*. Caldwell has serious sights set on her, and I know you and Mary Beth don't want her father handing her over to that snake. If you want that girl, you'd best figure out something quick. Ask for Nate's help; he'll give it."

The sandy-haired man scowled at hearing Travis's confirmation of his suspicions. "You're right, Trav; I'll take care of it soon. I sure don't want to lose her. A woman like her comes along only once."

Cody's hazel eyes widened in surprise when Travis handed him a sealed letter and told him to deliver it to Clarissa Caldwell that afternoon. "I'm sure you'll find her in town for the big celebration. We don't want her worrying over my second absence and nagging you again," he teased devilishly and winked at his two best friends. "Mace, you decide if you want any of the boys to have time off today to go into town. I know your bunch deserves it after that long cattle drive and ride home, but this is a bad time for too many of them to be off the ranch. A holiday would be the perfect time for a surprise attack."

"You're right, and I'm sure the boys will understand and agree."

"Nathan also thinks it would be best for him to stay around here. No need to let Caldwell rile him. And he doesn't want Rana bothered."

"How is Miss Rana? I haven't seen her around. You must be keeping her locked up. Mace and the boys are real anxious to meet her," Cody remarked playfully as he stuffed the letter into his pocket.

"Cody tells me Nate's granddaughter is a real beauty,

Trav. I bet you enjoy having her all to yourself. 'Course I would imagine Miss Clarissa Caldwell is not too happy about Miss Rana's return. She has heard the bad news, hasn't she?" Mace inquired with a grin. His sunny blond hair gleamed in the morning sunshine and his azure eyes glowed with undisguised curiosity. Being six feet three, Mace was at an eye level with Travis, and he studied his friend's reaction intently.

Not wanting to inspire romantic gossip about him and Rana during his absence, Travis shrugged and sighed. "Cody took a shine to her right off; too bad he already has a sweetheart. He's right, though; Rana Michaels is a real charmer, Mace, so you'd best be alert around Nate's granddaughter or you'll be following Cody's flowery path."

Cody laughed and wailed, "What's so bad about love and marriage? Especially with a radiant creature who'll inherit all this?"

"Aren't you forgetting I'm Nate's adopted son?" Travis teased casually, inspiring their laughter. "Besides, I've been working on Caldwell's only heir for years, and a man don't switch horses in midstream during a storm. I'll admit Rana is the prettiest vixen I've seen; she looks like that picture of her mother over Nate's mantel, and I've admired that beauty for years. But we all know that the most beautiful women are usually selfish and vain, and nothing but big trouble for a man."

Cody shook his head and protested amiably, "Not Miss Rana. I've never met a gentler or nicer lady. She's real smart and kind. I liked her right off, and I want her and Mary Beth to become friends."

Travis did not want to seem mean or suspicious, so he grinned and added, "You're right, Cody, but she's a mite young and willful for me. She's making Nate happy, so that's all that matters right now. You haven't been playing big brother to her, so you don't know how ornery

433

she can be. She's bullheaded and cocky, and she doesn't like to be bossed. You two keep an eye on her, 'cause she's a wild and restless filly. I guess you can't blame her too much, considering how she was raised. She thinks she can do anything a man can do, or better, so make sure she doesn't interfere with our problems or get into trouble. She's a real handful, and you two are probably the only ones who can handle her for Nate. She should be staying close to the house, 'cause Nate's got the schoolteacher coming over nearly every day to help her adjust to our white ways. She'll straighten out soon, but be alert for any mischief or danger. After what happened to Marissa, Nate would be crushed if anything happened to his granddaughter.''

"Don't worry, Trav, we'll look after Nate and Miss Rana for you," Mace replied seriously. "We'll also keep a sharp eye on the herds and fences. We've taken too many losses. You sure you don't want me to ride with you to look for those varmints? I feel responsible for losing that cattle money. I know what it means to you and Nate."

Travis empathized with his friend. "It couldn't be helped, Mace, and we don't hold you responsible. I will need your help with the payroll. We only have enough money to hand out about a third of their June pay, and I don't know what will happen this month. If you can get them to hold out for the rest of their money until the first of the month, I'll give each one ten dollars extra. Any man who has a problem with waiting, like Darby with all those kids, pay him what you can and leave off his and Todd's rent. We're all in for some rough times, Mace, so if any of the boys need to move on, tell 'em we understand and we'll get their money to them as soon as we can. If we don't recover that cattle money or get another loan, this place will be finished; then you boys will find yourselves working for Caldwell or moving on.''

"No, sir! We know Caldwell is behind this trouble, so how can you stand courting his daughter?" Mace inquired boldly. "From what I see and hear, she's too much like her pa. She doesn't deserve you, Trav. You need a good woman, like Cody's sweetheart."

Cody realized their talk was moving in a private direction, so he bid Travis farewell and dismissed himself. Travis and Mace walked a short distance for privacy. The foreman inhaled deeply, then slowly released the spent air. "Listen to me, Mace. I'm not going to search for those bandits; I'm sure you and the boys didn't overlook any clues, and I'm not riding to St. Louis to seek a new loan. I have another plan in mind, but it's dangerous and it might not work. Even if it does, it'll take me a month to check it over. I told the boys that false story because I can't risk anyone dropping clues about my whereabouts and business. Time's short, so I'll fill you in after I get back." When Travis revealed who and what Wes Monroe and Jackson Hayes were, Mace realized why Travis had to keep his impending journey a secret.

"You mean they're the ones who tried to kill you years ago?"

"That's right, but it doesn't seem as if they remember me or, if they do, they can't place me. When I return, I'm going to settle up with them. I'm telling you these things because I know you're one of the few men who would die before loosening his tongue and betraying a friend. Cody told you what happened over at the McFarland place, so you know Wes and Jackson have ways of making men talk. Watch out for those two gunslingers, Mace. I've got scars to prove bastards don't come any worse than them. As for Clarissa, that letter is only a trick to entice her to keep Caldwell off Nate's back while I'm gone. I'd bet she's as deep in this mud as her father is." He unflinchingly revealed the letter's contents to his best friend. "And as for Rana Michaels, between you and me, I plan to marry that little minx when I return."

Mace laughed heartily. "So I wasn't wrong about that sparkle in your eye. Is she willing to go along with your plans for her?"

Travis smiled and nodded. "It's strange, Mace, but the minute we met, it was like we had been waiting for each other all our lives and nothing could have stopped us from meeting. I can't explain how deeply that woman touches me. If any two people belong together and are perfect for each other, it's Rana Michaels and Travis Kincade. Lordy, I never thought I would be saying or thinking such things and surely not feeling them, but it's mighty nice," he admitted cheerfully. A worried look crossed Travis's face then, and he speculated, "You know the Caldwells think they might get this ranch through Clarissa and me marrying, so I don't want them viewing Rana as a snag in their plans. I detest that Caldwell bitch, but I'll do whatever's necessary to guard Rana and Nate from her and her father. Rana has enough problems as it is. Leaving the Indian camp to return home was hard on her, so do what you can to protect her and to help her adjust."

"I sure am glad you see through that wicked harlot. What happens if the Caldwells don't fall for your letter and deception? Miss Rana could be in real danger."

Travis mulled over that possibility. "If they get one look at her, they'll know I would never pick Clarissa over Rana. Unless Rana's really mean to me or she prefers another . . ." Travis's eyes brightened. "That's it: if she prefers another man, like the handsome and charming Mace Hunter," he suggested with a sly grin.

"You're joshing, aren't you?" Mace inquired.

"No, I'm not, old friend. If she can go along with my pretense with Clarissa, I can go along with her pretense with you." Travis related how they were planning to deal

436

with Clarissa. "Until Rana and I can openly express our feelings, you pretend to be her sweetheart to keep her safe. Will you do this for us, Mace?"

"You know I'll do whatever you ask, Trav, but isn't this a mite dangerous? If she's as perfect and beautiful as you and Cody let on, I might become captivated by her. If you're gone too long, we might forget we're playing a game. What if we fall in love?" he teased.

Travis retorted, "Keep reminding yourself she's mine and don't play the game unless it's absolutely necessary. Time's awasting. I have to tell her and Nate good-bye and get on the trail. Take care of them and the ranch for me. If something happens and I don't . . ."

Mace interrupted, "Don't even think it, friend. I'll be here, so don't worry about anything, or anyone. Take care of yourself, Trav. I don't want to lose the best friend I've ever had."

The twenty-seven-year-old foreman said, "Give me about fifteen minutes, then come to the house. I want to introduce you to Rana myself. Will you saddle Apache for me and load my gear? And I need another strong mount. I plan to switch horses while riding to prevent too many rest stops along the way. I need to get going and get back as quickly as I can."

Travis strode quickly into the house and proceeded to explain his discussion with Mace to an uncharacteristically quiet Rana and Nathan. When he had finished, Rana nodded her head and told him, "It is a clever plan. I am grateful that your friend wishes to protect me."

The three went over their plans and stories one last time, then Nathan left the room to await Travis's departure on the front porch, knowing his adopted son and his granddaughter would appreciate some time alone.

Rana slipped into Travis's arms and snuggled against his hard body. "Be careful and return to me," she

437

entreated in a strained voice. She had this terrible feeling that awful things were about to happen, but she did not want to worry or distract him with her fears and doubts.

Travis tightened his embrace and kissed her forehead, for he had those same feelings. Yet he knew his trip was vital. "I will, my love, and you be careful here. I promise, we'll be married real soon."

They kissed and hugged, then gazed longingly into each other's eyes, exchanging messages that held too much emotion for words to express. Finally, Travis murmured, "I have to go, love. We're running out of time. If I'm not back in twenty-nine days . . ." He sighed heavily and hugged her tightly. "Stay here and I'll bring Mace to meet you," he said.

Rana eyed the tall, handsome man who entered the room with Travis. He stood just an inch shorter than Travis and was two years older. His hair was the color of sunshine dancing on sand and his eyes were the shade of a blue pasqueflower. The creases around his mouth and eyes expressed his easygoing, happy nature and Rana found herself liking his compelling smile and genial manner. She sensed that before her stood a man of honor and prowess, much like Travis. The close friendship the two men shared was obvious in their demeanors, and she warmed to Mace Hunter immediately. He seemed a good man, and a dependable friend. They exchanged smiles and greetings.

After going over Travis's suggestion that they play sweethearts during his absence, all three left the room to join Nathan. Travis and the older man embraced affectionately, then Travis clutched forearms with Mace. Lastly and most tormentingly, Travis looked deep into Rana's eyes, then whispered, "I love you, *micante*," as he hugged her quickly.

Rana stood on the porch and watched Travis ride away, bravely holding back the tears that threatened to spill forth. She smiled and waved to Nathan and Mace as they headed off toward the stable. She knew Mace Hunter would return after her lessons to take her riding and begin their sham. She also knew that Rachel Raines would be returning to work the next day, and she looked forward to meeting Rachel and her husband. Study and keep busy, that was what she needed to do!

Harrison and Clarissa Caldwell were enjoying themselves immensely at the lengthy July Fourth celebration in town, but each kept a sharp eye for a certain, though different, person. The games, races, betting, eating, dancing, and drinking continued during the hot day without either person making an appearance.

Around two o'clock, Cody approached Clarissa with the letter from Travis, and she eagerly stole away to the livery stable to read it. She was astonished by the message and peeved over his sudden departure. She stuffed the letter into her draw-string purse to read again later, but before she could leave the secluded stable, Wes Monroe swaggered inside and attempted to have some fun then and there.

"Don't be a fool, Wes," she angrily scolded him. "We can't be seen together. This could look suspicious after you handle that job for me. Get rid of Jackson tonight, and I'll come to the cabin around ten," she offered, trying to prevent his anger or his refusal to help her.

"You're smart, woman. It would look strange for a gunslinger and a lady to be playing in the straw together. Don't be late tonight, and be ready to give me this man's name and why you want him killed."

When the celebration ended with enough time for the ranchers to get home before dark, Harrison was still tense and decided to stay in town and spend a few hours at the Silver Shadow Saloon. He had anticipated meeting

Marissa's double all day and had worked himself into a mental state of constant arousal, one that needed appeasing before he went home tonight. He shouldn't have been surprised by Crandall's failure to show up today, he told himself; after all, the man would soon lose everything. No doubt Nathan was plenty worried about now. Even if Nathan and Travis suspected he was responsible for the robbery, they couldn't prove a thing, and the ranch would be his within a month. Perhaps they could work out something reasonable, if Rana were another Marissa . . .

The day had passed busily for Rana. Despite its being a holiday, Mrs. Clara Dobbs had arrived that morning to deliver several items and to fit others. After the midday meal, Aaron Moore had arrived for her lessons, for the shy teacher cared little for rowdy celebrations and was eager to work with his delightful pupil.

At five, when she was waving farewell to Moore, Cody and some of the hands returned from their chores. At twenty-six, Cody was fortunate to hold such a position of authority. The smiling man cordially and politely introduced Rana to Darby and Bart Davis. Both men had dark brown hair and brown eyes, Rana observed, and neither had looks that would tend to catch the average woman's eye. Cody explained that Darby was forty-six, with a wife named Lettie and many children, and they lived in one of the rented houses a few miles away. Bart was forty, single, and lived in the bunkhouse. Clearly the two brothers were very close, Rana mused, in looks, feelings, and personalities. Though neither had had much to say, both had been friendly and polite.

Cody asked Rana if she wanted to go riding or spend time practicing her shooting. Just as she told him she was waiting for Mace, the affable blond arrived with Todd

Raines, who gaped at her as if seeing a ghost. For a time he stared at her transfixed, but Cody and Mace were too busy bantering to notice Todd's reaction.

Rana smiled at him and watched how his eyes glowed as they roamed her form from head to toe. She broke her spell over him by saying, "I am Rana Michaels, Marissa's daughter, Nathan's granddaughter. It is good to meet you, Mister Raines. Travis and Grandfather speak good words about you."

Todd murmured, "I can't believe it; you look just like your mother did years ago. They told me about you, but I wasn't prepared for this shock. I hope you'll forgive me for staring at you, Miss Rana."

Rana was delighted to meet this particular man and hoped they could become friends quickly so she could ask him about her mother. Todd was thirty-eight, the same age Marissa would have been had she lived. He had light brown hair, which some might have considered dark blond, and it shone in the approaching sunset with reddish gold highlights. His striking eyes were an unusual shade, appearing to be a mixture of silver and dark blue. His features were pleasing, and Rana speculated that his good looks had increased with age. How different Marissa's life and her own would have been if this man had won her mother's heart. She had been told his wife, Rachel, was barren and that the couple wanted a child badly. As it had been with Mace and Cody, there was something about Todd Raines that caused her to like him instantly.

Mace and Cody noticed the quick rapport and the ease with which Rana and Todd conversed. Todd explained that he had to pick up some barbed wire and head back to the men waiting for him, so he did not have long to talk. He smiled then and told Rana he would look forward to seeing her again, and she did the same. As he moved off, Todd glanced back at her several times and she watched him until he was out of sight. Their strange behavior caused Cody and Mace to exchange quizzical looks, for they had been too young to know about the fiery romance between Marissa Crandall and Todd Raines twenty years before. They only knew that after her hasty marriage and departure, Marissa had come to visit her father every two years, beginning in 1850, when Rana had been one. When she made her last, tragic visit in 1856, Cody had been fifteen, Mace, at eighteen, had only been with the ranch one year, and Todd had been married to Rachel for four years.

Still puzzled, Mace invited Rana to ride with him and, a short time later, when they had halted near a large pond to rest for a moment, Rana began asking countless questions about Todd Raines. Such excessive interest alarmed Mace. He casually stated, "I did tell you that Todd's happily married to a very sweet woman."

Rana glanced at him curiously, thinking to herself, Why would he . . . ? Suddenly Rana grinned, then laughed aloud. "I do not ask about him for myself, Mace Hunter. I asked because he was very close to my mother. I wish to become friends with him so he will tell me much about her. I was a small child when she was slain and I know little about her. Grandfather told me they almost married long ago. I think how different all would be if they had been joined. To learn about one she loved tells me much about her, and I wish to know all things. I must not ask such questions before his wife, for it would make her sad to hear him speak of another love. Do you understand?"

Mace smiled and nodded. "I understand, Rana. I never knew about Todd and Marissa, so I guess you were a shock to him since you look like your mother. I came to work for Nate when I was seventeen, so I only saw your mother once. But I can tell you, she wasn't one to forget," he murmured almost dreamily. Catching himself, he flushed lightly and said, "It's getting late. We should ride back." The sun was falling across her head, enhancing the color of her face, hair, and eyes. He smiled and remarked, "You know something? Travis is a lucky man. He said you were perfect and beautiful, and he was right."

"It is good he has a friend who knows and shares all with him, as Myeerah did with me in the Oglala camp. I miss her. Cody Slade says he will bring his love to see me and become my new friend. It is good."

Yes, Mace decided, Travis Kincade was a damn lucky man to have discovered this treasure first. He would take real good care of it for his best friend, and if Travis didn't return alive . . . No, Mace raged inwardly, nothing could and would happen to his best friend. "After you finish your lessons tomorrow, we'll do some target practice," he said aloud. "Just make sure you don't go riding without me or Cody, or Todd."

She smiled at Mace and mounted the pretty sorrel. "Did Travis forget to tell you I am very obedient and understanding?"

Mace's gaze met Rana's and they both laughed merrily.

Clarissa paced her room and read the letter again and again. The news was what she had desired, but could she believe it? Travis had been holding her off for years, so why this sudden change? Was the tough rancher going soft for her? Or was he getting worried about losing his ranch and all he owned? Did it matter to her that it was the only way she could have him? She read the letter one final time, then burned it.

It was probably a good thing he was gone right now, she told herself, for he might have been injured during her father's take-over, or he might have discovered the truth about her and her plans. And because he was gone,

443

Travis couldn't fall for that little chit of Marissa's! Once Travis lost everything, she would look like the best catch to him, especially if her father were dead and Travis could marry her and become the owner of a vast empire. No matter his motives, she would win him and tame him. But right now, she had another man to handle. Picking up a drying cloth, she made her way to the bathing closet.

When she returned to her room after her bath, she found Wes Monroe propped lazily on her bed. She hurriedly locked her bedroom door and went to him. Keeping her voice as low as possible though she was in a burning rage, she demanded, "What the hell are you doing in here? My father could return at any time. He would fire you and disown me!"

As he placed several pillows behind him and leaned against them, Wes playfully argued, "Nobody saw me sneak in and your door's locked. We're on the second floor, so nobody can peek in your windows. If you keep your voice down, nobody will know I'm here. Sit down and talk." He grasped her hand and pulled her down beside him.

"*Nobody* doesn't matter, only my father," she sneered. "If he finds out about us, he'll get suspicious and all my plans will be ruined."

"That's who you want me to kill for you, isn't it?" he asked calmly as he untied the sash to her robe, exposing her naked body, which was still damp from her bath. He noticed her uncontrollable reaction to his words, a response that left no doubt about her prey's identity or her character. He had watched and listened, and had added up the facts and clues. This woman wanted it all, and she would kill her own father or do anything to get it. That meant she was as cold-blooded and greedy as he was, and she couldn't be trusted.

"I told you I would come to the cabin later. I was getting ready to leave. This is too risky, Wes. We can't talk or meet here."

As he fondled her breasts, he suggested erotically, "Taking you here makes it more exciting, Clarissa. Riding you like crazy within a few feet of the man you want me to kill for you and knowing he doesn't suspect a thing . . . Knowing we can't make a sound even if our bodies heat up and burn to a crisp . . . Nope, woman, this ain't risky; this is feasting on danger and making all of your senses come alive. Don't you know how much pleasure and power you can get from other people's pain? Why don't you tell me what you've got in mind for your unlucky Papa while I take another payment?" His hands went behind her back and he pulled her forward so his mouth could devour her breasts.

Clarissa thought about his stimulating words as she watched him with fascination. Her father had taken Marissa many times in the room next to hers; now she would dare to have a lover in this very house! And the man who was going to murder him! Wes was right; danger was a heady aphrodisiac and so was victory. It was all falling into place for her, and that was intoxicating. As his hand slipped between her legs, she closed her eyes and was consumed by the blissful sensations that Wes was creating up and down her quivering frame.

Suddenly he halted and pushed her aside to rise and undress. She was eager to have him feasting and laboring on her body again, and she helped him remove his garments quickly. Tossing aside her light covering, she lay down, reached for him, and drew him down to her searing body. Few men she had known had been as skilled and generous as this crude beast. Until she was finished with Wes, she would make good use of him. Soon her head began to thrash on the pillow, for Wes was driving her wild with his bold actions.

He finally rolled to his back and whispered hoarsely, "Climb on top of me and ride me good, woman. We'll talk later."

Clarissa instantly obeyed. As she rocked back and

forth on him, a knock sounded on the door and her father called out, "You still awake, girl? I want to talk to you about something."

Clarissa froze and her heart pounded in fear of discovery. She gazed at Wes's wicked expression, unable to believe that he had devilishly begun to pinch her taut nipples and grin at her, knowing she could not cry out or scold him. Clarissa recalled the many times her father had hurt her and controlled her and, for a brief, maddening instant, she was tempted to cry rape and have Wes slain. But she needed him now, though she vowed she would repay him later. Harrison knocked and called out again, and Clarissa found her voice. "I'm tired, Papa; it was a long, hot day. Let's talk in the morning. I'm already in bed," she explained as she began undulating her body over Wes's again.

As Harrison argued, "It's only nine o'clock, and we have some plans to make," Wes seized Clarissa's hips and forcefully began to grind his manhood into her body. Then he pulled her forward to nibble roughly on her breasts, for the danger of Harrison's proximity and his power over her seemed to arouse him enormously. "Are you sure you don't want to get up and come downstairs for a sherry and a talk?" Harrison encouraged. He had heard about Travis's second strange departure and he wanted to learn if Clarissa knew anything about it.

Wes replaced his manhood with his mouth and hands. Tingles raced through her body. Her worst enemy was standing on the other side of that door, and, on this side, a dangerous villain was sensuously devouring her and promising to do her bidding. She felt as if she were vicariously punishing her father and she reveled in the feeling. Clarissa grinned salaciously. "I'm too tired and sleepy, Papa. I need to stay in bed tonight. I was just getting comfortable. I'll see you in the morning."

"All right, girl. We'll talk at breakfast. Have a good

446

night," he told her, bringing a wicked smile to her lips.

"I will, Papa," she murmured softly. "Sleep well." She focused her full attention on Wes, for soon she would have to get rid of him. Hopefully Travis Kincade was this good, or only half as good, in bed . . .

The next morning, Rachel Raines appeared for work. She was a willowy woman with dark chestnut hair and vivid green eyes. She and Rana seemed pleased with each other and soon established an easy rapport. Relieved at how well the two women were getting along, Nathan announced that he would be riding to the east pasture to see how the fence repairs were going in that troublesome area.

Rachel spent the morning teaching Rana about cooking and cleaning, and telling her about others on the ranch. Rana decided not to question the woman about her husband or their life together, at least not until they got to know each other better.

Aaron Moore arrived after the noon meal. While he and Rana worked at the dining room table, Rachel did the washing and checked on Nathan's garden, for she and one of the hands were responsible for tending it and gathering the vegetables and fruits. When Rana and Aaron took a short break from the lesson, Rachel told them she was leaving for the day and would see Rana the next morning. Rana was delighted to hear the woman had cooked a stew for supper and had left it simmering on the stove. Rachel also had biscuits ready to be baked later and had prepared tea and a cobbler with canned peaches.

Aaron Moore departed shortly after Rachel, and Mace appeared around five to take Rana to a nearby meadow for target practice. He was amazed by her natural skill with guns. As he instructed her and she obeyed, he told her many tales about the ranch and his friendship with

Travis. Rana felt at ease with Mace and told him many things about her life in the Oglala camp. Since the ranch was so sorely in need of money, she did not reveal how much Nathan and Travis had paid for her return, nor did she tell Mace that she and Travis were married under Indian law. He returned her just before supper time, then conversed with Nathan for a few minutes, and the older man invited him to stay for the evening meal.

Nathan cleverly suggested, "If anybody's watching us for Harry, it might be a good idea if you're seen around the house with Rana. Out riding, you might only look like her escort. And it wouldn't hurt none if you two were seen holding hands and eyeing each other."

That day set a pattern for many to follow, with Rana steadily increasing her knowledge and skills with her books, in the house, and on the ranch. Gradually she met the other hands and they were all taken with her, each offering to do whatever he could to help her. But as she and Mace played their deceitful parts, the other men were fooled completely and made sure they did not infringe on Mace's territory.

Mrs. Dobbs finished the new wardrobe and her congenial visits stopped, but Rana felt she had learned a great deal from the affable woman. Rana knew the clothes she had made were beautiful and costly, but some were very uncomfortable for a girl accustomed to wearing supple buckskins and going barefoot. Rachel, Nathan, and Mace often teased her about those bare feet and her amusing complaints. She had gotten used to the hard western saddle, but she still preferred riding bareback, which Mace and Nathan would not allow. She missed her daily swims and frequently begged Nathan and Mace to allow her that pleasure, but all she could manage to elicit was permission to go wading in a stream.

Whenever she and Mace went riding, he would point out and explain the various ranch tasks. This was a busy season for cowhands and ranchers, and only one man appeared to have decided not to wait out the current trouble. The others agreed to continue working with partial pay until Nathan solved his problems. Some hands were engaged in structural repairs or fence mending or rounding up strays or moving cattle between pastures. Others were occupied with branding calves and colts or guarding against rustlers or breaking wild horses.

Nathan did not extend or accept any neighborly invitations; he used lost work time and catching up from his long absence as excuses to continue guarding Rana's privacy for awhile. Anyone who dropped by was greeted outside and entertained there, and at such times Rana stayed out of sight. He realized people were curious about her, but he believed they should understand she needed time to get accustomed to a whole new life. Yet, with the hands' trips into town and to other ranches, news of her beauty and appeal spread quickly. To keep their friends and neighbors from getting too curious to contain themselves, Nathan sent messages to them saying he would hold a large barbecue on the tenth of August, at which time everyone would meet his granddaughter.

Each Sunday Nathan went to church with the Raineses and answered countless questions about Rana Michaels. Most seemed to understand why Nathan did not want her overwhelmed with so many new things and people, and told him they would wait patiently for the second Saturday in August.

It had been thirteen days since Travis's departure and Rana missed him terribly. So far, the incidents of wicked mischief had been limited to several fence cuttings, the rustling of fifteen to twenty head of cattle at a time, the strewing about of hay stacks—it would have been too dangerous to set them afire, for flames could spread wildly and rapidly in all directions during this sultry July weather—the plundering of small sheds, and the opening

449

of gates to allow horses to escape: problems that could be repaired or corrected, with the exception of the stolen cattle.

Rana had not yet been given the opportunity to speak privately with Todd Raines, but she often found him watching her intently. On this particular day, Rana turned suddenly to find Rachel observing the way she and Todd had been looking at each other. Tears glistened in the woman's green eyes and Rana followed her into the house and asked kindly, "Why do you weep, Rachel?"

Rachel dried her eyes and let them roam the features of the girl before her. "You look just like your mother, and she broke Todd's heart years ago. Every time he looks at you, he sees and remembers that pain. Your mother was . . ." Rachel held her revealing tongue.

"I am sorry my face brings such sadness and pain. Please speak, Rachel. Why did my mother hurt your husband? How did she do so? To understand my mother and myself, I must hear about the past."

Rachel answered reluctantly, "Todd was in love with Marissa Crandall and he believed she was in love with him. They were together nearly every day and they talked about marriage—until she suddenly ran off with that Raymond Michaels. It shocked everybody, 'cause he was . . ." Again Rachel fell silent and her face turned very red.

"Do not worry, Rachel, I know my father was a bad man. There is a reason why she married Raymond and died for her mistake. Why did my mother choose him over Todd Raines? It makes no sense."

Rachel's gaze wandered over Rana's entreating expression, and she knew the girl was serious. Rana's face was so much like the one that had haunted both Todd and herself for years, but there was nothing to dislike about this charming girl. The same had been true of Marissa, despite the fact that Rachel had wanted to despise the woman who had hurt her love so badly. Each time she had returned for a short visit, Marissa had seemed so sad, so lonely, so vulnerable, and so afraid. The girl whom Rachel had known during those visits long ago was nothing like the one described in the gossip she had heard then and later. And, Rachel reasoned, if Marissa had been as wicked and willful as the rumors claimed, Todd Raines would never have fallen in love with her. She wanted to help Rana, but she felt it would be wrong to reveal a mystery that would confuse and pain this sweet girl even more than she already was. Poor Marissa; something had terrified that beautiful creature and had driven her from home. But no one knew why she decided to run off with Raymond, including Todd and Nathan.

"That's something I can't explain, Rana; I doubt anyone can. I was working here during your last two visits, but I doubt you recall me. Todd married me after Marissa's second visit home in '52. I think he needed someone to help him forget your mother, but we've been very happy, except for having no children. Lord, how I wish I could give Todd a child. It would make us so happy. I used to watch Todd watching you and Marissa. I knew he still loved her and wished you two were his. I tried to hate your mother, but she made it impossible. She might have been wild and willful in her younger days, but she wasn't like that when I knew her. She was a kind, good woman, Rana, and she loved you dearly. I think she wanted to stay here on the ranch, but your papa wouldn't allow it."

Rachel peeked out the kitchen window to make certain no one was coming, then continued. "I couldn't blame Todd for his feelings, 'cause feelings are things we can't control. It took him years to get over losing her, then years to get over her death. He was one of the men who helped Mister Crandall search for you until they knew it was useless. The minute I laid eyes on you the other

451

week, I knew how you was affecting my Todd. My poor love! All those memories must have come pouring back when he looked at you, the good ones and the bad ones. Please don't talk to him about your mama. I promise you he don't know nothing that I ain't told you. Todd's talked about her plenty, asleep and awake. He don't know why she left; that's why he suffered so. Not knowing something important is like a festering wound that won't heal. Let him get used to having you around before you say anything to him. Maybe you'll help him accept the past and get over her."

"I will not speak of my mother to him until I know the truth; then I will tell it to him, for he has earned the right to know it. You are a good wife to him, Rachel. Do not let the spirit of a dead loved one come between you. He belongs to you; fight for him. My mother is not your enemy, and I am your friend. Do not be sad or afraid."

Rachel smiled through more tears. "That's what your mother said to me the last time she was home. I was so scared Todd would fall in love with her again, and I knew she was miserable with Raymond. I was afraid they would be drawn to each other like before. Marissa saw how I was feeling. One day she put her arm around my shoulder and told me not to be sad or afraid, to trust my husband, and to fight for him if necessary. She told me she had loved Todd long ago, but as a young girl. She said she knew she had hurt him deeply, but she couldn't change the past. She refused to talk to him because she said it was best if he kept terrible thoughts about her and hated her. She believed it would make it easier for him to forget her. She was a special woman, Rana. I wish she was still alive so you could know her like I did. If anyone tells you mean things about her, don't listen to them. Hardly anybody understood or knew Marissa, and that's plenty sad."

Just then Rana moved to answer a knock at the front door and accepted a fake telegram that was signed with

Travis's name. She did not bother to open it and read it, for she knew that the hired hand who had supposedly quit the ranch on July fifth was actually going from place to place to send such false telegrams to Clarissa Caldwell and Nathan as well, just in case Harrison had the telegrapher in his employ. The plan was that first a message would be sent from Springfield, then Sedalia, then St. Louis, then Springfield again, with the hopes of keeping Travis's whereabouts a secret.

Clarissa masked her outrage as she read the telegram that her father had opened and read first: "In Springfield. No good news. Sedalia next. Sending love and hope. Travis." She looked up at her father and asked, "Why did you read my mail, Papa?"

"It sounds to me as if you knew where he was going and why. Is that true, daughter?" Harrison asked coldly, angrily.

Her temper was rising and she fought to control it. "Nearly two weeks ago I told you he had left on another mysterious trip. He sent me a message by Cody Slade. I told you he said he was going to look for those bandits or try to get another loan. You read the telegram, so you know as much as I do. He hasn't found anything, and we both know he can't, so why are you angry and worried, Papa? You act like you think Travis and I are plotting against you instead of the other way around. I don't like being forced to defend myself to you."

"The whole damn thing seems curious to me!" he snapped.

"I know, Papa. That's why I told you about it. They're scared and worried over there, but we know they're trapped. Travis can't find that money because it's locked in your safe, and he can't get a loan with the debts they owe. You'll have their ranch by August first, so calm

453

down and enjoy your imminent victory."

"It isn't like Kincade and Nate to give up so easily."

"They're not, Papa. They think they're doing all they can. What has you so upset? Is it Mary Beth Sims? You haven't seen her lately," she suggested evocatively. "Is there a problem with her?"

"The devil take that mealymouthed child!" he exploded meanly. "She isn't fit to become a Caldwell or to bear one. I told Sims today that I didn't want his daughter. I told him to marry her off to that Cody Slade; a cowpoke's wife is all she's fit to be. I didn't like her anyway, and I got tired of her refusing me. I'll find me another woman, a better and a prettier one." Visions of Marissa filled his head and he wished he could catch one glimpse of her daughter. All he had thought about since learning about Rana's existence and arrival was Marissa and their past. Somehow he had to get his hands on that girl . . .

Clarissa glared at her father's profile. She detested the dreamy look on his face and the reasons for it: Marissa and Rana. At least Mary Beth was out of her way, and she would see to it that Rana didn't mar her beautiful plans. She advised maliciously, "I think it's time to get tough with that old buzzard on the Rocking *C*, Papa. That cocky Nathan is climbing high and he needs to be slapped down a few rungs. Don't take any chances. He could find someone to lend him the money, so you'd better make sure he doesn't want to pay off that debt in two weeks and stay around." She smiled wickedly. "I think it's time you turned your hired hands loose over there; that's why you're paying them, to run Crandall out. If you don't let them have some fun like they did with old man McFarland, they might get bored and leave, just when you need them. The timing is perfect with Travis gone. Nobody over there will stand up to Monroe and Hayes."

"You're right, girl. I think it's about time to show Nate

454

who's going to become the big boss soon. I'll send Fargo to fetch them. Yep, I'll make some plans with Monroe and Hayes this very afternoon."

Lone Wolf met Travis as he rode into the Oglala camp and reined in before his tepee. The two men looked at each other and smiled. "Come, sit, brother. Speak of my sister, Wild Wind, and speak of why you return to my lands when fires burn in your eyes."

Travis and Lone Wolf entered his tepee and sat on buffalo mats to talk. "There are many things I must tell you, Lone Wolf, my brother, but the words do not wish to leave my body. I must speak of much trouble in my past in these lands, and I must speak of great danger to us in the white lands. I come to seek the understanding and help of my brother, Lone Wolf, and I must return home quickly."

Lone Wolf read severe anxiety and doubt in the other man, and he knew something of great importance had brought Travis to him. "Speak, White Eagle; my heart is open to you and your words."

Travis slowly and painfully revealed his turbulent past in the Hunkpapa camp, and described all the tormenting days that had followed. "You have only my word, Lone Wolf, but I did not betray them and side with my father, whose heart was dark and evil. They left me without a people and a land and a heart for many years. They tried to take away my honor, my spirit, and my life. They left me no way to defend myself. If I had not run away, the truth would have died with me. Grandfather did not want it to end that way. He protected my life and sent me far away to find another land, people, and life. He returned my honor and renewed my spirit."

Travis explained the trouble and peril on the ranch. As had been the case with Rana, Lone Wolf had difficulty understanding white laws that prohibited Travis from punishing and slaying his enemy and recovering his belongings. Travis told the handsome and intrepid chief about the tainted gold, the "yellow rocks," which could save their lands. "Grandfather sent me into the lives and hearts of Nathan Crandall and his granddaughter, your sister, Wild Wind. I fill their hearts and lives, as they fill mine. When this danger is past and our enemy is defeated, Rana Michaels and Travis Kincade will join in the white land as Wild Wind and White Eagle joined in the Indian land. They are my heart, my life and honor, Lone Wolf, and I must defend them and protect their lands. To do this in the white world, I must have the gold, the yellow rocks, which have great value to the white man." He entreated Lone Wolf to go with him to the Hunkpapa camp and to help him convince them of his past innocence and persuade them to let him take the gold to save his lands from an evil white. This was something he hoped the Indians would understand.

Lone Wolf told Travis about the Hunkpapas' visit after Travis's departure with Wild Wind, and his words shocked and relieved the half-blooded man. "The Hunkpapas camp at a great distance from the Oglalas. We must travel far before the moon passes above us. When the new sun appears, we will finish our journey. Lone Wolf and White Eagle will speak with our Lakota brothers about the yellow rocks. It is good you come to ask for them and do not steal them. I say your words are true. But what will White Eagle do if the Hunkpapas refuse to let him take the yellow rocks?" he questioned gravely as they prepared to leave.

"I will trade all for them, Lone Wolf, for without them we will lose our honor, and perhaps our lives."

Chapter Fifteen

Travis recovered the last pouch of gold from its hiding place and packed it in his saddlebag; then met Lone Wolf's gaze and smiled. He glanced at the clear sky above them and inhaled deeply. "My heart is filled with joy and relief, my brother. My spirit chants this special *coup* of my Hunkpapa brothers. My mother's people have given back something very precious to me; they have returned my Indian heart and spirit. All has been made good again, Lone Wolf."

The young chief nodded. "It is as it must be, White Eagle. Grandfather has defeated the evil of the past. You are free of it."

"Free," Travis echoed dreamily. Yes, he was free of this tormenting part of his past. The Hunkpapas knew the truth and accepted it; he was one with them again, as it should be. Now it was time to cut the bond with this part of his life. Taking his knife, he severed the thong around his neck and removed his *wanapin*. He stared at it, then handed it to Lone Wolf. "Give this to your first son, my brother; it is a sacred bond between our two worlds. As he grows to a man, it will protect him in both worlds, as it protected me. One day the war lance will be broken between our two peoples, as the arrow is broken in the eagle's talons. He will be a leader of great power, like the thunderbolt in the eagle's grasp. He will end the bitter days of the War Bonnet Society; he will find the path to peace and survival. One day the children of Lone Wolf and Myeerah and the children of Rana Michaels and Travis Kincade will play and ride together in peace and love. They will share true friendship as we have, my brother."

Lone Wolf looked at the medallion that had been made by Medicine Chief Sitting Bull of the Hunkpapas. He understood what Travis was doing and saying. "It will be as you say, my brother. You live a new life, and the old one is gone forever. Soon such words may be true of all Hunkpapas and Oglalas. I will place this on my son's neck when he is born." Lone Wolf removed his *wanapin* and handed it to Travis. "Give this to your son, my brother. It will guard his life when he enters the Lakota lands many winters from this sun. Our hearts and lives will be joined forever, my friend."

"I must ride quickly, Lone Wolf. The days before my challenge pass as swiftly as the snows fall in winter. It is good I returned to these lands one last time. You are my friend and brother for all days."

The two men clutched forearms and locked their gazes briefly, each knowing this would be the last time they would see each other. By way of settling their old debt, the Hunkpapas had given him permission to take the "yellow rocks," and now Travis would have to get home in time to use them to thwart Caldwell. He could only pray he would make it home safely and rapidly, for it was now the eighteenth of July—two weeks before the bank loan was due—and many miles separated him from the ranch.

Lone Wolf watched Travis mount and ride away. He returned to his tepee and studied the gifts his friend had given him and his family: the *wanapin* for his firstborn

458

son, the hair ornament for Myeerah, which Wild Wind had worn in the painting that had led Travis and her grandfather to her, the buckskin garments that Travis had worn when he had come to stake a claim on his adopted sister, several guns and knives, boxes of ammunition, warm garments for Myeerah for the winter from her friend Rana, a mirror for his beloved wife, and a special blanket in which to wrap their first child.

Lone Wolf explained the significance of the gifts to Myeerah and smiled tenderly. "Wild Wind has returned to her destiny, my wife. She and White Eagle will join in the white way and be happy. It is good. We must pray for the Great Spirit to guide her husband to her safely." Lone Wolf closed his eyes and called to mind a vision he had had recently. He smiled. Yes, he reflected, there would be a strong bond between their children one day . . .

Rana was restless, for so much was happening all around her and she felt useless, restricted. She had been studying and working hard since her arrival, but she was unaccustomed to lengthy confinement. The only privacy she had came at night in her room, and the nights seemed unbearably long as she lay in her bed alone. With Travis gone, she felt there was no one with whom she could really talk, as she once had with Myeerah. She was always watching everything she said or did, and trying to be her very best so as not to disappoint her grandfather. She was used to being in and around nature, not trapped in a wooden structure, and she felt like a captive who could not come and go as she desired. Even more difficult to combat was the helplessness she felt at not being allowed to aid those she loved.

Aaron Moore had sent word that he was ill and could not come to the ranch for her lessons today. Rachel had taken care of her chores and had left early to assist Lettie

Davis with the early birth of another child. Todd Raines and several of the hands were busy mending a lengthy span of fence that had been cut the night before, while Cody Slade and others were trying to round up scattered cattle and horses. This time, in their haste, the malicious rustlers had left a carelessly concealed trail, which Mace Hunter and several men were following. If only they could catch one or two, Rana reflected, they might learn the identity of their leader, or prove it was Caldwell.

She was glad Nathan had left for a town called Dallas before this new offense had been uncovered, for he had been suffering too much during these trying days. She prayed it would not be difficult for Nathan to set aside his adoption of Travis Kincade, which would then allow them to marry. Nathan had told her he was going to Dallas to handle the matter so that Harrison Caldwell would not learn about it and become suspicious of their plans. Nathan intended to hire a lawyer there to dispatch the delicate legal problem, and he planned to return home late the following day.

Rana walked around the house several times, but there was nothing to do but wait and worry. Nathan had not realized she would be left alone today and tonight, nor had Mace Hunter when he had ridden off in pursuit of the rustlers and cattle. When word had come shortly before the noon meal that Lettie was in early labor, Rana had insisted that Rachel go to the woman and help her with the delivery. Lettie had two sons, eleven and thirteen, who would care for the smaller children, but they knew nothing of bringing a child into the world.

Rana halted near the front door and looked outside. Only two men were visible, and they were busy with chores. She was not afraid to be left alone in the house, for she knew how to defend herself. Yet worry and uneasiness plagued her and, as time passed slowly, she grew tense and irritable. Perhaps part of her distress and tension was due to the heat, for it was an oppressively hot, muggy day. What she needed was a refreshing, cooling swim.

Rana knew that the river was only a few miles from the house, and she believed she would be safe because the evil men had not attacked the ranch during the day. Why couldn't she ride there and enjoy herself for a short while? The hands would be gone for the afternoon, so who would know? Besides, she could take a gun and be very careful. Hesitating no longer, she decided to go.

Rana managed to get her sorrel and leave without being seen. She rode to a spot near the river where Mace had taken her several days before. After dismounting, she tied the reins to a bush and walked toward the inviting water. As she gazed at it longingly, she wondered if she were being rash, but before she could ponder her actions further, a man appeared from the trees. Rana drew her pistol and pointed it at him to let him know it would be unwise to attack her, if that were the motive for his approach.

The stranger did not seem alarmed or deterred by her action. He reined up near her and stared at her boldly, his mouth open and his eyes wide. As Rana studied him, she noted that he looked younger than her grandfather and was still an attractive man. His hair was dark, almost black, and his eyes were a mixture of green and brown. His body had a certain strength, but Rana could tell that he did very little physical work. She waited for him to speak.

"My God, you look just like her," he murmured in undisguised astonishment. He dismounted, dropped his reins to the ground, and came forward. He looked at the gun and her stance. "You don't need to be afraid, Rana. I'm your neighbor, Harrison Caldwell."

"I am not afraid of anything, Mr. Caldwell. The gun is for protection. Many bad things and people walk my grandfather's land. Why have you come to speak with me?" she asked bluntly, for she had guessed his identity and was therefore able to mask any outward show of emotion.

"I was out riding and I saw you standing here. I haven't had the pleasure of meeting you. Your grandfather is being very protective of you. I knew your mother, and I was shocked that you look so much like her," he replied smoothly, having mastered his surprise. "I imagine you're glad to be home again."

"Yes, it is good to return to my family and home. How did you know my mother?" she inquired politely.

Harrison laughed genially. "We were neighbors for years, Rana. Marissa used to come to my ranch to help my daughter, Clarissa, with her lessons, and sometimes she would watch Clarissa for me. It's hard for a man alone to raise a small child, especially a little girl. Clarissa and your mother were friends. She's looking forward to meeting you. Why don't you ride over one day and visit with us?" he invited.

Rana instantly thought of the safe that might be holding her grandfather's stolen money. If she could visit his ranch, she could see where it was located and how the house was arranged. If Travis could not get the gold, they could sneak into this man's house and take what belonged to them after his return. She smiled and nodded. "It is good to find new friends here. When my grandfather returns from this place called Abilene, I will ask him to bring me to meet your daughter. Grandfather went to speak with a man about horses," she lied convincingly, as she had been instructed by Nathan before his departure. "Is your ranch far away? Is it big like Grandfather's?" she asked with feigned feminine interest.

Harrison was fooled by her delicate, friendly facade and assumed that Nathan and Travis had not told her

462

about their problems. His eyes swept over the flaming head of hair that tumbled to her tiny waist. Her complexion was as smooth as silk and playful freckles danced across her pert nose. He gazed into those large, innocent-looking, gray-blue eyes. She was even more beautiful and desirable than her mother had been, and she possessed a sweetness and artlessness that Marissa had lacked. "You should not be out riding alone, Rana. We've been having trouble with rustlers lately."

Rana laughed at his mild scolding, and the sound of it washed provocatively over the man before her. In a skillfully controlled tone, she replied, "The rustlers do not strike when the sun is high and can reveal their faces. I have a gun, and I know how to use it. I am in no danger. Do not worry over me."

Harrison laughed too. "I see you're more like your mother than looks alone," he teased jovially. "Marissa was just as headstrong and brave as you are. Still, you should be careful."

Rana smiled deceitfully once more. "You are kind to worry, Mister Caldwell, but I can take care of myself." He was looking at her as if she were her mother, and the strange look mystified and intrigued her.

Harrison concluded that since Nathan was gone, it was unlikely that anyone knew this ravishing creature was out here alone. She was a vivacious, daring young thing, and he wanted to know all about her. His mouth was dry, his palms were sweaty, his body was quivering, his heart was pounding, and his manhood was pleading. He wanted this girl with every inch of himself. "If you like, you could ride over with me now and meet Clarissa. She was home when I left, and she didn't say anything about going out today," he lied eagerly, for he knew Clarissa would be at the dressmaker's all day and he would have this girl all to himself.

Rana sensed that the man was deceiving her, for he was

463

too caught up in his thoughts to realize that his gaze, voice, and behavior were giving him away. She noticed how he kept licking his lips and swallowing, and how his breathing indicated a racing heart. She had watched him dry his palms on his pants' legs several times. She saw the glow in his eyes and on his cheeks, and she observed how he kept shifting nervously from foot to foot. She noticed all of these things without Harrison's awareness. Rana knew she had this man duped and fascinated, and she found it impossible to avoid wondering if he had also been this taken with her mother.

She realized she was in no danger from him, at least for today. There was much she wanted to learn from him and about him, and the only way to do so was to accept his questionable invitation. "I will go with you, but I must return home soon. I must not worry those Grandfather left to protect me. Tell me about your daughter," she coaxed as they mounted.

Clarissa paced the cabin as she talked with Wes Monroe. "You're certain you left enough of a trail for them to follow without it looking odd?"

"Just like we planned, woman, so stop acting *loco*. By now, half the hands on the Rocking *C* should be chasing down that trail. When I see your papa later, I'll tell him we need to strike closer to the house tonight while those men are gone. Don't fret; I'll make sure that girl gets in the way of a stray bullet. I know my work; it'll look like an accident. Once it's done, ain't nothing he can do about it. You know this is going to cost you extra," he announced suddenly.

Clarissa halted to look at him and scoffed crudely, "Don't try that on me, you bastard. We both know how much you and Jack love killing people, including pretty women. All you have to do now is convince Papa to let you raid Crandall's stable."

"You worry too much, woman. He won't suspect a thing, not tonight or when I get ready to plug him for you. You want me to take him out quick and easy, or real slow and painful?"

"I haven't decided yet," she replied petulantly. "Right now, I just want to get rid of that little Michaels bitch before Papa gets any more silly ideas like he did with Mary Beth Sims," she explained, knowing it was Travis she wanted to protect from Rana's allure and not her father, for she had another way to halt anything that might start between Harrison and Rana.

Moving his tongue slowly over his dry lips, Wes commanded, "Forget all that for now and come here, woman."

Rana entered the house and looked around wide-eyed, as if she were astonished by its size and was appreciatively admiring it. She smiled and remarked, "Your home is very big and pretty. It is strange to live in a place with many rooms and belongings. It is much different in a tepee," she told him casually, knowing he was aware of the story of her past and concluding that her easy manner would disarm him completely. As if enthralled by the spaciousness and beauty of his home, she began to wander around, carefully studying the layout of the rooms and the objects in them.

Ushering her into the parlor, Harrison said, "I'm sorry about what happened to you, Rana. It must have been terrible for you, all those years with the Indians."

She halted her roaming to glance at him and answer, "It was not bad with the Oglalas. They stole me from the Kiowas when I was but eight winters. The Kiowas were very bad, but I was small and remember little about them. When I was taken captive by the Oglalas, Chief Soaring

465

Hawk made me his daughter. I was very happy and free with them. But I am glad to be home again. Still, there is much to learn. The white teacher comes each day to help me, and I work hard to learn quickly. I do not wish to shame my grandfather, for many think and say I am ... uncivilized, you whites call it. Yes?"

Harrison grinned. "Anybody who would call you a savage is blind and mean, Rana. But it isn't 'you whites,' because you're one of us."

She laughed merrily. "I forget. I was raised Indian, and change is hard and long. You are kind not to laugh at me. Grandfather knows that many people will; that is why he keeps me home until I learn much. I am brave and strong. It will hurt if they do not like me or they treat me badly, but words cannot slay a person. I wish to make Grandfather proud of me. He has been sad many years since Mother was killed. I wish to make him happy again. Where is your daughter? I wish her to tell me about my mother. I remember little about her."

Harrison replied, "She'll return soon. Why don't you look around?" he entreated. He watched Rana as she moved gracefully from one place to another as if she were on a magical journey. She was like a child filled with the wonder of Christmas. Several times her hand reached toward an object, then she would slowly withdraw it, as if afraid to touch the piece. She would ball her hands briefly as if warning herself she could break something precious or valuable. Recalling how long she had been with the Indians, he realized how new and different all of this would be for her. She was so alive and inquisitive, and he was feeling younger by the minute just observing her.

"You told me you weren't afraid of anything, Rana," he teased. "Pick it up and look at it," he encouraged when she wavered over a floral glass box and her exquisite gaze remained locked on it.

"I must not, Mister Caldwell. I would be sad if I broke something that belongs to another. I have never seen flowers that are not real, except painted ones. How strange and beautiful," she murmured, playing her naïve Indian maiden role with superb talent.

Harrison stepped forward, lifted the box, and handed it to her. "It's yours, Rana. Now you shouldn't be afraid to hold it."

Rana looked at the treasure in her hands. She widened her eyes guilefully and protested, "But I cannot take it without a reason."

"There are two reasons you should take it, Rana. First, because it's your first visit to my home and I wish you to have it; and second, because it was bought as a gift for your mother years ago, but she left before Clarissa and I could give it to her."

Rana looked at the fragile box and pondered Harrison's words. She believed it had been purchased for Marissa, but not as a gift from his daughter, and this strange perception alarmed her.

"Please take it, Rana. I will be sad if you refuse."

"I will take it because the Indians taught me it was wrong to refuse the generosity of a friend. I only wished to know why you wanted me to have it. Thank you. I will guard it carefully."

"I'll go see if any of my men know where Clarissa went and how long she'll be. You relax and I'll return shortly," he told her, pretending to know nothing of his daughter's absence.

Rana peeked out the window and watched him walk toward his stable to speak with the man working there. She hurriedly looked around his home once more, astutely memorizing where the doors and windows were located. She found his office and noticed the large safe behind an equally large desk. Excitement surged through her. She quickly studied the room, inside and outside,

467

then returned to the parlor and was feigning fascination with the pianoforte when he returned.

She glanced up quizzically when she saw that he was alone. She listened and nodded her head as he told her the stableman had said Clarissa had gone riding. Smiling, Rana rose from her seat on the oblong bench. "I must ride for home, Mister Caldwell. The others will worry if they find me gone. I will visit another day. You are most kind and generous."

"I wish you could stay longer, but I understand. I'll ride part of the way with you, to make sure you get home safely."

Rana smiled. "If it pleases you," she agreed.

Harrison bid her good-bye at the boundary to his ranch. He didn't want any of the men seeing them together and telling Nathan about their meeting, for Nathan would surely want to keep them apart. Since it was more than likely that Rana was not supposed to be out alone, chances were she wouldn't mention their meeting either, he reasoned. "Please ride over to visit us any time, Rana. I know Clarissa is anxious to meet you."

Rana reached the stable, then made her way to the house unseen, laughing inwardly at her cleverness. When she was finally safe in her room, she placed the floral box on her dresser and stared at it intently. She wondered why her mother had been a friend to those who were now enemies of her family. Clearly this Harrison Caldwell had been in love with her mother, and now he desired her to take Marissa's place. Perhaps it had not been Clarissa whom her mother had been visiting on the Circle C Ranch long ago . . . Was it possible that her mother and Caldwell had been in love and had wished to marry, but that something or someone had prevented it? Had her mother left home and married Raymond out of spite? There were so many unanswered questions.

Rana picked up the doll from her bed and placed it beside the glass box, then laid the heart-shaped turquoise and silver pendant next to it. Her probing gaze moved from one item to the next. "What is your secret, Mother? Why did you choose a cruel beast like Raymond Michaels over Todd Raines or Harrison Caldwell? Are you the reason Caldwell hates Grandfather so intensely? What happened to you before I was born? I am sorry if you loved him, but I must make him pay for hurting Grandfather," she vowed sincerely.

It was nearing eight o'clock when Mace knocked on the front door. Rana smiled at him and invited him inside.

"I don't think that's a good idea with your grandfather gone. We don't want people talking about us. I was just making sure you're all right," he explained.

Rana looked confused. "Is it not the plan to have them do so?"

Mace looked at her oddly, then grinned. "Yes, but not that way. It's fine for us to be seen outside together, but it isn't considered nice for a lady to entertain a man when she's alone."

She reflected upon his words, then reasoned, "Why not? If we do nothing wrong, why would they think badly of us?"

"Not badly, Rana, just . . ." He hesitated as he sought the right words. "It just isn't done like that down here. A man and woman just don't spend time alone in this situation."

"Travis and Rana spent time alone in this house," she argued.

"But you're family. That's different."

"No, Mace, we are not family," she corrected him.

Mace looked disconcerted. "I don't know how to

explain this to you, Rana. I just know it ain't right for me to come inside tonight."

"You whites have many strange ways, Mace Hunter," she teased.

"You whites?" he echoed mischievously.

She laughed, then asked, "Did you capture any of the rustlers?"

"Not a da . . . one, Rana. I sent a few men on ahead, but I think that trail was marked to mislead us. That makes me wonder what those bas . . . outlaws are planning tonight." Mace warned himself to calm down. He was so tired and annoyed that his tongue was hanging loose.

"You think the trail was a trick?" she inquired.

He nodded his blond head. "Yep, and I plan to put out lots of guards tonight. So if you hear anything, stay in the house and keep the doors and windows locked. And keep a gun nearby."

"It is too hot to close doors and windows, Mace."

"Then keep lights on in all the rooms so my men can see anybody sneaking around the house."

"I will. I am a light sleeper, and I can defend myself. Do not worry," she entreated confidently.

"I know you can take care of yourself. Travis told me how you and Nate fought off those deserters on the trail and how you saved his life. That's the only reason I'm not overly worried about you. He's a damn lucky man to have you, and I'm lucky he's my friend." Mace kissed her on the cheek then and left.

Nathan arrived home late the next afternoon and told Rana that the legal work had been set in motion and that the lawyer would notify him when it was time to pick up the papers in Dallas. He explained that it was a complicated matter, but he was confident it could be handled by the lawyer he had chosen.

Mace joined them for supper soon afterward and gave Nathan a detailed report of the recent events. "I can't explain it, Nate, but I was sure something was up last night. Who knows? Maybe they're watching our every move and knew we'd returned to the ranch and posted guards. Dang it! That Caldwell is a sly varmint. Doesn't look as if there's any outguessing him."

"He'll make an error one day, Mace, and when he does, we'll catch him, legally or otherwise. Presently I'm worried about Travis; if he made it, we should have gotten word from him by now." He glanced at Rana and frowned, annoyed with himself for his slip.

Rana smiled and squeezed his arm. "He'll be fine, Grandfather," she encouraged him tenderly, though she too felt something was terribly wrong. They had decided on a prearranged message to let Nathan and Rana know he had succeeded and was on his way home. There were less than two weeks remaining until their deadline, and the message had not arrived. Rana did not want to think about what that could mean.

After supper, Rana and Mace stood on the front porch in view of the hands near the bunkhouse and cook house, as if they were sweethearts sharing each other's company. As they talked, Mace slipped his arm around her shoulder and she rested her head against his chest. "Do you think he's safe, Mace?" she asked worriedly.

Mace comfortingly tightened his embrace for a moment, then answered, "I'm sure he is, Rana. We'll hear from him tomorrow; you'll see. Travis is cunning and smart; nothing can happen to him."

She looked up at him, her eyes pleading for reassurance. "But he's had time to send us word by now. Why has it not come?"

"I don't know, Rana, but it will." He kissed her forehead and snuggled her against him. He would not tell

471

her that he was plenty worried too. If Travis hadn't reached the Indian camp, retrieved the gold, and left by now . . . Mace sighed heavily. He almost wished Nathan hadn't told him Travis's secret plans. Damn, he cursed to himself, it was a crazy, dangerous scheme, and it had little chance of success. Even if Travis got the gold from the Indians, how could he get it back here safely by himself, and in time to save the ranch? Mace knew Travis could do most anything he set his mind to, but this task might be too much, even for Travis.

Clarissa sat staring at her father's back. Damn you, you bastard, she silently cursed him. He had refused to let Wes and his men go near Nathan's ranch last night. In fact, he had told them to lie low until he gave further orders. She wasn't fooled. She knew he hadn't wanted Rana Michaels frightened or injured. She had seen the way her father had behaved after Rana's visit yesterday—like a dog in heat! The more she thought about his weakness for Marissa and Rana, the angrier she became, and the more her hatred and bitterness increased. "Papa, I don't understand this hesitation. You should make every move possible while Travis is gone."

Harrison turned and looked at her. He scowled. "Stop trying to run my affairs, daughter. I know what I'm doing."

"What are you doing, Papa?" she asked sarcastically.

"I'm keeping them off balance, girl. When they think I will strike, I don't. When they think I won't, I do. Mace Hunter wasn't fooled by that false trail; he was back at the ranch before dusk. I sent Fargo over there to nose around. He said they had guards posted all over the place. If I had let Wes and the boys go there, there would have been bodies to throw suspicion on me. I sent Wes and Jack down to Abilene to make sure Nate wasn't down there trying to borrow money. If he visited any of those banks, I'll know by tomorrow, and that'll keep those two busy a couple of days. You just do as I tell you, and keep your little nose out of my business."

"How can I help you, Papa, if I don't know everything?"

"You know all you need to know, girl."

"What are you planning to do next?" she persisted.

"I don't know yet, but nothing for the next few days. Let 'em relax a little and drop their guards; then I'll strike again." Harrison looked at the hostile expression on Clarissa's face. He did not want her around when he brought Marissa—no, Rana—into this house to live. He detested his daughter and wanted to punish her, and he knew that the best way to hurt a woman was to degrade her. "I need you to do something for me, girl."

"Anything, Papa," she replied sullenly, rashly.

"Fargo is getting restless. Why don't you give him a reason to hang around and stay loyal to us? We need him, Clarissa."

"*We,*" "*us,*" her furious mind echoed antagonistically. "What kind of reason would hold him here, Papa?" she asked with what innocence she could muster.

"You know he has a hankering for you, girl. Why don't I go into town tonight while you invite him here? I won't come back until midnight," he informed her meaningfully.

"If I invite him, Papa, he'll get the wrong idea; then I'll have him hanging around me and the house all the time."

"They why don't I send him to the house with a message. You can offer him a drink while you read it, then let things proceed from there. You know he isn't gonna tell me he was sneaking into my daughter's bed while I was gone. You'll spark his interest, and he'll hang around waiting for another chance to get into your bloomers. Come on, girl, you're no silly virgin. You might as well enjoy your work. Before long, you'll be chained to a husband, so you'd best have fun now."

"Are you sure about this, Papa?"

"Just do whatever needs doing to keep Fargo around."

Late that afternoon, Fargo rode into town with Harrison. They stopped at the mercantile store so that Harrison could purchase some items for Fargo to deliver to Clarissa, and, shortly thereafter, Fargo was knocking at Clarissa's door, his arms full of bundles.

Clarissa answered the door in her night wrap, her hair pinned up and damp from a bath. "Fargo," she squealed as if surprised. "I thought Papa had forgotten something and had returned. I knew he said he wouldn't be home until midnight."

"He asked me to give you these things from the store," the man told her, making no attempt to keep his eyes off the way the thin garment clung to her wet body.

Aptly prepared for Fargo's arrival, Clarissa had made certain her hands would be full when she opened the door. She smiled beguilingly, her mirror and hairbrush held up before her, and asked, "Would you mind bringing them inside?" As he kicked the door closed and followed her, she pointed to the settee and said, "You can place them there. You're very kind to do this for me and Papa. Would you like a drink? I'm sure your throat is dry. This weather is so hot."

"Don't mind if I do, Miss Clarissa. Whiskey, if it's no trouble."

"Oh, it's no trouble at all." She walked to the liquor cabinet and pretended to search for the whiskey, which she had hidden earlier near the back. She knew Fargo was staring at her and becoming aroused. "Here it is," she announced and turned to him with a smile.

474

Fargo joined her and took the glass. When he downed it in two gulps, she refilled it, then glanced toward the door and whispered, "You won't tell Papa if I sneak a drink, will you?"

"'Course not," Fargo replied, filling his glass again.

After several drinks, Clarissa pretended to be drunk. When Fargo was filling his glass again, she casually loosened her sash, causing her wrap to gape slightly. "I think I'll find something cooler to put on," she announced. "This old rag is roasting me." She moved toward her room, knowing he would follow, and he did.

Clarissa struggled with the garment as if she were having trouble getting it off. "Let me help you," Fargo offered, removing it. He bent to kiss her neck and began running his hands over her body.

Soon he had her on the bed and was enjoying her to the fullest, and, to her surprise, she felt her body responding. They slaked their lascivious appetites until it was nearing midnight, then Fargo covered Clarissa's naked form and closed her door as he left the room.

Clarissa grinned as she heard him clearing away the "evidence" of his "seduction." She stretched and yawned. Fargo wasn't bad in bed, she mused, especially in the dark where she didn't have to look at his pockmarked face and squinty eyes. She thought about the times Raymond had forced Marissa to bed that ugly vulture, and she laughed. Perhaps the next time she did this favor for her father, she would ask Fargo a few questions about those degrading times. With a few accurate facts, she might be able to stir little Rana's memory . . .

By dusk the next day, Nathan, Rana, and Mace realized they would not be hearing any word from Travis for at least one more day. It was a very bad sign, for time was running out for them. Two hands had been ambushed and killed that afternoon, and a few of the others were getting worried. Alarmed by this added peril and dismayed by the extra work, Cody Slade suggested that the Sunday wedding he and Mary Beth had planned for tomorrow be postponed, but no one would allow it.

"If you don't do it now," Mace warned, "you might lose her. From now on, we'll post guards day and night around the ranch. I promise you she'll be fine over there with the Raineses and Davises. You've got everything set up in your new house. Do it, Cody."

"Mace is right, son," Nathan added. "Her pa is willing right now. But if Harry casts his eye on her again, it'll be too late for you."

Rana spoke up too. "Everything is ready, Cody Slade. How can you make her sad by refusing to show your courage and love?"

Todd told him, "Don't worry, Cody. Rachel and Lettie will look out for her. They keep loaded rifles ready all the time."

"That's what I'm talking about, Todd. That ain't no way to live."

"It won't be this way much longer," Todd replied.

"Then I should wait until it's better, and safe here for her."

"What you should do," Nathan advised sternly, "is snap her up while she's there for the taking. Listen, son, you know how Harry takes whatever he wants. You'd best claim her as your wife before he decides he wants her again."

"I guess all of you are right. We'll do it as soon as the preacher gets here after church tomorrow. Where do you want guards posted?"

Mace went over the evening's assignments, then everyone left except Nathan and Rana, who talked a few minutes before turning in.

*　　*　　*

Try as she might, Rana could not settle down. She lay across her bed, thinking distressing thoughts. In only twelve days her grandfather might lose his land and his heart. If Travis was not on his way back by now, he could not possibly make that deadline. And if he was on his way home, he would have sent word to them from one of the forts along the trail.

She went to her window, pushed against the thin covering, and gazed at the heavens to pray for her love's survival. He had taken such a great risk in going after that treacherous gold, she reflected.

Only a sliver of moon was showing and it was very dark outside. On such concealing nights, Oglala warriors had made secret raids on enemy camps, using skills and stealth she had persuaded her Indian brother to teach her. Long ago, on a dare, she had sneaked into an enemy camp, stolen a war shield, and sneaked home without getting caught; Lone Wolf had been furious with her and had tried to pretend he was not impressed, but she knew he had been secretly pleased that she had learned her lessons so well. He had taught her defense and escape and disguise using methods that had begun as amusing games, but there had come a time when her skills exceeded his, and his male pride had been injured. Often he had told her that these skills and practices would prepare her to meet and conquer her true destiny one day, and now she knew that the day had arrived.

Rana's keen mind began to whirl with daring plans. Saving this ranch was vital to her, because it was so important to the men she loved. She could live anywhere with them, but they loved this land and were a part of it. She truly believed it would be wrong and cowardly of her to do nothing while their enemy cleverly defeated them. If there were only a slim chance of recovering that money . . . She would not allow such speculations to continue. Her mind was set.

The daring redhead slipped into the dark pants she wore for riding and working around the house, then pulled on her darkest shirt. Taking another one of similar color, she secured it around her head to hide her flaming tresses. Strapping on her knife sheath, she concealed another, smaller blade in the long pocket that had been sewn into her knee-high moccasin, for she knew a gun might make noise and total silence was imperative. Remembering the bow and arrows in Travis's closet and confident of her skill with them, she went to fetch the quiet, lethal weapons. Cleverly and cautiously she obliterated any markings that would expose them as being Sioux, in case she was compelled to use one or more that night.

Perhaps she would not be able to reach the enticing safe or open it, but she could "nose around," as Travis called it. The more they learned, the more they would be prepared to deal with Harrison Caldwell when the moment of challenge came. She would not take any foolish chances or risk being captured, for she could imagine what that evil man would do or demand if she were to fall into his power.

The Caldwell ranch was fifteen miles away, but she could not risk taking a horse to ride there. Though she realized her stamina was not at its peak after having lazed around this house for three weeks, she knew how to travel across country and how to pace herself, thanks to Lone Wolf's training. Over this kind of terrain, she estimated she could travel a mile in ten minutes, which, allowing time for caution, would bring her there in less than three hours. Even if she could not steal a horse to ride most of the way home before releasing him, she would have time to get back before dawn.

Determined not to waste another moment, Rana climbed out her window and slipped around the house. Because she knew where Mace had posted the Rocking C

478

guards, she could easily avoid them, and, once she had done so, she took the shortest route to Caldwell's home. Gingerly adhering to her plan, she arrived at the Circle *C* Ranch within the time frame she had set for herself. Within the concealment of several trees, she rested as she studied the area around the house and the other structures.

It was Saturday night and Rana assumed that most of Caldwell's hands would be in town, for if her suspicions were correct, this ranch had nothing to fear or protect from the villains who had raided other ranches and were currently attacking her grandfather's. The men who were around all seemed to be gathered in the bunkhouse, which Caldwell had placed a good distance from his home. Rana began to slip from tree to tree as she circled the house. There were no lanterns burning upstairs, which indicated that either no one was up there or those who were were in bed. There were several lanterns burning downstairs and cautiously she peered into those windows. The kitchen and parlor were empty, but she found Caldwell sitting behind his desk in his office, counting money and making notes in a large book. As she surveyed the room, she noted with mounting excitement that he was alone and the safe was open.

She sat down behind thick bushes, knowing she could do nothing but wait, watch, and listen. Because of the location of his desk and the office door, it would be impossible for her to steal into the house and into his office unobserved. She needed a miracle. *Help me, Wakan Tanka*, she prayed fervently.

Time passed and Rana was about to give up hope of any success that night. Suddenly she heard the sounds of several horses galloping into the yard followed by the low muttering of men talking. She strained to catch the words but could not. Cautiously she peered around the edge of the window and watched Harrison rise to answer the

479

summons at his front door. Slipping to the corner of the house, she saw him join the men and begin a conversation. She assumed he did not want them to enter his office and see the tempting money on his desk. From his casual stance, she could tell he was relaxed, as if he were in no hurry to get the talk over with quickly.

Furtively she returned to his office window and climbed inside. She hurried to the safe and pushed wide the door to examine its contents. To the rear on the bottom shelf was a pair of saddlebags with rattle-snakes carved on the flaps. Seizing them, she fumbled nervously with the stubborn straps. She knew her time was short, yet her quivering fingers almost refused to work. Swiftly she removed the numerous, tightly bound packets she found within, cramming them into her roomy shirt and positioning them around her waist as she did so. Noting the many, small, decorative pillows on the settee in his office, she quietly retrieved two and stuffed one inside each saddlebag so that the missing contents might go unnoticed for a time. Then she refastened the straps and replaced the saddlebags. After carefully returning the safe door to its former position, she climbed out the window and concealed herself once more.

Her chest rose and fell rapidly with the forceful pounding of her heart, and she found it difficult to control her erratic respiration or ignore the dryness in her mouth. Her hands were trembling wildly and she felt as limp as a freshly skinned ermine pelt. No sense of power or smugness filled her; instead, she was almost overwhelmed by fear and tension. It was too soon for her to experience pride or relief or the sheer joy of success, for she was not out of danger yet. She had the stolen money, but she had to get away without being caught, stuffed as she was with the evidence of her "robbery." She prayed Caldwell would not look inside the saddlebags that night.

Feeling weak and shaky, she decided to risk riding home on a horse she would take from the corral farthest from the house and stable. She realized she would have to make her way slowly, for the paper money made a crinkling noise as she moved. Rana knew she would also have to wait until Caldwell's men had left the yard before attempting her trek to the corral, and, as she waited there in the darkness with the money packets tickling her waist, she gradually began to compose herself.

Eventually she heard Harrison returning to his office with one of the men. There the lawyer counted out some money and handed it to the other man, saying, "Pay the men for that excellent job, and make sure they hide those branding irons. We don't want Kincade or any of his boys finding them."

The other man replied scornfully, "Kincade ain't been around for weeks. What'cha think he's up to, boss?"

"I don't know, but very soon it won't matter. In two weeks the Rocking *C* Ranch will be mine," he boasted cockily. "When Monroe and Hayes return, make sure they come to see me immediately. I want to make certain they understand my orders and follow them to the letter." Harrison glanced up at his hireling and scoffed, "That Monroe bears close watching; he's an arrogant, dangerous son of a bitch. The damned idiot actually thought he had Mace Hunter fooled by that schoolboy trail he laid so he could raid Nate's stable. Hell, I really can't depend on anybody except you and Silas!" he lied to flatter the man. "Keep your eyes and ears open wide. I can't have any of my men's bodies showing up in the wrong places. I've worked too long and hard building this empire, and my final victory is at hand. I'll be damned if I allow some two-bit gunslinger to ruin things for me. I don't want any more burnings or shootings. It'll be my property soon and my cowpunchers. For now, I only

481

need to scare them and harass them from time to time. There's no reason to get real nasty unless Crandall finds another loan and gets stubborn about selling out, which he won't."

"Where's Miss Clarissa tonight?" the man asked in an eager tone.

"She went to that barn dance in town. She should be heading home soon. It wouldn't hurt if you rode that way to escort her home, if you don't mind," Harrison suggested nonchalantly.

"Don't mind at all, boss. I'll hide those branding irons in the barn, then be on my way," Fargo answered cheerfully.

"I'll walk you to the door," Harrison insisted.

The two men left the room. Fargo went outside and paid the waiting men, who then rode toward town to make the most of what was left of Saturday night by buying women and whiskey at the Fort Worth saloons. Whistling, Fargo headed for the barn with his horse's reins in one hand and the illegal branding irons in the other while, inside the main house, Harrison poured himself a drink and sat down to daydream about the vast empire he would soon control.

Without stopping to weigh the consequences, Rana set off at a cautious pace to follow the ugly man to the barn and see where he would hide the offending irons. She peered inside and watched him lift several boards to conceal the curved irons, which reminded her of the sliver of moon overhead and which easily altered the Rocking *C* brand into a Circle *C*. It was too simple for Caldwell to change their brand to his, she realized with sickening clarity. She would have to convince her grandfather to change his brand completely and into a pattern that Harrison Caldwell could not so readily alter. She moved out of sight as Fargo left the building and rode off on his horse, eager to encounter Clarissa Caldwell on her way home from town. Rana made no attempt to steal the irons, for she knew they would have to be found on Caldwell's property if they were going to serve as undeniable evidence against the villain. At least she knew where they were hidden and could tell Travis and Nathan, who would then tell the sheriff.

Rana made her way to the last corral and chose a horse. To conceal the fact of his theft, she left the gate open for others to slip out as well. She patted him for several moments and allowed him to get accustomed to her scent and touch; then she gently seized his mane and led him away from the inhabited area. He was sluggish and old, and because she was not intimidating, he went with her docilely. She mounted him bareback and guided him into a slow walk until they were out of hearing range; then she galloped toward the boundary line between the ranches. There she dismounted and left him nibbling grass, with no saddle marking to suggest he had been ridden.

Rana walked the rest of the way home, which took her over an hour in the mid-July heat. Her entire body was moist by the time she sighted the ranch, and she could feel the money sticking to her sweaty flesh. Not a breeze stirred to ease her discomfort. She was so weary, so thirsty, and she would have liked nothing more than to have been able to head for the river, strip off her clothes, and go for a soothing swim. But she did not dare. Skillfully avoiding the ranch guards, she slipped into the house and quietly made her way to Travis's room. Entering his closet, she closed the door and lit a candle. Carefully she climbed the wooden rungs that led to the attic. There she looked around for a place to hide the money until she could expose her daring deed to her grandfather.

A black trunk was positioned in one corner. She went to it and, withdrawing the packets from her shirt, stuffed the money behind it, assuming anyone who might come to search their house would look inside the trunk, not behind it. She removed the dark shirt from her head and crammed it on top of the packets to conceal them. Then she immediately proceeded to the water closet and took a long bath, hoping she would not make enough noise to awaken her grandfather. Either she succeeded or he awoke and assumed she was only trying to cool off from the stifling heat. Whichever the case, he never came to check on her.

Refreshed from the bath, she stretched out on her bed, naked and damp. It was done, she was home safely, and the money was recovered. It was nearing four o'clock in the morning and she was exhausted. Snuggling her old doll into her arms, she closed her eyes and was asleep in moments.

Travis continued his long journey between the Dakota Territory and Texas, traveling mainly at night. He found it was more comfortable to ride at night than during the heat of the day and he could more easily avoid the trouble that had begun to brew fiercely in this area if he rode under the protection of darkness. There were only twelve days remaining in which he had to cover a seemingly impossible distance. He had slept little and rested even less, but he forced himself to keep pressing onward. The telegraph lines had been cut by hostile Indians near two forts at which he had halted, and he could not afford to lose any more valuable time by seeking a place to send a telegram home. He could only hope that Nathan and Rana would realize there was a good reason why they hadn't heard from him.

Chapter Sixteen

The morning of Cody and Mary Beth's wedding
dawned bright and clear, and the beauty of the day caused
Rana to look forward to her second joining with Travis,
which she prayed would take place very soon. Activity in
the house had been hectic all morning, with Rachel
coming over to help with the preparations and Mary Beth
nervously dressing and waiting for the ceremony, and
Rana had not been given a chance to reveal her actions of
the night before. She knew her grandfather would be
furious with her at first, then proud and pleased over her
clever victory.

The day was cooler than the past few scorching ones
had been, and the sky was a tranquil blue, as if nature
were blessing the special ceremony that was now taking
place. Rana was wearing her loveliest gown in a flattering
shade of sapphire, and she received many admiring stares
and compliments. The defiant, daring Wild Wind seemed
lost forever in the poised, demure Rana Michaels who
charmed and deluded all present. With the radiant,
exquisite Rana nearby, very few kept their attention on
the pretty bride, but Cody and Mary Beth were too
entranced with each other to notice that they were not
the center of attention on their special day.

485

All morning and during the wedding ceremony, Rana had tried to conceal her apprehensions about Travis and about the grim situation with Harrison Caldwell, for she did not want anything to spoil Cody and Mary Beth's joining day. Yet, she was so worried about her love, and this silence increased her anxiety. For over two weeks she had told herself Travis could do anything and succeed, but panic was slowly eroding her confidence. Some perils were beyond even the bravest and cleverest man's prowess and power.

As soon as the talking and joking and celebrating began, Rana slipped away to her room to release some of the strain of her pretense. She could not imagine her existence without Travis Kincade, and she prayed for his return with all her might. How she wished he would ride up this very moment! The gold and the ranch were nothing compared to his life, she reflected despondently. She tried to tell herself she should be angry with him for leaving on such a dangerous journey, and alone. She should have gone with him! There might have been some way she could have helped him, or saved him. She remembered how she had aided him on the trail home, and she worried that another such difficulty might befall him and there would be no one around to rescue or assist him. She desperately wanted to believe he was safe and well, but if he was, why hadn't he contacted them? There was no way of knowing where he was on the trail, so she could not go searching for him as she had threatened and promised.

Mace knocked on her door and she let him come inside. "What's wrong, Rana?" he asked solicitously. "You've been in here a long time. Why don't you come back to the party? It'll be over soon. Has anyone said or done anything to upset you?"

"No, everyone has been kind to me," she replied sadly. "Why haven't we heard from Travis? How can I laugh and smile when he could be injured or in danger somewhere?"

Mace grasped her hand and squeezed it gently. Smiling, he encouraged, "You haven't known him as long as I have, Rana. I've seen him get out of pits and traps no other man could have escaped. He rescued you from the Indians, didn't he?" he reminded her.

"This time he is dealing with the Hunkpapas," she argued.

"But last time he defeated them," Mace returned.

Rana walked to her window and looked outside. "That was long ago and another helped him escape. What about those two men who attacked him before my grandfather found him nearly dead?"

"But your grandfather did find him, Rana, and saved his life, just like you saved his life when he was shot."

"That is what I mean, Mace. Each time someone helped him. This time he rides and faces evil alone. Something is wrong."

"Sometimes a man needs help, Rana, and other times he must face his challenges alone. I know he's all right and he'll return soon. You must have courage and faith. I promise you, there's a good reason he hasn't contacted us. You and Travis believe in the Great Spirit. Do you honestly think He would let you two be defeated?"

"The Great Spirit is a mystery. Sometimes His will does not match ours. Sometimes He does not answer prayers, or does not answer them as we wish. If He answered all prayers, my Indian people would not be suffering and dying at the hands of the whites. There are many things I do not understand."

"Locking yourself in this room and worrying yourself sick isn't going to change things, Rana. Come back outside and try to enjoy yourself."

As this conversation was taking place in Rana's room, Harrison Caldwell and two of his men were approaching

Nathan's stable on horseback. When they reached their destination, they reined in their horses and arrogantly waited for Nathan to come and speak with them. A hush fell over the wedding party and all eyes focused on the malevolent rancher. Nathan glared at the offensive man, angry at his bold intrusion. He told the others to ignore them and to continue with the happy celebration while he went to see what Caldwell wanted.

"What can I do for you, Harry? You can see we're busy," Nathan remarked coldly as his contemptuous gaze swept over the man who was trying to destroy his existence. "Surely you didn't expect an invitation to Cody and Mary Beth's wedding?" he scoffed pointedly.

Harrison laughed. "Somebody left one of my corral gates open last night and some of my horses got loose. If you find any strays, I'd appreciate your sending them over with one of your hands."

Nathan frowned. "If I have any extra time after fighting off these filthy rustlers and fence cutters, I won't use it to round up your horses. Why don't you send your new gunslingers out to gather 'em up?"

Harrison chuckled again. "If you'd hire yourself a few good men, you wouldn't be having so much trouble, Nate. I heard your men were robbed on the way home from Sedalia. Is that why you're being so nasty and inhospitable? Are you broke? If you wish, I could make you a personal loan, with . . . say . . . this ranch as collateral? Or anything else of value you might own," he suggested, looking over the group of revelers for Rana.

"You dirty bastard! Get your ass off my ranch and take your men with you! I'll die before letting you and your kind run me off my land. Our fight isn't over yet; I've still got eleven days to pay off my loan, you vulture."

"There's no way you can come up with that much money by a week from Thursday, so give it up, Nate. I'm a rich and powerful man; I'll make you a good offer. If you wait 'til the auction, I'll be the highest bidder and you won't have anything left. You're a fool not to bargain with me now, old friend. You don't want that beautiful granddaughter of yours thrown out in the cold, so to speak."

Nathan warned, "Leave my little Rana out of this! Lord's always provided for us in the past, and He'll do so this time."

"I wouldn't count on Him answering your prayers any time soon, Nate. I'm your only hope, and you aren't being very polite or grateful."

"And I won't be, no matter what happens around here. You've been gobbling up ranches for years, but you won't get mine. Mighty strange that the ranches that have trouble are the ones you want. Somebody's got to stop your greed, and I pray it'll be me."

Harrison eyed Nathan intently, then decided Nathan couldn't have had anything to do with the daring robbery at his home. *Robbery?* Harrison's warped mind echoed the ironic term. A man couldn't actually steal his own money. If Travis Kincade had been around, he would have known who to blame. But he had seen and handled the money since Travis's departure. Or had that cunning devil really gone? Harrison scolded himself for being so foolish. Travis would have to be gone; after all, he had sent Clarissa a telegram a few days before from Springfield, Missouri.

No, Harrison concluded, Nathan wasn't in on the theft of his own cattle money. He had no one with the skill or daring to pull off such a job, and he appeared too genuinely scared about losing his ranch to have that money back in his possession. This mysterious matter would need more study and investigation. The only person with access to his safe . . . No, surely his little bitch of a daughter wouldn't dare trick him!

"If you're finished staring at me, Harry, git off my

489

land. It ain't yours yet, and it won't be if I can help it."

Harrison's eyes drifted to the party in Nathan's front yard. He saw Rana leave the house with Mace Hunter. Gracefully she descended the steps on his arm, looking exquisite and delicate in a stunning gown. She appeared a little nervous, as if she did not wish to join the party and was being coerced into it. Perhaps crowds and strange occasions alarmed the Indian princess. She glanced toward the stable where he was still sitting astride his horse. She smiled and waved a greeting, then her cheerfulness faded suddenly as Mace spoke to her. She glanced his way again, a curious look on her face. Evidently Mace had disparaged him. After he took over this ranch, he would see to it that Mace Hunter couldn't find another job for a hundred miles!

Mace guided her over to the bride and groom, but she kept peering at him past the cowboy's sturdy body. She looked as if Mace had told her something that she could not quite believe and accept, and as if she were trying to determine the truth simply by looking at him. He wanted to believe that it troubled her to think those unknown charges could be accurate. Then Todd Raines captured her attention with his smiles and chatter. Harrison grinned sardonically, deciding that Todd was as smitten with Rana now as the younger Todd had been with her mother. Too bad, because Marissa had actually started falling for the handsome cowpoke years ago . . .

"No need to go studying Mary Beth now, Harry. It's too late. She's married to Cody Slade, and out of your filthy reach."

"Oh, I wasn't eyeing that little country lass. Who could notice her with Rana Michaels standing there? She's a beauty, Nate, a real beauty, more so even than her mother. Be seeing you around soon," he remarked, tipping his hat and riding away.

*   *   *

The celebration had ended and everyone had gone but Mace whom Nathan had asked to stay. Nathan told Rana he wanted to have a word with her, and now he paced the sitting room briefly before halting to look at her. He shook his head and exhaled loudly between parted lips. "Rana, I thought we'd explained to you about Harry. I don't want you smiling at him or going near him or being nice to him. Otherwise you might have him craving you as much as this ranch. He's bad, girl, real bad. He'd just as soon hurt or kill a woman as a man. Please, girl, steer clear of him."

"Your grandfather's right," Mace added. "Everyone noticed how friendly you were to him. In these parts, Rana, a man—or woman—is known by the company he keeps. You're new here, so people will wonder why Nathan Crandall's granddaughter is friendly with his enemy."

Rana looked from man to man, then smiled mischievously. "You must not worry. I will not be kind to him again; it was only to trick him. He will think you and grandfather told me bad things about him today. I did not wish him to see that I know the truth about him. He rode here to see how grandfather would look and behave today. You fooled him. I fooled him. He will think another stole the money."

Before Rana could take a breath and continue, Nathan asked in confusion, "Stole what money? What are you talking about, girl?"

"The money he stole from you, Grandfather. It was taken from his safe last night, from the saddlebags with rattlesnakes on them."

Mace stared at her oddly and inquired, "How could you possibly know about a robbery at Caldwell's place?"

"I took the money. It belongs to Grandfather. It is hidden in a room above us. He wished to see if you would act the same today. He does not suspect that you have the money or that I took it. Who would think a young girl

491

could sneak into his home and take the money?"

Nathan and Mace were gaping at her. Mace argued, "That isn't possible, Rana. You couldn't have gotten off this ranch last night, or gotten into Caldwell's safe."

Rana laughed. "You forget, Mace Hunter, I was trained as a hunter and warrior." Without boasting, she related how she had stolen off the ranch, onto Caldwell's, into his office, and into his safe to carry out her daring scheme, then explained how she had secretly returned home. "Come, I will show you the money," she offered.

In the attic, Nathan gaped at the money in the same way he had gaped at her earlier. "This isn't possible, girl."

She hugged him and vowed, "It is, Grandfather. I did not take the saddlebags with rattlesnakes because he would have noticed they were gone. I can show you where he hides the branding irons to steal your cattle. You must not let your voice and face tell him you have the money, or he will try to take it again. You can save the ranch, Grandfather."

Mace quickly counted the money, and the amount matched that which had been stolen. "It's all here, Nate. By Heaven, she actually did it!" he remarked in astonishment as the reality settled in on him.

She nodded and confessed, "Yes, it is so. I was very frightened, but I took no chances. It is done and the danger is past."

"Took no chances?" Nathan scoffed. "Girl, you could have been arrested or killed. Why did you pull something crazy like this?"

She looked into his troubled gaze and replied softly, "Because I love you, Grandfather, and I do not wish you to lose this land that you love. He is our enemy and must be defeated. We have not heard from Travis. I feared he would not return with the gold before your time was lost. I did not wish to anger you, only help you."

Nathan embraced her tightly. "I know, and I love you too, girl," he murmured in a choked voice. "But I could have gotten both you and Travis killed trying to help me get money to save this ranch. I love this place, Rana, but not as much as you two. Harry must have checked those saddlebags this morning and found my money missing." Suddenly Nathan laughed. "I bet he's as mad as a cat with his tail stuck in the door. And with Travis gone, he won't suspect a thing."

"He will if you start acting cocky," Mace warned. "You and Rana will both be in danger if he discovers you have that money back."

Nathan nodded in agreement. "I'll hold it 'til the last minute before I settle that loan. Now I can pay the boys, Mace."

"Not yet, Nate. If you go spreading money around, you might as well admit to Caldwell you have the money. The boys will wait."

Nathan handed Mace some cash. "I'll give you a little money just in case somebody needs a few bits. We'll leave it hidden up here in case Caldwell decides to have some of his boys check my safe. I think I'll leave it unlocked so they won't blast it open."

Mace suggested, "Now that you've got the money and know where those branding irons are, we could start looking for the McFarlands and Kellys. We'll need some witnesses to support our evidence."

Nathan nodded in rising excitement. "You handle everything for me, Mace. We don't want Harry getting too nervous now that he's lost this money, so we'd best lie low and keep on like we've been doing. As for you, girl, don't go near Caldwell or his place again."

"I will stay away from him, Grandfather, and I will not be nice again. But there is more you must know," she began, then told them about her visit to the Caldwell ranch several days earlier.

Mace looked over the exquisite girl who deceptively appeared so fragile. "You utterly amaze me, woman. Travis isn't going to believe this when he gets home." Mace chuckled. "No, I suppose he will; he's seen you in action before. At least we don't have to worry about you taking care of yourself or helping out."

"I must look like nothing more than a weak woman to all others. No one must see or guess my skills, for they may be needed again."

"You're right. Besides, who would believe the truth? Any chance there's another woman like you around?" Mace asked and they all laughed.

Clarissa returned from visiting and eating with friends after church. She was all smiles, thinking that after only one more Sunday, she would sweep into that church as the owner of a vast Texas cattle empire. She halted abruptly at the parlor door to question her father's expression.

"You know anything about the money missing from my safe?" he asked bluntly to shock her into exposing herself if she were guilty.

She was taken by surprise and bewildered. "What are you talking about, Papa? You know I never take money from the cash box without your permission."

"I'm not talking about the cash box, Clarissa. Nathan's money is missing from those saddlebags in the safe."

"Missing? But how, Papa? The safe is always locked." Her gaze widened, then narrowed. "You aren't suggesting that I took it?"

"I don't know what happened to it, but it's gone. I was going to use a little of it to pay Monroe and Hayes this afternoon. I opened the flaps to find pillows from my settee stuffed inside them. All I know is, the money was there last Saturday."

494

"But who could have taken it, and how? Surely Nathan doesn't have it back?" she demanded angrily.

"I'm sure he doesn't. I rode over there today and he's scared stiff about losing his ranch."

Before he finished talking, Clarissa interjected, "You went to Nathan's ranch during that wedding! What will people think, Papa?"

"Exactly what I told them; we had some horses get loose last night and we were tracking them down. Nate couldn't fool me, daughter; he's plenty worried. They were having a real nice party for Cody and Mary Beth. She looked right pretty, if anybody noticed her with Rana Michaels standing there. Strike me down, if she isn't the most beautiful woman alive. She would make me a fine wife," he suggested shockingly.

"You can't mean that, Papa!" Clarissa shrieked. "Don't start dreaming about Marissa's daughter. You can't have her."

"And why is that, my jealous daughter?" he asked sarcastically.

Clarissa knew this was not the time to use her ace in the hole, so she replied, "Because Nathan would never allow it. She's a little savage, Papa. She'll humiliate you before your friends and clients."

He laughed. "She isn't as uneducated as you seem to think, Clarissa. She was ravishing today. I think you've got something to worry about over there. You sure Travis isn't hiding around here somewhere? He's the only one with the guts and wits to steal that money."

"Don't be foolish, Papa. I received his telegram the other day. He couldn't possibly have gotten home by now. You said you had the money last week, so the timing is all wrong for Travis to be involved."

"What about Monroe and Hayes? You think they have enough brains and courage to pull something like this?" he speculated.

495

"I thought you sent them to Abilene. Have they returned?" she asked uncomfortably, not wanting Wes around without her knowledge.

"They should return today. It's hard to believe somebody could get into my home and safe without anyone seeing a thing!"

"What about Silas, Papa? Or that Fargo? They're around all the time, and you could have left your safe open by mistake."

"They wouldn't dare rob me or try to trick me," he scoffed.

"You set Fargo up to deceive you with me, Papa. How can you be sure that's the only time he's tried it?" she reasoned, having no further use for the repulsive man after her bout with him the night before.

"Taking my daughter behind my back isn't the same as robbing my safe, girl. But feel free to work the truth out of him if you want. I don't like having somebody around I can't trust, especially when I don't know who the traitor is. You keep your eyes and ears open good."

Clarissa was not deluded; she realized that Harrison was wondering if she were to blame for the theft. From now on, she had to be very careful, for he would be watching her, or having her watched. She believed the most likely person was Silas Stern, their foreman. She looked at her father and suggested, "Why don't I see if Silas knows anything? He's the one who could pull this off with the least trouble, and he has an eye for me."

"You do that, girl, but make sure Fargo doesn't see you and get jealous. And, while you're investigating this matter for me, make sure Fargo and Monroe are whistle clean."

"Papa!" she wailed in frustration. "I can't go bedding all those men at the same time just to ask questions."

"You want us to succeed with our plans, don't you?"

496

"Of course, I do, but—"

"No buts, girl. You have your talents, so put them to use to make sure this situation doesn't get out of control. We're too close to having it all, Clarissa. We can't allow anyone to ruin it for us."

As always, she raged inwardly, he was using his "we" and "us" strategy again! Oh, she would obey his orders, but for her own reasons. If the money was actually gone, she wanted to know who had taken it and how. *If* the money was gone . . .

Monday morning, Nathan refused to let Harrison enter his home to discuss the purchase of his ranch. The two stood on the front porch and argued. "This afternoon, I'm sending a telegram to the Cattlemen's Association in Dallas," Nathan told his unwanted visitor. "If I can't come up with the money to pay off that loan, I'll get them to find me a suitable buyer for the ranch. I won't sell her to the likes of you, Harry."

"You won't have any choice in the matter, Nate. I'll outbid anybody who comes to her auction."

"You mean you'll get those varmints you hired to scare off any other bidders," Nathan accused. "You think I haven't realized that nobody ever bids against you. You got Sam's and Harvey's and Jim's places, but you aren't getting mine. I'll see her burned to the ground first."

"We could come to a satisfactory understanding, Nate. You have needs and I have needs. Why don't we become partners? You sign half of this ranch over to me and let me take your granddaughter as my wife, and I'll pay off your debt. When you get enough money to pay me back, I'll turn my half of the ranch over to you."

"Lord help us, you're completely *loco*, Harry! I

wouldn't let you near my granddaughter, much less marry her. Get off my land!"

"What if Rana doesn't feel the same way, Nate? She might want to become the wife of the richest and most powerful man in this area. What will you have to offer her after next Thursday? Nothing!"

Having overheard their entire conversation, Rana crept out the kitchen door and signaled to Mace, who was heading in from the west pasture and was not yet in view of the porch. She ran toward him and related her cunning idea.

Mace grinned, reached down, lifted her, and set her before him on his horse. They rode leisurely toward the stable with their arms around each other. When Harrison glanced their way, they pretended not to notice him or any others as they kissed. At the stable, Mace eased her feet to the ground and then dismounted. Leading his mount toward the corral and keeping Rana snuggled close to his side, he whispered in amusement, "That should give Caldwell an eyeful and discourage his interest in you."

Rana looked up into his sparkling eyes and grinned. "It is good Travis has a handsome, unmarried friend to play this game with me."

"If Travis weren't my best friend and you were willing, we'd get hitched today," he murmured affectionately and chuckled. "I think we should ride somewhere until Caldwell leaves. We don't want him any madder at you than necessary." When she agreed, they mounted his horse again, this time with her sitting behind him and clinging to his waist, and headed off toward the nearest pond.

When they returned a short while later, Nathan laughed and remarked, "That was a clever trick, girl. You should have seen Harry's face when he saw you two all snuggly and kissy." Nathan then related the details of

Harrison's visit to Mace and the two men once again praised Rana's courage.

Clarissa returned from her shopping in town to make several infuriating discoveries. Harrison had read her second telegram from Travis from Sedalia, Missouri. Her father's jealousy and wrath had been inflamed by the apparent romance between Rana Michaels and Mace Hunter, and he was furious that his attempt to bargain for Rana's hand in marriage had been rejected so peremptorily. In his rage he had ordered Wes and Jackson to poison two water holes on the Crandall ranch.

"Papa, are you insane?" she asked, panting in alarm. "What happens when we take over that ranch? How could you do something so rash? That little slut isn't worth ruining everything!"

"You let me handle my business, girl," he replied sharply. "At least we know Kincade isn't in this area. That's a real sweet message. So he misses you, does he, and can't wait to get home? I'm going to fix Nate good, and that granddaughter of his won't get Mace Hunter. What have you learned about that missing money?"

"I saw Fargo last night and Silas this morning. I don't think either of them were involved. Do you think it's safe for me to fool around with that Wes Monroe or Hayes?" she inquired innocently.

"Do what you have to do, girl. Just find out where that money is," he demanded irascibly. "They should be back at their cabin by now." He watched with a total lack of emotion as his daughter turned on her heel and left the room.

Clarissa went directly to the cabin and asked to see Wes alone. Jackson eyed her curiously, then walked a short distance away. She explained to Wes why she had come to see him, and her reason surprised him.

499

"You mean that old fool's lost the Crandall money? And he sent you here to seduce information out of me? What kind of bastard is he? I told him it was crazy to poison those water holes. The lying bastard said he wanted to make certain nobody else wanted that ranch. And tell me, woman, why is this Kincade sending you telegrams?"

"He's afraid he's going to lose everything, so he's trying to court me to get Papa's holdings through me. I've been faking interest to get information about Nathan's situation."

"Like you're faking with me, maybe?"

"Don't be silly, Wes. If I didn't trust you, would I tell you such things? Papa's real upset over that money—Or, I should say, over who this traitor is. I think he suspects me the most, so we'll have to be really careful from now on. It'll all be over in two weeks. Once I fire Silas and Fargo, I'll be needing a new foreman and guard," she suggested provocatively, reaching over to fondle his chest.

"Who do you think took that money?" Wes probed.

"I don't know. Maybe no one," she declared, thinking aloud. "Maybe Papa's up to something. Silas and Fargo don't have enough courage or cunning to do a job like this. I was hoping it was you, Wes."

"Well, it ain't." Wes thought about the lost money, money he had intended would come to him, one way or another. Something strange was going on . . . His thoughts suddenly veered off in a new, more enticing direction as Clarissa began to disrobe.

Tuesday morning, Mace reported the grim news to Nathan about the poisoned water holes and dead cattle. "I've got Todd and some of the boys fencing them off and Cody's moving the cattle to another pasture. Seems like we made Caldwell real mad yesterday."

"Should I pretend to be nice to him again?" Rana suggested.

"That won't work, girl, 'cause he's seen you with Mace. Anyway, it wouldn't stop him from trying to pull us down. He wants to scare me into accepting his offer for the ranch and for you. We'll stand firm."

Around midnight, the hands were called out to battle fires in two wagons of hay that had arrived too late that afternoon to be unloaded and their contents placed in the barn loft. By the time the flames were discovered, it was too late to save the hay or the wagons. Luckily they had been left in a dirt clearing, which prevented the fire from spreading to nearby structures or the dry grass.

Nathan watched the flames slowly lessen and he cursed Harrison Caldwell. He had not alerted the sheriff to the poisonings and he would not inform him about this fire. It would not do any good, for there was nothing to connect Caldwell to either crime. At least no one had been injured and no structure had been destroyed. Nathan raged against Caldwell's game of harassment and intimidation, and prayed he could withstand it.

So far, two men had been slain, and the Rocking C owner hoped he could prevent any more deaths or destruction. Nathan called together his head men and ordered, "Mace, I want you to post more guards at every vulnerable area on this ranch. Cody, do whatever you can to keep any of the men from getting nervous and quitting like they did at McFarland's place. Todd, you set a man to watch the married houses. Post him near the fire bell so he can sound it if trouble strikes over there. Make sure you tell Rachel and Lettie and Mary Beth to be real careful."

On Wednesday, there were two more fake telegrams

501

from Travis: one sent to Clarissa and one to Nathan, both from St. Louis. The one addressed to Nathan was a trick to persuade Harrison that it was not a ruse at all, for Nathan suspected that Harrison knew about his telegrams and their contents. He hoped so, for both messages made Travis sound depressed and lonely. In them he confessed that he was failing in his tasks and would head home in a few days if nothing looked promising.

By eleven o'clock that night, Rana was so tense she could not rest or sleep. For some reason, she kept thinking about what had happened to the women on the McFarland ranch. She felt she had to make certain that Lettie, Rachel, and Mary Beth were safe, for she had this terrible feeling something was wrong over there. Dressing in her dark clothes once more, she collected her weapons and stealthily began her journey on horseback. She dismounted some distance away from the houses and walked to where the bell was located. To her horror, she found Darby Davis lying on the ground, his throat slit. Knowing there was nothing she could do for the unfortunate man, she cautiously crept to Darby and Lettie's home to discover that everything seemed peaceful within. She crept to the neighboring Raines house, but saw no one inside. Then she moved on to Cody's home to find that his new bride was not within. Alarm filled her.

Suddenly her alert ears caught a muffled noise from the trees not far away. She furtively headed that way and was stunned to see the two women, their hands bound and their mouths gagged, being taken away by four masked men. Their nightclothes were ripped and the men were running their hands over the helpless women as they urged them toward their waiting horses. Their intentions were obvious and Rana was consumed by rage. She gingerly moved closer, then fired several arrows at the villains.

There were too many trees and victims in the path of

her arrows for her to be able to do more than wound two of the men. She rapidly drew her pistol then and fired over their heads. In fear of being seen or caught, the cutthroats mounted their horses and fled swiftly. Rachel and Mary Beth ran toward the bell to ring out its warning, though the gunfire had been a sufficient call for help. Rana watched them rush into their homes to conceal their torn garments. Knowing they were safe and that others would arrive soon, she made her way to her horse and home in order to protect her identity.

In less than an hour, Nathan and Mace were back at the main house. They had guessed who the rescuer had been and wanted to find out what she had seen, for they knew what she had done. Still, they hadn't revealed her secret to anyone. Now the people of the Rocking *C* were as curious about this intrepid ghost's identity as were those on the Circle *C*.

Thursday morning Darby Davis was buried, and three hands were assigned to guard the women at night. That afternoon, a telegram arrived from Fort Wallace in Kansas saying that a rancher named Josiah Barns was not interested in buying a partnership in the Rocking *C* Ranch. Nathan, Rana, and Mace were overjoyed by the message, for it told them that Travis was safe and on his way home, though still far away.

"Even if he rode day and night, I don't see how he could possibly make it here by next week. Thank the Lord we got our cattle money back," Nathan remarked, then smiled at Rana. "Looks like that's what's going to save us. We need to defeat Harry soon, Mace, 'cause the chores can't get done with so many hands acting as guards all over the ranch."

"When Travis gets home, we'll handle Caldwell for good."

Rana was too excited to sleep much that night. The message had told them he was on his way home, but not how his mission went. She wondered what had taken place in the land of the Lakotas. She knew the men would be on full alert tonight, so she would not have to go riding. She could lie in bed and dream of Travis.

Thursday night saw no further trouble, to everyone's relief. Bart Davis moved in with his deceased brother's family to protect and support them. That afternoon, Nathan received another telegram, this one from Dallas. It informed Nathan that his papers were ready, and the rancher decided to go after them promptly in order to avoid any problems later. After all, he reflected, there wasn't anything he could do on the ranch between today and tomorrow. He told Mace to keep his eye on Rana and made her promise to stay home unless something terrible happened.

When disaster did strike late Friday night, there was nothing Rana or anyone else could do about it. The river was suddenly blocked by a dynamite blast, and all water flowing to Nathan's ranch was cut off. The poisoned water holes had been drained, and only heavy rain could fill them. The situation would become critical in a few days, after the streams dried up and the cattle became thirsty. But worse was yet to come, and on Saturday morning it did, in the form of Clarissa Caldwell.

Chapter Seventeen

Rana went to answer the door and found one of the
ranch hands standing there nervously with a woman
who, judging from her appearance and brazen manner,
could only have been Clarissa Caldwell. The wrangler
apologized for disturbing her and explained that the lady
had been most insistent. Rana smiled her understanding
and politely dismissed him. But before Rana could discourage Clarissa from visiting, the dark-haired woman
stated belligerently, "I came to talk to you about your
mother, and I'm not leaving until I do, so you might as
well let me come in."

Rana realized that Clarissa was in a mood to be
stubborn and hateful, and she knew this meeting could
not be avoided forever. Deciding it would be best to hear
the woman today and in private, Rana invited her into
the sitting room. She knew her grandfather would be
annoyed with her, but that could not be helped. "Speak,"
Rana said, as if giving Clarissa permission to begin. The
woman was silent for a time as she eyed the portraits
hanging over the mantel. Then Clarissa looked at her as
she had the portraits, coldly and with bitterness, like a
winter blizzard.

"I thought it was time we met and talked. Considering

how well I knew your mother, I can understand why everyone's been trying to keep us apart. I thought you might want to hear the truth about Marissa and Raymond, and I'm sure you'd like to have this," Clarissa speculated, handing Raymond's picture to Rana, who noticeably trembled and paled. "I see you remember the brutal bastard."

Rana stared at the picture of the gambler with black hair and brown eyes who had haunted her dreams for years. "Why do you come here?" she asked, looking at the antagonistic woman before her.

"I wanted you to know what a bitch and a whore your mother was. Do you know what those words mean?" she asked hatefully, then explained their meanings and how they applied to Marissa. She told Rana how Marissa had been forced to whore to earn money to support her daughter and husband. "Marissa slept with countless men, including plenty of those who work for my father. She's even slept with some of the men on this ranch, like Todd Raines. She had poor Todd believing she loved him and was going to marry him, but she got herself pregnant and had to run off and get married to hide her sin. When Raymond found out she had tricked him, he hated her and punished her by making her whore for their living."

"Tricked him? I do not understand. Why do you speak such evil lies about my mother? You were not her friend?" she probed.

Having decided to be crueler and more informative than she had previously intended, Clarissa echoed with an ugly sneer, "Friend? I hated her. Marissa was selfish and mean and bad. She stole the only man in my life; now her wicked daughter is trying to steal Travis or my father. Travis told me how you'd been trying to sneak into his bed. He knows you're nothing but a whore like your mother was. When he kept refusing you, did you give up and turn to Mace? You are a *bastard*, Rana Michaels. I

506

won't let you get my father or Travis."

Rana felt she could not trust this hostile, bitter creature to be truthful. "You must go. You speak with a false, cruel tongue," she declared, regaining her composure.

"Ask Todd Raines if I'm lying," Clarissa challenged. "He knows how bad she was. Or ask Fargo, who works for my father; he's spent plenty of money sleeping with her, and he told me and Papa all about her. Ask any of the men who paid Raymond to have her for a few minutes. And you'll never guess who your father is."

"I do not care, but I am glad it is not Raymond Michaels."

"If you don't convince Nathan to sell this place to my father, everybody else will care when I spread the word about you and your mother. People will be laughing at you and avoiding you. They'll think you're just like your mother. Or worse, you little savage."

"Even if you speak the truth, I will not ask my grandfather to leave his lands. Go away; do not return. Your heart is black and evil." To frighten and punish Clarissa, Rana threatened, "If you anger me, I will take your father and force you to leave home. He has asked Grandfather to allow us to marry. I see great desire for me in his eyes."

"It isn't you he sees and desires, you little fool! If you dare try to marry my father, I'll make you wish you had never been born. I know something very bad about Marissa that I haven't told you. Raymond and I were close friends, and he told me secrets about her, and about you. I could use them to destroy your family. I'm warning you, Rana, stay away from my father and Travis." With that Clarissa stormed out of the room and out of the house.

Rana went immediately to her room and flung herself across her bed. Memories mingled with the woman's words to torment her. Clutching her doll against her heart, she cried. She had slept little the night before and was exhausted. Slowly she drifted off to sleep.

Clarissa scolded angrily, "I don't know what's gotten into you, Papa! Why would you shut off the river to land you'll own next week? Poisoning water holes, burning crops, cutting fences, stampeding cattle, ordering excessive violence—such measures aren't necessary, Papa; you'll be able to buy that ranch peaceably next week. Why cause so much damage and ill will when the land and workers will soon be yours?"

Harrison glared at her. "I've told you, girl, stay out of my business. I'm tired of your meddling. Do things my way, or get out!"

His outburst shocked her, then enraged her. "How can I remain silent when you do such foolish things? Now I learn you're proposing to Rana Michaels!" she snapped, her temper flaring, for they had been quarreling for over an hour.

"How do you know that?" he demanded furiously. "If you're spying on me, girl, I'll whip you senseless, then kick you out."

"I saw her this morning at Nathan's ranch," she admitted freely.

"You little bitch! How dare you talk with Rana! You might as well know, I am planning to marry her. Tell me what you two said. And from now on, stay away from her; you could ruin my plans."

Clarissa glared at him. "Stay away? Why, Papa? Rana is my half sister. Or didn't you know Marissa was carrying your baby when she ran away with Raymond? You can't marry your own daughter. Either you're crazy with lust for Marissa's ghost or you're ignorant of the truth. Which is it, Papa?"

"What the hell are you talking about?" Harrison shrieked.

"Haven't you figured it out by now, Papa? You were gone for months when Marissa discovered she was pregnant. She had to get away before anyone guessed her secret. That dashing gambler came along and she duped him into marrying her and getting her away before she started showing her sinful secret. But Raymond found out she had played him for the fool, and he got even with her. Didn't you ever wonder why he hated her and abused her so cruelly? And didn't you wonder why Marissa was too afraid to disobey him or leave him? For goodness sake, Papa, he was blackmailing her, threatening to expose her sins to her father and everyone. And proud Marissa didn't want that. Raymond had slowly gotten her by the throat and knew too much about her. By the time she was desperate to be free of him, it was too late."

"How do you know such things?" Harrison demanded.

"You do recall we used to be friends and do things together? One day I heard Raymond and Marissa arguing when they didn't realize I was around, and the whole filthy story came pouring out. That's what he was using to blackmail her; you know, Papa, whore for his stakes or he would expose the dirty truth about her? Marissa did it a few times to appease him, but then Raymond started demanding more and more customers. By then, she was already soiled and she was in over her head, drowning in Raymond's revenge and her dark secrets."

"Why didn't you tell me about this?" he raged at her, seeing how fiercely she hated Marissa and Rana.

Her face was lined with hostility. "Tell you I knew Marissa had been secretly whoring with my father? Tell you I knew Rana was your bastard? No, Papa, I wanted Marissa and Rana out of our lives. If she had loved you and wanted you, she wouldn't have married Raymond.

She chose her prickly path and didn't try to change it. By the time I learned the truth, there was no way you could have married that cheap whore and claimed Rana as your child, and you can't claim her now. She would hate you and blame you for what happened to them. And such a revelation might cause a scandal, Papa, that is if Nathan didn't manage to kill you for what you did to his little Marissa. She wasn't much more than a child at that time, Papa. Some might suggest you raped her or misled an innocent young girl. They'll wonder why she ran off with that Michaels beast rather than marry you. Besides, if you lay claim to Rana, Nathan will disown her and she'll lose any claim to his ranch. If something did happen to block your purchase, Rana might be your only way of obtaining it."

"Is that all you care about, that stupid ranch? Did you tell Rana any of this?" he asked pointedly.

"Don't be foolish, Papa. Certainly not. I don't ever want her to know about us. Don't you realize that would give her a right to our holdings, if anything should happen to us. By revealing the truth, you'll offer them the perfect path to revenge and victory. We both know Travis doesn't love me or want me. What would happen to us if he thought he could have it all by taking the beautiful Rana as his wife? I thought maybe Marissa had confessed the truth to you and asked for your help in getting free of Raymond, but when you started talking seriously about marriage, I realized you didn't know about Rana."

Harrison had found the unexpected news staggering. "Leave me alone for a while, girl; I need to think about this," he told her, then went into his office and closed the door.

Clarissa stared at it, then grinned satanically. The old fool actually believed her! That lie would keep him distracted and mastered for awhile. If anyone were to discover who Rana's father really was, it would be a shock, especially to Rana, Travis, Nathan, Harrison, and Todd. Poor Todd; she had already been pregnant for a time when they had started falling for each other. And poor Marissa, who was too terrified and confused to realize that Todd would have married her and claimed the child. She thought about two lines from Scott's 1808 *Marmion:*

> "Oh, what a tangled web we weave,
> When first we practice to deceive!"

Terrible dreams began to fill Rana's mind. Her head thrashed wildly upon the pillow and she whimpered softly as she tried to halt them. Suddenly she cried out and aroused herself. She sat up panting and shaking. Clutching the doll tightly in her arms, she cried. Several of Raymond's statements returned to convince her that Clarissa had spoken at least part of the truth: ". . . me and that dark-haired vixen . . . greedy and wicked bitch . . . since you ain't . . ."; then Marissa's voice tormented her, "No more lies about me . . . once he's dead, the truth will be buried forever . . . terrible mistake, and I've paid for it . . . return soon . . . be free and happy . . ."

Raymond Michaels was dead, but Marissa's agonizing secrets had not died with him. Clarissa Caldwell knew them and would use them maliciously to hurt all of them if she did not get her way. Her grandfather would suffer again over Marissa's mistakes, and Travis and others would learn of her mother's past.

"What is the truth, Mother?" Rana sobbed sadly. As if Marissa were replying, Rana heard the words, *Inside the doll, little one.*

Rana shuddered and looked around the room, then glanced at the doll. She concentrated very hard to remember something her mother had told her several times: "Don't forget, little one, the truth is inside the doll. Never lose her and never tell anyone."

Rana bounded off the bed, seized her knife from its sheath, and cut off the doll's head. She stared at the rolled page that was wedged tightly within the rag stuffing, and she feared to remove it and read it. How she wished Travis were here to comfort her and help her. But she was alone, and she could not wait for his return. She closed her eyes and prayed. "Great Spirit, make me brave and strong. Help me understand. Do not allow bitterness and anger to blind me."

She pried the letter free and dropped the mangled guardian to the floor. Then she went to the bed and sat down weakly. Before unrolling the paper, she inhaled and exhaled several times to calm her racing heart and to steady her quavering hands. She had to prepare herself to confront this painful, enlightening message from the grave.

When she found the courage to read the letter, it was puzzling: "If you find this note, something is terribly wrong. Look for a final message from me in our hiding place. Remember, the little hole in the dark room, the place where we hid our treasures from the bad man."

Rana closed her eyes and tried to recall her mother's meaning. She envisioned them sitting on the floor in a small, dark area; then she saw a candle that cast glowing shadows over her mother's face. Marissa was smiling at her and her blue eyes were sparkling as she touched her finger to her lips to indicate secrecy. Marissa took a knife and pried loose a short board near the corner of a wall. She could see her mother placing things inside the black hole, then sealing it. Grasping her small hand, Marissa led her out of the darkness . . .

Rana's eyes widened, then she whirled to look at the closet in the corner of Marissa's old room. She leapt to

512

her feet, seized her knife once more, and ducked inside the closet with a candle. Crawling to the far end, she placed the candle on the floor and searched for the special board. As she worked to pry it free, she wondered if her mother's letter and "treasures" would still be hiding there after all these years. It was possible she had removed them during that last trip. It was possible someone else had found the hiding place and taken them.

The board squeaked and yielded, then fell noisily to the floor. Apprehensively she reached inside the black hole, grasped several objects and withdrew them: a bunch of dead flowers secured with a yellow ribbon, a lock of light brown hair with reddish gold highlights bound with another yellow ribbon, an oval locket that had a broken catch and held a picture of Marissa and Todd as teenagers, a leather pouch with money inside, and a time-yellowed envelope.

Rana replaced the lock of hair, the flowers, the pouch, and the locket. Taking the candle, she left the closet, deposited the candle on the hearth for safety, then went to sit on the bed. Carefully she ripped open the envelope and slowly unfolded the fragile paper, which crackled with age. Her heart began to pound heavily and her mouth went dry. Despite the heat of the day, her hands felt cold and shaky. She dreaded to begin this new torment.

My dearest daughter Rana,

Since you are reading this letter, my little one, then I have been taken from your side, for only you know how and where to find it. If things had worked out for us as I had planned, I would have recovered and destroyed this letter before you could find it and read it.

Even as I begin, I am not sure I am doing the right thing or if I know how to tell you what I must. I wish I were there to explain these matters, little one, but it cannot be. I beg you to read this letter with love and I pray you are old enough to understand what I must tell you and why, or how, it happened.

I must reveal the truth to you as I do not want you to go on believing Raymond Michaels is your father. He is a vicious and evil man, and I curse the day he entered our lives. I was so foolish and impulsive when I was young. I wanted to taste every treat life had to offer. I was spoiled and greedy. I was stubborn and willful. Many mistakes were of my own doing, Rana, and others happened because I was so naive and trusting, though I thought I knew everything. What cruel lessons life must teach us when we care more for ourselves than others. I only wish I had been allowed to bury the dark past forever. I can be thankful that only Raymond knows my secrets and I pray he has not and will never reveal them.

Before I was seventeen, I was called the most beautiful girl in Texas, and sadly I believed it and used my beauty and charms as weapons or for foolish tricks. Many boys desired me, but I was vain and blind in heart. I trampled upon their feelings and I was forced to pay for my meanness.

We had—and may still have—a neighbor named Harrison Caldwell, a rich, handsome man whose wife died many years ago. As a young girl, I tingled and blushed each time I saw him. None of the boys my age caused me to have such feelings, so I believed I was in love with him. One day I went to deliver a message to him from Papa, and my world became confused and upturned. He had flirted with me many times, and in my vanity I thought he was in love with me. At his house that day, he offered me a strong drink and I boldly and recklessly took it. It sent my head spinning as fast as my heart was pounding. He began to kiss me and touch me and strange feelings attacked me, and I wanted to kiss and touch him back. I let him take me to his room and make love to me. For many weeks I sneaked to his home to lie with him in his bed. I told myself it was because he ordered it and I feared he would tell Papa or others what I had done. He was a skilled lover and I was charmed by him and our actions. Soon, I had to admit I liked what we were doing and I enjoyed the power I held over him, for he loved me and craved me wildly. Perhaps I was in love with love or with the feelings of mystery and wickedness. It was so exciting to explore being a woman and to have such a powerful secret and to have a real man in my control. I felt as if I were living in an adventurous dreamworld.

Over a year passed. I had learned so much about men and life and my feelings, but I had learned it in a bad way. My lovely dream had slowly faded and I realized I did not love or want this man. He had ways that were vicious and wrong. He refused to release me from our secret affair. He wanted to marry me, to keep me as his property. We argued for weeks and I refused him in every way. And I did a terrible thing during this time to test my feelings for him, which I shall explain later. I told him I did not love him or want him anymore and I said many cruel and false things to him to force him to leave me alone. Then I began to see another man. He became very angry and jealous and vowed to have me or else no other man would. I threatened to tell Papa he had raped me and forced me to do his bidding to keep him from killing Papa. He left for many months, but said he would force me to marry

515

him on his return.

Now, I must tell you about the other man. One day my horse bolted and I was rescued by a boy my age named Todd Raines—he still works for Papa as I write this letter. When I gazed into his eyes as he held my trembling body, a feeling that I now know was true love washed over me. I wanted nothing more than to gaze into his eyes and stay in his arms forever. There was a quietness and gentleness about my feelings for him, yet he made my body flame with desire. We shared so many things, like a simple walk to gather wildflowers. We laughed as I cut his hair for a dance in town and he teased me about keeping a lock. He gave me a locket and placed our pictures inside. He was so kind and loving for one so young. How I wished I had been more like him. I kept those treasures hidden with this letter, for I could not bear to part with them. I loved him in that very first moment our eyes met and our bodies touched, and I knew he was the man I wanted as my own forever. Papa adored him and was happy for us. I hurt them both so deeply when I was forced to reject Todd. If you have found true love, little one, then you will understand what I am trying to explain.

Life had a cruel urge to punish me for my past wrongs. I discovered I was carrying a child, and I was terrified that someone, especially my beloved father or my cherished Todd, would discover the truth about me and my baby. I could not bear to tell them of my sins and past deeds, for they would hate me and think me evil. I had to break Todd's heart and reject him, and I shall never forget the pain I caused him or the love we shared. He has married another, but I know he suffers each time I return home and he sees me. But I suffer too, for I see what my sin has taken from me. How I wish I could tell him the truth, but it is too vile and destructive. How I wish you were his child—how lucky we would be today!

At times, I even wished Harrison Caldwell had been your father, so this burden would not have destroyed all I was and loved. How do I explain the truth, my little one, and not cause you to hate and scorn me as I despised myself until I almost let Raymond destroy me? How foolish I was to believe I deserved to be punished! How can I explain why I ruined our lives? I was a fool, a selfish, blind fool who made terrible mistakes. How do I explain them to myself or to you or to Todd? Your name is as close as I can ever be to him. Even now, I love him and I would give my soul for a second chance with him, but I cannot ruin his life again. I must let him go on hating me.

This is the hardest part of my confession. First, I must say I am sorry for letting you suffer at Raymond's hand. We tricked each other with our marriage. He wanted to get his hands on Papa's money through me, and I needed him to take me far away. When he learned I was carrying a child and I refused to beg Papa for money, he was very angry and mean. After you were born and he learned my secret, he became cruel and vindictive. To protect our lives and my secret, I am forced to lie with other men for money. I hate it and I hate him. When I tell you all, my little one, you will understand why I fear him and obey him. Today, we leave Papa's for the last time, for I shall kill him and return home to be free and happy, or he will slay me for trying. If he is still alive and near you, I beg you, Rana, run from him. Never let him near you. Never do anything for him. Never let him trick you or use you. He is bad and mean. Flee him, even if you must slay him. Otherwise he will destroy you as he destroyed me.

The secret he knew that held me under his control was about your real father. This was my biggest mistake and sin, my little one, not my reckless affair with Harrison or even surrendering to Raymond's brutality and blackmail. The only person who knew the truth besides me told Raymond, told him because she loved him and wanted him. How I hated her, for she was responsible for my wicked deed and for revealing it.

You see, my little one, when I was growing up I had a close friend whose father was a ranch hand for our neighbor, Harvey Jenkins, on the Lazy J Ranch. We did everything together until her parents were killed during the period of my secret affair with Harrison. She had no home or money, and she began to work at a private house outside town where men were entertained for a price. I sneaked over to see her one day and she was sobbing and shaking with fear. She owed the madam money for clothes and board and doctor bills, and the woman was demanding payment or she was going to throw my best friend in jail. Jail is a terrible place for a woman. We were young and gullible and did not know the woman was lying to frighten and gain control over my friend. I asked her what I could do to help, for I did not have enough money to pay her large debt.

We put all of our money together, but it was not enough. I knew Papa would not give me money to pay a whore's debt. My friend told me she had a man coming over that night who would pay her enough to finish off her debt; then she would be safe and she would leave to begin a new life elsewhere. But she was in her woman's way and could not lie with him. She begged me to take her place, for the owner was mean and had beaten her many times and the law does nothing to help or protect whores. She knew about Harrison and me and knew I was no longer a virgin. She pleaded and reasoned, telling me it was the only way I could learn if I truly loved and wanted Harrison, for I had lain only with him. I was enticed and convinced because she explained that the man always insisted on lying with her in the dark and without talking. He did not want to know her name or see her face, for he always pretended she was his lost love. She vowed that the man would never know I had lain with him in her place. It sounded so mysterious and romantic and exciting. We never saw each other or spoke that night. He was a gentle man with a very nice body, but he seemed so nervous and unsure of himself, and I could do nothing but lie there and wish the deed over. I regretted my actions that very same night and refused to see my friend again for lying to me about leaving that wicked life.

I had stopped going to Harrison's bed two months before that fateful night, and I met Todd a few weeks afterward, but we did not sleep together for a long time, for he loved me and held me precious. Two months passed, and I knew I was with child, from the night with a stranger in my friend's place. There was no way I could claim the baby was Todd's or Harrison's. Todd had taken me for the first time two weeks earlier and the experience had been glorious for we had been in love. He had been afraid to rush me, and I had been equally shy with him. He asked me to marry him the night of the day I learned my tormenting secret. I had to discover the identity of my baby's father and then decide what to do. I went to her and she tried to keep the truth from me, but I forced her to speak it, to my horror. How can I tell you without tormenting you as I was tormented when I learned the truth? Sobbing, she confessed that the stranger had been Nathan Crandall, who had made his last visit to her that night. She had been so frightened and selfish that she had tricked me into sleeping with my own father! How I wish she had lied to me about him. He is not your grandfather. He is your father.

When I learned this evil truth, my heart truly broke. I knew I had to leave quickly and go far away, where no one could discover my foul deed. I had met Raymond Michaels at several barn dances and he had been trying to win me and run away with me. I saw him as the answer to my prayers. I eloped with him before anyone guessed why I was leaving home. He told me one night—before he learned of my pregnancy and my deceit—that he had married me for my money and if I ever wanted to visit home again I would have to pay him a lot of money so that he could gamble with it. He was furious when he learned I had also tricked him.

By now, you realize why I could not ask Papa for money. I refused to return home to visit for a long time. I was ashamed to face Papa and Todd. But I was so lonely and afraid and I wanted to come home. Raymond met my friend and she told him my wicked secret, for she loved him and wanted to take him from me. He killed her, Rana, for he did not want anyone else to learn the truth. He used that truth to force me to lie with other men to earn his living. I was so scared and confused and believed I deserved this punishing fate. I did what he said for a long time. When I began refusing, he threatened to kill you and Papa after telling Papa the truth about you. I couldn't let him hurt Papa or you or Todd. I was the one to blame, the evil one, the one who should suffer. But I can no longer go on this way. Surely I have paid and suffered enough. My sins were committed far away, so no one here knows about them. I must never let Papa or Todd learn how I've been living for years.

I will try to kill Raymond as soon as we get away from the ranch. Harrison hates me and is being very cruel and vengeful. Todd is married and I cannot ruin his life again. And I cannot ask for Papa's help without telling him the truth. I have no one to turn to, my little one, no one to help us and free us. Each day I grow more afraid of Raymond. He has begun to tease me about no longer needing me. He says you are the rightful heir to Papa's ranch and that he can take it through you. I do not like the way he is beginning to watch you. I see such fear and suffering in your eyes. You're happy here with your father, my father. I must try to set us free of Raymond, or die trying. I tell you these things, because, if I am gone, you will have no one to protect you from him. You must not remain with him, and you must not be drawn to Harrison. Both are evil men and they will use you for their selfish needs.

Forgive me, Rana, and please try not to hate me or judge me too harshly. I know how wrong I was about so many things, but I love you dearly and I cannot allow you and Papa to suffer anymore. Only you can decide what to do with these tormenting truths, and I pray you have found a strong, special love who will help you do what is right and best and who will give you comfort against this pain I have brought into your life and heart. If you have met Todd, then you know why I love him and wanted him. Forgive me for pressing this burden on you. I

521

love you, little one. Do not ever doubt it or forget it.

The letter was signed, "Marissa Crandall, September, 1856," and had obviously been written during her final visit home before her tragic death. Rana read the letter again, trying to recall or understand the words that were strange to her. A variety of emotions coursed through her, but hatred and scorn were not among them.

Long ago, she had been as willful and selfish as her mother had been. She, too, had trampled on the feelings of men who had chased her. She had played with their feelings and rejected them unkindly. She knew what it was to love someone at first glance and touch, for it had been that way with Travis Kincade. How sad that she had truly loved and wanted Todd Raines, and he did not know it. She recalled how she had desired Travis that first night and wondered if that was how Marissa had felt, or thought she had felt, about Harrison Caldwell. How tragic that that mistake had led to another, more tragic one, for Marissa would not have taken her friend's place if it had not been for Harrison. Rana could not judge Marissa, for who could say what she might have done had Myeerah's life and safety been endangered? People were not invincible or perfect; only the Great Spirit was so.

She thought about Raymond Michaels and hated him even more. He deserved to die for using a helpless woman! If he had still been alive, she would have hunted him down and slain him herself.

She thought about Harrison Caldwell, who had begun the cycle of anguish that had caused her mother's torment and death. Now he was trying to destroy her grandfather—no, her father. He would pay for his evil, she vowed with fierce determination.

Her thoughts drifted to Clarissa, and she raged at the woman's maliciousness and spite. She mentally went over their conversation and wondered how much the woman knew about Marissa and her. Clarissa had said she knew "secrets about her, and you" and that Rana would never guess who her real father was. Rana prayed Clarissa did not know this destructive truth, but she feared she did. That wicked woman had pretended to be Marissa's friend, and possibly her mother had told Clarissa things without meaning to do so or because she had trusted her. If Clarissa held this awesome secret in her possession, what would she do with it? And had she revealed it to Harrison? Now she understood why Clarissa feared her father's attraction to her and what she meant when she said, "It isn't you he sees and desires!" Raymond had told Clarissa many secrets about them, but did she know about Nathan?

Nathan . . . She called his image to mind. Her father . . . Yes, she had his eyes and favored him. She could never tell him the truth, for it would destroy him to learn he had mated with his own child. How that secret must have tormented her mother. Yes, Marissa would have done anything to protect those she loved from its damage.

Travis . . . She desperately wished he were here to comfort her. What would he think about her mother's evil deeds? What if Clarissa spitefully told him everything? She was Nathan's daughter . . . How would he feel about that relationship? He loved her and she loved him, and she would tell him when the time was right, for such a secret could be harmful if it were kept from him, or if it were told to him by Clarissa.

Rana went to sit by the hearth. Lifting the candle, she burned the letter and note, then burned Raymond's picture. She took needle and thread from her sewing box and carefully repaired the doll, then laid it gently on her bed, understanding now why Marissa had left it behind. Finally she returned to the closet and concealed Marissa's hiding place. For now, she would do nothing with Marissa's "treasures."

Lost in thought she walked aimlessly around her room. Soon she realized that tears were rolling down her cheeks. Perhaps the Great Spirit had ended Marissa's suffering and removed Raymond's threat and evil, yet Clarissa's evil and threat remained. If she made an obvious move toward either Travis or Harrison, the woman might be tempted to wreak her evil vengeance. Rana doubted that Marissa had slept with any man around here other than Fargo, for she recalled that name from her bad dreams. At least Nathan and Todd had been protected from Marissa's secrets, and she would see to it that they remained so. Rana had been raised and trained to slay enemies and to seek justice or revenge. She vowed she would find a way to punish Harrison, Clarissa, and Fargo.

It was late when Nathan returned from Dallas with the papers that made Travis free to marry her. They agreed to keep them a secret until this difficult matter with Harrison was settled. Fortunately, Nathan was too busy and distracted by the damming of the river to notice how oddly Rana was looking at him and behaving. She had accepted him as her father in her heart and mind, and that reality did not trouble her. She smiled at him and hugged him tightly before he left to meet with Cody and Mace, knowing she could never call him "father."

On Sunday morning, Nathan and many of the others went to church to pray for strength and deliverance from the evil that had befallen them. Chores were being left undone as most of the men were assigned to guard duty around the ranch. Nathan had told them at a large meeting early that morning that Travis was on his way home, and he assured them that things would return to normal in another week.

Later that afternoon, Bart Davis married his brother's widow. Some might have disagreed with their decision as it came so soon after Darby's death and burial, but Rana did not. In the Indian camp, when a warrior was slain, a woman quickly took another husband to protect and to support her and her family. Bart and Lettie had been close friends for years and it seemed the best thing for all concerned.

On the Circle *C* Ranch, Harrison was still reeling from what Clarissa had told him the day before. He did not know what to do with or about the astounding information. But to make certain Rana would not be injured accidentally, he ordered all attacks to cease for the present. Matters would be settled Thursday, the first of August, the day Nathan's loan was due. If Nathan could not come up with the money, Wilber Mason's Mid-Texas Bank would foreclose on him Friday.

Clarissa sat at the dinner table, furtively observing her father. She had all of them right where she wanted them. Soon it would be over and everything would be hers. She smiled malevolently as she recalled her talk with Rana. Maybe she would visit her again, tell her that Nathan was her father, and threaten to expose them. If they gave her any trouble, she would. After all, there was no way Rana and Nathan could learn that Marissa was not really Nathan's daughter. She was the only one who knew that Marissa had not slept with her own father, as the troublesome slut had died believing!

Chapter Eighteen

On Wednesday, another false telegram came for Nathan and Clarissa from Travis, saying he was supposedly in Springfield and on his way home. The distance from Springfield was such that it appeared Travis would not return to the ranch in less than a week. This telegram delighted Clarissa because she felt everything would be settled in her favor by the time Travis arrived; then she could use her holdings and information to obtain her ultimate desire: him.

Because of the July heat, the poisoned water holes, the lack of rain, and the dammed river, the situation was becoming critical on Nathan's ranch and there was little fresh water for his cattle and horses. If not for the wells and the windmills, the people would soon have been suffering also. Mace ordered the men to dig trenches and to carry water to them to keep the animals alive until something could be done about the water supply. He also ordered guards posted on the windmills and wells, for he was very much aware of the consequences if Harrison ordered them poisoned or burned.

On Thursday, Mace helped Nathan sneak into town

527

inside a large box in a wagon. At the livery stable, they left the wagon and horse and stole out the back way to get to the bank without being seen by anyone Harrison might have posted as a lookout. Fifteen minutes before closing time, Nathan entered the bank to see Wilber Mason and was shown into the bank president's office.

He sat before Wilber's desk and stared at the man, who squirmed nervously in his chair, not wanting to do what he knew he must. "I'm sorry, Nate, but you know I can't extend that loan," Wilber began anxiously. He hated to see this good man broken, but he was helpless.

Nathan smiled oddly, then asked, "Tell me, Wilber, have you already made arrangements for the auction and drawn up the papers to hand my ranch over to Harry?"

Wilber Mason flushed a deep scarlet and looked down at his hands, which were writhing from his tension and guilt. "You know I would help you out if I could," he stated apologetically.

"You can help me, Wilber. You can cancel that auction and tear up Harry's offer," Nathan replied calmly. He began withdrawing packets of money from his jacket, shirt, and hat. He counted them and placed them before the astonished banker. "That should settle my debt, and you can deposit the rest of this money into my account. You do still want my business, don't you?"

Wilber's mouth dropped open and his eyes widened. "Where did you . . . get so much . . . money?" he stammered in surprise.

"From an old friend," Nathan responded, then grinned. "I do have some good friends, Wilber. Relax. There's nothing you can do but take the payment and inform Harry of his misfortune. He'll be furious, but he can't blame you."

Wilber's gaze met Nathan's. Suddenly a broad grin lit his face and he laughed heartily. It was obvious the banker felt great relief and joy. Without counting the money, he took his pen and Nathan's loan papers and marked them with large, dark words: "PAID IN FULL, August 1, 1867. Wilber Mason, President, Mid-Texas Bank."

As Wilber handed Nathan his copy, he looked at the rancher and warned, "Be careful, Nate. Harrison is determined to get your ranch. There's no telling what he'll do when he hears about this," he remarked worriedly, tapping the money and papers with a warning finger.

"I know, Wilber, but I wish men like you wouldn't help make it so easy for him. It's hard to stand against evil when you're standing alone. Harry's judgment day is coming; mark my words." He picked up his papers and walked out as Wilber hung his head in shame.

Nathan returned to his ranch and made his way around it, paying his hands their salaries and adding small bonuses for their loyalty. He warned each one to be especially careful tonight, for Harrison would soon be aware of his defeat.

But Nathan could not know that Harrison had other things on his mind. The man hardly reacted when the bank teller arrived with the shocking news. Somehow he had expected it to happen and he suspected it had to do with the cattle money vanishing from his safe, a mystery that still annoyed and baffled him. Apparently Nathan had hired a clever man who was working secretly to foil his plans, the unknown hireling who had stolen the money from under his nose and had thwarted the boys' attack on the Rocking C women. He knew Nathan was still in trouble, and he was confident he would eventually destroy him and take everything he held precious. After all, Marissa was not Nathan's daughter; therefore, Nathan had no claim on Rana. How he wished Marissa

529

had waited for his return years ago and had married him. Perhaps something had frightened her into fleeing swiftly. If he hadn't been so cruel to her on her final visit home, perhaps she would have confided in him that last night and he could have saved his love and his child. The problem was how to get his daughter without hurting her emotionally. Harrison desperately wanted the child whom Marissa had borne him, the girl who was her mother's image and his only rightful heir . . .

At two o'clock Friday afternoon, Travis galloped into town like a man pursued by demons. He hurriedly dismounted and rushed into the bank, demanding to see Wilber Mason. Inside Mason's closed office, Travis dropped his saddlebags on the desk and emptied them of numerous pouches that were bulging, as Mason promptly learned, with gold nuggets. Travis loosened the drawstrings on several to expose their contents and declared, "There's your money, Mason. And don't you dare tell me it's too late to pay off Nate's loan. You handle it personally and deposit the rest in Nate's account. Be quick and give me those papers. I'm exhausted and I want to get home."

Wilber looked from the shiny, valuable gold to the rugged man whose clothes were rumpled and dusty and who hadn't shaved for at least a month and probably hadn't bathed in that length of time. He did look exhausted and agitated. Apparently he had slept and eaten little in the past weeks, facts that the gauntness of his face and body confirmed. "Where have you been, Kincade, and where did you get all this gold?"

"From an old friend," he replied sullenly, using words that echoed Nathan's of the day before. "Hear me well, Mason; if you've set any foreclosure and auction plans in motion, you'd best end them here and now or you'll answer to me, and I'm not talking very nice these days. Now settle up Nate's account so I can be on my way."

"Evidently you haven't spoken to Nathan," he stated and smiled.

"I've been out of town since the fourth. I came straight here before you and Crandall got too busy stealing Nate's ranch."

"Like you've been stealing gold to save it?" Wilber probed.

"Not a nugget of this is stolen; it's all mine. I'll tell you what, Mason; if you hear of any gold robberies, you can notify the sheriff to investigate me. I'm sure he'll do a better job on me than he's done on all the crimes going on around here. All he'll find out is the gold is mine. Get busy 'cause I'm tired and hungry and mean."

"You can keep the gold or deposit it here, but you—"

Travis nimbly dodged around the desk, seized Mason's coat, and yanked the startled banker from his chair. Almost nose to nose, he warned, "Don't rile me, Mason. I said mark his debt paid."

"Nate's already paid off his loan!" Wilber shrieked. As Travis's hand loosened its grasp and Wilber sank weakly into his chair, he stammered, "I . . . I swear, Kin . . . Kincade. I'll show you the papers. He paid it all and deposited more money. Said he got it from an old friend, just like you did. Came in yesterday, a few minutes before closing time. I handled the transaction myself, but his ranch still isn't safe. He's had some big trouble while you were gone."

"What kind of trouble?" Travis asked as he wondered where Nathan had gotten so much money.

"The river's been dammed and there's been some burnings and shootings and water holes have been poisoned. You should have been here; he needed you," Wilber scolded, trying to regain his composure.

"Take care of this gold and make sure you weigh it

531

accurately," Travis cautioned pointedly, then rushed to his waiting horses. Mounting Apache and seizing the packhorse's reins, he galloped for home.

Not too far behind him, a bank teller rode swiftly toward Harrison's ranch to inform him of this curious incident.

Rana heard Travis's name shouted in the yard and ran out to greet him. She did not care how he looked or who was watching as she flung herself into his beckoning arms and hugged him tightly. At that moment, thoughts of their sham were forgotten by both. He embraced her fiercely and planted kisses all over her face.

"The message did not come for so many days and we were afraid for you," she told him as tears brightened her blue-gray eyes. She searched his face and body for injuries and was relieved to find none, but she saw that the swift, arduous journey had given him a terrible beating.

"I'm safe, *micante.* The telegraph lines were down most of the way, until I reached Fort Wallace. I couldn't spare the time to keep checking locations. What's been happening here?" he inquired anxiously.

At this point, Nathan and Mace rode up. They quickly dismounted and each gave Travis a bear hug. "You had me plenty worried, son," Nate declared, "when that telegram was so late."

"We need to talk, Nate," he stated seriously.

Nathan smiled and slapped him affectionately on the back. "No need to worry, son. I paid off our loan yesterday."

"I know. I just came from the bank. I left the gold there. We shouldn't have any money problems for a long time, if ever. But how did you come up with that cash?"

Nathan grinned and suggested, "Let's get inside.

We've got plenty to tell you. Mace, you come along too."

Travis listened with astonishment as Nathan, Mace, and Rana explained what had occurred during his absence. His emotions were mixed, and he kept glancing at Rana in surprise. Even though he had previously observed her mental and physical prowess, he could not help but be amazed at her feats. "We'll have to be real careful, son, 'cause I'm sure he's got his dander up by now. What we need to do is get those witnesses and branding irons and saddlebags. But tell us about your journey. You had us scared when we didn't hear from you, boy."

Travis went over the details of his trip and his accomplishments. He and Rana exchanged smiles as he talked about Lone Wolf and Myeerah. "That part of my life is finally settled," he remarked happily. His smile faded as he added, "Let's get busy settling our problems here."

Nathan told him, "As soon as we do, I have those papers that say you aren't my son anymore. Seems you two are free to marry."

Travis pulled Rana into his arms and whispered, "I love you, *micante*, and I sorely missed you." To the others he said, "We'll keep this quiet for now. We don't want Rana put in any danger. If I know Clarissa, she'll be furious, and she'll try to get her Papa that way."

After finishing their talk, Mace and Nathan left the room so that Rana and Travis could share a few moments alone. "I saw the look on your face when I mentioned her name. What is it, Rana?"

Rana told him about Clarissa's visit and his fury mounted. She smiled and nestled against his chest. "Do not worry, *mihigna*; I ordered her away. I told Grandfather nothing of her mean visit. She fears losing you and her father to me, and that fear makes her vicious, like an injured wolf. But soon the Caldwells will be defeated and we will marry."

"I need to get cleaned up and do some checking around. We'll talk about this later," he murmured, then smiled seductively.

"Yes, we will talk later," she concurred, thinking of what else she had to tell him and knowing that it was not yet the time or place.

Just as Travis was about to leave the house, a violent rainstorm broke overhead. Nathan rushed inside soaking wet and beaming with joy. Rana was here, and Travis was home safely, the loan had been paid, and the heavy rain would help replenish their vanishing water supply. He told Travis there was nothing he could do on the ranch this late in the day in stormy weather, and what he needed was a bath, shave, hot food, and a good night's sleep. Travis did not need much convincing and immediately set out to do what Nathan had suggested.

He had only intended to rest until Nathan had gone to bed, but he was so fatigued that he fell into a deep sleep and nothing aroused him—not the loud thunder or Rana as she sat on the edge of his bed and watched him for a long time. She made no attempt to awaken him; she only wanted and needed to be near him.

"See there, Papa, I told you it wasn't Travis hanging around here secretly and doing those things," Clarissa stated petulantly.

"Nor was he the one sending those telegrams, you fool. There's no way he could have gotten here today from Springfield. I don't know where he went or how he got that gold, but I intend to find out."

"Surely you can understand why he tricked me. He didn't want you to learn about the gold and rob him on the trail as you did the cattle money. What are you going to do now to force Crandall out?"

"I haven't decided, but I will. Don't you worry none, girl."

"You're hesitating because of that little slut, aren't you? You can't claim her, Papa; it would ruin everything we've worked for!"

Harrison slapped her and sneered, "That little slut, as you call her, is my daughter and your half sister. I've told you before, girl, let me handle my affairs." He stalked from the room then, shaking with anger.

I'll get you for this, you bastard, she vowed silently.

Harrison returned to the room suddenly and taunted, "Oh, yes, there's something I forgot to tell you about Nathan's recent trips to Dallas." He laughed wickedly as he related the pertinent information to a stunned Clarissa.

The next morning, Travis rode to the river to assess the damage. Seeing how it had been done, he also understood the only possible way to clear the blockage. All he lacked was dynamite, and he knew where to find some. He turned as he heard a horse approaching, and saw Clarissa riding toward him as if she had known where he would be.

She dismounted, ran to him, and tried to embrace him. He pushed her away and glared at her. "What's wrong, love?" she asked. "I've watched for you all morning. I thought you would be glad to see me."

"And I thought you'd keep your papa under control while I was gone," he retorted, slipping into the provoking role he was forced to play with her.

Assuming that Rana had not told him of her visit, Clarissa asked, "What are you talking about?" She unsuccessfully attempted to look and sound hurt and innocent.

He laughed harshly and demanded, "Get off that silly

535

horse, Clarissa. It doesn't ride with me. We both know Harrison Caldwell is behind all this trouble and destruction. I was hoping you cared enough about me to stall him until my return so I could fight him."

"Don't be mean. I love you, Travis. I would do anything to help you and make you happy," she told him, trying to snuggle closer.

"If that were true, you would be on my side," he argued.

"Then tell me how to prove my love and loyalty!" she cried.

He answered smoothly, "Give me evidence against your father so I can have him put in jail for his crimes. Once he's out of the way and you own his ranch, then we can talk seriously—not before."

Clarissa stared at Travis. If she agreed to help him defeat her father, Harrison would retaliate by leaving everything to his "daughter" Rana. Yet if she confessed her deceit about Rana's parentage in order to stop Harrison from changing his heir, she would be exposed as a liar—if her father could be convinced she had lied to him. Now that Travis had been disowned and disinherited, perhaps he would be more vulnerable to her offerings. She had to bluff him. "I don't know anything about Papa's affairs, Travis. He's always so secretive. I don't think he trusts me, because we're so close. Why don't you beat the truth out of him or one of his hirelings?"

"You really expect me to believe you don't know anything?" he scoffed in disgust. "If we can't get your father's place, then we'd have nothing," he told her, trying to sound vexed and flustered.

"What about Nathan's ranch? You'll get it one day," she responded innocently, though her expression told him she knew otherwise, as he had suspected.

"Not unless I marry that little savage of a grand-daughter! He's cut me off, hoping to force us together. If I let your papa take over, I won't get any part of this ranch, and it's mine, damnit! I'll fight him 'til one of us lands in hell, and I'll marry her if necessary."

"Never! That little bitch can't inherit Nathan's ranch because she isn't his granddaughter!" she shouted at him, then softened her voice to add, "Because Marissa isn't Nathan's daughter."

"What are you saying, woman?" he demanded eagerly, seeing she had made a rash slip in her anger.

Clarissa related the story of Ruth Crandall's death-bed confession to her mother, Sarah Jane Caldwell. "Marissa's father was a red-haired, blue-eyed outlaw! Mama told Papa, and he told me years ago, before he decided to seek another wife who could give him a son to take everything that rightfully belongs to me. I hate him and, if I knew anything that would help get rid of him, I would tell you. He can't live forever, Travis. You get Nathan's ranch by proving Rana isn't the rightful heir; then one day I'll get Papa's holdings. We'll marry and have the largest spread in this area."

Travis persisted in questioning her slip. "How do you know that it wasn't fever talking when Mrs. Crandall said such things to your mother?"

"Marissa was born six months after Nathan returned home from a four-month cattle drive, and she was fully grown as babies go. Hasn't anyone ever told you Ruth Crandall had black hair? How does black hair mix with blond to make a flaming-haired child? It doesn't."

"Obviously Nate didn't care that she wasn't his by blood."

"Nate didn't, and still doesn't, know the truth."

"And you expect me to tell him?" he inquired, fury lacing his words.

She stated coldly, "If you want the ranch badly enough, you will. Otherwise, Rana will steal it from you."

"Did Harrison threaten to expose Marissa as a bastard and she couldn't bear the shame? Is that what he told her to make her run away? Has he been trying to steal this ranch that long? Were you involved?" he demanded, attempting to evoke more answers.

"Don't be ridiculous! She ran away because she was pregnant. And she kept running because of all she had done to hide her sins."

"You certainly know a lot about her," he stated skeptically.

Clarissa's dark eyes narrowed. "I knew her and Raymond for years, but I never told her she was the bastard of an unknown Scotsman who had raped her mother. She died believing Nathan was her father."

"Did Raymond know she was pregnant? Was that his hold over her?" he probed, aware Clarissa was rashly exposing more than she had intended.

Clarissa's tone and gaze altered noticeably as she began to lie. "He made a deal with her. He was to get her away from her sinful past if she paid him money. When she tried to cheat on her part of their deal, he used it to blackmail her and to force her to whore for his gambling stakes. She should have killed the son of a bitch for beating her and degrading her. She was a fool and a weakling. She was willing to do anything to keep the truth from her father and Todd Raines!"

Although he was aware of what she had told Rana, he queried convincingly, "Todd? What does he have to do with this?"

"It seems he and Marissa discovered each other and fell in love, but, sadly, she was carrying another man's child by then. Since she hadn't been bedding Todd long enough, she couldn't tell him the child was his. She was afraid Todd and Nathan would hate her, so she bolted. She hoped to divorce Raymond and return one day, but Raymond realized what a good thing he had and used it. By the time she came to her senses, she had committed more sins and had gotten in too deep to dig her way out. Then, those nasty Indians got in her way."

"You mean she was really in love with Todd Raines?"

"Isn't that amusing? After all her running around, she found true love when it was too late. How pathetic."

He suggested doubtfully, "Something's strange here, Clarissa. I thought you said you two were friends. You sound as if you hated her."

"Why shouldn't I have? One of the men she was whoring with was my father—while she was pretending to be my friend and tutor. Why do you think he's so hot for Rana? Because she's her mother's image!"

Travis hated to think of Harrison's putting his hands on that lovely creature who had looked like his beloved. "Is Harrison Rana's father?"

"Thank heavens he isn't, or he'd leave her everything! Papa was back East during that time." She recalled what Marissa had told her friend, and what the traitorous friend had told Raymond, and what Raymond had told her about the timing of her breakup with Harrison, her affair with Todd, and her pregnancy. She had no doubt about when Rana had been conceived, but she couldn't imagine anyone else believing such a shocking accusation. "When Papa returned, Marissa was long gone and he was hopping mad. Papa had actually wanted to marry her, and he would have if she'd agreed, before or after Michaels. Haven't you figured it out by now, Travis? Revenge, that's what Papa wants with the Crandall ranch, revenge for Marissa's loss. Until he saw Rana," she added bitterly.

"Lordy, woman, what a tangled mess . . ."

"He wants Rana badly, Travis, and he would sacrifice

all of his schemes to marry her, but then they would have it all if Nathan conveniently died, if you understand my meaning."

So much for her alleged ignorance of her father's life and intentions, he mused. "Not if I get her first," Travis argued, knowing she would be vexed by his words.

Clarissa knew she could not tell him the lie she had told her father, for then Travis would also believe Rana had a claim on the Caldwell holdings. Travis was right; it was a complicated and tangled mess. Maybe she should get rid of her father now and take what she could. Whatever happened, she was more than ready to get rid of Fargo, Wes, Silas, and Jackson, before one of them started trouble.

"Let me mull this over and I'll see you in a few days. Since you don't know anything about your papa's business, keep a sharp eye and ear on him, and report anything suspicious to me." With this, Travis mounted his horse and waved his farewell.

As Clarissa watched Travis ride off, she felt her anger mounting. She had said too much, and she knew he had lied to her in those faked telegrams and about his trip. Like her father, he wanted Rana, and he was only using her to get his way! She was growing weary of all these deceits and setbacks, and her passion for him was waning . . .

It was after everyone else had gone to bed for the night that Travis and Rana set into motion their plan to unblock the river. "First we steal the dynamite, then we blow it to hell," Travis explained. "Let's get our weapons ready, *micante;* this is going to be a long and busy night." He smiled into her glowing eyes and caressed her cheek.

"I am happy you are taking me with you," she murmured.

540

"I think you've proven you're as good, if not better, than me," he teased, then kissed her. "Sorry about last night. I was exhausted."

Rana cuddled up to his firm body and ran her fingers up his back. "We will have many nights together when this foe is defeated."

Travis's passions were stirred by her touch and fragrance. He warned huskily, "If you don't stop that, they'll begin now."

Rana laughed softly and reminded him, "We must take the weapon tonight, before he thinks to hide it. You told me it is the only way to clear the river. We must wait, but we wait together."

"You're so smart and clearheaded. I should put you in charge of this assignment." He stroked her silky tresses and gazed at her.

"It is not so, *mihigna*. My heart beats as swiftly as the war drum, and my head spins at your nearness as if I had taken the peyote button. If you kiss me again, I fear all is lost for our raid," she cautioned playfully, even though she knew her words were accurate.

"Let's get moving, wife." He gathered his bow and quiver and slung them over one shoulder. Then he checked his two knives and stuffed a rawhide strip into his pocket, for this was a night for silent weapons.

Dressed in concealing dark colors and with Rana's flaming hair covered, they rode stealthily to within a mile of Harrison's home. They dismounted and left their horses tethered, and continued gingerly on foot. Having heard from Rana about the place where Harrison was hiding the branding irons, Travis decided to look there first.

As silently and secretly as Apache warriors, they made their way to the barn. It was Saturday night and most of the hands were in town. After pointing out the area to Travis, Rana stood guard while he pried loose the boards.

541

He grinned as his gaze touched on the branding irons and five sticks of dynamite. He removed only the explosives, stuffed them into a cotton sack, then replaced the boards.

"Let's go," he murmured against her ear, indicating his success.

They cautiously retraced their steps and headed for the dam. Rana stayed with the horses while Travis checked the blockage and carefully placed the sticks of dynamite. Time seemed to pass so slowly in the darkness and she wondered what was taking him so long. Her nerves were on edge and she continually licked her dry lips and scanned the shadows for him.

Suddenly a hand clamped over her mouth and a strong arm banded her body, locking her arms to her sides; it was not Travis's manly odor she detected and she froze.

A rough voice whispered in her ear, "Stay real quiet and still or I'll slice your throat. We finally caught you, you little sneak. Where's your partner? If you shout when I move my hand, you're both dead. Understand?" he warned, shaking her roughly.

Rana knew she had to stall for time. She nodded, then remained motionless. The hand slowly moved from her mouth. She knew the danger of shouting a warning to Travis, so she held her silence until he asked again, "Where's your partner? What's he doing?"

"Looking at the dam," she murmured softly, trying to disguise her feminine voice, forgetting her figure would give her away. She knew they could not sneak up on Travis with his keen instincts. What she had to do was entice one to go seek him; then she could battle the other one.

"Go find him and bring him over here," the voice commanded.

"It's probably Kincade. You go, Fargo, and let me guard this one," the other man argued nervously, unintentionally revealing her captor's identity.

542

Rana shuddered, for she knew that name. Hatred began to burn within her, and she silently vowed she would free herself and slay this man. Suddenly she was turned and shoved into the moonlight and her dark covering was yanked away. With surprise, she noted the effect of her appearance on the ugly brute.

"It can't be you. You're dead," he scoffed as he trembled.

Rana realized he thought she was Marissa, and she used that fear and hesitation to her advantage. "I have returned to punish all who harm those I love. Go from this place or I will strike you dead."

Fargo was pale and shaky. He stammered, "Don't go . . . go blaming me f-for what I did. It was . . . Mi-Mister Caldwell's orders."

"I will slay him, and I will slay you if you do not leave swiftly," she threatened, raising her voice slightly in the hope that he wouldn't notice but that Travis would be warned of their peril.

"Be quiet, girl," the other man hissed. "I'll go find her partner. Let's git this done, and git off Crandall's property. You know he's been posting guards ever'where, and that Kincade's back."

Fargo did not respond as he stared at Marissa's image in the flickering moonlight. Unaware of Fargo's involvement with Marissa, the other man frowned and slipped into the shadows to head for the dam, having been told by Harrison to check it every hour to make sure no one tried to tamper with it.

"Release me, dead man," she ordered harshly, glaring at him.

Unwittingly, Fargo obeyed. Without warning or delay, Rana yanked her knife from her sheath and buried it deep within his chest. Stunned, Fargo gaped at the knife butt protruding from his chest, then stared at the woman before him. Rana stared back, her eyes cold as ice.

"It weren't my fault," he wailed, then collapsed at her feet.

"He is dead, Mother," she whispered into the sultry night.

The other man leapt from the trees and grabbed her, striking her in the abdomen to disable her. Because of her years of Indian training, she took the blow without crying out in pain or surprise. Had she done otherwise, she might have drawn more attackers to the location, and a true warrior would never endanger his companions; he would suffer, or die, in protective silence.

The man was torn roughly from her by a leather thong around his throat. "You filthy bastard! Don't you ever touch her!" Travis warned, snarling like a wild dog. As the terrified man struggled, Travis tightened the rawhide rope until the man was dead.

He dropped the man's body to the ground, then reached for his beloved. "Are you hurt, Rana?" he asked worriedly.

She smiled and shook her head. "I knew we could conquer them," she stated confidently.

Travis glanced at Fargo's body and said quietly, "I see you got him." He was very much aware that even if one killed a man out of necessity, it was never easy, and he wondered what Rana was feeling.

She looked into his eyes and said mysteriously, "He is an old enemy. It was my right and duty to slay him. I will speak of it later."

Travis dragged the bodies into the dry river bed. "That storm has the river begging this dam for release. When she goes, she should take those bodies a long way off. You go back to the house like we planned. I'll send their horses running and cover our tracks. I'll give you twenty minutes, then I'll light the charges and get there as quickly as I can. We need to be seen there after the explosion."

"Be careful, my love," she told him as they embraced.

"You be careful, too. There might be other varmints around."

Rana quickly made her way home and slipped into the stable to return the horses to their stalls. They had ridden bareback to save time and to avoid the noise of squeaking leather saddles. Nathan had made it easy for them to move about the ranch by posting guards in places that allowed them to go and return unseen.

When she entered the house, Nathan seized her and hugged her to him. "How did it go? Are you all right?" he asked breathlessly.

"All is good . . . Grandfather. We must be ready to act." She hurriedly changed her clothes and awaited the blast, which would be heard and felt this distance away as well as on the adjoining ranch.

When it occurred, Harrison Caldwell was on his way home from town, from working off his frustrations in the Silver Shadow Saloon. He knew that if he raced to Nathan's house, he could see the guilty party returning to report. He clicked his reins roughly across his animal's shoulders and prodded him forcefully with the stirrups.

He sped to Nathan's stable, where hands were saddling horses and preparing to investigate the new blast. Nathan and Rana ran from the house toward the corral, and Travis was right behind them, buckling on his gun belt, his hair mussed from what seemed a recent arousal from sleep. They were all scurrying around like they were as surprised and puzzled as he was! If it hadn't been Travis, then who . . . ?

"What in tarnation are you doing here?" Nathan demanded.

"I was coming back from town and heard the explosion. I rode over to see what was happening." Harrison's eyes quickly went to Rana, and he smiled tenderly. "You all right, Rana?" he asked in a strange tone.

She looked at him with an inquisitive expression, then nodded. Turning away, she mounted and rode off between Nathan and Travis. As they galloped to the river, she suddenly realized why he had looked at her that way: obviously Clarissa had told him she was his child to keep him from marrying her! Would that woman do and say anything to get her way? she wondered. Stranger still, she mused, he had looked pleased!

At the river, everyone saw what had happened; the dam had been blasted away and the water was flowing rapidly and freely. Nathan twisted in his saddle to sneer at Harrison. "Looks like I have me a secret helper. Unless this is some new trick of yours, Harry. What's the matter, afraid you'll ruin the property you're trying to steal? You might as well give up, because I'm not leaving my land."

"Relax, Nate. I had nothing to do with this. But if I were you, I would find out who's responsible and learn why he's helping you. He might want your ranch more than I do." Harrison tipped his hat, then rode off. Something odd was going on, and he aimed to discover what it was and who was behind it. First, he would talk with Clarissa!

Nathan looked at Mace and suggested, "See if you can round up enough boys to move the herds near the streams. They should fill up fast. Tell 'em I'll pay 'em extra for working tonight. Things are looking sunny again," he stated, then laughed cheerfully.

Rana nestled against Travis's body and sighed peacefully, but as she recalled what she had to tell him, she stiffened slightly. Aware of her change in mood, Travis inquired softly, "What's wrong, *micante?*"

Rana told him about her mother's letter and what she

546

had remembered that enabled her to find it. She also told him what she suspected Clarissa had told Harrison about her. "The truth must be kept secret forever or it will hurt Grandfather deeply. I can never call him father. Do you understand and agree?"

Travis tightened his embrace and murmured, "Yes, my love, I understand and agree. But there's something I need to tell you, something your mother didn't learn before she died and Nathan still doesn't know: Marissa did not sleep and mate with her father; Nathan was not her father." He explained what he knew and how he knew it, allowing the entire mystery to unravel. "Marissa did what she did because she believed she had committed a terrible sin with her father. If she had learned that Nathan wasn't her father, things might have been different."

Rana cried softly as she told him why she had slain Fargo. "He believed I was Mother and that it was she who slayed him. It was my revenge. Now, I must slay Harrison for what he did to her."

"Let me handle him, love. Once he learns he's been duped, he'll be more dangerous than ever. We'll get the evidence on him and he'll be punished. If we kill him, we'll lose with him. We have to do this legally, love—under the white man's law," he clarified.

Rana's lips touched his, for she wanted him, not more talk. It was nearing dawn and they had so little time left together, and both were very much aware that it had been weeks since they had joined their bodies and spirits. Their hungers raged, yet neither wanted to rush these precious moments.

Travis eased off her gown and gently kissed each breast tip before drifting up to ravenously devour her parted lips. Between kisses, she murmured, "It is good to have you with me again. I am lost without you." Feverishly

547

she sealed her mouth to his.

The palm of his hand moved over her breast in a circular motion, stimulating it delightfully. Then he shifted to sear her quivering flesh with fiery kisses and burning caresses. His mouth explored and tasted her sweet desire and heady surrender. Aware of her unbridled passion, he labored lovingly and eagerly with lips and hands to arouse her to the highest peak before joining their bodies.

Her arms went around him and her hands drifted up and down his back, feeling the hardness and suppleness of his muscles and skin. He had set her entire body tingling and smoldering from his stirring actions. He tantalized and pleasured her from head to foot. Her body was aflame with need and scorching desire. Travis was controlling her, stimulating her to the center of her being. He whispered words into her ear that, coupled with his warm breath, caused her heart to race and her senses to soar like an eagle in flight. Each place he touched with lips or hands was highly susceptible to his skills, and he brought every inch of her to awareness and fiery life.

Travis's pleasure mounted as he was given free rein over her body and will. He loved her and wanted her to be a part of him forever. Her nearness, fragrance, and essence were driving him wild, but he wanted to enjoy and titillate her as long as possible. Rapturous sensations attacked him as her hands wandered over his body and her lips responded to his. Her fingers slipped into his hair and drew his mouth more tightly against hers, revealing her rising ardor.

Travis's hand enticingly roamed across her flat stomach to seek a flaming forest and a vital peak that summoned his exploration and craved his splendid skills. a place where he could heighten their desire and cause them to writhe together with barely leashed passion.

Rana's hands likewise wandered over his body, stirring

his flaming need to a brighter, higher level. Her fingers teased down his sleek sides and brazenly captured the prize of love's war that could send her senses spinning beyond reality, beyond resistance or inhibition. Gently and lovingly she stroked it and absorbed its warmth to create more heat. She delighted in its strength and prowess and smoothness. With great satisfaction she felt his body shudder and she heard a deep groan escape his lips as they worked upon hers. This act of total giving and taking and sharing was so much more than she had ever imagined in her girlish dreams.

Unable to restrain himself further, he moved between her parted thighs, where she eagerly welcomed his arrival and entrance. His body was tense and his control strained as he made that first staggering contact. He tried to move calmly, leisurely, but he found it difficult to master his urgency to ride ecstasy's undulating prairie with her.

As her hand trailed up and down his back, she could feel the rippling muscles that moved as his body did. She felt him enter and withdraw, slowly, then rapidly, then slowly again. She sensed the strain he was experiencing and she arched her body to meet his and set the pace for their entrancing climb. Her responses told him when she was approaching the blissful precipice and he worked skillfully and patiently to drive them over its edge at the same time.

When the triumphant moment arrived, he muffled her cry of victory with his demanding lips. Their mouths and bodies labored and came together as one as they conquered passion's peak; then like feathers on a gentle breeze, they rapturously floated downward into a peaceful valley of contentment. Still they kissed and held fast to each other, extracting every sensation and emotion their union could provide.

They snuggled together in her bed and held each other, wed by the greater closeness and deeper bond their lovemaking had inspired. The more they were together for any reason, the more tightly their hearts and souls were bound. Both realized how much they loved and needed each other, in every facet of their lives. Incredibly, each day they were together was better than the day before. They were friends; they were partners; they were passionate lovers. They could talk and share anything, everything. They trusted each other, depended upon each other, and gave to each other. They had grown and changed together, for the better. It was a special union, unique and strong.

Because each sensed how the other was feeling and what the other was thinking, their heads turned at the same moment and their eyes fused. This time they spoke without words, and they made love slowly, tenderly.

By the next day, Harrison knew his plans were coming apart, and he did not know who to blame. He suspected that Fargo and his other hand were dead. Their horses had returned to the corral, empty, and they had been assigned to guard the dam. Yet all he could think about was Rana, or Marissa. He had to get his child back!

Clarissa entered the room and observed her father. "They were all at church this morning, gloating over their triumphs. And here you sit like you're in mourning. We're losing, Papa, and you're to blame. I'd always thought you were so strong and clever, that nothing and no one could defeat you or crush you. Have you forgotten what Marissa did to you? She scornfully rejected you. She started sleeping with Todd Raines, then ran off with that gambler. She was selfish and no good, Papa. When are you going to accept that and forget her?"

"How can I forget her, girl, when our daughter looks just like her? You're a cold-hearted bitch, Clarissa. She's my flesh and blood, and I want her. I'm going to kill

Nathan and Travis; then she'll have no choice but to come home to me. Once she sees how much I love her and want her, she'll be fine. You're just worried about your inheritance, you greedy bitch. You'll have to share everything with your sister. And if you give us any trouble, I'll kick you out and she'll get it all. Do you hear me, girl?" he demanded scathingly.

Clarissa was pushed beyond control. She screamed at him, "I was crazy to lie to you to keep you from making a fool of yourself over Rana Michaels like you did with her whorish mother! That little savage isn't your child; she's Nathan's! That's right, dear Papa," she shouted contemptuously when he gaped at her as if she had gone mad before his eyes. She calmly clarified, "Rana is Nathan Crandall's daughter, not your bastard. Have you conveniently forgotten you were back East for months during that time? And you hadn't slept with her long before you left. That's right, dear Papa," she scoffed again, "I found out about you and Marissa Crandall when I was eight years old. Did you think I was blind and stupid? I knew about her countless visits to your room and I knew what you two were doing. How do you think I learned so much about sex and how pleasurable it is? From spying on you and her. All you cared about was her! You didn't love me or want me! I was glad when she left, but still you didn't shower any leftover love and attention on me, love and attention you gave her for nearly two years! I've done everything you've asked to prove my love and loyalty, but nothing matters to you. I hate you, and I hope they kill you!"

"My God, girl, you've lost your mind," he decided aloud.

"Would you like to hear the entire history of your beloved Marissa?" she asked, then shouted the shocking facts at him before he could respond. "You see, dear Papa," she finished, "Rana is Nathan's evil seed; and that flaming-haired bitch you loved so deeply was so wicked that she slept with her own father."

Harrison glared at her furiously for her deceit, for he knew she was telling the truth this time. "You forget, you malicious bitch, that Nathan isn't Marissa's father."

"What does that matter? She thought he was!"

"It was a girlish prank, a terrible mistake, and she paid for it. Are you forgetting how many times you've slept with men for a variety of reasons?" he taunted just to punish his malicious child. "Marissa was trying to help a friend, and that friend betrayed her. Nothing is worse than betrayal, Clarissa," he remarked meaningfully. "Frankly, I'm glad she isn't my daughter. I much prefer her as a wife."

"You wouldn't dare!" Clarissa screamed in outrage.

Harrison laughed coldly. "Wouldn't I? Just as soon as I can lure Nathan into a trap, I'm going to kill him myself. Then I'll sic Monroe and Hayes on Travis. Yes, I should be a happy bridegroom before winter. You'd best look hard for a husband, girl, because I don't want you around after I marry. Maybe I'll have a son this time." He strolled from the room, his laughter echoing satanically.

"Over my dead body, you bastard," she vowed. It was time to locate Wes and end this madness . . .

Chapter Nineteen

Early Monday morning, the fifth of August, Harrison handed Wes Monroe a sealed letter and told him to give it personally to Nathan Crandall without letting anyone see him or the letter. "I'm going to lure my annoying neighbor into a trap and kill him myself. I've ordered my hands out of the area of your cabin so Nate and I can meet and talk privately before I put a bullet in his head. I'll tell everyone he hunted me down and tried to kill me, and I was merely defending myself. Since he hasn't made any secret of his hatred and accusations, it won't seem suspicious. After I'm done with Nate, I'll let you and Hayes take care of Travis Kincade for me; then your jobs will be over."

"What about getting control of Crandall's ranch?" Wes asked, wondering about the abrupt change in plans and Caldwell's strange behavior.

"I have another way of carrying out my wishes. I don't want any more trouble over there until I tell you to get rid of Kincade. When that's done, I'll give you two a fat bonus and then you can be on your way to your next job. See me about ten tomorrow morning." Harrison watched with satisfaction as the cocky gunslinger mounted and rode off. Once Nathan and Travis were out of his way, he would settle matters with Clarissa before claiming Rana as his bride. Evidently she had beguiled Silas Stern into helping her with some plot against him. He was convinced they were working against him, for no one else could have gotten into his safe or known about his plans in time to thwart them. It had been a mistake to let Fargo and Silas fall under his daughter's spell, but he hadn't believed she possessed so much sexual prowess and allure, or intelligence and daring. She was a cunning, conniving bitch, and she had been plotting against him for years. Soon she would pay for her treachery and betrayal, he promised himself. He walked to his corral to fetch his horse. He had one task to handle before riding to the cabin, and he had plenty of time.

Wes rode off to find Nathan and carry out his curious assignment. As soon as it was done and Caldwell left his house, he would sneak in to see Clarissa and find out what was going on. He wasn't ready to leave the area, the job, or settle for only a "fat bonus."

Wes slid off his horse near Nathan's house. He hadn't noticed anyone nearby during his cautious approach, nobody except the graying blond man sitting on his front porch reading. Wes said, "Here's a message from Mister Caldwell. He wants a private meeting with you. He gives his word on your safety, so don't be afraid to go, old man."

Nathan stared at the villainous hireling who had delivered Harrison's surprising and mystifying message. Then he read: "Meet me in one hour at the shack near my eastern boundary and we'll settle our problems once and for all. I'll make you one final offer and if you reject it, I'll make certain you aren't troubled again. There are some secrets between us, Nate, and it's time we aired them. If you want to know the truth about why Marissa left home with Michaels, come alone and come quickly. Once you hear the truth, you'll know why I've hated you for years and sought revenge. I'm tired of all our fighting, and this is a better way to settle matters. I'll be waiting, if you're brave enough to face me."

Nathan watched Caldwell's man depart and read the message again. He wondered what Marissa had to do with their conflict. She had often visited Clarissa to help her with her studies or to watch her . . . Had something happened to his daughter over there? Was Harrison responsible for his child's running away? What "secrets"? he asked himself.

Rana and Travis were out riding. Neither Mace, nor Todd, nor Cody was nearby this morning. Harrison had told him to come alone, but he had not said to keep the meeting a secret. If Caldwell were planning to harm him, he wouldn't have sent a written message for others to see. Evidently Harrison wanted to play some clever word games. Why not? he speculated. Maybe he could withdraw some important information. After all, he had been letting others take all the risks and do all the work of saving his ranch. And that crude animal of a messenger had taunted him about being afraid, singeing his manly ego. His side had been winning all the victories lately; maybe Harry wanted to capitulate in private.

He stuffed the letter into his pocket and retrieved his gun belt. Strapping it on, he walked to the corral, saddled his horse, and left, carelessly forgetting to tell anyone where he was going or why. He wanted to be early so he could hide and study the meeting area. If Harrison were setting a trap, he would be very careful and not fall into it. Besides, he needed time to locate the cabin.

Silas entered the house and took the stairs by twos to see what Clarissa wanted. She was still standing at the window after inviting him to enter the room. Turning, she smiled seductively. "Silas, we have some business to discuss. I need your help with a little problem. How would you like to help me get rid of Papa so we can marry and take over this ranch?" she asked calmly as she removed her dressing gown and let it float provocatively to her feet. "Close the door and lock it. I'm sure you don't want to be disturbed while you're . . . talking to me."

Silas Stern gaped at the naked beauty who had made such astounding suggestions, unable to move or speak. He watched her come forward gracefully, then step behind him to close and lock the door herself. She moved before him and smiled enticingly as she began unbuttoning his shirt. "Relax, Silas. Papa will be gone for at least an hour. Surely you're tired of him bossing you around and treating you as if you had no brains or feelings. He's threatening to kick me out if I refuse to marry this old friend of his. I can't, Silas, because I want you. But if I tell Papa, he'll laugh at me and punish both of us."

When she started pressing kisses on his throat and chest, he shuddered and groaned. Once she had his shirt off, his hands went to her breasts and began to fondle them. Clarissa knelt to pull off his boots, then unfastened his pants and sensuously removed them with a wanton smile. As she slowly rose, her hands played ticklishly over his eager body. She drew him to the bed and pushed him down upon it. "You will help me so we can marry, won't you, my love?" she wheedled.

Silas smiled happily. "I'll do anything for you, Clarissa."

Grasping his head, she pulled it to her breast. "We'll make plans later, my future husband. Right now, I want you too much to think clearly," she lied provocatively, having decided that Wes was too dangerous and she was not sure she could depend on him or trust him. But Silas was weak and bewitched. He would aid her and then she would find a way to kill him.

Wes tied his reins to a corral post and walked to the Caldwell house. No one was around, so no one saw him or questioned him. He slipped inside the house and went looking for Clarissa. He stood outside her door and listened to the revealing sounds coming from within. Having heard enough, he returned to the front porch to await Jackson, who arrived shortly to meet him.

"It's time we had some fun around here, Jack, then moved on. That money's gone, so we can't get much from Caldwell. When he gits back home, we'll take what he has, kill the son of a bitch, then ride out. While we're waiting, I thought we could have us some fun with his whore of a daughter. She's in there now humping Silas."

"You ain't joshing, Wes?" the man asked excitedly.

"Nope. Fact is, old friend, you can have her first and last. Unless this stick gets hard and hot, I'll pleasure myself watching you hurt her real good," Wes Monroe told him, rubbing his taut groin.

"Let's go git her," Jackson Hayes urged in rising anticipation.

"Be real quiet. We don't want to give them no warning. Yessiree, Jack, you're gonna enjoy yourself today," Wes told him, grinning malevolently.

"Say that again, Rachel," Travis coaxed in disbelief.

"Some awful man came to the door and gave Mister Crandall a letter from Harrison Caldwell. He read it, got his gun, and left. I heard some of what the man said," she began, then repeated Wes's words. "I went to check on my stew, and he was gone before I could speak to him."

Travis and Rana hurried to the corral to claim their

horses, which had just been unsaddled and rubbed down. They mounted bareback and raced toward Harrison's house. Anticipating trouble and danger, they dismounted a distance from the house and moved toward it stealthily. Peering through the parlor window, they saw the obviously dead body of Silas Stern on the floor and Clarissa being tortured and raped brutally by Jackson Hayes while Wes Monroe watched and laughed. Before Travis and Rana could come to her aid, Jackson Hayes began stabbing her repeatedly as he climaxed.

Rana screamed uncontrollably as she witnessed the horrifying murder. Travis grabbed her arm and yanked her away from the window, knowing it was too late to save Clarissa's life and fearing that the noise had alerted the outlaws to their presence. Travis used Indian sign language to communicate silently with her. She nodded her understanding and hurried to obey, ashamed that she had committed such a terrible error in crying aloud.

When Wes and Jackson bounded from the house, Travis pounced on them. They struggled fiercely. To the cutthroats, Travis seemed to be nowhere and everywhere at the same time. "Where's Nathan Crandall?" he demanded as he struck one and whirled to deflect a blow from the other. "I'll kill you dirty bastards if you've harmed him!" He tripped Jackson and kicked Wes in the abdomen.

As the two men circled Travis, Wes taunted, "You'll never reach him in time. He's dead by now. Harrison lured him to our cabin to kill him. Come on, tough man, show me how you can whip me and Jack." Wes was too cocky and arrogant to draw his pistol. He assumed he could beat this man, especially when it was two-on-one.

"Then why don't you tell me where your cabin is?" Travis mocked. "I'll lick you both and be gone in a flash."

Wes tauntingly revealed its location as he drew his

knife and began to wave it threateningly in Travis's face. Travis grinned sardonically. He ventured, "I bet you don't remember where you got that knife and pistol." When Wes glanced at both, then back at the man between him and Jackson, Travis replied, "You took them off me seven years ago near St. Louis, when you were working for Elizabeth Lowry's father. Right before you raped and murdered an Indian girl, then tried to beat me to death. Then you went back and murdered Lowry and his daughter. You must make it a practice to kill your bosses and their families. The initials on the handle stand for White Eagle; that's me."

Wes hesitated as he listened to this incredible tale. That instant gave Travis the edge, and he delivered a stunning blow to Wes's gut and jaw. As Wes staggered backward, Jackson attacked Travis. Rana appeared with the horses, knowing they would have to hurry to save her father. As Travis spun to miss Wes's next blow, Rana lifted her gun and fired at Jackson, striking him in the chest and killing him. Within moments, Wes was dead and Travis had recovered his pistol and knife. He flung himself on Apache's back and they rode toward the cabin.

For awhile, Nathan remained hidden and observed Harrison as the man paced and fretted. Nathan wanted to make certain his foe was alone. He had never seen Harrison look so edgy or insecure. When he was certain no one else was around, he left his hiding place and joined him.

"You wanted to see me, Harry?" he asked as he walked to him.

Harrison turned and slowly eyed Nathan. "It's over, Nate. I finally win everything, your ranch and Rana."

"How do you see that, Harry?" Nathan argued insolently.

Harrison freely revealed his scheme to rid himself of Nathan. "I'll bet my ranch nobody knows you're here. So when I claim you came looking for me and tried to kill me, who's to prove me wrong?"

"Why didn't you hire one of your gunslingers to handle this?"

"Because I wanted the pleasure of killing you myself."

"Mind telling me why?" Nathan asked, stalling for an opening.

"Because you let Marissa marry that mean bastard and leave home. You're to blame for her suffering and death. You were too weak to control her and too damn stubborn to protect her. I was in love with her and I wanted to marry her, but that fancy gambler stole her while I was gone. You should have stopped them, Nate. She would be alive now if you had had the gumption to stand up to her or kill Michaels. You knew she was terrified of that bastard. Every time she came home, you saw she was in trouble, but you did nothing."

"You and Marissa?" Nathan murmured in disbelief.

"That's right, you fool. She should have been mine. Since she's lost forever, I plan to take Rana in her place."

"Like hell you will!" Nathan shouted in alarm, drawing his pistol and firing as Harrison simultaneously did the same.

Travis and Rana slipped from their horses and ran toward the fallen body of Nathan Crandall. He opened his eyes and smiled weakly at them. "I let him trap me," he confessed with remorse.

"Do not speak, Grandfather," Rana entreated with misty eyes and in a choked voice. "You must rest so your wound may heal."

"It's too late, girl," he murmured, then coughed as blood filled his lungs. As his strength and life began to

560

ebb, he coaxed faintly, "Marry and be happy, like me and my Ruthie. I'll see her soon."

"Do not speak so, Grandfather," she scolded him in panic.

"Travis knows I can't make it, girl. He'll take care of you. Harry said he wanted you like he wanted Marissa," Nathan told them. With lagging strength, he repeated what Harrison had said.

"He lied, Grandfather. He wished to hurt you before he killed you. Mother did not know . . . my father was bad when she married him. Afterward, she was too proud to confess her mistake. She caused her own suffering, Grandfather, but she was going to change things. That last trip home, she had decided to leave . . . my father and return to you. She knew you would love us and protect us. It was not to be. Do not blame yourself. You are innocent. This I swear."

Nathan smiled at her. "You're a good girl, Rana. I love you."

"As I love you, Grandfather. Do not worry. We will save you."

Nathan grasped Travis's hand. "You've been a real son to me, Travis. These past years would have been empty without you. Take care of Rana. I know you love her and want her. The ranch belongs to you two." He coughed again and grew paler.

Travis looked beyond Nathan and saw that Harrison Caldwell was dead, and in that moment he understood that there was no hope for Nathan Crandall to survive. He held the dying man's hand tightly and vowed, "Don't worry about her, my father. You saved us all from Caldwell's evil. We'll be married under the white man's law very soon. We'll name our first son after you, Nate. You changed my life, and I won't ever forget that. I love you."

Nathan smiled again. "I love you, son. It's all over

561

now, and you two can be free and happy. Don't mourn for me. I had a good life, a full one. You two made my last days happy. I can die in peace."

Nathan began to fade rapidly. His eyes fluttered and he called out, "Marissa, where are you, girl? Forgive me," he pleaded.

Rana glanced at Travis through tear-filled eyes and their gazes spoke. He nodded understanding, and she replied, "I am here, Father. I love you. I have come home to you."

"To stay?" he entreated, his mind dulled by imminent death.

"Yes, Father, to stay forever." Her heart thudded painfully.

"Will you forgive me for not helping you?" he pleaded.

"I forgive you, Father, if you will forgive me for hurting you."

"I love you, Missy," he murmured, using his pet name for Marissa.

"I love you too, Papa," she whispered in his ear and kissed his cheek. "Rest easy, Papa; I am home to stay."

Nathan smiled one last time, then relaxed in her arms, dying without every learning of the tragic misconception that had tormented Marissa Crandall Michaels and had driven her from her home and love. "I love you, Father," she whispered one final time, knowing that the tragic secret would be buried with him and the Caldwells. The dark past was ending, and a bright future for Rana Michaels and Travis Kincade was beginning.

"I'm sorry, *micante*," Travis told her as he knelt beside the man who had saved his life long ago and had changed it so drastically. "He was like a real father to me. I know how you must be hurting."

"It is best he did not learn the truth. I will think of him as my grandfather, as it should have been. He is at peace now, as is my mother. The dangers have passed, and we must begin a new life.''

By Friday, Nathan Crandall and the others had been buried. The sheriff had collected the evidence against Harrison Caldwell and notified the past owners or heirs of the Lazy *J*, Flying *M*, and Box *K* ranches to return and lay claim to them. Since Harrison Caldwell had left a will naming Rana Michaels as his only heir, Travis and Rana discovered they owned a large, connecting spread that would one day belong to the child Rana was now certain she was carrying. With the other ranches being returned to their rightful owners, the area could be at peace once more.

Travis held Rana securely and tenderly within the circle of his arms as they stood before the mantel, staring up at Marissa's portrait. ''She almost appears to be smiling at us,'' Travis remarked softly, nuzzling the side of her head.

Rana gazed into her mother's blue eyes, which did appear to be smiling down on them. ''She has found peace, *mihigna*. The past is over. We are home, and we must begin our life together.''

''I asked the preacher to come out Sunday after church to marry us. Cody and Mace are trying to keep it a secret, but they're planning a big party for us. We all know this is what Nate would have wanted us to do. Do you think we should tell everyone we're already married under Indian law?'' he inquired, patting her stomach.

''You have found peace here. I do not wish others to learn of your Indian blood and torment you. They can say no words to harm me while I stand in your shadow,'' she declared decisively.

''It doesn't matter anymore, my love. I'm not ashamed to be half-blooded. My friends won't turn against me and

563

others don't matter to me. I think we've all found peace, *micante*. You're not going to tell Todd anything, are you?" he ventured with mild curiosity.

"No, it is too late for such words to be a kindness."

"You sure you want to be doubly bound to me?" he teased, returning to a happier topic as he bent forward to nibble on her ear.

She quivered and warmed and leaned against him. "We are two people in each body; we must join two times."

"Good," he murmured as he turned her to face him. "That should make us twice as happy. White Eagle gets Wild Wind, and Travis Kincade gets Rana Michaels."

She looked into his eyes and smiled. "No, my love. I have you, and you have me. See, I have learned much English," she teased, then hugged him tightly. "Come, let us speak in a different way," she entreated, grasping his hand and leading him toward her room.

Saturday morning, Travis approached the family graveyard, which had been placed a mile from the house and beneath a lovely tree, whose sprawling limbs seemed to spread out protectively over those it guarded in their eternal sleep. The fence-enclosed space was a tranquil spot, and Travis had felt the need to visit it today to say a private farewell to Nathan Crandall.

Travis found Todd Raines standing over Marissa's grave, and he speculated that her funeral must have been a heartrending experience for Todd. Now there were three graves: Nathan's, Ruth's, and Marissa's. It had taken death to reunite them.

"I suppose I shouldn't be here," Todd murmured sadly. "It's the first time in years that I've allowed myself to visit her. It's hard to accept that they're both gone forever, Travis; they were such a big part of my life. I think the reason I could never get over her was because she left so suddenly; she left everything open and unsettled. I know a part of me will always love her and miss her, but I have a good wife who loves and and needs me more than Marissa ever did or could. If I just knew why she deserted me, then I would be free of the past."

"I know what it's like to be chained to a dark past, Todd, and I wish I could help you. It's something only you can resolve."

Todd laughed. "When you rode up, I was thinking about Nate and all he did for me. He was practically a father to me too. He taught me most of what I know, or made sure I learned it. Not long before Marissa realized I was alive and set her sights on me, I had never been with a woman. You might say I was the shy, serious type. Nate said I needed to become a whole man, so he sent me to this house outside town in his place. He told me the girl wouldn't know any difference because he always insisted on darkness and no talking so he could pretend she was Ruthie for awhile. He told me he wasn't ever going to visit that whore again, so he sent me in his place to be educated. I never knew who she was, but I could tell she wanted to be any place but in bed with me. I couldn't blame her. Lordy, I was so clumsy and scared, and she didn't help relax me or teach me anything. I never went back there either, but I've never forgotten that night. In less than a month, I was seeing Marissa, and she was the only woman I wanted. She nearly destroyed me, but I think the pain would cease if I only knew why she rejected me for that no-good gambler."

Travis looked into Todd Raines's gray-blue eyes and watched the sun bring out the reddish gold highlights in his hair. He stared at Todd's eyes, his nose, his mouth, his expression. The truth was as clear to Travis as the blue sky overhead: Todd Raines had been the stranger Marissa had slept with that night; Todd Raines was

565

Rana's father, not Nathan Crandall; and no one involved in that tragic incident had known the whole truth. Travis gingerly questioned Todd about that fateful night to make certain he was not mistaken. He was not.

Shortly thereafter, Travis returned to the house and told Rana what he had learned. She gave the matter careful thought and made her decision. "Perhaps I will be sorry one day, but I feel this must not remain our secret. To tell him I am his child gives him a new bond to the past, and that might be cruel, but he needs to hear the truth to be free. He is my father, and he has the right to know this. So many secrets in the past, and look what damage they have done. My mother's spirit cannot rest until it has made peace with the past, peace with her true love."

"You want me to bring him over here so you two can talk privately?" Travis inquired, knowing this would be hard on both of them.

Rana inhaled and nodded. "Yes, my love. Bring my father to me, and we will settle the past for all time."

"It's gonna hurt, Rana, but I think you're right."

She smiled at him. "As when you had to seek your past in the Hunkpapa camp, I must ride this lost trail alone and with courage. I will tell him all; then he can decide what to tell Rachel."

After Travis left to fetch Todd Raines, Rana retrieved Marissa's "treasures" from her closet. The wild winds that had blown destructively over Travis's life and over hers had been tamed and calmed. Their turbulent pasts were settled, and they had found love and peace together. It was time to allow Todd Raines, her father, the same opportunity for peace and contentment. She looked at Marissa's portrait and smiled. "Soon, Mother, you can rest peacefully. I have avenged the evil that befell you and I have returned your honor."

When Todd entered the room, his gaze first went to

Marissa's image, then to Rana's face. Love and anguish filled his gaze, though he quickly tried to conceal his emotion. Yes, she decided, this was the right thing to do. She went to him and smiled. Taking his hand, she led him to the settee. She told him softly, "Sit. There is much I must tell you about me and my mother, secrets that have harmed many of us. It is time you knew all, so the pain and sadness can vanish from your eyes and life, as they have from mine."

Todd looked at the portrait of Marissa Crandall above him and protested, "Miss Rana, I don't think we should talk about your mother. That was long ago, and it was a bad time for me."

"Yes, *Father,* we must talk about it. We must end the secrets that drove her from your arms, for I am proof of her true love for you. As are these," she added, placing Marissa's keepsakes in his shaky hands. She smiled and nodded when he gaped at them, then at her. She murmured, "It is true; you are my father, and she loved only you. Now I must tell you all of it . . ."

Epilogue

Deep in Dakota Territory, in the Oglala camp, Lone Wolf was playing with his son while Myeerah nursed their daughter. The twins had been born on the eighth of March and they had been named Moon Flower and War Hawk. For the present, peace and happiness abounded in his lands and in his tepee. He looked at the *wanapin* around his son's neck and imagined how the child would grow to wear it proudly. He thought about his friend, Travis "White Eagle" Kincade, and his adopted sister, Rana "Wild Wind" Michaels, and he smiled, for he believed they too had found peace and happiness.

Myeerah looked at her husband and asked, "Why do you smile so?"

"My thoughts are of Wild Wind and White Eagle. I long to see them and speak with them. Peace fills our lands and hearts this moon, but soon a time will come when it is no longer this way. When that moon comes, I will take you and our children to live with White Eagle and Wild Wind. The season of the buffalo and the Lakota is fading swiftly, my love. We must change, or we must die. I wish our children to grow and be happy, as we are

569

this moon. I wish them to know of their lands and people. White Eagle and Wild Wind will carry out my wishes. Many times I have dreamed of our children playing as one family. It will be so, Myeerah, for Grandfather has told me."

"Such evil days are far from this one, my husband. Forget them and share this flower of happiness."

Lone Wolf gazed into her eyes and smiled. "You are as cunning and quick as my sister, Wild Wind," he teased.

"Is that not good?" she playfully retorted, placing their daughter beside their sleeping son. They were children of one image, the image of Lone Wolf.

"Yes, it is good," he concurred, then drew her into his arms.

In Texas, on the Rocking *C* Ranch, Rana smiled at her husband as he entered the room. He strolled forward and looked down at her. "How're my two favorite girls today?" he asked. He watched Rana as she fed the tiny female child with fuzzy red hair and slate-colored eyes, and his heart overflowed with tenderness.

"We are fine, and happy, my love," she replied with a radiant smile. "Serrin Rose Kincade has been a very good girl today."

Travis looked at the tiny face and felt his heart lurch with joy. This bundle of bliss that had entered his life on the third of April had brought him great pride and contentment. He glanced at the shiny ring on Rana's finger, a wedding band made from the gold nuggets Sitting Bull and the Hunkpapas had allowed him to take. He had never told anyone where he had gotten them, and he never would reveal that secret.

One year ago this day, Travis had left her side to seek the gold. So much had changed during that year. Cody and Mary Beth Slade were expecting their first child.

Todd and Rachel Raines had adopted a jolly baby boy and were waiting to adopt another. Bart and Lettie were happy together. Mace had fallen in love with a girl from a new family that had taken up residence nearby. The owners or heirs of the adjoining ranches had returned and their spreads were flourishing. The Rocking C Ranch was prospering far beyond anyone's imagining.

"You know who's been on my mind nearly all day?" he asked. Without waiting for her reply, he told her, "Lone Wolf. I've been doing some checking, and things are calm in that area at the moment. They've got new treaties and they should keep peace for a time. Maybe we can visit them as soon as they complete those railroads. If things get bad, we can encourage them to come live on our ranch."

"You are the kindest and most generous man I know. Lone Wolf will never leave his lands. They are a part of him, as the air he breathes or the blood of his body. Once I felt that way, but you entered my life and changed me. You, Travis Kincade, did what no other could do; you tamed the Wild Wind."

Travis laughed skeptically. "You're bound to me in two worlds, but you're still as free as a wild wind, and that's as it should be." Travis glanced at his twin son, who favored him, and he jested, "You never do anything halfway. You've made me doubly happy, Rana Michaels Kincade."

Rana joined him beside the cradles and looked down at their twins. Her arm slipped around his waist as she whispered, "Tanner Crandall Kincade is as impatient and demanding as his father. He is always first in everything: eating, wetting, crying, and loving. He is spoiled like his father."

Travis pulled her into his arms. "They're beautiful like you, Rana. I never imagined I could be this happy. The past seems so far away," he stated dreamily as he began to

571

kiss a trail down her neck. "You aren't sorry you and Todd decided to keep the truth a secret?" he asked suddenly. "He's lost two ways; he can't claim his daughter or his grandchildren."

"He has another family and the truth would cause them suffering. The past is over." Rana turned to face him and mussed his sable hair. Her eyes met his and she coaxed, "The children are asleep, my love. Why do you not come and ride a wild wind?" She kissed him hungrily.

"Why not?" he teased. "If I can't tame it, I might as well enjoy it. I love you, Rana Kincade. Lordy, how I do love you!"

HISTORICAL ROMANCES BY PHOEBE CONN

FOR THE STEAMIEST READS, NOTHING BEATS THE PROSE OF CONN . . .

ARIZONA ANGEL	(3872, $4.50/$5.50)
CAPTIVE HEART	(3871, $4.50/$5.50)
DESIRE	(4086, $5.99/$6.99)
EMERALD FIRE	(4243, $4.99/$5.99)
LOVE ME 'TIL DAWN	(3593, $5.99/$6.99)
LOVING FURY	(3870, $4.50/$5.50)
NO SWEETER ECSTASY	(3064, $4.95/$5.95)
STARLIT ECSTASY	(2134, $3.95/$4.95)
SWEPT AWAY	(4487-9, $4.99/$5.99)
TEMPT ME WITH KISSES	(3296, $4.95/$5.95)
TENDER SAVAGE	(3559, $4.95/$5.95)

TODAY'S HOTTEST READS
ARE TOMORROW'S SUPERSTARS

DISCOVER DEANA JAMES!

CAPTIVE ANGEL   (2524, $4.50/$5.50)
Abandoned, penniless, and suddenly responsible for the biggest
tobacco plantation in Colleton County, distraught Caroline Gil-
lard had no time to dissolve into tears. By day the willowy redhead labored to exhaustion beside her slaves . . . but each night
left her restless with longing for her wayward husband. She'd
make the sea captain regret his betrayal until he begged her to
take him back!

MASQUE OF SAPPHIRE   (2885, $4.50/$5.50)
Judith Talbot-Harrow left England with a heavy heart. She was
going to America to join a father she despised and a sister she
distrusted. She was certainly in no mood to put up with the insulting actions of the arrogant Yankee privateer who boarded her
ship, ransacked her things, then "apologized" with an indecent,
brazen kiss! She vowed that someday he'd pay dearly for the lib-
erties he had taken and the desires he had awakened.

SPEAK ONLY LOVE   (3439, $4.95/$5.95)
Long ago, the shock of her mother's death had robbed Vivian
Marleigh of the power of speech. Now she was being forced to
marry a bitter man with brandy on his breath. But she could not
say what was in her heart. It was up to the viscount to spark the
fires that would melt her icy reserve.

WILD TEXAS HEART   (3205, $4.95/$5.95)
Fan Breckenridge was terrified when the stranger found her near-
naked and shivering beneath the Texas stars. Unable to remember
who she was or what had happened, all she had in the world was
the deed to a patch of land that might yield oil . . . and the fierce
loving of this wildcatter who called himself Irons.

*Available wherever paperbacks are sold, or order direct from the
Publisher. Send cover price plus 50¢ per copy for mailing and
handling to Penguin USA, P.O. Box 999, c/o Dept. 17109,
Bergenfiled, NJ 07621. Residents of New York and Tennessee
must include sales tax. DO NOT SEND CASH.*